To

Kathy

with Love

Keasa

THE PROTECTOR

Keesya Hill-Jones

authorHOUSE®

AuthorHouse™
1663 Liberty Drive
Bloomington, IN 47403
www.authorhouse.com
Phone: 1 (800) 839-8640

Published by AuthorHouse 05/23/2017

ISBN: 978-1-5246-9362-6 (sc)
ISBN: 978-1-5246-9363-3 (hc)
ISBN: 978-1-5246-9361-9 (e)

Library of Congress Control Number: 2017908160

Print information available on the last page.

This book is dedicated in memory of my father, Kenneth Hill.
He sacrificed so much so that I could dream and achieve.
He inspired me to believe I was capable of accomplishing
anything. I will always be grateful. Dad, I love you!!!!

CHAPTER 1

A cool, refreshing breeze blew through Dominique Wallace's sunroof as her sporty black 740iL BMW hugged the interstate at eighty-five miles per hour. Hiding behind her expensive black Chanel shades, Dominique was engulfed in the relaxing jazz sounds of Kenny G's music that poured through the crystal-clear speakers. She gripped the steering wheel, rejuvenated following an intensive workout. After her last trip to Brazil—having compared herself to the stunning native women and found herself lacking—Dominique had treated herself by installing a home gym, declaring the expense justified. She'd vowed to regain the admiration she'd once drawn from all eyes.

Dominique inhaled the fresh air as the view of downtown Richmond grew from a flat surface to a breathtaking skyline silhouetted by towering buildings. Excited to begin another day of upholding justice as an attorney in the system she believed in wholeheartedly, she raced toward the exit that was near her office building, mentally preparing for the next demanding case.

Dominique pulled into her assigned parking space, gathered her briefcase and purse, and headed for the elevator. She crossed the parking lot and spotted Shawn Silver, a well-known and respected Virginia state's attorney, and one of Dominique's closest professional colleagues. They worked together on several of the state's largest cases, and normally Dominique followed Shawn's lead. He was a trial veteran, surprising for a forty-year-old. His victories had come with painstaking battles against many large corporations, the most recent against a large cigarette corporation that had been previously untouchable in court. With his wit and endless research, Shawn exposed every negative piece of evidence he could dig up, winning this case almost effortlessly from the view of the uninvolved spectator.

Together, Shawn and Dominique were a courtroom powerhouse. Independently, they were just as fearless. Other attorneys' confidence buckled when they learned that Dominique and Shawn were prosecuting a case. And naturally the pair used it to their advantage, many times bluffing their way to a victory.

Dominique greeted Shawn as they stepped onto the elevator together. She admired his tailored black Italian suit, which he accented with a French blue dress shirt and a stately yellow tie.

"Good morning," Shawn responded as they both turned to face the doors. Dominique observed her own reflection in the gold finish as Shawn pressed the tenth-floor button for their floor.

She looked into his big bold eyes. "What are you working on now that the Carson case is over?"

"I have something major coming up. Matter of fact, I was going to bring it to your office this morning." Shawn grinned slyly.

"What is it?" She asked with a raised brow.

"It's going to be a very high profile case. The other attorneys thought it would be a good one for you to handle."

"Where was I when everyone was voting?" Dominique wasn't surprised that she was ignorant of the discussions surrounding this case until now.

It was their way of letting her know her place within the male-dominated legal clan. She was the only female attorney in her office and had created a remarkable reputation in the Virginia law system. She was sharp, determined, and won her cases. Harder cases came her way more and more frequently. Because of her hard work, it was only a matter of time before she would be allowed to choose which high-profile cases she would be willing to represent for the state. But obviously not yet.

"Why are you so sensitive, Dominique?" Shawn asked with a half-smirk. "You know it's not good for attorneys to be sensitive about minor details."

She saw the humor in his eyes, but one too many female sensitivity jokes had been thrown her way recently.

"Sensitive." Dominique snapped.

"Come on. Don't beat the messenger." He winked at her.

She raised an eyebrow, "What's the case, and why was I selected to represent it?"

"Believe me, it's going to be a really high profile case. Everybody thinks you've paid your dues."

She adjusted her bag and pierced Shawn with a glare. "Are you kidding? What kind of case is it?"

"Come to my office. I want you to review the file for yourself."

The elevator doors opened, and the two walked in silence to his office. Hoping this wasn't the case she'd heard rumors about last week, Dominique nevertheless was determined to keep an open mind.

"Close the door behind you." Shawn walked around his desk and picked up a folder from atop the clutter. He paused and stared at Dominique, expressionless, before handing it to her. "Just look it over before making a decision," Shawn said, releasing the folder.

The folder felt thin in her hands. She glanced at Shawn before opening it, hoping for some sign of what awaited her. But he stood stone-faced, waiting for her response.

Slowly, she read its contents, and her breath caught in her throat. Was she holding the keys to Pandora's box? The state wanted her to prosecute Michael Buchanan, one of the most influential businessmen in Virginia. He was being charged with sexually abusing his thirteen-year-old daughter, Kimberly.

Dominique wondered whether his reputation and connections would lead her into early retirement … or an early grave. There was no way she could keep this case quiet. She would be at the mercy of media scrutiny until the final verdict was announced.

Could she handle the pressure of being in the spotlight representing a no-win case? As she stood absorbing her possible demise, she felt a strange chill race through her body, an inner voice telling her to walk away. Normally, Dominique would accept all cases assigned to her without reservation, but there was something different about this one.

Shawn's face was still an unreadable mask. In a high-pitched voice, Dominique exploded. "You have got to be kidding me! This is a serious accusation being brought against Buchanan, and you don't have any evidence or proof that he's guilty."

Shawn nodded. "I was caught off guard, too, when I reviewed the material. What do you think?"

She let out a sigh and waved the folder in the air. "I don't know what to think. First, I want to know why you guys think I would be the best one to represent this case. And don't give me that 'because you've paid your dues' bull!"

Without hesitating Shawn answered, "You know Buchanan is a successful businessman. We think the jury will be more compassionate with you representing his daughter. So, we want you to play on the jury's sympathy. We think a woman representing Kimberly's case will have more impact. Come on. Don't act like you don't know." He raised both of his hands in the air.

She had no doubts that she could play on the jury's sympathy, but did she really want to? Before accepting the case, she would need more details than what Shawn had handed her. She wasn't a fool, and by no means was she desperate for victims to represent.

"The media will have a field day with this case," she said, shaking the folder at him.

"I knew you were going to be worried about the media dragging this case through the mud. I must admit, initially I shared your concern. I think you should at least speak with his daughter and hear her side before saying no. Will you do that for me?"

Dominique stared back in silence. She agreed that speaking with Buchanan's daughter was a must, but she also realized that it probably wouldn't be enough.

"I think this case is a personal set-up," she said, her voice rising again.

"This case isn't a set-up. I have every confidence in the world that you can win if he's guilty. Actually, I was the one who recommended that you represent the case. Brent was going to do it, but I thought you would have a better chance of winning. I'm certain you'll do fine. I plan to assist you, and you know how much I hate to lose."

Shawn wasn't lying about his dislike for losing. Like Dominique, he had earned a spotless track record, a track record any accomplished attorney would protect. And as far as she knew, he was achieving his status ethically and legally.

Calm again, she said, "I know. I hate to lose too. Have you spoken with his daughter yet?"

"No. I thought it would be best if you did. I think she'll be more receptive. I still don't know what her mental state is. She's in the hospital downtown."

Dominique shook her head slowly. "I'm not saying I'm going to take the case, but I'll at least speak with her and hear her side."

"Why don't you go down there now? We have to get going on this case as soon as possible. If Buchanan is guilty of this sexual abuse charge, I want him convicted. I don't want him on the streets another second." He licked his lips hungrily, like a lion about to attack. She had seen him perform this ritual many times before, when he felt that rush to conquer.

She agreed with him about getting Buchanan off the streets if he had committed this crime. And for a brief moment, she imagined Buchanan as a common criminal, not a powerful above-the-law citizen. Until now she had never allowed clients' reputations to affect her ability to accept their possible guilt and decided not to start with Buchanan.

She also knew Shawn was right. She had to speak with Kimberly. She only hoped the girl would open up to her. She knew from past cases that sexually abused people build protective walls around themselves because of everything they had suffered. This understandably makes it difficult for them to immediately trust someone.

Dominique wondered about Buchanan's wife's reaction to the accusation. Whose side was she taking? "What else do you know about this case besides what's in this folder?" She asked Shawn, snapping him out of his daze.

"Not much more. I do know his daughter has tried to commit suicide more than once. Somehow, until now, they'd managed to convince everyone that she was a problem child. I heard she's a train wreck. I also know Buchanan's wife is supporting him." He sat down behind his desk.

"I wonder why," she mused.

"If she does know he's been molesting their daughter, she'll wish she'd come forward to help her daughter," Shawn said, shaking his head. "I hate it when a parent finds out that the other parent is molesting their child and decides to do nothing."

"I'm going to go speak with Kimberly right now. I'll let you know what I decide." She headed for the door with the folder still in her hand. She left Shawn's office and walked past several cubicles crowded with state employees in idle chatter. This reminded her why she chose to practice for the state instead of taking on the overhead of a private practice and micromanaging her staff.

When Dominique approached her assistant's desk, she noted that Holly hurriedly got off the phone. Apparently she, too, was enjoying a personal conversation on the government's time. Dominique smiled tolerantly and instructed Holly to text her if anything pressing should arise while she was out visiting with Kimberly Buchanan.

CHAPTER 2

En route to the hospital, another chill raced through Dominique's body. She wondered whether the thought of having to prosecute Buchanan was troubling her subconsciously and continued to meditate on the information she had read. Maybe after meeting his daughter, Dominique would be able to pinpoint why her instincts were telling her to walk away.

She parked her car in the hospital deck and headed straight for the information desk to get Kimberly's room number. As she rode the elevator up to the fifth floor, she wondered what Kimberly's mental state would be. Thirteen is a critical age, and Kimberly could be mature or childlike. Either one would determine the direction and tone of her court attack.

Before knocking on Kimberly's door, Dominique took a deep breath. The strong fumes of disinfectant burned her nostrils as she glanced nervously around the hallway. Only when absolutely necessary would she make an appearance in a hospital and depart as soon as possible, feeling grateful for her present good state of health.

Trying not to succumb to her nagging doubts about the case, she reevaluated Buchanan's alleged sexual abuse of his daughter. He allegedly had committed a serious crime, and if he was indeed guilty, Dominique would have to work hard to convict him.

She knocked on Kimberly's door and stood straight. She wanted her new client's first impression to be that of confidence, not uncertainty. After several knocks with no response, Dominique assumed that Kimberly was sleeping.

As Dominique looked around, debating whether to walk in, a nurse approached, carrying a tray with medicines on it. "Are you here to see Kimberly Buchanan?"

"Yes, I am. I'm her attorney. Is she in her room?"

The nurse gave Dominique a quick look-over. "She's in there. I don't know if it's a good idea for you to speak with her right now. She's really edgy."

"Don't worry. I'm here to help her, not prosecute her. I promise not to push her." With a go-ahead nod, the nurse stepped back. Dominique knocked once more and entered. Closing the door behind her, she slowly walked into the half-lit room.

The blinds were closed. The only light came from the television screen that Kimberly was intently watching. Dominique was glad Kimberly had a private room. They would be able to talk freely.

Dominique approached the bed, where Kimberly was sitting propped up against a pillow. The flickering television light alternately illuminated then hid the small girl's sunken features. Kimberly didn't acknowledge her presence.

From all her years of experience, Dominique knew she would have to tread lightly and be patient with Kimberly. The girl would need constant reassurance that their relationship would be safe.

"Good morning, Kimberly. My name is Dominique Wallace. I'm your attorney," Dominique announced. She waited a few moments for a response, but Kimberly continued to stare at the television.

"Kimberly, I'm going to open the blinds. I want to see you better." Dominique reached for the string to open the blinds.

"I don't want the blinds open." Kimberly scowled at Dominique and turned back to the television.

"May I ask why? It's awfully dark in here."

"I don't want any light. I like it dark," Kimberly snapped back, continuing to stare at the television screen.

Dominique obediently dropped the string from her hand. "Kimberly, I know you have been through a lot, and I want you to know I'm here to help you. As I stated before, I'm your attorney." Dominique took a few steps toward the bed. "You may call me Dominique if you like."

"I don't need an attorney!" Kimberly shouted at Dominique while keeping her eyes glued to the television screen.

"Unfortunately, the state thinks you do. That's why I'm here." Dominique hoped she didn't sound arrogant.

This time Kimberly turned her attention from the television screen and stared directly at Dominique. "Is my father paying you to represent me?"

"No. Your father doesn't even know I'm going to be your attorney or that I'm here. The state appointed me. Your father has no control or influence over me. So, you can trust me, and you don't have to worry about him finding out." Dominique slid the lone vase of flowers aside, reached for the pitcher, poured the girl a glass of water, and offered it to her.

She waved away the glass. "My father has influence over everyone in this state. He's Michael Buchanan. Don't you know who he is?" Kimberly snickered at Dominique's ignorance.

"Kimberly, your father doesn't have any influence over me. This is one woman he doesn't control." Dominique placed the glass on the nearby table.

Disbelieving, Kimberly studied the woman. Kimberly wasn't sure whether Dominique was crazy or desiring to be as confident as she looked wearing her black Tahari dress and red patent leather pumps. Either, way she wasn't trying to open her heart to some stranger and find her-self vulnerable and hurt again.

"Well, you're the first," Kimberly replied sarcastically.

"I want to talk to you about what's been going on between you and your father." Dominique moved closer.

The teen turned her attention back to the television program and pushed the remote control to change the channel. "I don't want to talk about it."

"Kimberly, I know it must be tough talking about it, but it would help me put an end to what has been happening to you." Dominique avoided using the words "sexual abuse" or "molesting." She wanted to hear Kimberly verbalize the words herself to prevent any later accusation of coaching Kimberly's testimony.

Kimberly turned her attention back to Dominique. "Who really sent you here?"

"The state believes you need representation. I was informed that you tried to commit suicide. Why don't we start there? Tell me why you felt the need to take your life."

After a pause, the girl exploded, "Fuck you! I'm tired of living."

"You're tired of living? You have so much to look forward to. Besides, these are supposed to be the best years of your life." Dominique felt a pang. Growing up in the foster care system after her parents abandoned her, her own early life had been bumpy, yet she managed to survive.

Kimberly pointed a finger at her. "Maybe they were for you, but not for me. I've been living in pure hell for a long time. All alone. I don't need you coming in here trying to be my friend. You don't give a damn about me. I'm sure you're getting paid a lot of money to represent my case. So why don't you leave me alone?"

"I'm not here because of money. I'm here because I want to help you. I'm here to see that justice is served."

Kimberly snickered. "Please tell me how you plan to convict my father."

"With the information, you give me. Every piece of evidence I can present to the court helps me. Helps you. So you're going to have to trust me." Dominique reached for the glass of water and downed it herself. She wondered why suddenly this case was so important.

Kimberly looked away from Dominique and once again focused her attention on the television.

Dominique didn't want to push too much. Kimberly's cooperation was vital to the success of the case. Without it, it was like going into battle without armor.

Kimberly finally responded. "Does my mother know you're here?"

"No. Neither your father nor your mother knows I'm here. Why?"

"Mother doesn't believe me. She thinks I'm lying about everything. I hate her." Kimberly raked her fingers through her long, stringy blonde hair.

"How do you know your mother doesn't believe you?"

"She told me so. She thinks I tried to commit suicide to draw attention to myself and to hurt my father. All she's concerned about is what people are going to say. She doesn't give a damn about me either. She never has. All she cares about is maintaining her luxury lifestyle."

"I'm sorry to hear that. But you're not alone. A lot of other parents have chosen to ignore what's going on under their roofs. But you can't allow your mother's feelings to keep you from doing the right thing. You owe it to yourself. You do know that what your father has done to you is not your fault?" Dominique leaned in closer to Kimberly.

Kimberly kept staring at the television.

Breaking the silence, Dominique asked, "Have you spoken to your mother or father since you were admitted to the hospital?"

"My mother came by, but my father hasn't. I don't want that sick bastard near me ever again." Kimberly gripped the sheets in her scrawny hands.

"I can take care of that. I'll issue a protective order. Your father won't be able to write, phone, or visit you during the trial. How do you feel about that?" Dominique scribbled a note in her planner.

Dominique waited a second or two. "Just give me the word and it's done." Dominique reached over the girl's bed rail and turned the volume down on the television.

Kimberly glared at Dominique. Only her IV lines seemed to prevent her from coming after Dominique. "You think you can just stroll in here and win my trust. Are you crazy? I don't know you! Besides, I've heard it all. I know I'm just a game to all of you. Who's going to reach little Kimberly? None of you give a damn about me. I'm tired of playing games with all of you!"

Kimberly rolled her eyes and neck. "You're obviously out of your league. I don't know why the state chose you, but I think they're trying to make an ass out of you just like they think they will out of me. You'll never be able to convict my father. He's too damn important. Get out of my room and leave me alone!" Kimberly pressed the remote button and turned up the volume.

Her sudden outburst disarmed Dominique. She didn't know what to make of it. Kimberly had good reason to be bitter. The system had let her down, and Dominique wasn't sure if she would be able to redeem the system in Kimberly's eyes. But she had to try.

Dominique raised her voice over the noise. "Kimberly, trust me, I'm here to help you."

Kimberly reached for the buzzer. "Do I need to call a nurse to escort your behind out of here?"

"No. That won't be necessary." Dominique gathered her purse and Kimberly's case folder. She walked briskly into the hallway, headed toward the elevator, and pressed the elevator button, steaming with frustration and determined to convict Buchanan.

CHAPTER 3

As Dominique stood waiting for the hospital elevator, her thoughts began to drift back to her own childhood. She had been abandoned by her parents and spent the only youth she could remember in foster care. Now the pain and anger bubbled up inside of her.

She remembered lying in bed late at night, crying, trying not to wake anyone, confused as to why her parents had given her up. She questioned her self-worth and why she was even born. She'd prayed to God for guidance but constantly felt ignored.

Dominique had questioned her faith until the day Eric Wallace, now her husband, entered her life. Since that day, she had a sense of peace and hope that gave her strength.

The elevator doors opened, but Dominique turned around and marched back to Kimberly's room. If Dominique could make it after her own miserable childhood, there was hope for Kimberly. Dominique walked straight into the room without knocking and opened the blinds. She wanted Kimberly to see her clearly. And this time she would make her intentions very clear.

Kimberly sat up, hiding the tissue she'd been using to wipe her cheeks. "Didn't I tell you to get out of my room? I don't have anything else to say to you. Get out!"

"Calm down. You've made it very clear that you don't trust me. And I can understand why. I just waltzed in here demanding your trust. But I assure you, Kimberly, that your father doesn't influence me. He has a lot of connections, but not with me. There is nothing your father can say or do that will prevent me from giving you fair representation. I will do everything in my power to help you, but I can't if you won't trust me."

"Please!" Kimberly rolled her eyes. "You're no different from the rest."

"I don't know what other people you're referring to. I can only speak for myself. I know how hurt you must feel because I've been hurt in my life, too." Dominique's chest ached as she considered what could have driven the fragile girl to suicide. She handed Kimberly a fresh tissue from the box on the bedside table.

"So now you're going to tell me you've gone through what I have?" Kimberly took the tissue and wiped her nose.

"No. My father and mother abandoned me. I can't even remember what they look like. I was put in foster care when I was six years old. From then on, I moved from family to family, and none of them wanted me. So my life was no joy ride. I know how it feels to be hurt." Dominique took a tissue for herself, clutching it in one fist.

"So, what?" Kimberly snapped. "I would have preferred for my father and mother to have abandoned my ass. I would have been better off. Your parents did you a favor."

"Maybe so, but I would've liked to have made that decision myself. I've had to work hard for everything I have today. No one gave me anything. Your father's money and influence mean nothing to me. I've learned how to survive the hard way, and from the looks of things, you have, too." Dominique pulled the lone chair closer but did not sit down. "Kimberly, I can't erase your years of pain, but I can give you my all while prosecuting your case. I can make your father regret ever harming you. I'll guarantee you that much. I can't represent you properly if you won't trust me."

Kimberly stared at Dominique, her face softening. Dominique plunged forward, praying that Kimberly would take the leap of faith with her.

"The sooner you give me the okay, the sooner I can help you. Like I said earlier, I can prevent your father from coming in contact with you during the trial. Just give me the word." Dominique walked over to the phone and lifted the receiver.

Kimberly finally responded, sounding defeated. "If you can do that, I'll tell you whatever you want to know."

"Consider it done. I'll call my office now, and my partner will start the process right away."

Dominique quickly dialed Shawn's office number and summarized what had transpired. His excitement echoed over the phone as he accepted the assignment for the case. Dominique ended the conversation as quickly as possible.

Kimberly sat up in her bed. "When will he get that restraining order?"

"Today. You don't have to worry. I have everything under control," Dominique repeated. "I have no intention of helping your father," still trying to reassure Kimberly.

"Ms. Wallace, if I tell you everything, will I have to repeat it again in front of everybody in the courtroom?" Kimberly fidgeted with the tube extending up her forearm.

Dominique couldn't protect the girl from having to take the stand unless her father would plead guilty. "If I can get your father to confess before we go to trial, maybe you wouldn't have to."

"He won't confess. I know he won't. He'll deny it until the end. I hate him so much. He's ruined my life, and he doesn't care. He's hiding behind all his money and power." Kimberly threw her crumpled tissue onto the floor.

"He won't be able to hide behind all his money if you tell me everything. I need to know every little detail so I can make your case strong and solid. Then his only option will be to confess. Kimberly, I assure you I'll do everything in my power to see you through this. Please trust me and give me a chance." Dominique pulled a notepad and pen out of her purse.

"I don't know." Kimberly raised her hands to cover her face. "I don't know."

"This is difficult to talk about, for sure, but Kimberly, your father's actions were sinister and evil." Dominique hoped the words would linger in Kimberly's mind whenever she would have second thoughts.

"He's a sick bastard who needs to die!" Kimberly shouted.

Dominique watched as Kimberly removed her hands from her face to rub her arm. Tears rolled down her face. "I'll never be the same. He has ruined my life. That sick bastard has been forcing me to have sex with him ever since I was eight years old."

Bingo! Dominique shouted inside. As Kimberly poured her heart out, and as Dominique listened, she became more and more convinced that she had made the right decision to represent Kimberly. Dominique prayed that the girl would be able to put her life back together after the trial was over.

Dominique pulled out her tape recorder and began taping and writing feverishly what Kimberly told her. Then she started to ask questions.

"Your father started forcing you to have sex when you were eight years old?"

"Yes." Kimberly responded, with tears still in her eyes.

"Did you tell your mother the first time your father forced you to have sex with him?"

Kimberly shook her head from side to side. "No. He told me if I did, he would kill me."

"The first time he forced you to have sex was where?"

"In my bedroom. My mother was out of town." Kimberly wrapped her arms around her chest.

"Was there anybody else at your house while your mother was away?"

"Yes. Our housekeeper, Maria, was there. She lived with us then."

"Do you think there is the slightest chance that Maria knew what was going on?" Dominique tapped her pen against her teeth.

"I don't know. If she does, she won't admit it because she'd be too afraid she'd be sent back to Mexico. It wouldn't surprise me if he forced her to have sex with him, too." Kimberly looked away, mumbling something only she could understand.

"Why would you say that?" Dominique probed.

"She was always nervous when he came around. I noticed that right after she started working for us. I think my mother noticed it, too."

"She used to live with you. What happened to her?"

"My mother said Maria wasn't working out. She's gone through so many housekeepers it isn't funny. Nobody does anything the way she likes, so she complains all the time. My father told my mother to stop complaining and just do the housekeeping herself. But we both knew Miss Princess wouldn't dare lift a finger to clean or do anything that would make her sweat. I think that's why my father is fucking me — because my mother is so afraid of getting sweaty."

Kimberly's brutal candor slammed Dominique in the chest. "I hope not. How many different housekeepers do you think your family has had?"

"I don't know." Kimberly paused to think. "Maybe five. Ms. Jennings lasted the longest, but she got really sick and had to stop working. She was the only person my mother never complained about."

"About how long did the other housekeepers last?" Dominique continued to take notes.

"Usually they lasted a year or two maximum, if they were lucky. I really thought Maria was going to make it. I even told my mother I liked having Maria around, but my mother still let her go."

"Do you know where Maria is now?"

"No, but I'm sure I can find out. Our chauffeur liked Maria, too. I think they still stay in touch." Kimberly smiled for the first time since Dominique had met her. Her smile was sweet and distinct as her pearly white teeth shined along with her large dimple on the right side of her cheek.

"Do you think your chauffeur would be willing to speak with me?"

"No way!" Kimberly shook her head emphatically. "My father would kill him, and he knows it. None of my father's employees would ever tell on him. They're very loyal."

"Kimberly, I want you to give me the first and last names of all the housekeepers your family has had over the years."

As Kimberly named them, Dominique carefully wrote down the information. She would have someone speak with each of them. But Maria would be her personal quest. She had a hunch that Maria would play a key role in her conviction of Kimberly's father.

"When did you first notice the change in Maria's behavior when your father was around?"

Kimberly tilted her head back as she tried to recall the approximate time she noticed Maria's nervousness around her father. "I think it was about two months after she started. Maria was a real quiet person, but we talked to each other sometimes when my parents were out of the house. She was only seventeen years old. She sent most of her money back home to her family. They really relied on her to help. My father gave her a big bonus one holiday so she could send it back home. My family knew what she was doing and felt sorry for her. I even gave her some money for Christmas. I told her not to tell my parents. I didn't want them to know."

"Kimberly, that was really nice of you. Who actually fired the housekeepers?"

"My mother. My father never got involved with hiring or firing any of them. My mother handled all that stuff."

Dominique paused for a moment before asking any more questions. She reviewed her scribbled notes to make sure her facts were straight, even though she had her tape recorder for backup. "I need to know more details about the first time your father forced you to have sex with him. I want you to take your time, and be as specific as you can." Dominique prayed that the painful memories would not send Kimberly back into her hard, protective shell like a turtle.

But Kimberly didn't hesitate. She spilled out more details as if she was relieved that someone actually cared to hear them.

"My mother was out of town. So, it was only my father, Maria, and myself at the house that night. I didn't even know he was home. I thought he was out of town on business. When he came into my room, he told me, he was just coming to tuck me in. I remember smelling alcohol on his breath. I didn't think too much of that, because he always drank around the house. I was already in bed, but he insisted on making sure I was comfortable. Then he told me he wanted to play a game. I didn't think too much of that either. He used to play games with me all the time when I was a little girl. So, I went along.

"Up to then, my father had never touched or approached me in the wrong way. He told me we were going to play a secret game under the sheets. So, he took off his clothes and got in the bed with me. He told me to close my eyes while he started the game." Kimberly paused, and Dominique watched as tears filled Kimberly's eyes and her face became flushed. She continued telling her story as she lay her head back onto her pillow and closed her eyes. Tears rolled down Kimberly's face as she relived each horrible detail of that night. Kimberly's words crippled Dominique's note-taking and made her hands shake. She watched Kimberly wipe the tears away from her face as she freed herself of the horrible night.

"He told me not to make a sound because he didn't want to wake Maria. After he finished, he threaten me if I told anybody, he would kill me because it was our little secret. I didn't know what to do. He made me change the sheets on my bed because blood was everywhere. He took the bloody sheets with him. The next day he brought me a big stuffed animal and told me he loved me more than anything in the world. I don't understand how you can tell someone you love them and do what he's been doing to me. You can't love your child that way. It's wrong. I hope he goes to hell for what he's done!"

Dominique responded, "If I have my way, he'll think he's in hell. I plan to send your father to prison for a long time."

After Dominique and Kimberly had wrapped up the questioning and Dominique turned off the tape recorder, she gave Kimberly her private telephone number and told Kimberly she could call anytime.

"Ms. Wallace, I don't know why I told you everything. For some reason, it just came out. You're easy to talk to. You've been the first person I feel really cares about me. Everyone else has accused me of lying about everything, or they were secretly trying to protect my father's reputation.

"I'm telling the truth. Why would I make up something as horrible as this? My mother tells everybody I'm doing drugs and sleeping around. I'm not sleeping around. The only person I'm having sex with is my damn father!" Kimberly winced and rubbed her arm.

Dominique noted in her mind that Kimberly didn't say she was *not* using drugs. And if Buchanan's team of attorneys was sharp, they would use it to discredit her.

"Kimberly, do you, or have you, ever used drugs?"

"Yes, I've used drugs. I've had to use drugs to deal with all this shit. I don't care if you don't approve of me using drugs. I had to in order to survive." Kimberly's chin came up and her spine stiffened.

"I'm not here to judge you. I'm here to help you. I can understand why you felt a need in the past to use drugs, but you must promise me that you won't use them anymore, especially during this case. I don't want your father to be able to use that against you."

Kimberly relaxed, her small shoulders slumping forward and nodded to agree.

Dominique continued, "I'm going to arrange for you to stay here in the hospital. I think it would be very helpful for you to undergo therapy now. How do you feel about that?"

"I'm sure my mother has already started telling family members their side of the story. I hate them." Kimberly's lip curled in disgust.

"Well, let's not worry about them. The truth will come out in the end, and they'll know you've been telling the truth. I want you to get some rest now."

A sudden thought entered Dominique's mind. "Kimberly, before I go, I want to let you know that the media will try to visit you as soon as they discover where you are. I don't want you to talk to anyone about your case without me being present. I'll ask the nurse assigned to you to monitor your door to make sure no one tries to come in and bother you."

"What do you mean, 'the media?'" Kimberly sat upright in her bed. "I don't want everybody to know my father has been having sex with me. I've been humiliated enough already."

Kimberly's demeanor had changed abruptly, and Dominique would have to think quickly not to lose her. "Kimberly, your father is a very influential man in this community. They are going to be very curious about whether or not he is guilty. I think we can use this in our favor, but I want you to stay away from them. I don't want them to see or speak with you at all. I think the public will have a lot of sympathy for you because your father took advantage of you. Besides, you tried to commit suicide to escape all of this traumatic abuse. As a third party, I would feel complete sympathy for you, not him." Dominique was on slippery ground in bringing up the suicide. The media could try to spin the suicide attempt as a sign of the mental illness of a child who lies.

"Ms. Wallace, you don't think I'm lying? My mother has already told me she's going to tell everyone that I've been nothing but trouble if I go public with this."

"When did your mother tell you that?"

"Yesterday, when she stopped by. She's going to support my father until the end. She doesn't give a damn about me, and she never has. All she cares about is herself. She's an old bitch." Although Kimberly's words and voice contained venom, hurt was painted all over her face.

Dominique decided to address Kimberly's vulgar language with her later, but not now, for fear of jeopardizing their new relationship.

"Kimberly, don't worry about what your mother will say to others. The truth will come out during the trial. So, let her go right ahead. We can let that work in our favor, too. The court will feel even more sympathy toward you when they find out your mother has chosen to support your father, knowing he's guilty."

"She'll never admit she knows he's guilty. She'll go to her grave with that secret. My family is full of secrets and lies. I just want out!" Kimberly cried.

Dominique lightened the tone. "I understand, but the next time you decide to check out, please contact me first. I don't want you to do anything to yourself because of them or anyone else. You have a lot to live for, and I plan to see that you have an opportunity to experience it for yourself."

"May I call you Dominique?"

"Sure." Dominique smiled at Kimberly warmly.

"Dominique, can I ask you a personal question?"

"Go ahead."

"Do you have a daughter?"

"Yes."

"If she came to you and told you her father or anyone else was sexually abusing her, would you believe her right away?"

Dominique pondered Kimberly's question. Knowing her husband as she did, she would have difficulty believing that Eric would do such a thing. Then she stopped herself. She would definitely investigate for her daughter's sake. Devin was her flesh and blood, the only blood family she knew. From her experiences with practicing law, Dominique had learned that no one was above committing crimes.

"Kimberly, I would support my daughter. I would definitely do some investigating to verify the charges against my husband. As far as I can tell, she wouldn't lie to me, but she's just a little girl. I pray she will never have to go through what you have." Dominique patted Kimberly's arm.

Kimberly responded softly, pleading, "I do too. Promise me you'll always believe your daughter. No matter what."

"I promise. I have to leave now, but I'll come back to check on you tomorrow. I want you to get plenty of rest and please call me if you need to talk. I'm here to help you. Remember, you're not alone." Dominique waved goodbye.

Slowly she walked down the hallway to the nurses' station and left instructions that only those on her list be permitted to visit Kimberly. As she stepped onto the elevator and pressed the button for the garage level, thoughts raced through her head. She rode down alone until the elevator doors opened to the third floor. A very tall, muscular male wearing a faded blue jean shirt and pants stood before her.

"Going down?" He asked in a heavy voice, leaning toward Dominique.

"Yes."

As the two traveled down in silence, she shivered unaccountably. Dominique glanced over at the man, uncomfortable in his presence. Quietly she eased backward into the corner of the elevator, gripping her briefcase tightly. Her body started to tremble as she stared at the gold trim surrounding the doors, certain the man was watching her and waiting for the perfect moment to attack her.

As the doors slid open at the garage level, her heartbeat echoed loudly in her ears. She waited for the man to move.

As he stepped off, the man slowly turned his head and glanced over his shoulder at Dominique, who was still paralyzed in the corner of the elevator. The doors slowly closed in between them as Dominique breathed a sigh of relief and moved to get off.

Then a strange hand reached in between the doors, stopping it from closing

CHAPTER 4

Dominique's heart began to race, and she prayed desperately that it wasn't the tall, muscular man returning to fulfill his deed. Her eyes followed the strange hand to the face and took a deep breath when she realized it belonged to an elderly nun smiling at her.

"Miss, are you okay?" the nun asked as she reached out to comfort Dominique.

Without saying a word, Dominique raced past the nun before the doors closed, leaving the nun in the elevator alone. In a full sprint, she headed for her car, gasping for air, praying silently that no one was following her. Her hands shook as she reached into her purse and struggled to locate her keys.

Ah, there they were! She unlocked the car door, lowered herself into the driver's seat, and hastily locked the door. Just as she turned the key in the ignition, a loud ringing sound filled the air. Where was it coming from?

Her senses returned, and she recognized the sound was her cell phone ringing inside her briefcase. By the time, she pulled out the cell phone to answer it, the caller had hung up.

Dominique checked her caller ID and finally exhaled. The caller was her husband, Eric. She pressed the redial button.

Eric answered after the first ring. "Hello."

"Hi. Did you just try to call me?" Dominique's voice quivered.

"Yes, I did. Are you okay? You sound funny."

"I'm fine. What's up?" Embarrassment set in. She'd worked herself into a panic over nothing.

"I just wanted to call my beautiful wife to tell her I love her."

"Thank you and I love you too."

"How's your morning going so far?"

"Good. I've just agreed to represent a very high-profile case." The pride in her voice was apparent. She proceeded to back out and exit the garage deck. She continued to small talk with her husband as she drove back to her office.

She parked her car and headed directly to Shawn's office, and spent the remainder of the morning and part of the afternoon in his office. Then she retreated into her own office to review the notes from her conversation with Kimberly. When she finally remembered to look at her watch, it was five o'clock.

She drove home, savoring the fresh breeze coming through the sunroof as she tried to forget the panic episode in the elevator earlier that morning. She found the whole ordeal strange but quickly discarded the unsettling thoughts. She was eager to tell Eric about her new case.

When Dominique entered the house, Devin wrapped her short, chubby four-year-old arms around her mother's legs and proceeded to rattle off the childish events of her day.

"Mommy, I helped Ms. Anderson make cookies. She allowed me to mix the cookie dough like you do. Then I played with my dolls today. I had a tea party. Ms. Anderson allowed me to put real tea in my teapot to serve everyone," Devin rattled off without taking one break to take a breath.

As Dominique listened, her attention drifted back to her earlier conversation with Kimberly. At the same time, she hoped that Devin would continue to share things with her, good or bad, and that she would be honest and forthright in answering the questions that inevitably would arise.

Dominique instinctively reached down and gave Devin a hug and kiss. Giving birth and watching Devin grow had given Dominique the self-worth that she once had questioned and the peace that she had not known during her childhood.

"I have something I want to tell you," Dominique said suddenly.

"What is it, Mommy?" Devin looked up at her with a big smile on her face.

Dominique leaned over to tell Devin face to face. "I missed you today, and I want you to know how much I love you."

"I missed you, too." Devin nodded with a big smile on her face.

"I guess you don't love me?" Dominique joked.

"I love you, Mommy. I love both you and Daddy." Devin said playfully.

"Oh, I was just checking. Finish telling me about your day."

"I made you a picture to hang in your office." Devin pulled Dominique by the arm and led her mother into the sunroom. She walked over to her drawing table, picked up the colorful picture, and handed it to her mother with an enormous grin on her face.

Dominique glanced over the picture and kissed Devin on the forehead. "Sweetheart, this is absolutely beautiful. I can't wait to hang it up in my office. Thank you so much."

"You're welcome, Mommy." Devin was pleased with herself and with her mother's gratitude.

"What else did you and Ms. Anderson do today?"

Ms. Anderson was Devin's babysitter, a responsibility that had evolved into cooking, cleaning, and just about anything else the family needed over the years. Ms. Anderson had proven to be a family treasure.

She came up behind the pair, removing her apron. "Is there anything else I can do before I leave for the evening?"

"No, nothing that I can think of." Dominique walked Ms. Anderson to the door and stood watching her back out of their driveway.

No sooner had she left with a goodbye honk of the horn than Eric turned into the driveway and parked.

Devin jumped off the porch. "Daddy's home! Hello, Daddy!" she shouted. In full sprint, she headed in his direction.

"Hello, sweetheart." Eric stretched out his arms to receive Devin's embrace and picked her up.

Dominique chimed in from the doorway of their house. "How was your day?"

"It was okay, but it's a lot better now that I'm home with my two favorite ladies. How long have you been home?" Eric lowered Devin to the floor.

"Not long. Are you hungry?" Dominique leaned toward her husband and kissed him gently.

"Sure am. I didn't have lunch. The only break I had all day was when I called you. I've been working nonstop since this morning."

"I can't wait to tell you about my new case," Dominique said as she followed Eric into the kitchen. "Michael Buchanan is being charged with sexually molesting his thirteen-year-old daughter, Kimberly. And I'm going to be representing her!"

Eric stopped in his tracks and turned to face her solemnly. "Are you sure you want to represent this one?"

"Yes." She nodded, "I wasn't sure when it was first presented to me, but after speaking with his daughter, I knew I had to." She paused. "I really believe he's guilty, Eric."

"How did you get the case? I'm sure she didn't just walk into your office."

"No, she didn't. The state assigned me. Kimberly tried to commit suicide. She's in the hospital right now."

"How do you know she isn't lying about everything?"

"I don't think she is. Her story seems credible. I have a feeling he's forced at least one of the previous housekeepers to have sex with him, too."

"Did Kimberly say that?" Eric's eyes widened.

"No. But she did mention that she noticed one of their housekeepers was nervous around her father. I got a strong impression that he forced that woman to have sex with him. I think his wife found out and fired her, like she ended up doing with all the other housekeepers, because this one no longer works for the family." She added, "I have to find her and talk to her."

Dominique went on, "Kimberly gave me the names of all the housekeepers that were let go over the last few years. I'm willing to bet they were fired for more than not cleaning the house the way Mrs. Buchanan wanted." Dominique lifted the lid of the pot on the stove and savored the aroma of Ms. Anderson's homemade spaghetti sauce.

"So, what's Mrs. Buchanan's position in this case?"

"From what I can tell so far, she's supporting her husband's story. Kimberly doesn't get along with her mother. I bet Mrs. Buchanan knew something was going on, but I can't prove that until I have a chance to speak with her one on one."

"Do you think you'll be able to get him to admit he's guilty out of court? You know the media is going to have a field day with this." Eric leaned back against the kitchen counter.

"I know. I told Shawn the same thing." Dominique pointed to herself. "I'm going to be the lead prosecutor on this case, and he's going to assist me. Everybody thinks I would generate more sympathy from the jury as a woman. I'm willing to run with it if it works in my favor." Dominique had finally adopted the strategy she once questioned.

"Good luck. How soon do you think the former housekeepers can be located?" Eric took three plates from the cherry cabinets and set them on the table.

"I'm not sure. I'll have some people working on that—I'm hoping before the end of the business day tomorrow, if I'm lucky. I also think the housekeepers were illegal. Kimberly mentioned that one of them probably wouldn't say anything because she was afraid of being sent back. If I'm able to find her, I'll try to get her citizenship papers in exchange for her testimony against Buchanan."

Eric took the silverware from the drawer. "Good luck."

Dominique drained the spaghetti and heaped a generous serving onto each plate. Then she ladled some of the sauce over the steaming pasta.

"This spaghetti and meatballs smell delicious." Eric pulled up chairs for himself and his wife. Devin, already in place, dug in with her fork.

"Mommy, what does 'sex' mean?" she asked, with a strand of spaghetti dangling from her mouth.

Dominique choked momentarily. She looked over at Eric for support. He smiled back, pointing at his own mouth full of spaghetti. The question was Dominique's to answer.

"Sex is when two people who love each other sleep together."

"Mommy, why is Kimberly's daddy in trouble for sleeping with her? Daddy sleeps with me sometimes when I can't go to sleep. Will he have to go to jail too?"

Devin's eyebrows bunched together and she frowned. Obviously, Devin's father wasn't sleeping with her in the same way Kimberly's father was sleeping with his own daughter. At least Dominique hoped not. A gnawing anxiety entered her mind fleetingly, and she looked over at her husband anxiously.

"Dominique, I think you should explain the difference to her." Eric put down his fork to listen to Dominique's explanation.

Dominique smiled broadly at Eric and turned to address Devin. "Kimberly's father was sleeping with her in a different way. He made her do things she didn't want to do when he was in bed with her. He would hurt her in bed, and she didn't like that. Daddy doesn't make you do things Kimberly's father was making her do. Daddy doesn't hurt you."

"I still don't understand," Devin responded.

"Remember when we went to the zoo and we saw those snakes all wrapped up together?"

"Yes. You said they were mating. They weren't in a bed. They were in a glass box."

Dominique was always so amused at Devin's level of intelligence and curiosity. Maybe Dominique should have paid more attention to the details about Kimberly she was relating to Eric in her daughter's presence.

"The difference between Kimberly and the snakes is that Kimberly and her dad were in the bed doing the same thing. But animals don't sleep in beds. They sleep together on the ground. Do you understand now?"

"Maybe. Do you and Daddy wrap up like the snakes?"

Dominique nodded yes without speaking.

"That's nasty." Devin stuck out her tongue in disgust.

Eric and Dominique both burst out laughing, relieved. They hoped their daughter would continue to feel that way until she was old enough to really understand.

"You're right," Eric joked. "It's nasty. I don't know why your mom likes to do it."

"Eric, stop it! Your daddy is just playing with you, Devin, and please don't repeat what we've talked about this evening? You have to keep what you heard about Kimberly and her father a secret. No one is supposed to know."

"I know. I don't want you to get in trouble at work." Devin parroted what she'd heard from Dominique the last time she'd eavesdropped on her parents discussing work.

"You're right. Good girl." Dominique jumped at the chance to change the subject.

CHAPTER 5

The next morning Dominique was sitting at the mahogany desk in her downtown office, reviewing Kimberly's case notes, when her telephone rang. Anticipating more information to use against Buchanan, she answered before it could ring a second time.

"Good morning. I have Maria Gonzales's address." Shawn eagerly shared.

"Great! Please give it to me. I want to speak with her as soon as possible." Dominique scribbled the information on a yellow legal pad. "Shawn, I need to get going." She hung up and without removing the phone from her ear, pressed the extension of her assistant.

"Holly, please print me the directions to 3201 Shamrock Street. I'll pick it up on my way out."

"Are you leaving for the day?" Holly asked.

"No. I have an important errand to run, but I'll be right back. Page me if you need to." Dominique grabbed her pocketbook and a half-used notepad and headed for Holly's desk out front.

"Thanks," Dominique acknowledged as she took the address to Maria's house that Holly handed her.

The directions were easy to follow. Dominique drove in silence as she passed block after block of boarded-up buildings with trash and old, abandoned cars left out front. Many years ago, this had been an affluent and safe neighborhood, a neighborhood with much pride, but death and depression had raised their ugly faces. And now life wasn't as comfortable in this part of town, and hardship was plastered all around for anyone to see. Had it not been daytime, and with the mace container in her pocketbook, Dominique might have asked for backup. Instead, she parked in front of a small frame house marked by the number 3201 and observed the surroundings.

Through the front windshield, she noticed a group of young boys loitering in front of the corner store. One of the young boys approached a car, quickly exchanged something, and returned to his original position with the others. Dominique assumed she had witnessed a drug deal, but she didn't care to investigate.

Then she noticed across the street another group, a mix of boys and girls, sitting on the steps of an apartment building about half a block away. They were pointing excitedly at Dominique's car. Under normal circumstances, Dominique enjoyed attention to her sporty black 740iL, but today their glances were making her squirm.

She slowly got out of her car and locked it, then cautiously approached Maria's door and knocked. There was no answer.

Dominique looked down at her watch. It was still early afternoon. She strode back to her car with her head up. She had been told that alertness and a sense of purpose were signals for anyone who might entertain thoughts of harming her to stay away.

She decided to pay another visit to Kimberly.

As she drove to the hospital, she wondered how many of the kids she had seen congregating in Maria's neighborhood would live to see their thirtieth birthday. And if they were lucky enough to see their thirtieth birthday, it would probably be behind bars. She'd seen one or two make it, but they'd been the exception.

After finally snaring a space in the crowded parking garage, Dominique entered the building, where the smell of disinfectant assaulted her nose. The familiar smell normally indicated cleanliness, but here it was just a cover-up for all the sickness within.

As she doubled-checked the number on Kimberly's door, a man in a white jacket approached. "Excuse me, miss."

"Yes?" Dominique wondered if he was Kimberly's doctor.

"That's a private room. The patient has requested that we not allow anyone inside."

"I'm Kimberly Buchanan's attorney, Dominique Wallace. I was the one who requested that no one be allowed to enter her room unless their name was on the list." Dominique searched the white jacket for the doctor's name, but his pen case flap obscured it. "Are you Kimberly's doctor?"

"May I see some identification, please? I just want to make sure."

Dominique reached into her pocketbook and produced her driver's license.

"Thank you. I'm Dr. Ellis, and yes, I'm Kimberly's doctor." He handed back the license.

"Good," Dominique smiled at him. "I'd like to talk to you about her condition. Have you performed a complete physical examination on Kimberly yet?"

The doctor did not return her smile. "Yes, we have. I just received the preliminary results."

Dominique moved back from Kimberly's door. "What did you find?"

"Kimberly has indeed been sexually active. Her test results show that she has been penetrated recently, and she has a case of gonorrhea. I haven't told her yet. I was just about to go in and see her." The doctor lowered his voice further. "She's really lucky to be here today. When they brought her in, she had lost a lot of blood from her suicide attempt."

"Do you know how long she's had the STD?"

"It's not possible to know, but further testing of her father would reveal his current status. I'm going to start treating her right away." Dr. Ellis held Kimberly's chart close to his chest.

"How soon could I have Buchanan's test results if he were required to take a physical examination?"

"This type of testing could produce quick results."

"Good." Dominique nodded. "Do you mind if I'm present when you tell Kimberly about her test results? I think she's going to need some support when she finds out she has gonorrhea. And some explanations, too." What did a thirteen-year-old know about STDs?

Dr. Ellis hesitated.

"I'll have to assess her condition. Will you wait a few minutes?"

Certainly, she would.

Much sooner than Dominique had expected, the doctor stepped outside the door and invited her in. Kimberly was smiling and looked perkier than she had the previous day.

The doctor began. "Your lawyer asked to be present while I tell you about your test results, and I've agreed to her being present. Is that okay with you?"

Silently, Dominique thanked God that Dr. Ellis hadn't told her Kimberly was pregnant. At least with gonorrhea, she could be treated and move on with her life. A baby would really complicate matters. She was just a child herself.

"First, we have your blood pressure under control. You lost a lot of blood the other day and gave us quite a scare."

After pausing, Dr. Ellis added, "However, we did find gonorrhea present."

"What's gonorrhea?" Kimberly leaned forward quizzically.

"Gonorrhea is a disease transmitted by sexual contact." The doctor's face was neutral, but his eyes conveyed kindness.

Kimberly burst into tears. "I can't believe that dirty bastard gave me a disease. Oh, my God! I hate him! I hate him! I want to kill him!" Kimberly reached for the hand Dominique held out.

"It's going to be okay, Kimberly. They can treat the gonorrhea and get rid of it. Please don't be upset."

Dr. Ellis interjected, "From a medical viewpoint, it would be best for you to stay calm."

Dominique embraced Kimberly's trembling body until she stopped shouting and surrendered to the tears that erupted like a waterfall. Dominique could only imagine Kimberly's anger and frustration.

"Dominique, promise me he'll go to prison. I want him to pay. He's ruined my life. If I had my way, that motherfucker wouldn't live another day."

After a pause, Kimberly continued. "Please don't make me tell anybody about this. I don't want anybody to know." She clutched at Dominique's shoulders.

Dominique turned to Dr. Ellis, confirming the girls' wishes. "A guardian has been assigned to Kimberly until the case is over. Information about her condition is not to be shared beyond the guardian and us."

After explaining the treatment protocol to Kimberly, Dr. Ellis left the room.

Kimberly resumed shouting, "I can't believe he did this to me." She threw her arms above her head, her fists in tight balls. "Actually, yes I can.

He doesn't give a damn about me. Look at me! I have a disease now because of him. I wonder if my mother has gonorrhea, too?"

"I would like to know also. I'm going to have your father tested to see if he has gonorrhea. I probably won't be able to test your mother, but I can request that your father be tested. If his test shows he has gonorrhea, it will definitely help confirm your charges against him."

"What if his test doesn't show that he has it? What if he doesn't have it anymore?"

"Excuse me for a second, Kimberly." Dominique dialed Shawn's number and asked if he would request that Buchanan be tested right away. A positive test result would be crucial in the prosecution.

"I'll stop by tomorrow, Kimberly, but if you need to talk before then, please call me," Dominique reminded Kimberly as she left.

Dominique almost collided head on with a woman on her way to Kimberly's room. By the look of the chic attire, Dominique could tell she wasn't part of the hospital staff. Maybe a news reporter wanting to interview Kimberly?

"Excuse me. No unauthorized visitors allowed."

The petite woman looked squarely at Dominique.

"I'm Kimberly's mother. Who are you?"

Momentarily taken aback, Dominique responded, "I'm Kimberly's attorney, Dominique Wallace. May I speak to you about your daughter's case?" Dominique reached out to shake her hand. Mrs. Buchanan did not return the gesture.

"I have nothing to say to you. If you have any questions, you need to speak with my attorney." Mrs. Buchanan backed away.

Dominique decided to be direct, to disarm the woman. "I have something I want to share with you regarding Kimberly's current condition. Dr. Ellis just shared some disturbing test results with Kimberly and myself. I would prefer if the whole hospital didn't hear our discussion." Dominique moved sideways toward the waiting room without removing her eyes from Mrs. Buchanan for very long as they made their way to the empty waiting room.

"Mrs. Buchanan, Kimberly tells me you don't believe your husband has sexually abused her. I would like to know why."

Mrs. Buchanan took a deep breath before responding.

"I'll tell you this. Our daughter has a history of lying. I'm furious about what's she trying to do to her father and to our family's name."

"Mrs. Buchanan, your daughter doesn't want you to visit her. She's requested that you not be allowed to see her while she's at the hospital."

Mrs. Buchanan stepped back from Dominique.

"I'm still her mother. I have every right to see her."

Dominique was firm. "I have to respect her wishes. You are not allowed to visit."

Mrs. Buchanan dropped her head.

"I'm not sure what lies my daughter has told you. But we have done nothing to hurt or harm her. We've tried to do everything we can to give her a good life. We've made sure she has had the best of everything. I don't know what else we can do for her." Mrs. Buchanan tossed her chin upward in a gesture Dominique had seen Kimberly use.

Dominique decided to be blunt.

"You can help her. Stop ignoring the fact that your husband is sexually molesting your daughter! Mrs. Buchanan, we're able to help her and you if you're willing to testify that your husband has been sexually molesting Kimberly. We have organizations and programs available for people in your situation."

Mrs. Buchanan stuck out her chest. "I don't think you understand who my husband is. I have nothing to confess. My daughter is obviously telling you lies, and I refuse to listen to this drivel any longer." Mrs. Buchanan stalked out of the room.

"Mrs. Buchanan. Wait!" Even as she spoke, Dominique realized it would be a waste of time to go after Mrs. Buchanan.

Dominique looked at her watch. It was already after six o'clock, and the sun would be setting soon. She would have to rush to return to Maria's house with the hope of speaking with her.

Dominique drove slowly as she entered Shamrock Street again. She parked and glanced around to see if anyone was watching her. Seeing no one, she got out of her car, proceeded up the sidewalk and knocked. This time Maria answered the door.

CHAPTER 6

As the woman appeared in the doorway, Dominique looked approvingly at her tall, slender body clad in a white uniform. Her long, dark hair framed her anxious face. "Good evening. Are you Maria Gonzales?"

"Si … yes."

"My name is Dominique Wallace. I'm a state's attorney." Dominique held her hand out to Maria.

Maria stepped back inside her doorway, ignoring Dominique's reaching hand. Dominique hastened to reassure her. "Maria, you're not in trouble. Actually, I need your help."

"Sorry, Señora, I cannot help you." Maria started to close the door in Dominique's face.

Dominique quickly placed her hand on the door and held it open.

"Maria, please hear me out. If you listen to what I have to say, I can help you become a citizen." Dominique pleaded with her eyes.

Maria's face flushed, and she pulled her hair back away from her face.

"I am a citizen. I don't know who told you I'm not." She again pushed against the door.

"Kimberly Buchanan." Dominique allowed the name to sink in. "She's the reason I'm here today. She needs your help."

"I don't know anything. I told you. I got my papers after I worked for her family." Maria's hands shook, but she seemed convincing.

"Maria, Kimberly tried to take her life." Dominique hurried on, knowing that Maria could turn her away for good at any moment. "She confessed her father has been sexually molesting her. I think he has forced other women to have sex with him, too. If he has, I need to know so I can have him put away."

34

Maria leaned out of her door and quickly peeked in both directions. "Does Señor Buchanan know you came here asking me these questions?"

"No, he doesn't know. I'm here on behalf of Kimberly. She likes you a lot and she wants me to help you become a citizen."

"I like Señorita Buchanan, too. She was nice to me." Finally, Maria stepped back and motioned Dominique to come in.

"You said Señor Buchanan does not know you are here. How did you find me?" Maria's brows were knitted, and she rubbed her hands together nervously.

"I have ways of finding people in my job. Don't worry. I won't let Mr. Buchanan know where you are. If you're really worried, we could help you find another place to live."

Dominique was surprised at Maria's quick response. "Bueno! If you found me, he can too." Maria obviously had no qualms about leaving her neighborhood either. "Why does Señorita Buchanan want me to help her?"

Dominique chose her words carefully. "Mr. Buchanan has been hurting Kimberly. We think he might have hurt you, too, in some way. Did he ever force you to do things that you didn't want to do … personal things?"

Maria started to pace on the worn rug.

"I can't talk. He will try to send me back to my country. I lied. I'm not a citizen." Maria ran her hands through her hair.

"Maria, I need you to tell me the truth about everything. What he did to you? I can't help you unless you tell me everything."

"How do I know that? Why should I believe you?"

"Well, you have to. Maria, you know I can turn you in now."

Maria's body shook and she burst into tears. Head down, she mumbled something in Spanish.

"Maria, can we sit down and talk about this? Can you do that?" Maria stared at Dominique for what seemed like minutes. Finally, Maria lowered herself onto a worn, stuffed chair, and Dominique sat down on the threadbare sofa facing her.

"Si. He did that … sex … It was awful. And he told me if I told anybody, he would kill me. He has power. He will come back to punish me." Maria cried out as tears started to form in her eyes.

Dominique reassured her. "What you are doing is the right thing. I'll protect you. Will you tell me how many times that happened? How many times did he do sexual things to you?"

Maria's eyes were still full of tears. She answered nervously. "I can't remember. Many times. He waited until Señora Buchanan was asleep. Then he would come to my room."

"Why did you leave the Buchanan's home?"

"Senora Buchanan let me go. She knew what was going on. She gave me some money to leave and told me if I ever told anybody she would have me sent back to my country."

"When and how did she find out?"

"I think it was the night Senor Buchanan thought his wife was going to be out of town, but she came home early. She knocked on my door, and Senor Buchanan told me to tell her I was getting dressed and that I couldn't open the door.

"She asked me if I knew where everybody was. I reminded her that Kimberly was staying with a friend and I didn't know where Senor Buchanan was.

"He made me wait a few minutes before opening the door so he could slip out without her knowing he was in my room. I thought that almost getting caught would stop him from coming to my room again, but it didn't. He continued to come just about every day until Senora Buchanan fired me. She said I wasn't doing a good job, and it was taking me too long to catch on. I didn't argue with her. I was glad to be leaving that place. The only thing I was worried about was being sent back to my country.

"Senora Wallace, my family is counting on me to send money back to help them. I can't afford to get into trouble. I can't go to court because I will be sent back if I don't have my citizenship papers."

"Maria, don't worry about that. I will get you your citizenship papers. Were you aware Mr. Buchanan was sexually abusing his daughter, too?"

"Si," Maria answered as she lowered her head.

"How did you know?"

Maria took a deep breath. "I saw Senor Buchanan watching a videotape of him and his daughter having sex."

"A videotape," Dominique repeated in disbelief.

"Si. He taped it himself."

Dominique was spellbound by the news of the videotape and celebrated her victory silently. She couldn't believe Buchanan would be reckless enough to make a videotape of himself and his daughter. Kimberly never mentioned anything about any videotapes. More than likely Kimberly didn't even know her father had taped them. And she dreaded the thought of having to tell her of its existence.

"Maria, did Mr. Buchanan tape the two of you having sex too?"

Maria dropped her head and shamefully answered. "Si."

"Did you know he was taping you?"

"No. He hid the camera in the room somewhere. I don't think Kimberly knew he was taping them, either." Maria paused. "I snooped around the house when Senor and Senora Buchanan went out of town. I found his videotape of us. He's a sick man, Senora Wallace."

Dominique agreed, but she wanted to finish discussing the videotapes. "Where did you find the videotapes?"

"They were in his office. He had them hidden in the floor. I don't know who else knows. The only reason I know about the secret hiding place is because I saw him go to it one day while I was cleaning outside of his office. I peeked in when he wasn't looking. I never told anybody else about the secret place."

"Are you sure he doesn't know you saw him that day?" Dominique prayed he hadn't noticed and moved them somewhere else.

"Si. I was really quiet. He didn't even know I was in the hallway cleaning. Senora Buchanan never liked us to make noises in the house. We had to do our work quietly. No singing or talking around the house. She said it would disturb the members of the house if they were working or resting."

"How many videotapes were down in the hole that day?"

"There were about five videotapes in the hole then. I'm not sure how many are still there. It's been about two years since I last worked there. I took my videotape out of the hole while they were gone. I prayed he wouldn't notice it." Maria shook her head side to side.

"Where is the tape now?" Dominique asked, praying she hadn't destroyed it.

With a sigh and a proud smile, she replied, "I destroyed it."

"Damn," Dominique blurted out.

"I'm sorry. I didn't want anyone to see it. I only pray he doesn't have any more of me in that hole," Maria said, with tears streaming down her face. "I didn't get a chance to check before I left their home the last time. Señora Buchanan made me pack my things and leave that same day." A worried look crossed Maria's face. "Does that mean you won't be able to use the videotapes against him?"

"I'm not sure. I have to get my hands on the other videotapes."

Dominique paced the floor trying to figure out her next move.

"If you do, who will see them? Will they be shown all over the news?" Maria asked with a very worried look on her face.

"No. Normally evidence such as sexual tapes are not shown in open court because of the nature of the material. However, I can't guarantee that the media won't get wind of it and plaster the information about them being used as evidence all over the news. But if I'm lucky, Mr. Buchanan will plead guilty and no one will hear about the videotapes other than his attorneys, my team, and the judge."

"When are you going to get the other videotapes?"

"As soon as I can."

"I'm afraid Senor Buchanan is going to find me and kill me. I can't stay here." Maria twisted the hem of her shirt in a state of panic.

"I know. I'll arrange for you to be relocated now. In the meantime, I'll start the process to get your citizenship papers approved as I promised."

Dominique tried to comfort Maria. She nodded without saying a word.

"Excuse me for a moment." Dominique pulled out her cell phone to call Shawn in order to make arrangements for Maria to be placed into protective custody. After she hung up, she continued to ask Maria more questions about Buchanan. "Do you think Mr. Buchanan knows where you are working now?"

"I don't know. I remember him telling me one day, if he ever wanted to find someone, it wouldn't be hard. He has connections all over the world. Senor Buchanan is a very powerful man, Señora Wallace." Maria dropped into an extremely worn easy chair and rubbed her forehead.

"I know, but I'm a very powerful attorney," Dominique boasted boldly. "Don't worry about a thing. I will take care of it."

Until now, Dominique had no idea how ruthless Buchanan could be. Before yesterday, she knew very little about him, but she was quickly getting the impression he was someone to fear. And leaving Maria exposed without proper protection was asking for an accident. She would have to keep Maria safe.

"I need to get a few things before we go." Maria rose, suddenly seeming calmer than she had before.

"I'll wait out here while you pack." Dominique sat on the worn couch as she waited for Kevin Dunbar, her police assistant, to return her call informing her of the details for Maria's relocation. Over the years, Kevin had proven to be trustworthy, unlike some corrupt policemen Dominique heard about. Because of the severity of this case, Dominique didn't feel she could trust just anyone with Maria's safety.

Maria disappeared down her hallway into a bedroom. Dominique saw no need to follow and watch Maria pack her belongings. She would give her privacy as she waited for her call.

A loud crash echoed from down the hallway.

"Maria, are you okay?" Dominique yelled from the front room, but there was no response. She ran to the end of the hall and entered the bedroom.

The bedroom was empty. Long, bright, sheer curtains swung in the wind from the open window. Dominique rushed across the room and looked out. There was no sign of Maria anywhere. Dominique knew she was scared. To her, running probably seemed like the best option.

Dominique's cell phone rang and she jumped. "Hello?"

"Hello, Dominique. I have the information you requested."

"Kevin, my girl just bailed on me. I got a runner. Guess I acted too prematurely?" She sighed. "I need you to locate her again." Dominique gave Kevin Maria's description and hung up.

She was upset with herself for allowing Maria to slip through her fingers. She never considered for a second she would jump out of her window and run after she promised to put her in protective custody and get her citizenship approved. She thought everything was going to be fine. She'd get Maria's testimony, help convict Buchanan, and Maria would become a citizen and go scot-free. But now things were more complicated—unnecessarily, in Dominique's opinion. Now the police were going to be looking for an illegal alien instead of protecting her, making Dominique's argument to grant Maria's citizenship more difficult.

Afraid of what was waiting outside of Maria's apartment, Dominique cautiously opened Maria's front door and peered out.

Several teenage boys stood around her car looking inside. Her heart raced, and her hands started to shake nervously. She didn't know what to do.

She debated calling the police for assistance and questioned whether they would even come to her aid in this neighborhood. She tried to think positively as her nervousness climaxed. Maybe they were honestly admiring her car.

Dominique took a deep breath and stepped out of Maria's front door, praying she hadn't made the wrong decision in trusting the teenage boys' intentions. She approached her car, pretending to be calm and unaffected by their presence. She pressed the unlock button on her key chain.

"This belongs to you, Mommy?" One of the boys asked Dominique with a Hispanic accent. He backed up to make space for Dominique to open her car door.

"It sure does."

"You took a risk leaving it around here, Mommy." Another boy came forward to lean on the rear passenger door.

"I guess. Thanks for watching it for me." Dominique opened her car door and got in. Still trying to look calm, she started her engine and pulled off, her hands gripping her steering wheel tightly. She was thankful things hadn't gone differently, but next time she would bring Shawn or someone else with her for backup.

Dominique turned onto the interstate and accelerated in the direction of her neighborhood. More relaxed now, she dialed Shawn's cell phone number and told him about everything. He immediately called to get a warrant to search Buchanan's house before he had a chance to remove the videotapes.

Dominique raced home and waited for the phone calls telling her the videotapes and Maria were safely in the state's possession. And if Maria couldn't be found right away, she prayed she would at least be able to get her hands on the videotapes as evidence.

Dominique ate her dinner and tried to stay up as long as she could, but her eyes started to become heavier with each passing hour.

Eric, clothed in his pajama pants, leaned into their office doorway. "Dominique, are you going to come to bed tonight?"

"Yes. I was trying to wait up for some important information." She wiped her tired eyes and stood. "I'm so tired."

"Then go to bed. They'll call you with the information. Don't they always?" Eric was joking, but Dominique didn't respond. Yes, she did receive calls at all times. That was the nature of her position. And Eric's executive position was just as demanding. His company required him to be available at a moment's notice. And fortunately for them, they were both very accepting of each other's careers.

Dominique followed Eric upstairs to their bedroom, undressed, and got into bed. She fell into a deep sleep as soon as her exhausted body touched the cool, comfortable sheets on their bed, never even hearing the telephone when it finally rang.

"Dominique?" Eric shook her sleeping body.

Half asleep, Dominique answered. "What?"

"I think it's the call you were waiting for." He held the telephone beside Dominique's ear.

Dominique immediately reached for the telephone and answered with a raspy voice. "Hello?"

"Sorry to call so late, Dominique."

"Kevin."

"I think you will be glad to know what we retrieved from Mr. Buchanan's house!"

"What did you get?" Dominique sat up in the bed, now wide awake.

"We retrieved a total of five videotapes. Buchanan had quite a collection. We haven't been able to watch them all, but the ones we've been able to view, you definitely will be interested in. We have him and his daughter on one videotape. The others are with other women. None happen to be his wife."

"Great. I definitely need to see the one with his daughter and him."

"I will have the conference room set up for you first thing tomorrow unless you want to come down now and view them." Dominique glanced at her alarm clock, saw that it read two thirty a.m., and decided to wait to view them later that morning. They would keep a few more hours.

"I'll be in around seven. Kevin, thanks for calling me with the news."

"My pleasure."

"Do you have any leads on the whereabouts of Maria Gonzales yet?"

"Not yet, but we are doing our best."

"Call me when you hear anything."

"I sure will. See you later."

"Good night and good work."

Dominique handed the telephone back to Eric. "I got him now." Dominique jumped up out of the bed and danced around.

"What's going on? You never told me what was so important."

"I had a warrant issued to search Buchanan's house. I got a lead he had videotapes that would show him sexually abusing his daughter. I can't believe the fool videotaped himself with everybody."

"How did you find out about the videotapes?" Eric sat up, fluffing the pillow behind himself.

"One of his previous housekeepers told me. The only thing is, I lost her today. She jumped out of her window while I was in the other room. I have the police looking for her now. I only hope we can get to her before Buchanan does. And I hope he's smart enough to plea out of court before the press gets wind of the videotapes."

"Did his daughter know she was being videotaped?"

"No, I don't think so. Maria told me that she didn't know she was being taped. She accidentally found out one day while she was cleaning up the house. He was watching it in his study. I thank the Lord he didn't see her and move them. There's no way he can deny the charge now that I have those videotapes in possession. He has to plead guilty if he has any sense."

"I wonder what he's doing now?" Eric asked, shaking his head in disbelief.

"I don't know. I'm sure he's wondering how I found out about them. If it hadn't been for Maria, I wouldn't have known about his collection. I wonder what he's telling his wife and attorney."

"That's a good question."

"I hope his wife realizes he is guilty and will be angry enough to testify against him." Dominique found it hard to believe she was okay with ignoring the truth. "Earlier today when I spoke with her, she was dead set on supporting him. Unfortunately, I couldn't force her to talk because she's protected by the spouse's clause, the law that protects spouses from having to testify against the other in court." Dominique shared with Eric, knowing he could be trusted one hundred percent.

"Did she tell you why she doesn't believe her husband is guilty?"

"She says Kimberly is lying, but I really don't think she is. Today, Kimberly's doctor told me she has contracted gonorrhea. So, I'm having her father tested now."

"You're kidding. Did his test come back positive for gonorrhea, too?"

"We haven't gotten his test results back yet. Hopefully, his results will be back soon."

"Well, if he has given his daughter gonorrhea, his wife must have it too. I find it amusing how all this stuff is going on around us and we have no clue. What a sick bastard."

"Eric, you'd be surprised to know some of the crimes people commit. I don't understand it myself. I'll never understand how someone could do something as awful as having sex with their own child. I would kill you if you ever did anything to hurt Devin."

"Well, you don't have to worry about me. But I would like to start working on another child." Eric turned his body in her direction and pulled her closer.

Dominique allowed her body to be embraced by Eric's strong hold, escaping to a place of pure pleasure. Eric was gentle and passionate as he entered her. He filled her and Dominique felt his abundant love explode inside of her. Completely satisfied, they held each other tightly until they drifted off to sleep.

CHAPTER 7

Dominique rose around six and dressed, trying not to wake Eric. Then she drove to the police station to review Buchanan's videotapes before his bond hearing.

"Good morning, Kevin." Dominique stood in Kevin's doorway and watched him working on some paperwork at his desk.

Kevin immediately looked up. "Good morning." He checked his wristwatch.

Kevin stood from his desk and told Dominique to follow him to a private conference room. She was amused to see how many people were being questioned at seven. Trying not to stare, she made eye contact with a young pregnant girl wearing a provocative dress. Dominique assumed she was a working girl. Still pulling tricks while very much pregnant? From the look of her protruding stomach, she had to be at least eight months along. Dominique wondered what the young mother-to-be's plans were after the birth of her baby. Would she stop pulling tricks and raise her child, working a more suitable profession? Or would she give the baby up for adoption at birth? Or would she just continue to pull tricks to make a living as she raised her baby? Dominique prayed silently for the young pregnant mother and baby's future.

Dominique thought about how lucky she had been growing up, without the proper influence of her parents, knowing her life today could have been similar to the young lady before her. Maybe after the young girl's arrest today, she would decide to call her parents for help. And if she was lucky enough to have parents that still cared about her, they would come and rescue her from her personal destruction and provide the baby with a suitable upbringing.

Kevin pulled a chair away from the conference table for Dominique while he started the VCR. Videotape after videotape, Dominique watched in silence, completely disgusted as Buchanan enjoyed sexual pleasures with women who were clearly obeying his command. But tears started to fill her eyes when she watched Buchanan demanding sex from Kimberly while she cried.

Dominique looked down at her watch. It was already nine o'clock, and in two more hours she would need to be in court. Before leaving, Dominique made sure the videotapes were placed in top security at the police station. She wanted Buchanan's videotapes to be the catalyst that proved his guilt because she couldn't imagine a jury in the state of Virginia that wouldn't convict him of his charges after viewing them.

Dominique entered her office building and noticed Shawn standing by the security desk. She headed in his direction to brief him on everything she had just seen at the police station.

"Excuse me." Dominique politely interrupted.

"Good morning." Shawn acknowledged, turning to greet Dominique.

"I need to speak with you before we go into court."

"Sure." Shawn excused himself and began to walk with her in the direction of the courtroom.

"Sorry, but I really need to talk to you about Buchanan's case. I just left the police station after viewing his videotapes."

"I went down last night after Kevin called me. I can't believe how lucky we were to find those tapes. There is nothing he can say that will convince the court that he's not guilty. He was so stupid."

"I know. It's almost too good to be true. Unfortunately for the young ladies, their personal lives might be plastered all over the news. I know he must be dying to know who revealed his secret hiding place."

"I wish I could have been there to see his face when they pulled back the rug in his study and took possession of his videotapes. Kevin said he went insane and they had to restrain him. I wonder what he told his attorney." Shawn paused. "Dominique, I'm surprised they haven't called us yet."

"I'm surprised too. They're probably trying to decide what type of deal they want to make. I want him to pay dearly for what he's done. He needs to be made an example."

"I agree."

They exited the lobby area of their office building and headed for the courtroom. Dominique and Shawn both knew Buchanan would get out on bond, so they didn't waste any time trying to prevent it. Their energy was better spent getting enough evidence against him to ensure an indictment during the grand jury.

The courtroom was filled when Dominique and Shawn entered. The news had traveled fast about Buchanan's case. But she wasn't surprised. The news industry, without fail, always managed to get leads on everything. She was concerned only about Kimberly watching her personal life on the news before she had a chance to prepare her. She prayed the news wouldn't send Maria into deeper hiding.

Dominique, with Shawn at her side, proceeded to their designated section in the courtroom and sat down to wait for the magistrate to enter and begin the bond hearing. She glanced over her shoulder at the defendant's table. She recognized Buchanan's attorneys, Mark Jennings and Larry Peters. They were partners at one of the top law firms in the state—Courtney and Bushey—and they, too, demanded a lot of respect in the courtroom. But now that she had Buchanan's videotapes in possession she felt more at ease. She had a very strong case and Buchanan by the balls. When she relocated Maria and got her to testify, she was certain she would be able to convince the court without a doubt.

Dominique continued to look in the defendant's direction. Behind Mark and Larry, she recognized Mrs. Buchanan, who was wearing an attractive lime silk suit. Her hair was pulled back from her face ever so neatly as she calmly stared straight ahead.

Dominique redirected her gaze to Mark and Larry. Buchanan, examining her from his chair, didn't show any facial expression, just cold observation.

Dominique welcomed Buchanan's examination as she checked out his inordinately clean-cut appearance. He wore a navy suit that accented his broad shoulders. Under normal circumstances, Dominique would have admired his disposition, but today she was there to prosecute this well-dressed man. Dominique continued to stare back. She watched Buchanan whisper something in Mark's ear and return his attention to the front. Mark immediately turned and made eye contact.

"Good morning, Mrs. Wallace." Mark grinned from his defendant's table. "Seems you have been a little busy lately."

"I guess I have been. Collecting enough evidence is vital to a successful conviction." He was referring to Buchanan's videotapes she'd retrieved. She was surprised how calm he was with her having them because now his job would be more difficult.

"You're definitely right about that. Seems to me you've been learning from the best. We need to talk." Mark's arrogant grin disappeared from his face. Dominique didn't appreciate his comment or his tone, and she certainly wasn't going to entertain his arrogance.

Before Mark could say anything else, the judge entered the courtroom. Everyone was told to stand. Judge Clarence Bacon took his seat and motioned for everyone to sit.

"Good morning, court," the judge greeted everyone from his chair. "Good morning, attorneys Wallace and Silver."

"Good morning," Dominique and Shawn responded in unison.

"Good morning, attorneys Jennings and Peters."

"Good morning," Mark and Larry returned.

"Is the defendant ready to proceed?"

"Yes, sir," Mark and his team answered.

"How do you plead?"

"We plead not guilty," Mark answered in a confident tone, staring Judge Clarence Bacon straight on.

"The defendant has pleaded not guilty to sexual abuse charges," Judge Clarence Bacon informed the court. "Has the defendant made arrangements for a bond?"

"Yes, Your Honor, we have." Mark proceeded with the details of the bond. "We have made agreements with the district attorney at four hundred thousand dollars."

"Okay. I will set the preliminary hearing for two weeks from today. I request that the defendant have no contact, physical or verbal, direct or indirect, with the victim and shall not initiate any contact with the victim. Mr. Buchanan, I'm setting your bond at four hundred thousand dollars."

Shawn whispered in Dominique's ear as they gathered their belongings. "I can't wait to hear what his reasons are for pleading not guilty."

"I'm interested in hearing his story, too," Dominique whispered back as they rose from their seats to exit the courtroom.

"I want to put as much pressure on him as possible, and the media definitely will be able to assist with that." Shawn hoped the negative publicity would change his plea.

She was surprised Buchanan's defense hadn't requested a speedier trial themselves. They were going to allow the media to have a field day with this case, the longer it took. But now Dominique needed to know why he had pleaded not guilty, especially after he knew she had the videotape of him and his daughter.

"I'll need to prepare Kimberly after the hearing this morning," Dominique said to Shawn as they headed toward the exit of the courtroom.

"Do you want me to come along? I haven't met her yet."

"No. She's still a little uncomfortable about talking to anybody. I plan to stop by the hospital after we speak with Buchanan's team."

The camera lights almost blinded Dominique as she exited the courtroom. The reporters circled around them like a gang about to attack. Reporter after reporter directed their questions at Dominique, practically pushing their microphones down her throat.

"Mrs. Wallace, is it true Mr. Buchanan forced his daughter, Kimberly Buchanan, to have sex with him? What has been Mrs. Buchanan's response to everything? Do you think you will have enough evidence to convict Mr. Buchanan?"

Dominique tried to claim her space among the reporters as the heat from the camera lights and crowd of people suddenly drained her strength. She could feel her legs becoming weak under her as a strange sense of fear swept through her body, similarly to what she experienced in the hospital elevator. Afraid of drawing attention to herself again, she responded rapidly. "No comment at this time. Please let me by."

She pushed her way through the crowd, leaving Shawn behind. Dominique rushed out of the courthouse, headed straight for her office, and slammed her office door behind her to create a barrier for her retreat.

She stood in the middle of her office floor, gasping for breath. Confused by her sudden discomfort, she questioned its origin. Had the crowds of people created an artificial sense of fear for her, as the closeness in the elevator with the stranger had? Still not sure, she paced to soothe her edginess. "Calm down, girl. You can handle this. You're a veteran," Dominique whispered to herself as she continued to pace.

A loud knock at Dominique's door stopped her. As her fear resurfaced and intensified, she realized she was afraid to open it.

"Dominique, open up." A muffled voice from the other side of the door called. Dominique dropped her briefcase and backed away from the door, her breathing becoming laborious.

"Dominique?" The muffled voice called out again.

Dominique's heart pounded as she tried to remember whether she locked her office door. She was too afraid to check. So she maintained her distance as she watched her doorknob turn. Without warning, her body slipped into a convulsive state, as the fear invaded her body like poison running through her veins. Her door swung open, and the muffled voice entered her office. The flashing camera lights created an illuminated background.

Shawn burst into her office and closed the door behind him. "Wasn't that great? I just love all the attention from the press. Our pictures will be all over the front page tomorrow. I can't wait to see what they say." Now alone with Dominique, he noticed her convulsive state and rushed to her side.

"Dominique, are you okay? What's wrong?" Shawn frantically tried to help her sit down. "Don't go amateur on me," Shawn pleaded with her as he held onto her body, probably afraid to leave her side to get help. Her body shook uncontrollably in his arms, and he prayed her seizure would subside soon.

After a few minutes passed, an eternity to Shawn, Dominique calmed to a steady quiver. Slowly, she began to regain her control. She recognized Shawn's worried face. Disoriented, she pulled away from his hold and adjusted her clothes. She could tell by the look on his face that something had happened. But what?

"Dominique, you never told me you have epilepsy." Shawn backed away from Dominique, giving her space.

"I don't." Dominique replied, confused.

"Then what happened out there in front of the news reporters? You ran away like a bat out of hell and freaked out in here. Did I miss something?"

"No. I'm not sure. I just started to feel real funny all of a sudden. I can't explain it," Dominique admitted, still trying to get her bearing.

"Are you okay now?"

She nodded. "I am now."

"Are you going to be okay to meet with Buchanan and his team?" He asked, worried she might have a repeat attack during their meeting.

"Yes."

"I don't want them to sense anything wrong when they see us," Shawn lectured.

"I know. I'm ready. Let me get my things together," Dominique said as she bent over to pick up her scattered papers from the floor.

"I'll get them. I want you to catch your breath. Don't worry about the case. We have him. Now that we have his videotapes, there's nothing he can do but try to plead out, if he's smart."

"I'm not worried about the case." She started to pace the floor. "I can't explain it. I felt like a defenseless little girl when everyone surrounded us out there. Then the heat from the lights started making me feel like I was suffocating. It was the weirdest thing," She confessed, still curious as to why.

"Dominique, is there something you haven't shared with me?" Shawn stepped back to get a better look at her.

"What do you mean?"

"Is this case to close to home? You know you can talk to me if you need to." Shawn reached out to caress her shoulder.

"No, this case isn't too close to home. I'm fine. Don't worry about me. I have everything under control." Dominique touched Shawn's hand to reassure him.

"So are you ready to meet with Buchanan and his team?"

"Yes, I'm ready. Let's go." Dominique bounced to her feet.

When they reached the meeting room, Buchanan and his team were waiting. Dominique noticed Mark and Larry talking between themselves, but they made eye contact with her and Shawn as soon as they entered the room and took their seats. Buchanan was sitting back in his chair with a smirk on his face.

How dare he smile? Dominique thought, knowing what he has done— knowing if she were in his shoes, she would be too embarrassed to make eye contact with anyone. Dominique and Shawn took their seats, eager to hear Buchanan's defense of not guilty.

"Guys, let's get down to business. As you know, my client, Mr. Buchanan, has pleaded not guilty."

"Yes, we heard. And we are very interested to know why he pleaded not guilty when we have evidence in our possession of him committing the crime. Evidence Mr. Buchanan knows we have." Dominique looked Buchanan directly in the eyes.

Mark responded: "My client has admitted to suffering from an awful illness that he is unable to control at this time. Because he is unable to control this illness, he has agreed to complete extensive therapy to resolve his present condition, if all charges are publicly dropped against him. As you know, Mr. Buchanan is a very important figure in our community. Charges such as sexual abuse would not be good publicity for him. Mr. Buchanan is also prepared to donate a large sum of money to the organization of your choice. My client has made me aware of the videotapes you have of him and other participants. Those tapes were made when Mr. Buchanan was not himself."

"Mark, I'd hardly refer to the women on those tapes as participants," Dominique interrupted. "They are victims of Mr. Buchanan's sick sexual appetite. Excuse me … *illness*. I agree Mr. Buchanan is clearly suffering from an illness, but we, the prosecutors, are not sure if completing therapy and donating money to a charity are just punishments. Mr. Buchanan's daughter, Kimberly, is presently trying to recover in the hospital. She has been severely affected by your client's repeated sexual abuse. Unfortunately for my client, once she has completed therapy, there is no guarantee that she will be completely recovered from the traumatic experience inflicted upon her by Mr. Buchanan, her father."

"Dominique, we're not disputing that what Mr. Buchanan is being charged with is serious, but he has agreed to complete therapy and to donate money to support other suffering victims, in addition to paying for any necessary expenses Kimberly Buchanan might incur during her recovery. We feel that will be appropriate punishment and settlement." Mark laced his fingers together on the table.

"Mark, regrettably, we disagree." Dominique copied his gesture with his hands.

"I hope you aren't thinking about making an example out of Mr. Buchanan. I would strongly discourage it. We've come to the table with a reasonable offer." Mark rocked back and forth in his chair.

Dominique sat upright. "Mark, Mr. Buchanan became an example when he committed his first sexual crime." Then Dominique directed her attention back to Buchanan as she continued to speak. "His only problem this time is he got caught. Mr. Buchanan has no intention of stopping. If Miss Buchanan had not tried to commit suicide this last time, he would have continued to sexually abuse her."

"I've done everything to make that little bitch's life comfortable for her," Buchanan shouted out. "She has been a troubled child all her life."

"Michael calm down. Let me handle this." Mark touched Buchanan on the shoulder.

"That 'little bitch' is your daughter!" Dominique leaned across the table toward Buchanan. "Regardless of her past behavioral problems, she didn't deserve to be forced to have sex with you. She's your daughter, and in case you didn't know it, fathers don't have sex with their daughters."

"She's a liar!" Buchanan railed at Dominique from the other side of the table. "I've never forced her to have sex."

"I don't think so. I saw a young girl coaxed into having sex with you. Your daughter was crying as she performed sexual acts. And she was not crying because she was enjoying herself, she was crying because she was afraid of what you might do to her if she didn't obey.

"Mr. Buchanan, your daughter had no idea that you were videotaping her, nor did any of the other women. You have committed more crimes just by taping them without their knowledge. Those will be another case in itself. I'm very certain if we question each and every woman on those tapes, they would be very surprised to know you taped them. Completing therapy, paying for your daughter's treatment, and donating money isn't enough, Mr. Buchanan. You need to pull some time and think about how you have affected your daughter's life."

"Mrs. Wallace, correct me if I'm wrong: You haven't lived a perfect life yourself. I've done some research on you myself. I've discovered that you weren't born with a silver spoon in your mouth." Buchanan half smiled and sat back in his chair.

Dominique was furious with Buchanan for attempting to expose her personal business in front of her colleagues. "Let me stop you now," Dominique interrupted, leaning across the table in Buchanan's direction. "You need to remember I'm not on trial for sexual abuse. You are. My past has nothing to do with your case. I have videotapes that will bring your case crashing down around you faster than you can blink your eyes. So, don't play with me, Mr. Buchanan. I'm not one of those weak women you've been able to have your way with. I'm much stronger than that. It's this type of attitude that won't allow me to let your sorry behind get away with therapy and a little throwing around of money. You won't learn a thing." Dominique stood. "Mark, Larry, we'll see you at the preliminary hearing."

Buchanan leaned across the table and calmly cleared his throat. "Mrs. Wallace, I only pray you don't find yourself in a situation you can't get yourself out of."

"Is that a threat?" Dominique leaned in toward him. She felt her eyebrows rise.

"No. Just words of advice," Buchanan replied menacingly, continuing to stare.

"I think you better concern yourself with your situation and not worry about me." Dominique redirected her attention to Mark. "See you all at the preliminary hearing," she said as she gathered her belongings and left.

"Dominique, way to go!" Shawn cheered as they turned the corner.

"I can't believe that son of a bitch. Shawn, I want him behind bars."

A reporter jumped from around the corner in front of them. "Excuse me. I would like to get any statement from you about Mr. Buchanan's case."

"The only thing I will share with the press at this time about Mr. Buchanan's case is this: Be present at the preliminary hearing. Have a nice day." Dominique gritted her teeth, still furious with Mr. Buchanan's comments.

"He really ruffled your feathers in there. Is there something I should know about your past that he could use against you?" Shawn asked as they stepped alone into the elevator.

"No. I just resent the fact he thought he could bring up my past as a weapon against me."

"How could he use your past as a weapon against you?"

Dominique allowed the elevator door to close, securing them from roaming ears before answering. "I was raised in the foster care system. I never knew my parents or anything about my biological family. No, I didn't grow up with a silver spoon in my mouth, but it's because of that I have had to work hard and have earned everything I've gotten."

Shawn nodded slowly. "Personally, I think that will work in our favor. You'll be able to get the sympathy of the jury when they find that out. They will feel sorry for you, too."

"Shawn, I don't care for the jury to know about my past. I want them to respect my work as an attorney, not see me as an orphan who deserves sympathy because she doesn't know who and where her family is. I'm a good attorney. I don't need to have some jerk like him dragging my past into this case. Besides, this case is about him, not me, and let's not forget that."

"Dominique, I'm sorry. You're right, and for the record, I know you're a great attorney. If you don't want to represent this case, I will understand."

Dominique didn't hesitate. "I wouldn't dream of walking away from this case. I want to be the one who convinces the jury this bum needs to rot in prison."

She wasn't going to allow Buchanan to threaten her. He wanted her to get emotional and walk away from his daughter's case. She refused to give him that satisfaction. Her abominable past produced a fighter and survivor. She was eager for him to experience it firsthand in court as she convicted him.

"Sounds good to me. You know I have your back," Shawn assured her.

"Shawn, I need to stop by the hospital to see Kimberly. I want to bring her up to speed. I need you to locate Maria and get her citizenship papers approved in time. I need her testimony."

"Consider it done. Go take care of Kimberly. I'll handle the rest." Shawn hesitated for a second.

"Dominique, you did a great job today. You know I'm here if you ever need to talk about anything."

Shawn was referring to her past. And she didn't feel like discussing that with anyone right now. If she discussed her past with anyone, it would be with her psychiatrist, Dr. Martin, who had been helping her for the last fifteen years. Next to Eric, Dr. Martin was the only other person who

Dominique trusted when it came to her personal welfare. Her sessions with Dr. Martin were now a normal routine in her life, a routine that Dominique felt was necessary for her everyday survival.

As Dominique got off the elevator, she stepped to the side and waved goodbye to Shawn. She had another appointment today, but she couldn't remember where or when, so she found her schedule and discovered she had an appointment with Dr. Martin in thirty minutes. She rushed to her car and drove to Dr. Martin's office. Today she would have a lot to discuss. And she was anxious to have Dr. Martin help her work through her frustration regarding Buchanan's distasteful attempt to discredit her in front of her peers.

And after her appointment with Dr. Martin, she would go visit Kimberly and share the news with her. Surely, Kimberly wouldn't hear too much about this morning's events before then.

CHAPTER 8

The receptionist ushered Dominique to Dr. Martin's office as soon as she arrived for her appointment. A glance at her watch told her she was a couple of minutes late.

Dr. Martin was a tall, muscular man. He obviously worked out, Dominique noted as they exchanged greetings. His black hair was cut close to his head, and he sported a neat goatee, which complemented his bold brown eyes. To top it off, he unfailingly wore a warm, comforting smile.

Dominique perched on the edge of the couch.

"So, what are we going to discuss today?" Dr. Martin walked around his desk and took the chair across from her.

Dominique allowed her body to fall back into the soft cushions. "I have this case I'm working on now, and it's stirred up a lot of unsettling emotions for me."

"What do you mean by 'unsettling emotions?'" Dr. Martin pulled out a notepad.

"One minute I'm extremely emotional, the next I'm fine. It's the strangest thing."

"How is this case different?" Dr. Martin asked.

"For starters, this will be my first high profile sexual abuse case. It has already drawn attention with the media, because of the defendant's identity. I guess I allowed myself to be distracted by the defendant's reputation when I was initially asked to represent this case."

"Would you like to share whom you are representing?"

"I'm representing Mr. Michael Buchanan's daughter, Kimberly Buchanan. The state is charging him with sexually abusing her."

"So, you think it was because of Mr. Michael Buchanan's well-known reputation that you hesitated taking the case."

"Yes. That had a lot to do with it. I actually questioned whether someone of his stature could commit such a crime. But after speaking with his daughter and hearing her side, I knew right away he was guilty. If you could have seen how emotional she was reliving the horror he put her through … I was absolutely outraged. Then I became even angrier when I found out Mrs. Buchanan was siding with her husband." Dominique shook her head in disgust.

"Why did you become angry?"

"Because their young teenage daughter tried to take her life to escape. Parents are supposed to love and protect their children. In this case, neither parent is holding up their obligation. Her father is sexually abusing her while her mother refuses to believe it. A part of me cried for her when she shared her painful history with me, and I still do now."

"Why is that?" Dr. Martin jotted down some notes.

"I was brought up in the foster care system, as you know—a system that can be unpleasant for many, as it was for me. I always felt alone with nowhere to go. So, I could relate to her pain all too well. For years, Kimberly had been trying to tell her mother or anyone who would listen to her what was going on, but no one believed her. I think what was the worst for her was knowing her mother was aware of the situation and did nothing to stop it. Her mother even accused her of lying. There was no way I could turn my back on this poor young girl. She needs someone to help her."

"How do you know no one else has tried to help her before now?"

"She told me."

"Did she reveal her painful history with you freely?"

"No. At first she was very reluctant, but I managed to convince her. She even told me she felt comfortable telling me afterward. She said that for the first time she felt someone really cared about her. That made me feel good because I really do care about her welfare. She's not just a case for me. And I know she is counting on me to help her."

"Does she have a strong case against her father?"

Dominique nodded. "Yes. I think we have a good chance of winning and an even better chance if her mother would testify against her husband. But I know I can't count on that."

"Have you spoken with Mrs. Buchanan yet to hear why she is siding with her husband?"

Dominique nodded again. "Yes. She told me she was upset with her daughter for trying to destroy their family. I find it absolutely amazing how she can completely ignore what is going on."

"Why do you think she's choosing not to believe her daughter?"

"I think there are several reasons. First, I don't think she wants to accept the truth. It's easier and less painful to deny it. Second, I think she doesn't want to lose everything she has. Third, I think she's like so many other women in similar situations who don't believe they are strong enough to challenge their husbands. And then, of course, there's the fear of public embarrassment. I think Mrs. Buchanan is a classic case of all four. Mr. Buchanan is a very wealthy and well-respected man."

"How do you feel about Mrs. Buchanan?" Dr. Martin asked as he crossed his legs at the knee.

"Resentful." Dominique pointed to herself. "I know if it were my daughter, I would give my life to protect her."

"How do you know, deep inside, she doesn't want to help her daughter?"

"I don't, but if she does, siding with her husband makes it extremely hard for me to see that." Dominique watched Dr. Martin scribble more notes.

"How do you feel about Mr. Buchanan?"

"I'm very angry with him for what he has done to his daughter. I'm angry that he has robbed her of her innocence and youth. His daughter will never be the same again. When I look at Kimberly, I know he has destroyed a very special part of her that she will never be able to get back," Dominique paused. Her mind drifted to the bond hearing. "And after talking to him, I realized he doesn't care. He thinks he's above the law. And what's so sad is I know he's not the only person of his stature who thinks that way. I only wish the law wasn't as selective and would punish them accordingly."

"How do you know he think he's above the law?" Dr. Martin tilted his head to the side.

"He sat there in court and pleaded not guilty, knowing full well he's a hundred percent guilty! I have a videotape of him having sex with his daughter, and he knows it. Then he had the nerve to say his daughter deserved it. I told him no one deserves to have sex forced upon them. He had the audacity to throw my past in my face during the closing meeting."

"How was he able to throw your past in your face?"

"He said he had me checked out. I think he found out I was raised in the foster care system."

"Will that be a problem for you representing this case?"

"No. But I didn't appreciate him sharing that personal information with my peers."

"Did anyone else question you about your past after he brought it up?"

"Yes, my co-worker did, but I assured him that he didn't need to worry because it won't affect our case in the least bit. Me being raised in the foster care system has nothing to do with me representing this girl. If he wants to make an issue out of it, I will have to address it when that time comes. Until then, I choose to keep my personal life separate from this case and any other I happen to represent."

"Let's recap. You feel empathy for Kimberly and resentment toward her parents?"

"Yes." Dominique played with her necklace.

"How do you think your emotions for this case are different from those in your other sexual abuse cases?"

"I don't know. I've represented other sexual abuse cases in the past where I didn't feel anything. I just did my job and moved on. But from the very beginning, I had a bad feeling about this one. I've tried to get past who he is and just concentrate on the facts."

"Have you managed to do that?"

"After my meeting with him earlier today, I know I can. I have to."

"Maybe Kimberly's case hit a nerve."

"Maybe." Dominique didn't rule out the possibility. "I just remember so many times asking God what I had done to deserve the childhood I had. But now I have a wonderful husband, child, career, and great health. Back then I would never have thought any of this would be possible. I just want her to be able to experience it too."

"How often did you ask God 'why' when growing up?"

"A lot," Dominique answered as she nodded her head. "I had a very hard, lonely childhood. I don't wish what I went through on anyone. I remember crying on many days, trying to understand why my parents didn't love me enough to keep me, wondering what I did wrong. Then I looked at the families the foster care system placed me with. They didn't want me either. They only wanted the money the state gave them. They made sure I ate, but anything more than that was out of the question. I didn't get new Sunday dresses like other little girls. I didn't get my hair done. Nothing! And I was told to be grateful someone wanted to take me in. I just thank God for staying with me during that awful period in my life."

Dominique's chest ached from reminiscing about her painful childhood, knowing somewhere out there someone else was feeling now as she had back then.

"Did you ever try to kill yourself?"

Dominique searched her memory. "No. I can't remember ever trying."

"Have you thought about it recently, as an adult?"

"No. Once I was released from the foster care system, I felt free. I used to wonder about my birth family, but now I don't. I've just grown in faith and moved on. I've accepted my plight."

Dominique smiled. She felt grateful that everything in her life had turned out as positively as it had, regardless of her past circumstances.

Dr. Martin paused to write a few more notes down before speaking again. "Good. Do you think you are too emotionally involved with Kimberly's situation because of your past?"

"No. I think my feelings for Kimberly will help me focus and be more determined."

"Have you felt any other types of emotions besides sympathy and resentment?"

Dominique thought. She remembered how funny she'd felt in the elevator and in front of the news reporters.

"Yes. I've had two weird episodes. The first one was in the elevator the other day when leaving Kimberly's hospital room. I got on the elevator with one other person, a man I didn't know. I could feel myself becoming afraid of him. He never spoke or even looked at me while we were riding down together. His presence just bothered me."

"Did he resemble anyone you know?"

Dominique shook her head slowly. "No. I can't even remember how he looked. He was a plain-looking man with his back to me. He didn't do anything physically to threaten or harm me. It was just his presence."

"You said you were leaving Kimberly's hospital room. Do you think talking to her about her father created your fear?"

Dominique thought for a moment. She wasn't afraid of Buchanan. She just wanted to convict him.

"I don't think so."

"Tell me about the second episode."

"It happened right after Buchanan's bond hearing. As I left the courtroom, news reporters surrounded me, asking questions. I've been subjected to that type of attention before, and I've always been fine. But this time I started to panic, so I ran to my office to escape. It was the strangest thing."

"Was it a particular question that bothered you?"

"I don't think so. I just felt boxed in and all the lights bothered me."

"Were you tired?"

"No. I felt fine before then."

"You said you started to panic?" Dr. Martin shifted in his chair and stroked his goatee.

"Yes."

"Was your panicky feeling similar to your fear in the elevator?" Dr. Martin asked.

"Yes. Both times I felt myself losing control. But the second time I think I had a full blown panic attack in my office."

"Explain what you mean by 'full blown panic attack.'"

"My associate walked in, and he even questioned whether I am epileptic. As far as I know, I don't have epilepsy."

"Have you ever experienced an attack of that nature in the past?"

"No."

"How do you feel now?"

"I feel fine." Dominique shrugged her shoulders.

Dr. Martin nodded and paused. "I don't want to make a big deal about your two episodes, because you haven't had a history of them. But I'm going to ask you to pay close attention to your body reactions and how they might be tied to what triggers anything unusual."

"I'll do that."

"Good. Is there anything else you'd like to share?"

Dominique felt tired and empty. "No."

"If you do have another episode," Dr. Martin instructed, "please call me right away."

Dominique smiled warmly. "I promise."

"See you next week," Dr. Martin said, his brows knitted.

In the past, he had mentioned his concern that she showed some signs of burnout. This was common in her profession. But by recognizing the early warning signs, it could be headed off. This time was different though. Dominique didn't indicate the usual signs of burnout. She just felt confused by the odd attacks.

Putting the unsettling thoughts behind her, Dominique headed for the hospital.

CHAPTER 9

As Dominique stepped off the elevator onto Kimberly's floor, she spotted Dr. Ellis walking toward Kimberly's room. She quickened her pace.

"Good afternoon, Dr. Ellis." Dominique reached out her hand.

Dr. Ellis smiled and grasped her hand firmly. "Good afternoon, Mrs. Wallace. I was going to call you later this afternoon and give you Mr. Buchanan's test results."

"I saved you a phone call." Dominique looked at the doctor with anticipation.

He looked directly at her. "The test was positive for gonorrhea."

Dominique nodded affirmatively. She would be able to use his positive test results in conjunction with Kimberly's at the preliminary hearing. "Could you have copies of the results sent to my office right away?" Dominique handed the doctor her business card.

"I'll have my nurse courier take them over this afternoon." Dr. Ellis placed her business card in the pocket of his white jacket. "Well, I need to finish my rounds."

"Dr. Ellis, thank you so much for the information." Dominique turned and moved to knock on Kimberly's door.

Hearing her name, Dominique turned and saw Mrs. Buchanan approaching her. Dominique extended her hand, but Mrs. Buchanan didn't return the gesture.

Dominique decided to be blunt. "Mrs. Buchanan, I'm not sure if you've been made aware. Your husband was ordered to take a physical examination. His test results came back positive for gonorrhea. I would advise that you get tested."

Mrs. Buchanan's face turned red.

"Both your daughter and your husband tested positive." Dominique paused for a few seconds. She wanted her to digest what she just told her. "Their results will be used in court along with the videotape of your husband with your daughter—in addition to the videotapes of other women having sex with your husband. Mrs. Buchanan, the media will have a field day with those. If you don't convince your husband to plead guilty, you'll be under the spotlight, too."

"I don't know why you're trying to destroy my husband." Mrs. Buchanan wrapped the strap of her purse around her knuckles and blinked rapidly.

"He destroyed himself when he forced Kimberly to have sex with him and she contracted a venereal disease from him. For God's sake, we have videotapes of them in the physical act. What other evidence do you need?"

"I've heard enough." Mrs. Buchanan turned and rushed away.

Dominique stood in the middle of the hallway, watching her turn the corner. How could she ignore the obvious? The test results alone should have been enough for her to question her husband. And if that wasn't enough, there was the videotaped evidence. But for now, Dominique had to focus her attention on her client.

She knocked on Kimberly's door, but there was no answer. Slowly she pushed the door open. The room was dark, and she could barely see. She moved across the room and quietly opened the blinds.

Kimberly was lying in bed, her eyes closed. Dominique moved to her bedside. Kimberly's skin looked pale, so Dominique placed her hand on her forehead. Kimberly's skin felt cold and clammy. With trepidation, Dominique folded Kimberly's bedsheets back to feel for her pulse.

A large bloodstain saturated Kimberly's sheets.

Dominique rushed out of the room to the nurse's station. "Kimberly is bleeding! Please come."

Dominique stood back as the nurse raced to Kimberly's bedside and paged Dr. Ellis.

"What happened?" the nurse inquired brusquely, adjusting Kimberly's IVs.

"I noticed that Kimberly looked pale when I came in, so I checked her pulse. That's when I noticed the bloodstain on her sheets." Kimberly looked even more pale, so frail and vulnerable.

The nurse eyed Dominique with suspicion. "Who are you? This is a private room."

"I'm her attorney."

Just then, Dr. Ellis entered the room, and the nurse asked Dominique to leave the room.

Dominique felt helpless. What could have precipitated this? Had the news of the videotape reached Kimberly already? But if so, how? Only a few people knew about the videotape, and the media had not received this information.

Dominique's thoughts drifted back to her own childhood, a childhood that could have led to her own suicide at times. One day she had been sitting on a rusty old swing set during a thunderstorm, praying that the lightening would strike her. She wanted to die that day because she saw no way out. She was twelve years old.

"Mrs. Wallace?" Dr. Ellis's voice snapped Dominique back to the present.

"Yes? How is she?"

Dr. Ellis looked somber. "She's in critical condition. She's slipped into a coma."

Dominique's chest tightened. She had let Kimberly down.

The doctor continued, "The next few hours will be crucial. I'm going to have our staff watch her around the clock. It's a good thing you showed up when you did."

"Can I see her?"

"No. Maybe tomorrow." Dr. Ellis said and turned to go back into Kimberly's room.

Dominique stared at Kimberly's closed door before moving. She prayed her condition would improve. Dominique dropped her head and slowly walked towards the elevator as she waited for the doors to open. She stepped into the elevator, pressed the garage floor button and watched the floor indicator descend to the parking garage level. Remembering the earlier episode, she reached for her car keys. When the elevator door opened, she peered into the sea of cars, looking for movement.

She hurried to her parking space, pressing the unlock button on her key chain as she neared her car.

In an instant, a hand grabbed her face from behind, trapping her against the car. She tried to scream, but the huge hands were so large they covered her mouth and nose. She gasped for air.

The male body was much larger than hers, and it wrapped around her backside. He pulled her body deeper into his, and rubbed against her. Dominique could feel him growing hard. She drove an elbow into his rib.

The man's hot, stale breath filled her ear. "Don't fight it. A good friend wants me to show you what happens to bad girls when they betray him. You'll be better off if you just calm down. You know what I want, so stop fighting and it will all be over soon."

The words pierced her ears. Was Buchanan the "friend" who'd sent this horrible man to attack her?

She thrashed about wildly, but the strength of her assailant overtook her more with every second. She tried to bite the palm of his hand, but his grip was too tight. His rough hand crept up her skirt.

He cupped her vulva in his hand and squeezed. Pain coursed through her body as he repeatedly squeezed her vulva, and tears filled her eyes as she fought to endure the pain in silence. He ripped at her stockings and underwear. Her heart raced as the cold air hit her naked flesh. She prayed desperately for someone to come to her rescue.

Her vision blurred as he pulled her body to the concrete. She managed to pull off one of her shoes and struck his head with the heel. For a brief second, he loosened his grip on her mouth, and she sucked in several deep breaths. With all the strength she could muster, Dominique swung the shoe at him again and again. His groans propelled her.

Suddenly she was free. Renewed, she kept pounding and pounding on him. Blood poured from his head. He wasn't moving.

Dominique crawled backward away from the man and toward her car, her lungs burning and heart pounding. She was free and everything seemed blurry. When Dominique wiped her eyes, a teenage boy appeared behind the man on the ground. The boy's clothes and face were covered with blood. He held a bloody object in his right hand and pointed it at the apparently lifeless body. Was she hallucinating? The boy stared at her, smiling as he approached her.

Desperately, Dominique tried to struggle to her feet, but her legs were like jelly under her, and she fell back to the ground, exhausted. All she could do was scream out in the dim light.

The boy continued to approach her. "Please don't be afraid. I won't hurt you."

"What do you want?"

Dominique's voice quavered.

"I just want to make sure you're okay. That's all. I won't hurt you." He threw down the bloody object. Dominique winced as it hit the concrete and echoed through the garage. The boy maintained his distance.

"What are you doing here?" Dominique cried out.

Without answering, the boy turned and ran.

A security guard appeared in the dim light and hurried toward Dominique, holding a walkie-talkie. "What happened? Are you all right?" Before Dominique could react, the guard turned his attention to the body lying on the pavement and kneeled to check his vital signs. "He's still alive, but his pulse is weak." He reached for his walkie-talkie.

Disoriented, Dominique asked, "What about the boy? He had blood all over him."

"What boy?" The security guard swiveled and visually searched the garage.

"He ran away. But he was just here." Dominique pointed to the area the boy had occupied.

"Maybe he heard me coming." The guard glanced around the garage again. He didn't see anyone. He looked back at Dominique, sitting against her front tire.

"What did the boy look like?"

"He might be about twelve or thirteen and was wearing a blue baseball cap, T-shirt, and jeans, everything covered in blood."

The security guard repeated the description to whoever was on the other end of the walkie-talkie while Dominique tried to stand again. Her legs failed her.

"I want to get in my car." Dominique demanded.

"I think you should stay put until I can have someone from the hospital examine you."

"No. I'm fine. Please help me up," Dominique demanded again.

The security guard helped her to her feet and opened the car door.

Dominique collapsed onto her leather seat and took stock of her condition. She looked better than she felt, having pulled up her stockings and put her shoes back on. To her surprise, there was little blood on her.

Dominique looked down at the bloody body. She didn't recognize the man, but she knew deep inside that Buchanan was responsible for the attack on her. Now she, too, was his victim. Her assailant's voice echoed in her head: "A good friend wanted me to show you what happens to bad girls when they betray him."

Police cars were arriving. They seemed to fill the parking garage. The hospital staff carried her assailant away. She lost track of time.

A knock on her car window snapped Dominique out of her daze, and she rolled down the window.

"Excuse me, ma'am, do you need medical attention?"

"I just want to go home," Dominique responded. She wished Eric was there to comfort her.

"You look pretty shaken," the hospital attendant stated.

"No, I'm fine. I just want to get out of here," Dominique responded with a shaky voice.

A police officer joined the hospital attendant.

"I do have to ask you some questions first." Captain Lewis pulled out his notepad and pen. The hospital attendant moved to the side and allowed Captain Lewis to draw Dominique's attention.

"Please tell me everything that happened. Start at the beginning."

Dominique recounted every painful detail but assured the officer that she had not been raped.

Captain Lewis interjected, "You said the boy threw something away. Where did he throw it?" He instructed the other policemen to search the area where she pointed.

"I have to tell you, you did quite a job on your attacker!"

"Do you think he's going to live?" Suddenly Dominique was worried about the possibility of being a killer. That thought was alien to her.

Just then her phone rang, startling her. It was Shawn.

"Dominique, I just heard the great news about Buchanan's test results. How did Kimberly take it?"

"Shawn, right now isn't a good time to talk."

Shawn could hear the sirens in the background. "Jesus, Dominique, what's going on?"

"I've just been attacked in the hospital parking garage." Dominique's voice hitched.

"I'm on my way. Have you called Eric yet?"

"No." She hiccuped and covered her face with her free hand.

"Dominique, don't move. I'm on my way. I'll take you home."

Dominique tossed her cell phone onto the passenger seat and tried to ignore the commotion surrounding her. The loud voices and sirens filled her head, and she became nauseous. She pushed the button to lower the seat back and lie back against it. She sat quietly waiting for Shawn's arrival. Her nerves were still rattled by the events.

She jumped with shock when Shawn finally knocked on the driver's window to get her attention. "Dominique?" She squinted first at Shawn, then at the dashboard clock. She couldn't believe how quick it took him to get to her.

"I want to get out of here."

"Dominique, I think you should be seen first. Let's have the staff here check you out."

"No. I just want to go home."

Shawn looked to Captain Lewis for support. But Dominique was adamant, she wanted to go home without being seen.

Captain Lewis thanked Dominique for her help, and they exchanged business cards for follow-up.

On the way to his car, Shawn squired her through the growing crowd of the curious.

Beside Shawn's car, she bent over and allowed her nausea to climax. Weak and light-headed, she wiped her mouth, slid into Shawn's passenger seat, and laid her head back.

Dominique listened as Shawn dialed Eric and informed him of her misfortune. She felt disjointed, as if they were talking about someone else.

When Shawn pulled into the driveway, Eric was waiting anxiously. He rushed to her side and pulled her into his arms. She could feel his body shaking as he held her tightly. "Dominique are you okay?" He brushed her hair back from her face.

Dominique started to cry. To herself, she sounded like a helpless little girl. But she was safe now in Eric's arms.

She didn't want to think about what had happened to her. She whispered into Eric's ear, "Please take me inside."

"Thanks so much, Shawn," Eric acknowledged and carried his wife to their bedroom and laid her across the king-size mattress. She knew he wanted to hear the details, but she was too drained to talk.

He wiped her tears with the side of his hand. "Can I get you anything?"

"No. I just need to get out of these clothes, take a shower, and rest." Fortunately, Devin was already asleep, allowing Eric to concentrate on his wife.

"You don't have to pretend to be brave for me. I'm your husband. I'll go start your shower while you undress."

Dominique heard the shower being turned on, and the creak of the linen closet door told her Eric had gathered her towels and washcloth. She wobbled toward the welcoming shower.

"Eric, would you mind getting me a glass of wine?" Dominique called from the bathroom. "Today has been one hell of a day but nothing a good shower, clean clothes, a glass of wine, and a good night's sleep can't fix."

"Now you're sounding like my girl," Eric responded and paused. "Dominique, I love you," he said in parting.

Dominique lost herself in the soothing, cleansing shower. Stepping out, she reached for the towel. In the steamy mirror, she saw the bathroom door open. A bolt of fear raced through her. Her chest tightened, and she began to shake uncontrollably. She instinctively knew that the person standing in the doorway meant to harm her. She felt herself starting to feel faint. Her towel and body fell to the floor.

When Eric entered the bathroom, he noticed Dominique was lying on the bathroom floor in a fetal position, shaking with tears streaming down her face.

"What happen?" Eric's voice pierced her terror.

"Eric, please don't leave me." Dominique cried as she allowed him to bring her helpless body into his arms.

He gently helped her to her feet. "I promise I won't leave you." He held her tightly.

They walked slowly to their bed, where her glass of wine awaited her on the nightstand. Dominique climbed into the bed and tried to gather herself. She still felt unnerved, but she didn't want to worry Eric. She looked over at him staring at her helplessly. She tried to fight back the tears. She turned her stare away from him and looked for the remote control. She wanted to change the worry mood in their bedroom.

Dominique picked up the TV remote control and pressed the power button. A colorful high-def image emerged on the wide screen television. The TV was a recent birthday gift from her to him. She only wished he had more time to enjoy it. Long hours and days came with his job. He co-owned a computer company.

Dominique handed Eric the remote control. He hastily took the remote and flipped through the channels, stopping to hear the sports updates on the news. A newscaster broke in with a bulletin about an attack downtown. Eric turned the television off.

CHAPTER 10

Through the window, the early morning light lit the bedroom. Normally, the light wouldn't wake Dominique, but this morning she rose along with the brightness of the day and glanced at her alarm clock - six thirty. She rolled over and looked at her husband sleeping peacefully beside her. She decided not to wake him and instead slipped out of bed and tiptoed downstairs. She fixed herself a cup of coffee and selected an apple from the basket on the kitchen counter and headed into the sunroom.

She stretched out across the chaise, closed her eyes, and took a deep breath. When she reopened her eyes, and reached for the coffee cup, a movement in the backyard caught her eye. A boy stood watching her.

Dominique recognized him as the same boy from the night before, but this time his clothes were clean.

The boy spotted her and waved. Dominique opened the door and stepped outside.

"Hello?"

The boy smiled. "How are you doing?"

"I'm fine. How about you? You had a lot of blood on your clothes last night." Dominique didn't wait for an answer. "What were you doing there?"

"Just hanging out. Then I saw that man grab you, so I tried to stop him. We showed him!" The boy grinned broadly.

Dominique searched her memory. She didn't remember seeing him during her actual struggle. It was only afterward.

She probed. "If you hadn't been there, no telling what would have happened to me."

She had a sudden thought. "Would you like to come in and have some breakfast?"

The boy didn't have to be coaxed. He followed her inside.

"Do you like pancakes?" Dominique handed the boy a glass of milk.

"I love pancakes." Then, shyly he said, "You're very pretty."

"Thank you. What's your name?" Her back was to him as she prepared the pancakes. He didn't answer. She forged ahead.

"Where do you live?" Still no answer.

The boy asked, "Where's your family?" as he took a seat at the kitchen table.

"They're still asleep." Dominique marveled when it hit her: She wasn't afraid!

"You have a really big house," the boy observed, "much bigger than mine."

Dominique figured he didn't live nearby because all the houses in her neighborhood were at least as large.

Dominique pulled their plates out of the cupboard, along with forks and knives and placed one set in front of the boy. She set a place for herself next to him and brought the plate of pancakes to the table. The boy helped himself to three pancakes.

"Butter? Syrup?"

The boy poured a healthy stream of syrup over the stack of pancakes.

"How did you know where I live?" Dominique asked.

He continued to eat hungrily, once again ignoring her question. At the sound of footsteps on the floor above, the boy stopped eating and pushed his chair back from the table.

Dominique rose to get a plate. She knew it was Eric. She started to prepare him a plate for breakfast. When Eric entered the kitchen, he walked over to Dominique standing in front of the stove and bestowed a quick peck on the cheek.

"You fixed your famous pancakes?" he said approvingly.

"Yes, there's someone I want you to meet." Dominique turned around, but the boy was gone without a trace.

"Who is it?"

At the risk of sounding odd, she asked, "Did you see a boy sitting at the table when you came in?"

Eric stared at her quizzically. "Dominique, you've been through a lot lately. You must be exhausted. I think you've been working too hard."

"I'm fine, Eric, really," she responded wearily. Not only was the boy gone, but she didn't even know his name, where he lived, and how he had found her.

"Please call work today and tell them you're going to take today off at least. They'll understand, especially after what happened last night."

Dominique nodded. "Just today, though. I've got a case I can't leave. Kimberly really needs me."

Eric broke in. "How do you know Buchanan didn't have something to do with what happened? Maybe he was trying to send you a message?"

"Eric, whatever happened, I'm not going to let him push me around. He wants to intimidate me so that I'll get out of his way, but I won't. When I finish with him, he'll wish he never laid eyes on me. End of conversation."

Eric knew that tone. He threw his hands in the air and mumbled, "Whatever. But I don't have a good feeling about this."

Dominique searched her husband's eyes. "I'll take some time off after this case. I promise."

"Good. It will give you some more time to spend with Devin." Eric kissed Dominique on the forehead.

Dominique knew Eric wanted her to stay home with Devin while she was still young, but he knew better than to ask her to give up her career. She loved her daughter dearly, but she also loved practicing law.

Just then, Devin bounced into the kitchen carrying her favorite doll with matching pajamas, something Dominique had found one day at an outlet mall.

"What were you saying about me?"

"After I finish this case I'm working on, I'm going to take some time off to spend with you at home."

"Goody, goody!" Devin stopped short as she noticed the scratches on her mother's face. "Mommy what happened to you?"

"Someone tried to hurt me last night," Dominique answered quietly, trying to sound calm.

"But she's fine now," Eric interjected. But Dominique knew by his set mouth that he wasn't done with the assailant. That's the kind of man he was, and that was just one reason she loved him. He lifted Devin and hugged her.

"I made you pancakes." Dominique set a plate in front of her daughter.

Dominique pinched Eric on the cheek and finally sat down to her own breakfast.

CHAPTER 11

Dominique called her office receptionist to tell her that she wouldn't be in the office today, but Shawn had already told her not to expect Dominique. She didn't pursue the conversation.

She had just settled down with her family in the backyard when the doorbell rang. Eric jumped up to answer. It was Captain Lewis.

"How is Mrs. Wallace today?" Captain Lewis asked him.

"She's fine now, but she did have a rough night. I'm concerned about her."

"Mrs. Wallace is probably going to have some more rough nights for a while remembering what happened. Sometimes attack victims aren't able to put it behind them for quite some time. Fortunately, she wasn't raped."

Dominique appeared in the hallway. "Eric, who's at the door?"

"It's Captain Lewis."

"Hello, Captain Lewis. I don't know what else I can tell you." Dominique reached out to shake his hand.

Eric stood close to her. "If you don't mind, I'd like to be present."

"I don't mind if Mrs. Wallace doesn't mind."

"Not at all." Dominique replied. "Why don't we go to the sunroom and talk? So, we can keep an eye on our daughter while she's playing outside?"

"Sounds good to me." Captain Lewis followed Dominique into the sunroom, and Eric followed.

"Captain, would you like something to drink?" Dominique asked.

"Actually, a glass of water would be great," Captain Lewis answered, taking a seat.

Eric excused himself. "I'll get it. And I'll tell Devin we have company."

"Mrs. Wallace, you were most helpful to me last night, but I want to make sure we have all the information. So, if you could just tell me again what happened from the beginning, I'd really appreciate it." Captain Lewis pulled out his notepad and pen.

Dominique took a deep breath and began. Her stomach tightened as she repeated the chilling words whispered in her ear during the attack. She felt strongly that Buchanan was somehow responsible, and she emphasized this point to Captain Lewis.

Captain Lewis listened tentatively until she reached the part about the boy appearing and interrupted. "Let's stop there. The security guard said he didn't see anybody else at or leaving the scene when he approached you."

"I know. He told me the same thing. But the boy I saw ran away when he heard the guard approaching. I don't know why, but he did."

Captain Lewis stared at her. "Mrs. Wallace, I don't know how to tell you this, but I went back to review the security tape, and there were only two people at the scene until the security guard showed up; you and your attacker."

"I know I'm not crazy. I saw him. I talked to him. How do you explain that?"

"I'll go back and review the tape again. I have to admit the lighting was poor, but we didn't find anything lying around the scene that the boy could have used as a weapon, either."

"I don't know what to tell you, but I saw the boy. I know I'm not crazy."

"Mrs. Wallace, no one's trying to imply you're crazy. I'm just telling you, we cannot place him at the scene, that's all. If he was there and helped you, you were extremely lucky." Captain Lewis's eyes met Eric's.

"I know," Dominique answered.

"Captain Lewis, is that going to create a problem?" Eric asked.

"Not really. The tape clearly shows that Mrs. Wallace was attacked from behind and she reacted in an appropriate manner to protect herself. Anyone who reviews the tape will see that."

"Do you think you'll be able to trace her attacker to Buchanan?"

"We'll try. The guy is in the hospital, but he's expected to recover. As soon as we can, we'll put a lot of pressure on him to confess. But even if we are unable to make the connection with Buchanan, we'll be able to convict him from the evidence on the tape alone. He'll pull some time."

Dominique stared at Captain Lewis. Her thoughts and concerns were not about her attacker. She was more worried about the boy who was now an invisible part of her life.

"Getting back to the boy," Dominique spoke out, "he stopped by here this morning to see how I was doing."

Eric did a double take. Captain Lewis asked, "How did he know where you live?"

"That's a good question. I don't know. He said he just wanted to see how I was doing."

Eric leaned forward in his chair. "Where was I when he stopped by?"

"You were still asleep," Dominique answered. "I fixed him breakfast, and we talked a little. But he wouldn't tell me anything about himself."

"Did he tell you why?" Captain Lewis asked.

"No. He ignored my questions. Then he left abruptly when he heard Eric's footsteps coming down the stairs."

"You did ask me if I saw a boy," Eric interjected.

Dominique repeated, "He just left."

Captain Lewis put his hands together. "He seems to have a habit of running when anyone else comes around. Possibly he's a runaway. We have a lot of those. If by chance he comes back to visit, will you try to get some information about him for me?" Captain Lewis folded over a sheet of paper on his notepad.

She nodded yes. "Would you mind if I come down to the station and review the tape myself? I'm one hundred percent sure he was there at the scene." She felt better now that Captain Lewis sounded as if he believed her.

"When would you like to come down?" Captain Lewis asked.

"What about tomorrow?"

"Call first, though, so we can have everything set up for you."

"Mrs. Wallace, I'm through. The information you gave me is exactly the same as the information you gave me last night. If I need anything else, I'll be in touch." Captain Lewis added, "Until then, please take it easy." He stood.

"We appreciate your hard work." Eric shook Captain Lewis's hand.

"No problem. I'm just glad things turned out the way they did last night. It could have been much worse."

"So am I." Dominique rubbed her sore shoulder.

"I'll see you out." Eric motioned for Captain Lewis to follow him.

The officer offered in a confidential tone, "Mr. Wallace, I want to remind you that Mrs. Wallace will have more bad days, and this is common."

"I appreciate the advice." Eric lowered his voice. "What do you make of the boy? I didn't want to say anything to upset Dominique."

Captain Lewis shrugged his shoulders. "To be honest, I'm not sure. After talking with your wife, I believe she's in her right mind, yet the boy seems like a phantom. She's the only one who saw him. Then there's the episode this morning. In any case, if he appears again, it's important for her to get as much information as possible from him."

Eric said, "It seems so strange how he keeps running away when anyone else comes around."

"He's probably a runaway and afraid of authority figures."

Eric looked down. "I'm still uneasy."

"What makes you uneasy?" Dominique asked as she joined the two men at the front door.

"The whole attack," Eric responded quickly.

"Well, I'd better get going." Captain Lewis walked out, leaving Dominique to relax with Eric and Devin by her side the remainder of the day.

CHAPTER 12

Dominique lay awake in her bed thinking about her discussion with Captain Lewis. She couldn't believe no one had been able to confirm the boy's presence from the garage videotape. The more she thought about that night, the more she wanted to go down to the station and view it for herself. But until that happened, she'd try to convince herself that the poor quality of the tape had prevented the officers from seeing the boy.

Dominique glanced over at the alarm clock. It was only three o'clock in the morning. She glanced over at Eric, who was sleeping peacefully. She wanted to wake him, but she remembered Devin sleeping in the next room. She didn't want to drag her out of the house this time of morning, so she stared at the ceiling wishing the time away.

Dominique thought about her case. Anger started to boil inside of her. How dare Buchanan attempt to threaten her? Then she remembered her session with Dr. Martin. She would have to find a way to hide her true feelings until the case was over. Physically, she felt exhausted. For some reason her mind drifted to her first semester at law school.

She'd felt awkward and self-conscious among all the rich and well-traveled students. She was driving a second-hand family car the Franklins had given her for graduation. Her classmates drove expensive foreign cars. Their wealthy upbringing was transparent as they infested the small town housing the private campus. They were everywhere, and they made sure the local community knew their money was responsible for the community's survival.

Dominique smiled. Her first day on campus, she'd immediately been overwhelmed by all the people unpacking their things, even by those out enjoying the warm August sun.

She answered a newspaper ad for a roommate, someone wanting a female law student to share a three-bedroom apartment. Dominique figured they were probably looking for someone to study with, but as a first-year law student she didn't know how much help she would be.

She rang the apartment doorbell anyway. Nervous, she waited on the front steps for someone to welcome her. Dominique was dumbfounded when an unshaven and smelly guy named John answered the door. He was tall and skinny, with short black hair and a beard that seemed to overrun the bounds of his strong face as his clothes hung off of him. She was almost afraid to enter the apartment after he opened the door, but with nowhere else to go, she entered cautiously.

Dominique was confused. The newspaper ad specified they were looking for a female roommate to share a three-bedroom apartment with two other females. She wasn't comfortable sharing an apartment with a male. But being too afraid of making waves her first day, she remained silent and reminded herself the rent was excellent on her little budget.

Later, her roommates explained to her how John had become the third roommate. It had been a last-minute arrangement, when Nancy, one of the original two roommates, discovered the other roommate, Julie, had packed and left during the night, leaving only a note behind informing her the pressures of law school had been too much. This had left Nancy in a bind and desperate for a replacement. John had been only too eager to replace Julie due to the cheap rent.

Dominique didn't know it at the time, but she would find herself feeling the same way shortly after starting her law classes. She cried just about every night her first semester. She wasn't sure if she had made the right decision. She had a lot of reading assignments and she wasn't retaining the information. When she went to class, it seemed like everybody else was able to keep up and she was the only person struggling. She was enrolled in five classes and failed her first test in four of them. She didn't have anyone to talk to about how she was feeling and entertained thoughts of dropping out of school and just getting a nine-to-five job. She convinced herself that no one would ever know she didn't complete law school.

Then one night, while all her friends were out partying and celebrating, Dominique sat alone on the back steps of her apartment, crying because she was failing and wasn't sure whether she would be able to do any better on the final exams. She battled with feelings of isolation and depression.

"Hey, it can't be that bad. Don't cry," a strange voice had uttered. She quickly wiped her tears away, embarrassed she had been caught crying. The last thing she wanted was someone feeling sorry for her.

"What could be so bad that you would cry about it?" The owner of the strange voice was tall, handsome, and well-built.

Dominique was speechless when she saw how handsome he was. She immediately recognized him from the college calendar. He was one of the football players, and he was the model for May. She finally forced her mouth to answer. "I'm just having a bad day."

"I don't mind listening. Sometimes it helps if you can talk about it. It works for me. By the way, my name is Eric Wallace. What's yours?" Eric sat down beside her before she could answer.

Finally, extremely embarrassed that he'd caught her crying, she answered. "Dominique Shepard."

At first, Dominique was hesitant to share anything with him, but as the evening went on, she found herself feeling very comfortable. She really liked Eric. They sat for hours, laughing and talking. During the remainder of the semester, he played a very important role in Dominique's life. He listened and encouraged her when there hadn't been anyone else in her life to do that.

Eric worked his way into her life and eventually asked her to marry him. She didn't waste any time accepting his marriage proposal. She loved him and was very thankful God had brought him into her life.

Sometimes when she was alone, she would wonder what her life would have been like if he hadn't found her that night. Would she have finished law school? Would she have married and had a wonderful little daughter?

Snapping back to the present, she glanced over at Eric, still sleeping peacefully beside her. She watched as he breathed rhythmically, prayed nothing would take him away from her. He was her anchor in life and kept her grounded. He taught her how to love and be loved. He taught her to trust, to be open, and not to be afraid. At times, she felt like a child just learning how to live. Eric had shown her so many things in such a short period of time, things that took people a lifetime to learn. She owed him so much, and she prayed she made his life as complete as he made hers.

Dominique placed a kiss on two of her fingers and gently placed them upon his heart, wanting him to feel her love while he slept.

She laid her head back against their headboard. She wondered how many other women had been in Eric's life and how many women he had truly loved. She wondered where they were now because he never talked about his past relationships. He dealt only with the present. He told her he didn't believe in living in the past because it would only hold him back from enjoying the present. Dominique tried to adopt the same philosophy in her life. She didn't have anything in her past she needed to remember, so it worked out perfectly for her.

She glanced over at her alarm clock. It read five thirty a.m. She didn't realize so much time had passed, but she still wasn't sleepy. She couldn't wait until Eric woke up. When he did, she was going to ask him to go with her to the police station and review the tape. She would leave Devin with Ms. Anderson.

Still very restless, Dominique decided to force herself to sleep, so she turned her lamp off and slid down under the sheets. She closed her eyes and lay there until she drifted off. When she opened her eyes again, it was eight thirty. She had managed to sleep for three hours. She felt rested and immediately turned over to face Eric. He was already up and had been watching her.

"Good morning." Eric smiled from his side of the bed.

"Good morning. How long have you been up?"

"Not long. I just got up. How did you sleep?"

"Not well. I couldn't seem to fall asleep. I just lay here thinking about how we met."

"What made you think about that?"

"I was thanking God that I have you in my life."

"I thank Him every day for you, too." Eric smiled. "You want some breakfast this morning before we go down to the station?"

"No. I can make you and Devin some if you like."

"No, I'm fine. What are your plans after we go to the police station? I hope you don't plan on going into the office today?" Eric sat up.

"No, but I do want to go visit Kimberly."

"She's in a coma. Why don't you just call the hospital to check on her?"

"I could, but I want to speak with her in person. Who knows? Maybe I will be able to get her to respond." Dominique walked into their bathroom.

"Well, I'm going with you."

"Eric, I don't need you to babysit me." Dominique leaned against the doorway.

"Dominique, I mean it. I'm going to take you and that's that. I don't know what you are trying to prove, but I'm really worried about you." Eric rolled out of bed and walked toward the bathroom.

She didn't feel like arguing. She didn't care whether he took her or not. All she wanted to do was visit Kimberly. And if that meant Eric taking her, so be it.

"You win. You can take me. I want to go right after we leave the station."

"We can leave as soon as Ms. Anderson arrives."

When Ms. Anderson arrived, Devin was awake and in their bedroom, pleading to go with them.

"Where we're going isn't a place for little girls to visit," Dominique explained to Devin. Then she and Eric kissed Devin goodbye.

Eric and Dominique listened to music in silence as they drove to the police station. Eric found a parking space close to the entrance and pulled in. He immediately got out of the car and walked to Dominique's side to open her door, something he started when they first began dating. His traditional values were another thing that really attracted Dominique to Eric. Being with him made her forget her dysfunctional upbringing.

Before Captain Lewis started the videotape, Eric questioned Dominique a final time about whether she was okay reliving that whole night because this time it would all be replayed live in front of her. Psychologically, it could cause a total relapse or be the turning point that changed her fear to unbridled anger.

As the tape began to play, Dominique watched closely. The visual quality of the videotape was poor, making it hard for her to see even herself clearly. She became frustrated when she couldn't spot the boy's presence and demanded that Captain Lewis replay the videotape several times with no success.

When she was done, she questioned how security had been able to determine what was going on after they reviewed the videotape. She wanted to make an official complaint to the hospital garage manager, and have them upgrade their video equipment. She might not prove her point, but she could save others from a similar fate.

Dominique left the station deeply disappointed. She rode in silence, wondering what Eric was thinking. Was he disappointed she hadn't been able to identify the boy and was just too afraid to say anything?

"Eric, do you believe me when I say I saw a boy that night?" she asked haltingly.

Keeping his attention on the road, Eric responded. "I don't know what to think. I watched the videotape with you and I didn't see anything. How do you explain that?"

"I don't know. All I know is I saw a boy standing across from me. I even spoke to him. He spoke back. And how do you explain his visit at our house?"

Eric shook his head. "Dominique, I don't know. I saw only two people until the security guard showed up. I must be honest with you: I don't know what to think. I can't tell you I believe you, and I can't say I don't. I've never known you to just make things up. All I know is I wasn't able to see him, nor was Captain Lewis, or anybody else who saw the videotape at the station. As far as our house, I truly can't explain his presence."

He had a point. She gazed out the window, feeling even more disappointed now that she knew Eric questioned her story. How was she going to prove to Eric and everybody else that the boy had been present that night now that the videotape failed to corroborate her story? The only way she would be able to confirm her story would be to bring the boy in. That would be the only way they would believe her. More importantly, Eric would believe her. So, she prayed the boy would come by to visit with her again.

When Dominique and Eric stepped off the elevator on Kimberly's hospital floor, Dominique noticed Mrs. Buchanan standing in the hallway, talking to a nurse. Afraid Mrs. Buchanan might create a scene in front of Eric, Dominique insisted he wait for her in the waiting room while she spoke with Mrs. Buchanan and visited with Kimberly.

Dominique quickened her pace in Mrs. Buchanan's direction before she noticed her approaching. She was eager to see if her support had changed now that her daughter lay in a coma.

"Good morning, Mrs. Buchanan. How is Kimberly?" Dominique asked cautiously, trying to start an amiable conversation.

When Mrs. Buchanan turned to face Dominique, she froze, speechless as she observed Dominique's colorful facial bruises.

"She's about the same," Mrs. Buchanan answered slowly. Her face tilted downward to the floor.

"I'm really sorry to hear that. I was hoping she would have shown some improvements."

"Mrs. Wallace, I know you are probably judging me. However, I do love my daughter." Mrs. Buchanan raised her face and looked Dominique squarely in the eyes. Dominique noticed her tears.

"I'm not here to judge you. I would expect that, as a mother, you would love your daughter. I love my daughter and there isn't anything I can think of that would change that."

Mrs. Buchanan wiped her eyes. "It's been really hard raising her. I've tried to be a good mother."

"Kimberly needs you more than anything right now. When she comes out of the coma, this is your chance to show her how much you love her. Show her that you're concerned about her welfare first by testifying against your husband," Dominique urged.

She reached into her bag, withdrew one of her business cards, and handed it to Mrs. Buchanan. "I want you to call me if you need anything. I'm here for Kimberly and I will be here for you too if you want."

"Mrs. Wallace," Mrs. Buchanan said, and paused abruptly, staring back at Dominique, tears rolling down her face. Dominique hoped she had managed to touch a soft spot. "I'm sorry about what happened to you. I'm glad you are okay. I need to go." Mrs. Buchanan rushed past her to reach the elevator.

"Mrs. Buchanan?" Dominique followed.

"Just leave me alone. If you continue to bother me, I will consult my attorney," Mrs. Buchanan said while never looking back.

Dominique followed her and continued to speak. "I didn't mean to upset you. I just want to help, that's all! You see what your husband is capable of. Why are you trying to ignore it? Look at me. He had someone attack me. Who else are you going to allow him to hurt?"

Mrs. Buchanan pressed the down button and turned to face Dominique. "The only way you can help me is to convince Kimberly to drop the charges against her father. Otherwise, there is nothing you can do."

"Mrs. Buchanan, that's ridiculous. I can't do that. Unfortunately, I'm forced to protect Kimberly's interests because no one else will." When the elevator doors opened, Mrs. Buchanan stepped inside the elevator and faced Dominique as the doors closed between them.

Dominique stared at the doors, wondering how she had managed to lose Mrs. Buchanan. For a brief moment, Mrs. Buchanan had seemed to entertain the possibility of testifying against her husband, but all of a sudden, she snapped and ran away again, leaving a cold and disheartening aura behind.

Dominique headed toward Kimberly's room, grateful Eric hadn't witnessed her disagreement with Mrs. Buchanan. She sat with Kimberly for half an hour. Caressing her fragile shell, Dominique prayed Kimberly would return now that she was by her side.

She combed Kimberly's stringy blonde hair away from her thin pale face and placed a gentle kiss upon her forehead.

Dominique rode in silence from the hospital to their home. What was going through Mrs. Buchanan's mind now that she saw how violent her husband could be? Once home, Dominique went outside to relax to escape the disappointments of her day.

"Hello," whispered a soft voice from the bushes. Dominique didn't recognize it. It didn't sound like Devin or Eric. She rose and glanced over at the bushes from her chaise. It was the boy from the attack. She was so glad to see him again. She wanted to introduce him to Eric right away to prove she wasn't insane.

"Hello!"

"Sorry, I didn't get a chance to say thank you for breakfast yesterday."

"You're welcome. I wanted to introduce you to my husband, but you left before I got a chance. Where did you go?"

"I had something to do." The boy kicked a wild daisy with his foot.

"What made you come back?" She wasn't sure if she was going to see him again after the way he left the other day.

"I wanted to see how you were doing today." He smiled shyly.

"I'm doing fine. I want to introduce you to my husband so you can tell him how you helped me the night of the attack." Dominique noticed a frown appearing on the boy's face.

"No way."

"Why not?" Dominique saw no harm in her introducing the two of them.

"I'm sorry. I can't help you with that. I only came by to see you. I don't want to talk to anybody else." The boy ran back through the bushes.

"Stop! Please don't leave!" Dominique raced behind the boy. She was angry with herself for running him off. Now what was she going to do?

"Dominique!" Eric ran toward her.

"What's wrong?" She responded, as she turned around concerned by his tone.

"What are you doing? Didn't you hear me yelling your name?" Eric asked as he stopped.

"No. I didn't hear you calling me. I'm sorry. What do you want?"

"What were you doing in the bushes?"

"That boy was here again. I was trying to convince him to allow me to introduce him to you, but he ran away again."

Eric didn't say anything at first. He stared at Dominique and looked over at the bushes.

"Dominique, what are you talking about? I didn't see anybody out here with you. I think you need to sit down and relax. I know you're disappointed you weren't able to confirm your story earlier this morning, but that's over now. You need to let it go."

"Let it go! Eric, I know what I saw. I saw a boy that night. He was just here!" His lack of faith irritated her. What reason would she have to lie? What would she stand to gain?

Eric raised his voice. "Dominique, sit down. I think you've had too much excitement these last few days. I want you to calm down."

Dominique didn't appreciate his tone. He was trying to use reverse psychology on her and she didn't like it. "I don't need to sit down. I'm fine. I can't believe you don't believe me, Eric. I'm really offended."

Dominique rushed by him, into the house, and upstairs to their bedroom to be alone. She felt light-headed. Was the lack of sleep now taking its toll? She closed the bedroom door behind her and stretched out across the bed to nap. She hoped Eric wouldn't come upstairs to apologize because she wasn't in a forgiving mood.

When Dominique woke up, it was already dinnertime. Feeling

rejuvenated, she went downstairs to join Eric and Devin. They had already finished eating dinner and were watching TV in the family room.

"I fixed you a plate and left it in the microwave," Eric said.

"Thanks." Dominique headed for the kitchen to eat her dinner alone.

Afterward, she returned to the family room and sat beside Devin. She didn't want to be near Eric right now. She was still upset with him from earlier today. As long as Devin was awake, they would have to wait to discuss their differences.

"Sweetheart, it's time for bed." Eric patted Devin's leg.

"Please, can I stay up a little longer?" Devin pleaded.

"No. You know the rules. You have to give Daddy his kiss good night."

Devin didn't argue. She stood up and kissed her father good night like a good girl. "Good night, Daddy."

"Good night."

"Good girl. Let's go take your bath." Dominique held Devin's hand and led her upstairs. Devin selected her nightgown. Now that Devin was getting older, Dominique wanted to nurture her ability to make decisions for herself.

Devin finished her bath and dried off before brushing her teeth. Dominique couldn't believe how much Devin had grown. She was getting taller and her hair was growing longer. It seemed like only yesterday she was starting to walk and talk. Next year she would be starting school. And before long, she would be graduating from high school and leaving the nest for college. The thought made Dominique sad, but she promised to enjoy every moment she could with Devin.

Dominique put Devin in bed and read her a Bible story, a luxury she often missed because of long hours practicing law. But tonight, she would enjoy the opportunity. She read about God's truth and love. As always, Devin fell fast asleep before Dominique finished.

Dominique closed the Bible and kissed Devin on the forehead. She watched Devin sleeping peacefully. Dominique envied how carefree Devin behaved. Her days were filled with fun, away from the world's cruel pressures.

Devin had been a wonderful blessing in her life. She had also taught her how to love as Eric had. Dominique kissed Devin on her forehead and left the room. She slowly walked down the hallway to her own bedroom.

She wondered if Eric had come up. What would they say to each other? It had been a long time since they had a disagreement. Somehow, they had managed to keep a peaceful marriage, friendship, and household. Working out their disagreements had come easy, but today was different. He had let her down. He was asking her to admit she was wrong and she couldn't give in and deny what she believed, nor should he expect her to.

Eric was already in bed, watching TV. She prayed he wasn't waiting up for her. She didn't feel like talking. She undressed without saying a word. She slid into bed and turned her back to Eric. She tried to fall asleep.

She felt funny not saying anything to him. Especially knowing they had vowed never to go to bed mad with one another or without resolving their differences. But if he still believed she hadn't seen the boy, they would have nothing to discuss this evening.

"Dominique," Eric whispered from behind her.

Butterflies flew in her stomach. What was Eric going to say? Would they get into another disagreement? "Yes?"

"Will you please turn over so we can talk?"

Dominique slowly turned over to face him. She didn't want to, but she figured she would at least listen to what he had to say.

"Dominique, I know you are upset with me about this afternoon. I'm sorry. I didn't mean to hurt your feelings. Believe me, I didn't."

"Well, do you believe me now?"

"I don't know. Dominique, I thought about everything you told me about the night of the attack. I thought about what I saw on the videotape today and how you couldn't identify the boy, either. I can't honestly say I believe someone else was there. I didn't see it on the videotape. Neither did anyone else. How do you explain it?"

"I can't. I just know what I saw. I'm not crazy. He was there. He spoke to me. Let me ask you this: How do you explain him showing up here twice since the attack?"

"Again, I can't. I never saw him. Only you have seen him."

"So, you think I'm making it up?" Her blood pounded in her temples.

"I'm not accusing you of anything. I'm just telling you that I'm not sure. Maybe if I could see and talk with him myself, I would feel differently. But right now, I have to be honest with you, Dominique, I can't support your story, no matter how badly I want to. I just want you to understand my position."

"Well, I can't. You're supposed to be my husband. A husband is someone who believes in his wife no matter what."

"I do believe in you. I just can't believe what you're telling me this time. I'm not sure of all the facts. I can't support something I don't understand. Why would you want me to?"

"Because I'm your wife and I'm asking you to. I've never lied to you, and I don't plan on starting now. I don't know what else to say, knowing how you truly feel about everything. I appreciate you being honest, but I'm very hurt and disappointed."

"I'm sorry. I had to be honest. That's how I've always been with you. I don't plan on changing that either."

"I guess we don't have anything else to discuss." Dominique turned her back again.

"Dominique!"

She glanced over her shoulder. "I'm sorry. Was there anything else you wanted to discuss?" Dominique asked transparently, letting Eric know she was through discussing the matter.

"Have you forgotten our vow that we promised each other never to go to bed without resolving our differences?"

"No. Unless you can tell me you believe me, we won't be able to resolve our differences this evening." Dominique laid her head on her pillow.

Dominique waited until she heard their bedroom door shut behind him before allowing her tears to fall from her eyes. She was disappointed in Eric, too. She couldn't understand why he couldn't believe her. What reason would she have to make something like this up? She continued to cry until the telephone rang. She wiped her face and reached across the bed to answer it. "Hello?"

"Good evening. Is Mrs. Dominique Wallace available?" a female voice asked.

"Speaking," Dominique answered, unfamiliar with the voice. "Who is this?"

"Mrs. Wallace, this is Katherine Buchanan, Kimberly's mother."

Dominique immediately sat up. She wondered why Mrs. Buchanan was calling her after today. Was she going to try to talk her out of prosecuting her husband again? That would be useless. Besides, it was out of her hands anyway. The state was counting on her to represent Kimberly's best interest. Right now, Kimberly's best interest was prosecuting her father, Mr. Buchanan.

"Yes, Mrs. Buchanan, how can I help you?"

"I need you to meet me at the corner bar on Sixty-Second and Broad Street in thirty minutes. I think it would be in your best interest not to be late. I have some information you need to win Kimberly's case." Mrs. Buchanan hung up.

Dominique hung up, jumped out of her bed, and dressed. She rushed downstairs, grabbed her keys and pocketbook, and raced to meet Katherine Buchanan. Halfway there, Dominique realized she hadn't told Eric where she was going. The more she thought about it, the more certain she was about not calling to tell him. He would be upset with her for leaving this time of night to meet someone at a bar, especially someone affiliated with Buchanan. If he wasn't questioning her mental state already, he definitely would be now.

When Dominique arrived at the bar, the parking lot was filled with automobiles. She pulled her car in between two trucks and checked to see if anyone was outside hanging around before getting out. She needed to be cautious.

She rushed toward the entrance of the bar and slowed upon entering to hide her nervousness. Without asking for assistance, she looked around the smoky bar for Katherine Buchanan.

"I'm glad you made it," Mrs. Buchanan whispered from behind her.

Dominique quickly turned around. Mrs. Buchanan's dress attire was very different from the previous times she had run into her. She was dressed down considerably. Dominique assumed she had done that on purpose to blend in with the bar crowd. But she still stood out, wearing a black Michael Kors top and blue jeans. Dominique quickly acknowledged her and followed her to a table in the corner.

"What exactly do you want to discuss?" Dominique wanted to make sure Mrs. Buchanan wasn't going to try to talk her out of representing her daughter's case. If that was the goal, Dominique wasn't going to stick around and argue. She would go back home to her warm, comfortable bed and call it a night.

"Please have a seat over here." Mrs. Buchanan sat down and crossed her legs at the ankles.

Trying not to cause a scene, Dominique seated herself opposite the woman. She placed her pocketbook on the table and waited for Mrs. Buchanan to tell her why she insisted she meet her.

"I'm glad you made it, Mrs. Wallace. Would you like to order something to drink?" Dominique detected a slight slur in her voice. She must have already had a few drinks before Dominique arrived.

"Mrs. Buchanan, I would like to know why you had me rush down here this time of night." Dominique abruptly slapped the table.

Mrs. Buchanan sipped from her drink before she answered. "I've been thinking about our conversations these last few days. I know you think I'm an awful mother, but I'm not. I love my daughter. It's been hard these last few years living with Kimberly and her father. I've tried to be everything they wanted me to be, but I couldn't." Mrs. Buchanan blinked rapidly.

"I don't think you're a bad mother. I have no idea what you have been through these last few years." Dominique placed her hands palms down on top of the table. "You are not the first mother to go through something like this, and unfortunately, you will not be the last."

"You have no idea how hard it was for me to dial your number this evening."

"May I ask what changed your mind?"

"Several things. The first thing, I know my husband, and I'm trying to be a few steps ahead of him. I have learned a few things from him over the years. You don't wait for the hunter to spot you. You get the hell out of Dodge before he gets his gun out of the gun rack." Mrs. Buchanan had assumed a southern accent.

"The second thing was when I saw how bad he hurt you. I know you're trying to help my little girl. I thank you for that. You have taken on a responsibility that I should have long ago.

"The third thing was when you told me about Kimberly testing positive for gonorrhea. I knew there was no mistaking it. I suspected he was sexually abusing our daughter for years, but I was too ashamed to say anything to anyone about it.

"I also contracted gonorrhea from my husband. I never told anyone. I tried to pretend it was nothing and everything would be okay if I just took care of it. I guess you could say I'm like a lot of wives who know their husbands are sleeping around, but they tell themselves they are the special one because he always comes home to them in the end. I know this is very different. But he has been sleeping around outside of the house, too." Mrs. Buchanan paused to take another sip of her drink.

"For a while I thought I could handle it, but eventually it got to a point I couldn't deal with it anymore. I started to notice everyone whispering when I enter a room. I knew it wasn't just because I was married to one of the richest and most powerful men in the state, but because he was sleeping with half the state. Mrs. Wallace, I hope you never have to experience the embarrassment I have had to endure all these years. I've confronted Mike about his affairs and he always promises to stop. But I know now that he can't."

"Why do you think your husband can't stop?"

"My husband has a large sexual appetite. One woman can't satisfy him. He's slept with so many women … It's different when your husband is having sex with someone you don't know, but to have sex with someone you know under your own roof is another thing."

"Mrs. Buchanan, are you telling me you knew about Mr. Buchanan having sex with your housekeepers?"

"Yes. I'm sure Kimberly's shared with you that we have employed several housekeepers over the years. I had to get rid of some of them because I suspected something. There was one young lady named Maria Gonzales. I really liked her, but she was one of the ones I had proof on. I had to be the only woman in our house. I was not going to allow him to disrespect me in our home. I couldn't allow that." Mrs. Buchanan took another sip.

"So, you knew Mr. Buchanan was having sex with your daughter and your housekeepers?" Dominique clarified.

"Yes." Mrs. Buchanan burst into tears. "Yes, I knew. When I found out about our housekeepers, I would just fire them. But how do you confront your husband about having sex with your child?" Mrs. Buchanan wiped her tears.

Dominique patted Mrs. Buchanan's free hand. "Mrs. Buchanan, I know it must have been difficult for you, but you're doing the right thing now by telling me this. The important thing is you are finally doing something to stop it. That's what I will tell the court. Please don't blame yourself. Your husband is to blame for what has happened. Neither you nor Kimberly is to blame," Dominique insisted.

"Well, explain to me why I feel like shit right now. If someone else had told me they had gone through something like this, I would've asked them why in the hell they hadn't done anything. There were days I wanted to kill myself because I wasn't strong enough to do anything. My husband is a very powerful man. He has a way of making you feel you need him."

"Men like your husband like for you to feel like you need them. That's how they get so powerful. They must control all those around them. Obviously, he has lost his control over you, because you called this evening. You have to remain strong for Kimberly. She needs you to be strong for her. You have to be her voice." Dominique waved away the waitress who slowed near their table.

"I've lost my daughter, Mrs. Wallace," Mrs. Buchanan said, shaking her head. "I'll never have her back again. She's gone and it's all because I didn't stop it." She looked up at the ceiling as if praying. "God, I pray she comes out of that coma. I will never forgive myself if she doesn't."

"Let's think positively. Kimberly's going to come out of her coma, and you will be able to tell her yourself that you were the one who helped convict her father. I know she'll forgive you."

"I hope so. I've never been one for praying, but lately I've been doing a lot of it. It feels good, but I'm not sure if God will answer my prayers. I haven't been the best follower."

"Trust in God, who holds no animosity toward his children. He will see you through."

"The Devil has had me for so long." Mrs. Buchanan smiled wryly. "I don't know if I can be Kimberly's voice," she uttered with uncertainty in her voice.

"Yes, you can. You're stronger than you realize. You told me you loved your daughter. Now is a great time for you to show her and the rest of the world. You have to do this for her and not yourself. You also have to let your husband know he can no longer control you. He can't destroy your daughter's life any longer. She doesn't deserve to be treated the way he has treated her. Your husband has been forcing your daughter to have sex with him!" She wasn't going to pacify Katherine Buchanan's feelings any longer.

It was about time for her to be angry about what her husband had done. "Mrs. Buchanan, can I count on you to testify against your husband?"

Mrs. Buchanan scanned the bar, wiped her eyes, and redirected her attention to Dominique. "My husband will kill me." She shrugged as if those words explained her position.

"Your husband will not be able to hurt you if I put you in protective custody. I won't allow him to hurt anyone else. Your husband will pay for ordering someone to attack me, too. I will see to that, but I want to convict him for sexually abusing your daughter first."

"Mrs. Wallace, may I call you Dominique?" She leaned in, lowering her voice.

"Yes, by all means."

"Mike believes in loyalty and eliminating anyone who does not honor it. Anyone who knows him well will tell you that. I know that he will view my testifying against him as an act of disloyalty to him. He's going to be outraged with me." Her voice became increasingly shaky.

Dominique found herself suddenly curious. "Have you talked to your husband about the videotapes and about him testing positive for gonorrhea?"

"Yes. He knows I'm furious. He knows this will bring embarrassment to me."

"What did he say?"

"He told me he didn't care if he embarrassed me, because he made me. Mike doesn't give a shit about anybody but himself. I've always known that, since the first day I met him. A part of me wants to see him pay for all the pain he has caused all these years, but I'm trying to think about my daughter right now. I know she needs me more than ever. I have to admit you struck a nerve in the hospital. You made me realize for the first time this isn't about me but about my daughter," Mrs. Buchanan delicately blew her nose.

"Good for you. That's how you must see this. This isn't about you. It's about your daughter who needs you more than ever. Remember your daughter is in the hospital as we speak, fighting for her life. She has tried on several occasions to kill herself. She hasn't even begun to live. You owe her this opportunity when she comes out of her coma. She needs to know you were by her side in her time of need.

"I think your testimony will allow you and your daughter to get a new start on building a new relationship together. It might not happen right away, but give her some time. The two of you have been through a lot, and healing must take place first. I want you to consider counseling with your daughter, as well as for yourself. I think it will be very beneficial for both of you."

Mrs. Buchanan chuckled. "I'm already in counseling. I've been in counseling for several years. That has been the only thing that has saved me. Kimberly's been in counseling ever since she was a little girl. She's always been a little different from most children her age. I used to think it was because we didn't spend enough time with her because Mike and I were so busy with our lives outside of the house—Mike with his career and me with my volunteer activities and groups. I thought all those things were important, but now I know they were not. My family should have been first.

"It's funny how we allow society to dictate our lives. What a shallow world we live in. Or is it just shallow individuals?" Mrs. Buchanan laughed and sat back in her seat.

Dominique was glad Mrs. Buchanan had come around. She would have to make quick arrangements to keep Mrs. Buchanan safe. She couldn't afford to lose a very important witness, even with all the other evidence.

A loud commotion across the room drew their attention to two scruffy-looking people arguing. Simultaneously, Dominique and Mrs. Buchanan agreed it was time for them to wrap up their meeting and get somewhere else where it would be safe.

"I need to make a few calls and secure a safe house for you. I don't want to take any chances." Dominique pulled her cell phone out and started making arrangements.

"Dominique, I really would like to see my daughter. I want to tell her I'm sorry for not doing anything sooner. I need to tell her that now and in person before something happens to me," Mrs. Buchanan confessed as they walked to Dominique's car.

Dominique was glad Mrs. Buchanan had taken a cab to the bar. All she had to worry about was getting her to the designated spot and pray Buchanan would have no way of tracing their steps.

"Nothing's going to happen to you. You're going to be safe," Dominique tried to reassure her.

"You never know. Please grant me this wish," Mrs. Buchanan pleaded.

"I will do my best to arrange something. But I need you to promise you won't try to see her before I make the arrangement for you. I don't want to compromise your safety."

Dominique entered the interstate heading toward their designated drop off point.

"Yes, I promise. I really want to see my daughter. God, I pray she comes out of that coma."

CHAPTER 13

When Dominique awoke the next morning, she was still alone in their bed. She wondered whether Eric had returned last night after she left unexpectedly to meet Katherine Buchanan. Tired from her lack of sleep, she rolled out of bed and dragged herself into the bathroom to wash up before going downstairs.

Dominique stood before the mirror, amazed at the dark circles around her eyes. She looked and felt bad as she stared back while considering her martial situation. It, too, was in bad shape. She couldn't believe they'd actually gone to bed without resolving their differences. She was unsettled that they broke a vow made so many years ago. How would it affect their marriage? They'd always been able to resolve their differences, but this time was different. She wasn't willing to budge and neither was he.

Dominique dressed and peeked into the guest bedroom to see if Eric had fallen asleep in there. The bed had not been slept in. She tiptoed downstairs to see if he had fallen asleep on the couch, but there was no sign of him in there either.

"Are you looking for me?" Eric strode down the hallway from their office.

Dominique jumped and turned around to face him. "Yes."

"How did you rest last night?" Eric's eyes were bloodshot red, as if he had been drinking all night long.

"Fine. I didn't have any difficulty sleeping." Dominique wondered whether Eric knew she left last night and was hinting around for answers.

Eric's shoulders slumped. "Well I didn't. Our conversation bothered me all night long. In case you didn't realize, last night was the first time we've gone to sleep without resolving our differences. That bothered me because we promised each other long before we married that we wouldn't do that. But it seems you didn't have a problem with it at all because you just turned over and went to sleep,"

She heard the anxiety in Eric's voice. She didn't want Eric to think she didn't care, but she still couldn't accept his position and let it go. She was sure of what she saw that night. The boy was real.

"Eric, I'm bothered about last night. I'm upset we went to bed without resolving our problem, but I'm not sure we can." Dominique realized he had no idea she'd left last night and thought it would be best if she didn't mention it, for fear of escalating the situation at hand. Right now, they had more than enough to deal with.

"Dominique, while you slept, I thought about everything. I love you too much to allow us to be mad with each other over something like last night. I thought about all the years we have been together and all the things we have been through. Somehow, we always managed to work things out. Regardless of what you might think, I don't like it when we don't agree or get along. It bothers me.

"So, I've decided to trust that you really saw a boy that night. You've never lied to me before, and I can't believe that you would now. You're my wife and I'm your husband. We are supposed to believe and support each other 'until death do us part.'" Eric stepped closer to Dominique as he stared directly into her eyes.

"I value my vows and pray you do too. That's why I'm telling you now, I will support you all the way. I love you, Dominique, and I don't want to lose what we have over some disagreement. It's not worth it." Eric's chest heaved with emotion.

Dominique's heart stung. She wasn't prepared for Eric's impassioned comments. She hugged him, kissing his face and neck. She loved him more than ever, knowing he believed in her. "Thank you, Eric, for believing in me. It really means the world to hear you say the things you have."

Eric sighed and pulled her from him. "I need to ask one favor of you."

"What is it?"

"I need you to introduce me to this boy the next time he comes over. I want to talk to him myself and ask him what happened that night. Can you promise me you will do that for me?"

"Yes. The only thing is I'm not sure if he's going to come back. He ran off when I asked him before. I think he's afraid of meeting you."

"Maybe. If there is a next time, you need to convince him. Let him know it would really mean a lot to me." Eric gave Dominique a small smile.

"Eric, I'll try."

"Good. Would you like some breakfast this morning before I go to work, or would you prefer me to work from the house today?"

"Oh, no. I'll be fine. I have a lot of work to do on my case, so don't worry about me."

"Are you sure you're fine with me going into the office for a little while? I probably won't stay the whole day. I have some stuff I really need to take care of that I can't do from here."

"I completely understand," Dominique assured as she leaned over to give Eric a kiss on the lips. "Go. Devin and I will be fine."

"What do you want for breakfast before I go?"

"I'm not hungry. I'm going to eat a banana. I'll fix Devin something when she gets up."

"I'm going to run upstairs and get dressed." Eric returned her kiss and hurried upstairs to get ready for work.

Dominique wandered into the kitchen, sat down at her kitchen table, and peeled a banana. She opened her briefcase and retrieved some of her casework to review.

Thirty minutes later, Eric came into the kitchen and kissed her again before leaving for his office. When the front door closed behind Eric, she started to think about their earlier discussion. Knowing Eric now believed in her made her feel better. She prayed her young friend would return for her to totally convince him.

She moved into her sunroom and gazed out of the window in a daze until Devin interrupted her.

"What would you like for breakfast this morning?" Dominique asked.

"Nothing." Devin squatted to play with her toys on the floor.

"You have to eat something in order for you to grow." Dominique stood, watching Devin.

"Can I have the rest of your banana?" Dominique finished peeling the banana and handed the remaining fruit to her daughter. She would have preferred that Devin eat a full breakfast, but she didn't want to force the child to eat if she wasn't hungry.

"Can I go outside, Mommy?" Devin asked, finishing her breakfast.

"Sure," Dominique answered as the telephone rang. Dominique answered it.

"Good morning, Dominique. How are you feeling?" It was Dr. Martin, and he sounded worried.

"I feel fine." Dominique was a little shocked that he was calling her at home.

"I heard what happened. I'd like to come over this afternoon if you don't mind."

"That will be fine. I'll be here all day." Dominique didn't question where he'd gotten his information. She didn't remember Eric telling her that he'd called Dr. Martin or anyone else about her attack.

"I saw it on the news," he disclosed, anticipating her confusion.

Dominique couldn't believe it. Her attack had been broadcasted on the news? Suddenly, she remembered Eric changing the station the other night. She hadn't thought anything about it, but now she was uneasy.

"I just want to make sure you are okay."

"I'm fine. Thank you for calling. I'll be glad to see you later this afternoon." She stared at the phone a moment after hanging up.

She looked outside at Devin playing by herself in her sandbox and marveled at how peaceful and innocent she looked. She prayed Devin would remain that way forever. She decided to join Devin outside while she worked on Kimberly's case. The weather was perfect, and she could use the fresh air. She placed her folders on the glass backyard table and gazed around the large yard. Her garden flowers had grown out of control, and weeds had begun to take over. Unable to concentrate on Kimberly's case, she decided to pull a few to relax herself.

"Good morning," a little voice called out to her from the bushes. She recognized the voice. It was the young boy.

"Good morning to you. How are you doing this morning?" Dominique asked in a cheerful mood. She would play it cool since she needed him to agree to speak with Eric.

"I'm doing fine. How are you?"

"Great. It's a beautiful day, and I'm so glad to have my health." Dominique gave her new friend a big smile and breathed in some fresh air. She noticed he was wearing the same clothes as yesterday. They appeared to be clean.

"I'm glad you're feeling fine. You didn't look too good yesterday."

Dominique had to agree with him. The day before her bruises had been a shock to several people, but today they weren't as startling.

"Well, I feel better even though I might not look like it. What brought you back today?"

"I just wanted to see how you were doing. I'm your little protector, remember?" The young boy joked.

"Yes, I remember."

"What are you doing?" He started to walk around Dominique's flower garden, examining all the work that needed to be done to it.

"I'm trying to pull the weeds out of here so you can see my pretty flowers. What are you going to do today?"

"Nothing much, I was planning on hanging out with you if you don't mind." He refocused his attention back to Dominique.

"I don't mind. I could use your help if your mother doesn't mind you being here."

"She won't care. My mother doesn't care about me," he replied with a bit of resentment in his voice. He looked away from Dominique.

She stared back at the young boy, praying he wasn't living in a neglectful and abusive household. Over the past few years, Dominique had noticed the increasing number of abused children from different backgrounds. No longer were only children from low-income families being abused but children from well-to-do backgrounds were now victims, too. Or maybe those with money had just hidden it better. The numbers were staggering and were steadily growing every day.

"Don't say that. I'm sure your mother cares about you."

The young boy lowered his head. "No she doesn't. She's never been there for me."

Dominique felt sorry for him. She didn't understand why his mother wouldn't care about such a sweet young boy who seemed to be very caring and thoughtful.

Her mind drifted to the relationship between Kimberly and her mother. Kimberly felt the same way about her own mother. Dominique felt sorry for both children. And she could relate personally. Dominique never knew her mother nor her father. So, like her new young friends, she understood their frustrated feelings toward their parents.

"I'm sorry to hear that," Dominique finally replied.

"Me too," the young boy responded jokingly.

"Actually, my mother wasn't much of a mother to me either when I was a little girl." Dominique yanked a particularly stubborn weed.

A curious look appeared on his face. "What did she do?"

"I never knew my mother or my father. They abandoned me when I was a little girl, so I was raised in the foster care system."

"Did you have any sisters or brothers?"

Dominique hunched her shoulders. "I don't know. I've been by myself for as long as I can remember." It had been a long time since she'd talked about her past. She tried to keep it suppressed. She didn't like to remember her childhood.

"Who knows? Maybe I'm your long lost brother." The boy smiled strangely.

"Maybe." Dominique smiled back, allowing herself to entertain the idea of him knowing where her parents were. But she knew it was only wishful thinking.

"I bet you are a good mother."

"I try to be a good mother. But I can always do better, and I have every intention of doing so." She exhaled, proud of the small pile of weeds. "Well, if you are going to be coming by to visit me, you have to tell me your name." Dominique waited for his response, but he looked through her without answering.

"You do have a name, don't you?"

Dominique sensed from the look on her young friend's face that he didn't find it very amusing.

He looked as if he'd been accused of a crime. "Why do you need to know my name?"

"I always like to know the names of people I associate with or invite to my home."

"I don't like my name." The boy dropped his head and looked away.

She laughed a little. "You don't like your name?"

"No."

"Well, let me hear it anyway. I'm sure it isn't as bad as you think."

He shrugged his shoulders. "What is your son's name?"

"I don't have a son. I have a little girl. Her name is Devin."

"If you did have a son, what would you name him?"

Dominique thought for a moment about what she would name her son. Before Devin was born, she remembered making a list of boy names for Eric to select from. "Maybe Jonathan, Aaron, or Shawn."

A smile appeared on the boy's face.

"Is one of those names I mentioned, your name?"

"My name is Shawn." Dominique didn't know whether to believe him.

"No, that's not your name."

"Yes it is," he insisted.

Dominique smiled, but she didn't believe him by the way he said it. "What's your last name then?"

"That's not important. I've told you my first name. That's enough."

"I didn't say it was enough for me." Dominique gave up her weeding.

Without hesitation he answered, "I meant it was enough for me."

Still not convinced, she proceeded with questioning him, "No it isn't. You just told me you didn't like your name. Shawn was one of the names I told you I liked. So, what's your name? I want you to tell me the truth. If we are going to be friends, you have to be honest with me. So what's your real name?"

Irritated now, he answered. "I told you it's Shawn. I came here to see you, not argue about my name."

Sensing his irritation, she thought it might be best to drop the discussion before he ran away again.

"Is Devin your only child?"

"Yes, Devin is my only child."

"She's lucky to have you as a mother," he said politely.

"I like to think so too." He wondered what he would do if she tried to touch him.

"Shawn, how old are you?" Dominique asked.

"I'm twelve years old." He proudly pushed his chest out.

"You're a bit young to be wandering around by yourself. Where do you live, Shawn?"

"Nearby." he answered vaguely.

"Nearby where?"

"Not too far."

"What's not too far?"

"Not far." His voice became irritated again. "I like coming to see you, Dominique, but you make it such a struggle with all these questions. Why can't you just enjoy my company without asking me all these questions?"

"I like you coming, too, but I'd like to know who I'm spending time with, that's all. Besides, I don't want your mother to worry about you."

"She won't, believe me." He started to walk around Dominique's garden, presumably to assess the work needed to restore it.

Dominique could tell from Shawn's responses that his relationship with his mother wasn't too pleasant.

Dr. Martin, her psychiatrist, would be a good person for Shawn to speak with, to help him deal with some of his frustrations toward his mother. But for now, she would have to befriend him before suggesting any introductions.

"Don't say that. I'm sure she cares about you." Dominique watched him circle her garden.

"I know she doesn't," he responded, dismissing her comment.

"Would you like to talk about it?" Dominique asked, trying to be supportive.

"No. I just want to spend time with you." Shawn's voice was calm.

"Sure. You can help me pull up the weeds."

Together they pulled weeds from her garden. Occasionally, Dominique would look up and gaze at Shawn as he worked diligently. As the day went on, she started to feel there was something familiar about him, but she couldn't put her finger on it.

Dominique heard a loud growling sound from Shawn's direction like she heard the first morning he stopped by to visit. She looked at her watch and realized it was lunchtime. She was surprised Devin hadn't come over to tell her she was hungry too. She looked over in the direction of Devin's sandbox, but she wasn't in it. Dominique assumed she must have gone inside to use the bathroom. She would have to go check.

"Would you like some lunch, Shawn?" Dominique got to her feet, but Shawn continued to pull weeds.

"Yes."

"What would you like?"

Shawn shrugged his shoulders. "It doesn't matter. Whatever you have."

"I'll be right back with some lunch for us." Dominique left Shawn in the garden. When Dominique entered through the sunroom, she noticed Devin asleep on the floor with her toys scattered around her. That explained why Devin hadn't come over to tell her she was hungry. Dominique picked Devin's sleeping body up from the fluffy carpeted floor and laid her on the soft, cushioned couch before preparing lunch.

Trying to eat light, she made some chicken salad sandwiches. She was sure Shawn would be hungry after working so hard in the garden. So, she put extra helpings on his sandwiches and placed everything on a tray. She quietly exited the sunroom, trying not to wake Devin from her afternoon nap. When she exited, she noticed Shawn looking through her folders.

"Did I give you permission to look through my things?" Dominique asked, disappointed that he had taken it upon himself to prowl through her belongings.

"I'm sorry," Shawn apologized. "It was just lying here on the table."

"Well next time, get my permission to read my papers."

Shawn's head dropped. "I will. Thanks for lunch."

"You're welcome," She responded cheerfully to change the mood. "I hope you're hungry. I put extra helpings on your sandwiches,"

He raised his head and gave her a smile. "Thank you. I'll need it. I'm a growing young man, can't you see?" He made a muscle with his right arm.

Dominique laughed when she saw his little muscle pop up in his arm.

"I sure like it around here," Shawn said, his mouth full with food. "I bet you wouldn't let anything ever happen to her."

"I do my best to keep her safe." Dominique wondered where that statement had come from.

"If I lived with you, I would keep her safe, too. You would never have to worry about her when I was around. I would make sure no one would ever hurt her." He took a sip of his glass of cold lemonade.

"When Devin wakes up I want to introduce you to her," Dominique hoped he was feeling more comfortable now, so she could introduce him to her family.

"I don't want to meet anyone yet. I just want to hang out with you." Shawn sipped his lemonade again.

Dominique wondered whether he was running from somebody. If so, she wanted to help him. "Are you sure everything is okay?"

"Yes. But what if I needed you to protect me, would you?"

"Yes. I would try."

"Can you keep a secret?"

"Yes."

"What if I told you something you had to keep a secret to save my life. Would you be able to keep it without trying to go behind my back and getting help?" Shawn asked, his face serious.

Dominique stared back at Shawn before answering. She didn't want to answer too fast, without thinking about his question completely. As a lawyer, she knew she had to keep what her clients tell her in confidence. But Shawn wasn't one of her clients.

"You don't think you would be able to keep my secret, do you?"

"Yes, I would be able to keep your secret if it would save your life, but I can't imagine what you could tell me that I would need to keep a secret like that," Dominique finally answered.

"You never know. I don't have anything to tell you, but I just wanted to know if I ever did that you would be able to keep my secret," Shawn explained to Dominique with a smirk.

"Shawn, I know we just met, but I want you to feel comfortable coming to me if you ever need to talk to someone. I'll do my best to listen and help you if I can. I'm also an attorney, and my job is to help and protect people."

"That's all I needed to know." Shawn gave Dominique a big smile of approval. "How is that girl Kimberly, in your folder?" Shawn asked, changing the subject.

"I can't talk about her case with you. You have to promise me you won't repeat anything you've read in her file," Dominique insisted.

"I won't. How did you get her case?" Shawn asked, even though Dominique had just told him she couldn't discuss the case with him.

"The state asked me to represent her."

"The state?" Shawn responded with a puzzled look on his face.

"I'm an attorney for the state."

"Where do you work?" Shawn asked, filling his mouth with more of the sandwich.

"I work downtown."

"Who were you visiting at the hospital the night of the attack?"

"I was visiting with Kimberly. What's with the million questions?" Dominique asked, feeling interrogated.

"I just want to know more about you if we're going to be friends. I told you my name. It's only fair," Shawn joked.

Dominique realized her young friend was quite clever.

"When will Kimberly be able to leave the hospital?"

"I'm not sure. She's really sick now," She said. Sighing, she added, "Shawn, I really can't talk about Kimberly with you. I could get in a lot of trouble."

"I hope she'll be okay." Shawn removed some mayonnaise from the corner of his mouth with his tongue.

"I do, too." Dominique wiped her mouth with her napkin.

"I hope you make her father go to jail for a long time. One last question, I want to know why you took her case?"

"Shawn, I can't talk about it."

"Please, just answer this last question for me. Why did you take her case?"

Seeing no harm in answering his last question, she granted his wish. "She needs someone to help her. What her father has done to her is wrong and I must help her prove that in court. If I'm good—and I am—he'll have to serve a long sentence in prison where he can think about what he has done to her all these years."

"Would you be my attorney if I needed you to?"

"Do you need an attorney?"

"No, but I might one day. So would you represent me?"

"Sure, I would. If I felt I couldn't help you properly, I'd make sure I found someone else who could."

"Dominique, are you sure you are okay to help her? You still seem a little shaky."

Dominique was surprised by Shawn's comment. If she hadn't been looking at him directly, she would have thought he was Eric talking to her.

"I will be just fine."

"You're stronger than me. I probably would have to take some time off to regroup after an attack like yours. I'm surprised your husband hasn't asked you to take some time off and let someone else handle her case."

"He has, but I'm not going to do that right now. I'm fine."

"How are you able to forget your attack so fast? You were really shaken-up that night." Shawn asked.

"I know what's best for me," Dominique said sharply.

"I'm sorry if I upset you. We're family now after all we've been through. You're like a sister to me, and I wouldn't want anything to happen to you." Shawn searched Dominique's face for acceptance. "I hope you can understand that."

"I can. Shawn, I appreciate your concern. And I do plan to take some time off after this case is over." She patted his shoulder. She was amazed by his maturity.

"Dominique, I don't want you to take this the wrong way. But I remember watching a program on television one day that talked about people who were attacked. They talked about how important it was for attack victims to allow themselves time to get over everything. The victims who did not take time, condition worsen."

"I've given myself time to deal with my attack."

Standing to his feet, Shawn said, "Well, I have to go, but I will come back another day."

"When are you coming back?" She asked, glad to know he would be returning since Eric didn't get a chance to meet him.

"Soon. Remember me asking you if you could keep a secret if it would save my life?"

"Yes," She answered.

"Well, I have a secret I need you to keep confidential for my safety." Shawn looked around the backyard as if to make sure no one else was listening.

Dominique found herself eager to hear his secret. "Tell me."

He paused before answering and stared back at her with a blank facial expression. "I need you to promise not to tell anybody about me coming to visit you."

"Why, Shawn? Is someone after you?"

"I'll be fine if you don't tell anyone about me? If you don't promise, I won't be able to come around anymore." He shrugged his shoulders.

"I don't like the way that sounds, Shawn. If you're in trouble, please let me know so I can help you," Dominique pleaded.

"In time, I'll be able to tell you more. But for now, please don't tell anybody about me. Remember, I'm your little protector," Shawn joked with a big smile on his face.

"I remember."

"I knew I would be able to count on you."

"How did you know?" Dominique was deflated that he'd trapped her into making a promise that would cause her to break her promise with her husband.

"I guess you could say my intuition told me so. It's like I've known you all my life," Shawn said, smiling back at Dominique.

She too felt there was something familiar about Shawn. But prior to the attack, she had no knowledge of his existence. The night of the attack was the first time she'd ever seen him. Even then, he wouldn't tell her who he was. How had he known her? How had he known where she lived? She had so many unanswered questions about him.

CHAPTER 14

Dominique heard the doorbell ringing. She excused herself and ran to answer it before it woke Devin from her nap. When she opened it, she was surprised to see Shawn Silver from her office.

"Hello, Shawn," Dominique greeted him, with a little question in her voice.

"I hope I'm not intruding because I didn't call before showing up." Shawn stood in the doorway with a bouquet of assorted flowers for her.

She gave Shawn a welcoming smile and motioned for him to enter the house.

He handed her the beautiful bouquet. "These are for you. The whole office pitched in to get them."

She took the bouquet of flowers and raised them to her nose to smell them. "They're absolutely beautiful. Tell everyone I said thank you. I really appreciate the thoughtfulness." She gave him a kiss on the cheek.

"You're welcome. I only wish we had gotten them for a different reason, but I'm really glad to see that you are doing well now."

"I'm doing great. I was just about to start working on Kimberly's case." Dominique walked toward the kitchen to place the bouquet of flowers on the kitchen counter.

"Dominique, I wanted to come by to make sure you are up to working on the case. I will completely understand if you want me to take the lead. Nobody will blame you either, especially after what has happened to you," Shawn assured her, patting her on the shoulder.

"I'm fine." She placed the bouquet of flowers on the kitchen counter and faced Shawn, standing across from her in the kitchen. "Shawn, what's really going on?"

"Nothing. I just wanted to give you the option of taking some time off. If you were my wife, I would demand that you do so, but you're not. I don't want you to feel you have something to prove to me or to anybody else at work."

"I don't feel like I have anything to prove to anyone. I promised Kimberly I would help convict her father, and I plan to keep that promise to her." Dominique propped her arm on the edge of the counter.

Shawn nodded. "Just know I have your back, Dominique, with whatever you decide."

"I know. Actually, I am planning on taking some time off after the case. I promised Eric I would, and I think I could use the time off, too."

As they entered the sunroom, Shawn said: "I agree. Just let me know when and what I can do to help you tie up any loose ends back at the office. Thanks for calling me about Mrs. Buchanan's change of heart. I want you to know I'm doing everything I can to make sure Buchanan will be prosecuted for what he did to you." Shawn's voice expressed certainty.

"I appreciate knowing that." Dominique gave him another hug.

"I've been trying to play back everything you told me about the events of the attack in my mind. I remember you telling me about a boy being present at the scene."

"Yes. What about him?" Dominique asked, worrying where he was going with his question.

"Well, I'm wondering if he heard what your attacker said to you when he told you who sent him. Do you think he might have overheard him and would be able to testify in court?"

"I don't know if he heard anything or not. I can ask him."

"You know where he is?" Shawn responded with a shocked look on his face.

"Shawn, he's here right now. The thing is, he just made me promise him I wouldn't tell anybody about him. So I don't know if it would be a good idea for me to ask him while you're here." Dominique hoped he wouldn't push the issue.

"Are you kidding? I need to speak to him." Shawn demanded.

"What about this: Let me ask him, and I will call you as soon as I find out." Dominique was trying to stop his pursuit of the boy. Shawn replied, "I don't want the court to say you coached him into saying anything. If I hear it for myself, I would be a witness when he tells you what he saw and heard that night."

Shawn had made a valid point. Maybe the boy wouldn't be too upset once he found out why she broke her promise.

"Follow me. He's outside in my backyard." She headed toward her sunroom to go outside.

"How did you two find each other? I spoke to the police and they still have no leads on him," Shawn asked as he followed behind Dominique.

Still curious herself, she chuckled. "He actually found me. He just showed up."

"He just showed up? Don't you think that's a bit strange?" Shawn asked, a bit concerned.

Dominique tried to downplay Shawn's reasonable question. "Kind of. I've been trying to get information out of him, but he won't tell me much."

"You mean you can't get him to answer your questions? I definitely want to meet this boy. Finally, you've met your match." Shawn laughed, trying to make light of this new situation.

Joining Shawn's laughter, Dominique smiled. "You know what else is so funny about all of this?"

"What?"

"His name is Shawn, too."

Together they laughed out loud as they exited the sunroom into the backyard. Dominique realized immediately that Shawn was gone. Once again, he'd left without saying goodbye. She didn't understand why he continued to disappear. She looked around her backyard for any sign of him, but he was gone.

Devin was up from her nap and busy eating her chicken salad sandwich. Dominique thought maybe she would know.

"Devin, did you see where Shawn went?" Dominique asked.

"Funny, Mommy," Devin laughed. "Shawn's right behind you." Devin continued to laugh as she took another bite of her sandwich.

Dominique just smiled. Surely Devin had seen Shawn out in the garden with her. There was no way she could have missed him. But then again, she didn't know his name was Shawn. She hadn't formally introduced them to each other either.

"No, not this Shawn—the boy who was helping me in the garden. Did you see where he went?"

"No," Devin answered with a funny look on her face.

Dominique couldn't understand how Devin could have not seen where he went. He was just outside with her. Then Dominique remembered Devin had been sleeping while they worked in the garden together earlier.

"He must have left." Dominique turned to Shawn Silver, now standing beside her, also disappointed. "This is the third time he's left, and no one has been able to meet him. I'm really worried about him. He keeps telling me he doesn't want to meet anyone."

"Dominique, you know as well as I do: Sometimes people disappear when they don't want to be found."

Dominique had to admit that was what it was starting to look like to her too. He was also making it hard for anyone to believe her. But now she was worried he was in trouble because of how paranoid he was about meeting anybody other than her.

"You might be right." Dominique bit her bottom lip in worry.

"So much for that." Shawn Silver patted Dominique on the shoulder. "Well, before I go, I want to give you another opportunity to walk away from this case without feeling bad."

She was determined she was going to represent Kimberly's case no matter what. "I appreciate your thoughtfulness, but I have every intention of staying until the end. Then—and only then—I plan to take some time off."

"Dominique, you and I both know you have definitely proven yourself."

Though she felt no need to validate her work, she still wanted Shawn to know how she felt. "I sure hope so. I've worked my behind off for the state."

"Dominique, I'm home," Eric called out to her as he walked outside carrying Devin on his back.

"Daddy's home, Mommy!" yelled Devin as Eric placed her on the ground.

"Hello. How was your day?" Dominique greeted Eric, startled by his entrance. She hadn't heard his car in the driveway, nor had she noticed that Devin had left to go inside and greet her father.

"Fine." Eric leaned over to give Dominique a kiss on the lips.

"Hope you don't mind me just dropping in on your wife, but I wanted to see how she was doing and insist she take it easy if she was refusing to listen to you." Shawn extended his hand to Eric.

"I'm trying to help her relax, but you know Dominique." Eric was comfortable with Shawn stopping by. They'd spent many late nights working at their dining room table, going over case information before a presentation in court.

"I'm taking it easy," Dominique interjected jokingly.

"I didn't get a chance to tell you, but your garden looks great." Shawn stared at a now weed-free garden.

"Thanks." Dominique glanced in the direction of her garden, too. It had been a long time since either she or Eric had done any gardening. Their careers had been so demanding the last few months that simple pleasures such as yard work had gone on the back burner.

"I like what you've done. It looks like you pulled every weed in the garden." Eric smiled with gratitude because now he wouldn't have to do it.

Dominique smiled back, hesitating to tell Eric that her young friend Shawn had assisted her in pulling all the weeds out of their garden today—especially since she promised to introduce them the next time he came over. Afraid of being accused of breaking another promise, she decided to remain silent.

"It's been so long since I've had time to devote to my gardening," Dominique said, glancing down at her watch. "Did you finish all your work at the office?"

"Yes. I told you I wouldn't be long. How are you feeling?" Eric wrapped his arms around one side of Dominique's body as the three continued to stand around causally.

"I feel fine." Dominique laid her head on Eric's shoulder gently.

Shawn cleared his throat. "Well, guys, I'm not going to intrude any longer. I just wanted to stop by and see how Dominique was doing. If the two of you need anything—and I mean anything—please don't hesitate to call me. You know I'm just a telephone call away." Shawn moved toward the door.

"Thank you very much. I appreciate the offer. I'll see you in the office tomorrow." Dominique gave Shawn a big hug.

"You don't have to come in tomorrow. My visit wasn't to rush you back." Shawn glanced at Eric to set the record straight.

"I know. I want to." Dominique shrugged. "Besides, I'm going to have to face the office eventually, and tomorrow is as good as any other day. Why delay it?"

"You heard her." Shawn threw his hands up in the air.

Eric smiled back at Shawn. "I appreciate you for trying. She's agreed to take some time off after this case, and I plan on holding her to that." Eric's expression made it very clear to Dominique that he wasn't going to allow her to break her promise.

"She's definitely earned it. I'm only sorry she's taking it because of the unpleasant circumstances," Shawn consoled with a half-smile on his face.

"Me too," Dominique joked. "Shawn, thanks for stopping by." She motioned for him to follow her to his car.

"No problem." Shawn leaned in to hug Dominique goodbye and left her and Eric standing in the front doorway of their home.

Dominique had grown to admire his honesty and caring characteristics. She was glad Shawn hadn't allowed the system to corrupt him.

"Dominique, are you sure you don't want to reconsider Shawn's offer? I'm sure Shawn can easily finish this case for you since he's been working so closely with you." Eric's eyes conveyed he was hoping she would reconsider as they closed the front door.

"I don't want that. I want to finish out my case, Eric," Dominique regretted her angry tone as soon as she'd spoken the words.

Eric accepted defeat and gave Dominique a kiss on the lips. "I love you very much and I don't want anything to happen to you."

"Eric, I love you too." They walked to the backyard to relax while Devin continued to play in her sandbox.

"Dominique, I want you to take it slow when you take off. I don't want you to try to rush back to work," Eric said cautiously, trying to avoid upsetting her again.

Dominique gave Eric a smile to assure him she would consider his request. "I don't plan on rushing myself either. I'm looking forward to the time off. I've already started to think about things Devin and I can do together while I'm home."

"Dominique, I have to be honest with you. I was afraid to leave you here with Devin this morning while I was gone."

"Why?" Dominique asked.

"I was afraid you might have another attack while you were here alone with Devin. You and I both know Devin is too young to understand what is going on." Eric wouldn't meet her eyes.

Dominique grabbed his arm, forcing him to face her. "I know, but Eric, I'm really feeling fine. I think the reality of what happened just came crashing down on me and I couldn't handle it. I feel I have full control of the situation now. I've had time to think about everything, and I've started putting it behind me. I want you to do the same."

"I will try, but I can't promise you I won't worry about you," He said with a sincere look on his face.

"I know, but don't treat me like I'm helpless."

"I just want you to understand how I feel right now. I felt helpless the other night, and I didn't like it. And I didn't like what I saw in the bathroom that night either. You really scared me."

"Eric, I know, and I pray it won't happen again."

"Daddy?" Devin approached Eric and Dominique as they sat down on the chaise together. "Why are you so worried about Mommy? Are you afraid that bad man who hurt Mommy is coming back to hurt her again?"

"No. He won't be coming to hurt Mommy ever again." Eric picked Devin up and put her on his lap.

Dominique gently rubbed Devin's leg. "Mommy wasn't feeling well the other day, and Daddy was worried if I was feeling okay today. That's all and I don't want you to worry either." She kissed Devin on the forehead.

"Okay," Devin said, leaning into Dominique's arms from her father's lap.

Eric rose to his feet with Devin in his arms and started to swing her around in the air.

"Eric, stop! You're going to make her sick," Dominique said. Then she heard the doorbell. "Eric, someone's at the door." Dominique tried to distract Eric as he continued to swing Devin in circles.

"Do you want me to get it?" he asked now standing still with Devin in his arms.

"No. I'll get it," she sighed and headed for the front door.

Dominique smiled when she realized it was her psychiatrist. "Hello, Dr. Martin," Dominique greeted and led him to the backyard to meet her family. "Eric and Devin, this is Dr. Martin."

"Hello, Dr. Martin. I have heard a lot of good things about you. It's finally nice to put a face with a name," Eric reached out his hand to welcome their guest.

"Nice to meet you, too." Dr. Martin shook Eric's hand. "So, I finally get to meet the beautiful Miss Devin Wallace. Your mother raves about you all the time." Dr. Martin shook Devin's hand, earning an impish grin.

"Nice to meet you, too." Devin giggle.

Dr. Martin gave Dominique a warm smile, "Thank-you for allowing me to stop by this evening."

"No. Thank-you for stopping by." Dominique directed him to sit down on her lawn set. "Eric, Dr. Martin and I need to talk a little. Do you mind keeping an eye on Devin?"

"No. I'll take her in and we'll find something to get into—won't we?"

"Yes. I'll beat you into the house." Devin started running.

"Dr. Martin, I really appreciate you making a house call today. Have a seat."

"No problem. I'm making both a professional and friendly call today. I was deeply concerned when I heard the news. So how do you feel right now?" Dr. Martin kept his focus on Dominique.

"I feel fine. I feel blessed to be here in one piece." Dominique, use to the office couch, laid back on her chaise.

"Have they identified your attacker yet?"

"Yes, and I have a strong feeling he is one of Buchanan's men. He said something that led me to believe that." She shifted her body weight on her chaise.

"What did he say?" Dr. Martin eased back in his chair.

Dominique thought back to that night and tried to remember the exact words he'd whispered in her ear. "He told me not to fight it. He said a good friend of his wanted him to show me what happens to bad little girls who betray him. And I would be better off if I just calmed down. He said I knew what he wanted, so if I stopped fighting, it would all be over soon." Dominique closed her eyes to ease the pain of reliving that moment.

"How did you feel when he told you that?"

"I remember feeling terrified, afraid that he might rape me in that garage and no one would know. I felt helpless," Dominique admitted. "I couldn't scream because he had my mouth covered. And I couldn't run

119

because my body was pinned in between his body and my car. It was awful. I pray I never have to experience it again." Dominique felt herself starting to shake just thinking about the evening.

"That's awful to hear."

"I know, but I'm not going to let him scare me from representing Kimberly Buchanan. I'm even more determined to win now." Dominique straightened up a little.

"Why?"

"He tried to make me a victim, too. Luckily for me, I was strong enough to stop him. But Kimberly wasn't. She's just a child." Dominique said passionately, "She trusted him with her life, and he took advantage of that trust. He crossed the line, and the law must protect her from him."

"Can you tell me more about Kimberly's situation with her father? Like how did it start? And how long has it been going on?"

"She told me he came into her room one night and he wanted to play a game. She didn't think anything of it because they were really close. She loved playing with her father. Then, he took off all his clothes and got in bed with her."

"Did she think anything was strange about that?"

"She said she never thought he would hurt her the way he did. So, after he took off all his clothes and got under the covers with her, he made her do things to his body and then he got on top of her. He made her promise never to tell anyone. Kimberly said she didn't know what to do, so she kept it a secret. After he got away with it that one time, he continued to come back to her for sexual favors."

"That's awful. Did she ever try to tell anyone before now?"

"Yes, but she said no one believed her when she finally said something. Her own mother didn't believe her until now."

"What do you mean 'until now?'"

"She called me last night and agreed to testify against her husband."

"So, what changed her mind?"

"Several things. She was remorseful that her husband had me attacked, also to discover her daughter had contracted gonorrhea from her father. There is no disputing the evidence and reality of what her husband has been doing. He is guilty and she knows it. Besides, he'd also given her gonorrhea, but she'd never told anyone. She knew her husband was sleeping around, but she was in denial about him sleeping with their daughter."

"Does Mr. Buchanan know his wife contracted gonorrhea?"

"No. She never told him."

"So, did Kimberly's mother confess when you told her that her daughter had gonorrhea too?"

"No. She called me late last night and asked me to meet her at a bar downtown. When we met there, she agreed to testify against her husband. She said she knew after the hospital test that he was one hundred percent guilty of the charges and she wanted him to be punished for what he had done to their daughter. And to her."

"How do you feel about Mrs. Buchanan changing her mind?"

"I'm greatly relieved. I think she's doing the right thing."

"That's something." Dr. Martin shook his head sadly. "So does her husband know she's going to testify against him in court?"

"I'm not sure. I've placed her in protective custody for her own safety."

"Let's get back to the attack. I want you to tell me more about that."

Dominique adjusted her weight to get comfortable and recounted all the details about her attack.

"You mentioned there was a boy who was present at the scene who ran away?"

"Yes."

"Who was this boy?"

Dominique was tired of talking about Shawn's presence at the attack. "I didn't know at the time."

"Do you know where he came from that night?"

"No. I didn't notice him until I broke free from my attacker. Then I noticed he was covered in blood too."

"Did he say anything to you?"

"Yes. He asked me if I was okay, but he ran away when he heard the security guard approaching."

"What did the security guard do when he saw him running away?"

"Nothing because the security guard never saw him."

"So why do you think the boy ran away?"

"I guess he was afraid the security guard would accuse him of hurting me. If it hadn't been for him, I might have been raped. He must have stabbed the attacker several times in order to help me."

"About how old is he?"

"Twelve years old."

"I'm assuming the attacker is an adult?"

"Yes, the attacker is an adult."

"Have the police found the boy? You did say he ran away before they had a chance to question him?"

"No, they haven't, but I have seen him since the attack."

Dr. Martin raised his eyebrows in surprise. "When did you see him again?"

Dominique responded slowly. "He showed up at my house the next day."

"He came *here* the next day? How did he know where you live?"

Dominique still wasn't sure how Shawn had managed to find her house. She remembered asking him and him avoiding her question. She would try to get that information out of him when he returned to visit. There were so many unanswered questions.

"I don't know. I asked him and he completely avoided the question. I haven't asked him again. I just let it go, but I'm still curious to know myself."

"Are you going to ask him the next time you see him?"

"Yes. I'm going to try. He's so sensitive about things. I'm always afraid I'm going to run him away."

"How is he sensitive?"

"He gets upset and defensive when you ask him for personal information. I have to be careful not to scare him off."

"Why is he coming to your house?" Dr. Martin asked, measuring his words carefully.

"He said he's concerned about me."

"How thoughtful of him," Dr. Martin commented.

Dominique gave Dr. Martin a smile. "I thought so, too."

"Did he tell you his name?"

"His name is Shawn, but he wouldn't tell me his name at first, not until the second visit. I'm not convinced that's his real name," Dominique admitted. Dr. Martin took a notepad and pen out of his jacket and started writing down some notes.

"Why do you think it's not his real name?"

"I don't know." Dominique shook her head.

"Why wouldn't he tell you his real name?"

"He doesn't want anybody to know his real name, I guess."

"Not even you? After all, he did help save you."

"I know. He's afraid to let anyone know anything about him."

"Whom do you think he's afraid of?"

"I don't know yet." Dominique's mind drifted from why Shawn was behaving the way he was to her thoughts about her argument with Eric. She wanted to discuss that whole ordeal instead.

"Dr. Martin, Eric and I had an argument, and I want to talk to you about that today, too."

"What was your argument about?"

"Eric doesn't believe I saw Shawn the night of my attack."

"Why doesn't he believe Shawn was there?"

"I haven't been able to prove it. We went down to the police station yesterday to view the videotape of the attack, and I wasn't able to point him out, nor was anyone else."

"What videotape?"

"The hospital security camera recorded the attack, but it wasn't very clear."

"Who saw the tape with you?"

"Eric, Captain Lewis and several other officers at the station, no one was able to see Shawn on the tape. I can't explain it. All I know is I saw him there. Why would I lie about him being there?"

"I don't know," Dr. Martin answered, not having a logical answer. "What did Eric say after he saw the tape?"

"He didn't say much. He just sat there."

"When did he tell you he didn't believe you?"

"Later that night, he confessed he didn't believe Shawn was there, after he and everybody who viewed the tape was unable to verify his presence. He told me he couldn't honestly tell me he believed me because there was no proof anywhere. Dr. Martin, I felt Eric betrayed me." Dominique was still feeling disappointed.

"Why?"

"Eric has always supported me. This is the first time he has ever questioned me. It was bad enough that the police didn't believe me. But my own husband doesn't believe me either? He eventually told me he would support me. The only reason he changed his mind was because we went to bed without resolving our disagreement." Dominique shifted her weight again on her chaise. "Eric and I made a vow when we first married to never go to bed without resolving our disagreements. I broke that vow when I refused to discuss it any further. I felt there wasn't anything more to say after he told me he couldn't believe me. So, I went to sleep."

"What did Eric do?"

"He left our bedroom and slept in another room for the night."

"So, when did Eric tell you he changed his mind?"

"He told me the next morning. He said he didn't want us to argue about it anymore. It wasn't important enough for us to destroy our marriage over it. He was really affected by me breaking our vow." Dominique closed her eyes, fighting the image of how bothered Eric looked and sounded this morning.

"So how do you feel now, knowing Eric supports you?"

"At first I was happy, but the more I think about it, I'm not so sure I am."

Dr. Martin paused to write down more notes before continuing. "Why aren't you sure about how you feel?"

"Because he did it only to make me happy, not because he really believes me. Dr. Martin, I value my husband's support, and to know he really doesn't want to support me bothers me."

"Dominique, don't you think it took a lot for Eric to change his mind?"

"I guess. I want him to believe me. I don't want him just pacifying me to keep the peace. I want him to believe me," She repeated.

"I understand." Dr. Martin nodded his head. "You said Shawn has been here more than once?"

"Yes."

"Why haven't you introduced Eric to him?"

"Shawn always leaves before I get a chance. He won't allow me to introduce him to Eric."

"Why?"

"I don't know yet. He says he doesn't want to meet him or anybody else."

"I think you need to convince Shawn it would be a good idea for you to at least introduce him to Eric. If he is so interested in how you are doing, let him know you would do better if your husband could believe your story about him being there."

Dominique wished it was that easy. She already tried that route and it hadn't worked. "I'll try. I hope he'll come back to visit. I never know when he's coming over. He just shows up."

"See if you can arrange for him to come when Eric is home."

"I'll try."

"I know you are working on an important case, but are you going to take some time off now?"

"I'm going to finish Kimberly's case. Then I plan to take some time off."

"Why are you waiting until after Kimberly's case is over?" Dr. Martin crossed his legs.

"I don't want to abandon her now. She's counting on me to be there for her."

"Do you feel up to it, or are you pushing yourself to prove something to her father?"

Dominique tried to convince Dr. Martin of her position. "Both. I want to be there for Kimberly. I'm the first person who has managed to reach her, and I'm not about to let her down. She really needs me, and her mother does too."

"Dominique, I just want you to make sure you're able to handle what comes next. From what you have told me about this Mr. Buchanan, I don't think he's going to stop with one attack. I want you to think about that. You have a lot at stake. You have a husband and a daughter who are counting on you. Please don't forget that."

"I won't. I haven't forgotten that either. Dr. Martin, I'm going to be fine. I promise you. I'm a survivor." Dominique smiled proudly at Dr. Martin.

"I want you to call me if you ever need to talk. You know I'm available for you."

"I know and I appreciate it."

"Dominique, one last question. Have you had any more panic attacks since we last talked?"

She immediately thought about the scare in her bathroom. She'd almost forgotten to tell him about that. "Yes. I had one the night I was attacked."

"What happened?"

"I'd just finished taking a shower, and I was standing in front of the mirror, looking at myself drying off, when my bathroom door opened up behind me. I saw someone enter my bathroom but I couldn't see who. Then I started to feel very nervous."

"Who do you think it was?" Dr. Martin started to write again.

"I don't know. It looked like a man, but I wasn't sure. Whoever it was, I watched him move closer and closer to me in the mirror. I remembered not being able to move or scream. I just stood there frozen. Then I fainted," She was still confused by the memory.

"Did the figure resemble your attacker that night?"

"I don't know. I couldn't see a face. As soon as I saw him enter the bathroom, I started to panic. It was bizarre, but my mind and body knew to be afraid. That's all I could remember."

"Were you alone?"

"When I snapped out of it, Eric was there."

"Do you think you might have mistaken him in the mirror?"

"I don't know. That's possible." Dominique considered the possibility of mistaking Eric in the mirror. It would make logical sense, since he was in the bathroom with her when she finally came to.

"Where was Eric when the panic attack started?"

"He was in our bedroom waiting for me to finish my shower."

"What can you remember from when you finally snapped out of it?

"Being on the floor, curled up in his arms, while he continued to ask me if I recognized him."

"Did he say whether you were talking during your panic attack?"

"Not really. He said I was pushing him away and I wouldn't allow him to touch me. All I remember is waking up in his arms—crying and shaking. After I closed my eyes and fainted, I can't remember a thing."

"How did you feel after you calmed down? Did you still feel nervous?"

"I felt a little shaky, but I wasn't afraid anymore. Just a little disoriented.

Eric helped me get in bed, and I went to sleep. The next morning, I felt fine."

"What else can you tell me about your panic attack?"

"Nothing. That's all I can remember about the attack that night."

"Sometimes when people have experienced something as traumatic as your attack, it takes them some time to relax again. Maybe you were still in shock from everything." Dr. Martin uncrossed his legs. "Have you had another panic attack since then?"

"No."

Dr. Martin frowned at Dominique. "I definitely want you to take it easy. Your body is trying to tell you something, but you're refusing to listen."

"I promise to take some time off after Kimberly's case."

"I want you to make sure you keep all your appointments with me while this case is going on. I want to keep a close watch on you."

"Okay, I promise." Dominique said while laughing silently to herself as she thought about all the promises she'd had to make over the last twenty-four hours.

Their session together concluded, Dr. Martin stood. "Good. I'm going to leave now so you can spend some quality time with your family. I also want you to get some rest. Your body is trying to tell you something, and I don't want you to find out the hard way. It's okay if you have to take a leave of absence for a while. People do it every day, and you have my permission to do it, too."

Dominique started to stand up. "I promise to take it easy after the case."

"I'm planning on holding you to that," Dr. Martin said jokingly, pointing at Dominique with his finger.

"I know you will, and so will Eric." She smiled at Dr. Martin.

"Set up an appointment with my assistant tomorrow." Dr. Martin followed her to his car. "Please take care."

"I will." Dominique gave Dr. Martin a hug and watched him drive away. She spent the remainder of the evening with Eric and Devin, watching television and taking it easy as ordered.

CHAPTER 15

Dominique had to admit her first day back in the office was more awkward than she had anticipated. She felt everyone's curious eyes staring as she moved around the office. At times, she wondered what they were thinking or whispering about her as she desperately tried to focus her attention on preparing for Kimberly's case. Occasionally some brave soul would offer an apology when they thought no one else was paying attention. And almost as if rehearsed, she would downplay the whole attack to comfort their curious minds. She didn't care for all the negative attention. She prayed something else would happen in the office and her attack would be considered old news there.

There was a knock at Dominique's door. She looked up from her desk and stared at her office door. "Who is it?" But there was no response. Instead she watched as her office door opened. She promised herself that if it was a news reporter, she would make that person regret bothering her.

But it wasn't. It was her young friend Shawn. And once again she wondered how he had found her.

"Shawn, what are you doing here?" Dominique asked.

"I wanted to see how your first day back to work was. I figured you must have been here when I stopped by your house today and you weren't home."

Dominique glanced at the clock on her desk. It was only two in the afternoon, and surely school was still in session. "Why aren't you at school right now?"

"I didn't have school today, so I decided to visit you instead."

"Shawn, how did you know where my office is?" Dominique leaned back in her desk chair and allowed it to rock back and forth as she waited for his answer.

"You told me yesterday where you worked. I just asked the lady at the front desk where your office was. It wasn't that hard. Is there a problem with me stopping by?" Shawn closed the door behind him.

She was happy to see him, but she was more surprised than anything. "No, there isn't."

"Well, you don't seem happy to see me. Maybe I should leave." Shawn reached for the doorknob.

"No, don't leave. I just find it strange how you've been able to find my home and workplace so easily."

"You're not hard to find. Why do you have to question everything?" Shawn frowned.

"Because I'm an attorney, and it's my job," Dominique answered, still rocking in her chair.

"Well, I'm not one of your clients, so drop the probing questions, will you?" Shawn released the doorknob and looked around her office. "When are you leaving work today?"

Wrapping up her day did sound good. "Actually, I think I'll call it a day right now." Dominique gathered the papers scattered all over her desk and placed them in a folder.

"Are you going to go straight home from here?" Shawn asked as he surveyed her office.

"Yes. Do you need a ride home?" Dominique thought she would take advantage of this opportunity to find something out about him.

"Not really. If you don't mind, I'll just ride to your house and walk home from there."

Disappointed but not surprised that she wasn't going to find out where he lived, she probed again. "Are you sure?"

"Yes." Shawn gave her an innocent smile.

"Are you ready to go?" Dominique gathered the last of her things.

"Yes. I will meet you downstairs by your car. Where did you park?" Shawn waited for her instructions than he left ahead of her.

Eager to leave herself, she finished up rapidly and headed for the elevator.

"Dominique!" When she heard her name being called, Dominique turned around in the elevator. It was Shawn Silver, who was racing down the hallway to catch her before the doors closed.

"Are you leaving for the day?"

"Yes. Is there something you need before I leave?"

"No. I'll walk you to your car."

"Sure. Come on." Dominique held the elevator doors open for him to join her.

"How was your first day back?" he asked as if she had been away for a long time.

"Same as usual. I managed to get a lot accomplished today," she replied as the elevator door closed in front of them.

"Are you free for lunch tomorrow, so we can prepare for the preliminary hearing."

Dominique pulled out her planner and looked at her schedule. As far as she could tell, she was free. "What time do you want to meet and where?"

"What about eleven thirty at Charlie's?"

"Sounds great. I'll meet you then." Dominique wrote the information in her planner. The elevator door opened and they both stepped off. She glanced in the direction of her car, looking for her young friend Shawn, who was supposed to be waiting for her there, but wasn't. She scanned the parking garage as she approached her car.

"Is there something wrong?" Shawn Silver asked.

"You remember that boy, Shawn, I told you about?"

"Yes."

"He stopped by the office this afternoon and told me he was going to wait for me by my car."

"What's he doing here?" Shawn asked, surprised.

"He wanted to see how my first day back to work went."

"Well, maybe he saw me and decided to run again."

"Maybe so," Dominique responded, unconvinced.

"Are you sure he's real?" Shawn joked as he stood by Dominique's car, waiting for her to get in.

Not finding his comment amusing, she shot him a sharp stare. "I'm positive. And don't you start with the doubts. He's very real. He's just a little nervous about meeting strangers." Dominique opened her car door to get in.

"Good luck. I wish you well with trying to convince someone who doesn't want to be found," Shawn teased. "Have you asked him if he heard anything yet?"

"No, but I will."

"Please do. We really need his testimony if he did. Are you coming in tomorrow?"

"Yes."

"I'll see you tomorrow. Drive home safely." Shawn closed her car door.

Dominique started her engine and slowly backed out of her parking space. She was convinced her younger friend Shawn was still in the parking garage somewhere, so she started canvassing the place as she proceeded for the exit. His disappearing acts were starting to get old. He was creating a phantom character for himself, and she didn't like him doing it at her expense.

One car away from exiting the garage, young Shawn jumped in front of her car and tapped her hood to get her attention. Then he ran around to the passenger side of the car and knocked on the window for Dominique to unlock the door so he could get in. She reached over to her door control panel and pressed her unlock button. Shawn jumped in.

"Shawn, where did you go?" she asked as she waited for him to put his seat belt on.

"I couldn't find your car, so I figured I would meet you here instead," Shawn answered, breathing hard.

She didn't believe him. "I told you where it was. I don't understand how you could have missed it."

"I just did. What's the big deal? I finally found you." Shawn sat up in his seat, checking out the interior of her sporty BMW.

"I was worried about you."

"You don't have to worry about me," Shawn corrected her. "I've been taking care of myself all my life. It's you who you need to worry about.

"I love your car. Maybe one day you can teach me how to drive it?" Shawn asked as they accelerated onto the interstate.

"You must make a lot of money to afford a car like this," Shawn observed, staring at Dominique while she concentrated on driving in all the traffic.

"I'm comfortable," Dominique answered with a smile. Together she and Eric were making well into six digits. Eric was doing an excellent job of managing their money. Their savings and retirement were doing well. They would be able to retire comfortably at an early age and still be able to send Devin through college.

Traffic was heavy on the interstate, so Dominique decided to take the scenic route home. Normally, she would stay on the interstate and drive straight to her front door, but today she wasn't in the mood for sitting in traffic. Besides, the beautiful scenic route would be a change for her and her company.

All the way home, they laughed and enjoyed the beautiful scenic, sights. When she turned into her driveway, she saw Eric's car. Excited to have an opportunity to finally introduce Shawn to Eric, she grabbed her briefcase from the back seat as Shawn got out on the passenger side.

"I want you to come in for a minute to meet my family." Dominique looked at Shawn over the top of her car.

"No. I need to get home. I have a lot of homework I need to do before school tomorrow. I'll see you later. Thanks for the ride home." Shawn waved goodbye as he ran down her street.

"Dominique, what are you looking at?" Eric stood in the front doorway, still wearing his suit from work.

"I was watching Shawn run down the street." Dominique turned to head in his direction.

"Shawn from your office?"

"No, Shawn from the attack."

"What did he want?" Eric looked puzzled.

"He actually showed up at my office today and rode home with me," Dominique stepped onto the porch.

"He showed up at your office today. How did he know where you work?" Eric's voice reflected his anxiety.

"I told him I worked downtown and he just figured it out. So, he decided to stop by to see how I was doing and to make sure I got home safely. I thought that was sweet of him." Dominique hurried past Eric and entered the house.

"Dominique, I thought you told me the next time you saw him, you were going to introduce us. What happened?" Eric was on her heels.

"He had to get home, so I didn't get a chance this time." Dominique placed her briefcase down.

"I don't feel good about him just showing up at your office. Don't you think it's a little strange?"

Dominique tried to downplay Shawn's surprise visit. "No. I think he was just worried because he saw what happened to me that night. Remember, he was there."

"Dominique."

"What?" Dominique waited for Eric to say the wrong thing and cause another argument.

"Nothing." He sighed loudly. "I don't know if I like him just showing up at your office and here unannounced." Eric chose his words cautiously.

But she could tell he wasn't being truthful with her by the anxious look on his face. "Are you sure that's all you're worried about? Or do you still believe he doesn't exist?" The silence was telling.

"Dominique, I don't want to argue. I'm just trying to be honest with you about not feeling comfortable. That's all."

"Are you sure?" She wished he would say what he really wanted to say.

"Yes," he answered, but he looked defeated, and she hated that.

As they lay in bed later that evening, Eric informed Dominique he had to go out of town for three days, "Are you going to be okay?"

"Don't worry about Devin and me. Ms. Anderson will be here during the day, and I'll try to come home earlier from work." Dominique was used to Eric's frequent trips. They came with the job.

"Are you sure? If not, I can call Ron and ask him to handle the meeting without me."

"No, you don't have to do that. I'll be fine. Please don't start babying me again." Dominique settled down to go to sleep.

"I'm not. I'm just worried, that's all. I have to leave tomorrow evening."

"Try to call me at the office before you leave."

"I will. And I'll call you as soon as I get to the hotel," Eric promised as he kissed her on the forehead.

CHAPTER 16

"Dominique, are you awake?" Eric slid his feet into his slippers.

"Yes," Dominique answered, barely awake.

"Why don't you go in late this morning so you can sleep in a little longer?" Eric must have heard the exhaustion in Dominique's voice.

"No. I'll be fine. I need to get up." Dominique forced her eyes wide open. She reached for the remote control on her nightstand and turned on the news.

"Don't forget I'm going out of town this evening and won't be back until Friday. Are you sure you're going to be okay with me going out of town?"

"I'm positive," she replied, becoming annoyed with his repeated questions. She slid out of bed and joined him in the bathroom.

When Dominique arrived at work, there was a message on her voice mail from Shawn Silver. He needed a rain check on their lunch appointment today. Something important had come up, and he would share the details with her later.

Dominique decided to order in for lunch. She spent the time combing through all her notes. When she glanced up again for a break, her clock read four forty-five, and she decided to call it a day.

She was surprised she hadn't heard from Eric by now and decided to call his cell to see what time his flight was leaving. His voice mail was full, and she was unable to leave a message. She hung up and pressed her assistant's extension to inform her she was leaving.

Mentally exhausted, Dominique tossed her briefcase in the back seat of her car and slid into her front seat. Anxious to get home and unwind, she started the engine and flipped her favorite jazz CD into her CD changer.

The tapping on her passenger window startled her. Her young friend

Shawn was staring back at her, waving for her to unlock the door for him. Dominique smiled and pressed the button to unlock her passenger door so he could get in.

"Did you have a good day today?" he asked as he jumped into the front seat.

"What are you doing here?" She placed her seat belt on and waited for him to do the same.

"I wanted to see you."

"Oh, you did? Did you go to school today?"

"I sure did," Shawn answered, tossing his backpack on the floor between his feet and placing his seat belt on.

"Good, I will drop you off at home today."

"No. I'll get out at yours. What did you work on today?"

"Case work. Nothing you would be interested in." If he wasn't revealing details, neither would she.

"You mean Kimberly's case, don't you?"

"Maybe."

"Is she still in the hospital?"

"Yes. Why do you ask?"

"I would like to go by and see her one day."

"I don't think that would be a good idea, Shawn." Dominique didn't take her eyes off the road.

"Why?"

"She has a restricted guest list." Dominique's cell phone rang. She glanced down at the caller window and recognized Eric's number.

"Hello. Are you there yet?" Dominique asked after pressing the button.

"Not yet. I just landed in Dallas. I'll call you when I get to LA."

"Be careful."

"I will. You need to be careful, too, and I love you."

"I love you, too." Dominique hung up.

"Mushy, mushy. I guess that was Eric?" Shawn teased.

"It sure was!" Dominique nodded, smiling ear to ear. "He has to go out of town for a few days, and he just wanted me to know where he was."

"Can I spend the night while he's away?" Shawn sat up.

"No!" Dominique replied firmly as she glanced over at Shawn, almost swerving into the next lane.

"Are you trying to kill us?" Shawn shouted as the car next to them blew its horn.

"No. Sorry." Dominique straightened the wheel and moved into her own lane again.

"I think Eric would be glad to know there was a man in his house protecting you and Devin while he was away," Shawn said, trying desperately to convince her.

Dominique didn't know how Eric would feel about Shawn staying at their house. He still hadn't met him. What would his parents say, anyway? Surely, they wouldn't give him permission to spend the night without knowing anything about her or her family.

"I don't think your mother would say yes. She doesn't even know me," Dominique said, keeping her eyes on the road this time.

"I'm telling you, she doesn't care. Half the time I don't stay home anyway."

"What are you going to do for clothes? How are you going to get to school?"

"Don't worry. I can go home and get some clothes. As far as school goes, I can walk."

"I don't know. I have to run it by Eric first."

"You promised me you wouldn't tell anybody I was coming over to visit you. That means Eric too," Shawn reminded her.

Dominique had to tell Shawn she wasn't going to be able to keep that agreement because she promised Eric she would introduce them. "Shawn, I can't hide your spending the night from my husband. It wouldn't be right. Besides, your mother probably wouldn't give you permission."

"I'll make a bet with you. If my mother gives me permission to stay with you, can I stay?"

"I still have to tell Eric."

This time, he didn't challenge her. He sat back, looking out of the window silently.

Almost home, Dominique remembered she still hadn't asked Shawn whether he overheard anything the night of the attack.

"Shawn, I need to ask you something about the night of the attack. Do you still remember the details of that night?"

"Some. Why?"

"Do you remember hearing anything the man said?"

"No. Why do you ask?"

"I was hoping you would be able to testify about what you heard."

"You think Kimberly's father is responsible for your attack, don't you?" Shawn asked with a blank look on his face.

"Yes. He's not a nice man." For the first time she wondered about the possibility that Buchanan had been sending Shawn. "Shawn, do you know Mr. Buchanan?"

"No."

"Has anyone working for him ever asked you to do anything for him?" Dominique asked while glancing over at Shawn for his response.

"No. Why do you ask?" Shawn rested his head back against the firm leather seat.

"I just wanted to know."

"You think I'm one of his hit men waiting to strike again?" He made a gun with his hand and aimed it at her. "Bang."

Dominique felt a little uncomfortable with Shawn's response, but she didn't want him to notice. "No. I just wanted to know if you knew him or anyone who knows him."

"I don't." Shawn dropped his hand gun and laughed out loud. "I hope you don't think I would do anything to hurt you. I don't hang out with people like him. Are you afraid he will try to hurt you again?" Shawn asked softly and with an anxious look.

"No. I just don't trust him." Dominique looked at Shawn again with a serious look on her face.

"That's more reason for me to spend the night while Eric is away. Dominique, how do you know he doesn't have someone else following you?" To reinforce his point, he turned around to see if he noticed anyone following them.

"I don't know," Dominique admitted, never having considered the possibility. She glanced in her rearview mirror to spot any unwanted followers.

"I know. So, what are you going to do now that I told you I didn't hear anything?" Shawn searched through the back window worriedly.

"I don't know. I pray my attacker will break and talk."

"I wouldn't hold my breath. Buchanan probably paid him a lot of money to hurt you and to keep his mouth closed. Come on, Dominique. Don't make me go home. Please! Pretty please!" Shawn begged.

Dominique felt herself giving into Shawn's pleading and decided to allow him to spend one night. That would be it. If he stayed any other night, he would have to allow her to tell Eric. "Just tonight, but you have to get permission from your mother. So, tell me where you live so I can speak to her."

"Honestly, my mother doesn't care where I stay."

Dominique didn't feel comfortable just allowing him to spend the night without her asking his mother. But there was something about him she couldn't resist. She convinced herself one night's stay wouldn't hurt anything if his mother wasn't aware where he was half the time anyway. She turned onto her block and slowed down to pull into her driveway. "We're here."

"I need to go home and get some clothes for tomorrow. I'll be right back." Shawn ran down her street with his backpack swinging in the wind.

"How long will it take you?"

"Not long. I'll be back right before dinner," Shawn yelled.

She pulled her briefcase and purse from the car. Still mentally exhausted from working on Kimberly's case, she headed for her front door and was greeted with a loving bear hug from Devin when she entered.

"Mommy, I missed you. When is Daddy coming back?" Devin squeezed her mother hard.

"In a few days," Dominique answered. "What have you been doing today with Ms. Anderson?" She gave her daughter a little kiss on her forehead.

"We played and made cookies today. I made you some too." Devin pulled her by the arm and dragged her into the kitchen to see the cookies she baked.

"Ms. Anderson, it smells absolutely wonderful in here. What did you fix for dinner?" Dominique allowed the wonderful aroma from the kitchen to fill her nostrils.

"I fixed ravioli and garlic bread. And Devin helped me prepare dinner. She's quite the little helper now." Ms. Anderson washed her hands and dried them with the folded kitchen towel next to the sink.

"I can't wait to taste everything." Dominique laid her briefcase on the kitchen counter. She watched Ms. Anderson finish cleaning up the kitchen. "Ms. Anderson, thank you for preparing this wonderful dinner for us. Eric is going to be just sick when he finds out he missed your ravioli."

Ms. Anderson smiled back at Dominique. "Oh, I almost forgot: Dr. Martin called. You forgot your appointment and he wants you to call him."

"Thank you." Dominique pulled her planner out of her briefcase and flipped through the last few days. Indeed, she had forgotten her appointment with Dr. Martin. She checked her watch and figured it was too late to call his office. His answering service would probably be answering by now. She promised herself she'd call him first thing in the morning.

"See you ladies tomorrow," Ms. Anderson said, waving goodbye as she left the kitchen.

"Take care, Ms. Anderson. See you tomorrow."

Dominique heard the telephone ringing from the living room.

"Mommy, Daddy is on the telephone for you." Devin held the telephone in her hand.

"Thank you, sweetheart." Dominique took the telephone. "Hello."

"What are you doing?"

"We're about to have dinner. Ms. Anderson made her famous ravioli. Where are you?" Dominique listened to the voices and commotion in the background.

"I'm still in Dallas. I should be in LA in a few hours. You miss me yet?"

"Sure, we do. Do you miss us?" Dominique started to set the table for dinner as she talked with Eric until he boarded his next flight.

After Dominique and Devin finished eating dinner, Dominique allowed Devin to watch television in the family room while she washed their dinner dishes in the kitchen. As she finished the last of the dishes, she heard someone knocking at her sunroom door. Nervously, she peeked out the corner of the kitchen window to see who it was before acknowledging their presence.

Shawn had returned for the evening. This time he was carrying a tote bag in addition to his backpack. Eager to welcome him in, she rushed into the sunroom and unlocked the door.

"Sorry it took me so long." Shawn entered the sunroom out of breath.

"What took you so long?"

"My dad was acting like a jerk this evening. He makes me sick." Shawn walked past her and entered the kitchen like he was at home.

"Did something happen at home?" She followed him into the kitchen.

"Something is always wrong at home. That's why I hate it there." He sat down at the kitchen table.

"What happened?" Dominique wanted to hear all the details.

"Nothing different from usual." Shawn responded. "Have you eaten yet?"

"Yes. Have you?"

"No. But I'm starving!" Shawn tossed his bags on the floor beside the chair.

"I'll prepare you something," Dominique made him a hearty plate of ravioli. She sat down across from him and watched him eat.

"Shawn, I want you to know if you ever need to talk to someone you can talk to me. I know growing up can be tough. Just know you aren't by yourself. A lot of people have tough times in their lives, but it gets better. Trust me, I know."

"My life can get better only if one thing happens." Shawn responded with his mouth filled with food.

"What is that?" Dominique asked curiously as Shawn finished the last bit of food on his plate.

"If you let me live with you." Shawn answered as he crossed the kitchen to place his empty plate in the sink.

"Shawn, I don't think that's possible. I want you to sit down so we can talk." Dominique motioned for him to sit back down. She wanted to learn more about Shawn's situation and why he was so unhappy.

He sat back down across from Dominique. "Why can't I live with you?"

"Because you already have a home and a family that loves you."

"No I don't. They don't love me," Tears were starting to form in his eyes.

"Why do you say that?" Dominique was becoming more curious about his situation.

"They don't because if they did, they wouldn't do the things they do."

"What do you mean?" Dominique feared they were dealing drugs or doing something worse that would land them in jail.

"Things. I don't want to go into details." Shawn seemed agitated by her persistent questioning.

"You never answer anything I ask you. Why can't you be truthful about anything?" There was frustration in Dominique's voice.

"Why is it such a crime? I don't want anybody knowing my business. Why can't you respect that?" Shawn responded, equally frustrated.

"I'm not just anybody. I thought we were friends. Please correct me if I'm wrong." She hoped her reverse psychology would work on him.

"Yes, you are my friend."

"Then why don't you trust me like a friend?"

"I don't trust anyone." Shawn slumped in his kitchen chair.

"Friends are supposed to be able to trust one another. Besides, I owe you. You were there for me the night of the attack. Now I want to be there for you."

"I don't know. I already have the police looking for me because you opened your big mouth about me being there the other night. I think you've done me enough favors already. Besides, I'm not ready to tell you all my business. And I sure don't want to talk to anybody else. So don't mention my name again."

Dominique couldn't agree to that. She'd promised her husband she would introduce them. She had to keep her promise to him. But now she was afraid of losing Shawn's trust in her. Dominique stared through him, thinking of how she was going to respond to his request.

"Dominique, what's wrong?"

"Shawn, I have a favor I want to ask of you."

"What is it?"

"I promised my husband before you asked me to keep you a secret that I would introduce the two of you. Well, I haven't done that, and it has caused a lot of problems around here. I know you don't want anybody to know about you, and I'll respect that wish. I only ask that I be allowed to at least introduce you to my husband. Right now, he thinks I'm going crazy or something, because I couldn't identify you on the security tape at the police station."

"They have me on tape?" Shawn gasped and leaned toward her.

"Not really."

"What do you mean 'not really?'" Shawn asked for clarification.

"We couldn't see you. The tape wasn't very clear. I want you to tell the police, but convincing Eric is more important to me right now."

"I told you I didn't want anybody to know about me. That includes Eric." Shawn stood up from the table to leave.

"Shawn, please wait." Dominique followed behind him into the sunroom.

He dragged his bags behind him. "No!" He shouted back.

"Shawn, I really need your help with this matter. Please allow me to just introduce you to my husband."

"I don't trust him. What if he goes to the police and tells them about me?"

"Eric won't tell anybody if I tell him not to. You can trust him."

"How do I know that? I don't know if I can trust *you* yet. You already failed your first test." Shawn twisted his face in frustration.

"Come on, Shawn," Dominique pleaded desperately.

"If you ever want to see me again, I would advise you not to tell anybody else, including Eric, that you have seen me."

"Shawn, who are you hiding from? Are you in some kind of trouble? Because if you are, I can help you. Remember, I'm an attorney, and I know a lot of people who might be able to help you. But you have to tell me the truth."

"Forget it. You're just like everybody else. You'd sell your soul to get what you want. Well, I won't allow you to sell me out." He turned his back to her and headed for the door.

"Shawn, you're wrong. I'm not like that. You obviously don't know me. I've devoted my life to helping people." Dominique grabbed his arm.

"Let me go!" Shawn screamed as he pulled away, dropping his bags to the floor and holding the area where Dominique grabbed him.

"Shawn, I'm sorry. I didn't mean to hurt you." Dominique reached out to comfort him, but he quickly moved away from her, holding his wounded arm. "Shawn, let me see."

"No. Don't touch me!" Shawn snapped at her.

"Shawn, I didn't mean to hurt you. I only wanted to stop you from leaving."

"You're just like my father." Shawn slowly backed toward the door.

"What are you talking about? I didn't try to hurt you on purpose.

I would never try to hurt you." Dominique was starting to regret her decision to allow Shawn to come over this evening.

"I don't have to tell you anything. You're not my mother. You're not even my friend anymore."

"Shawn, please tell me what is going on with you. Did someone hurt you before you came here tonight? Is that why you're holding yourself where I grabbed you?"

"What do you care? All you care about is people not thinking you're crazy. You don't care if it will cost me my life. I was really hoping you were different." Tears rolled down his face.

Dominique felt awful. She pleaded with him. "Shawn, I am different. Please believe me when I tell you that."

"I'm afraid I can't," he responded as he shook his head.

"Calm down, let me see your shoulder." She reached out again to examine his arm.

"No!" He pulled further away.

She took a deep breath. She didn't want to upset the situation any more than she had. "Let's go into the kitchen and start over."

"Why? So, you can convince me to tell your husband and everybody else about me?"

"No. I don't care about that right now. I'm thinking about you and your arm."

"My arm is okay." Shawn continued to hold it tightly.

Dominique didn't know what to do, but she wasn't ready for him to leave. She wanted to know what happened to his arm. She had to figure out how to get him to calm down and trust her.

Dominique stared at Shawn, who was looking at her helplessly and with tears rolling down his face. She knew she was making a mistake, but she was allowing her emotions to get the best of her tonight. "Why don't we just let it go and get ready for bed? I'll run you some bath water so you can take a bath before you get in bed." She now noticed how filthy his clothes were. "Would you like for me to wash your clothes while you take a bath?"

"Sure. Do you have one of those big tubs that make bubbles?" He asked as he allowed his arm to fall back to his side.

"Yes, in my bedroom I do. I'll let you take a bubble bath in my bathroom so you can see how it feels to take a bath in a jet tub. Follow me."

As they approached the family room, Dominique remembered leaving Devin watching television. There was no way she could avoid them not meeting one another. She prayed Shawn wouldn't get upset and think she was trying to trick him.

Devin was gone from the family room. So, Dominique led Shawn upstairs to her bathroom, where she started to run his water, assuming Devin had already gone upstairs to her own bed.

She pulled out one of Eric's T-shirts and drawstring shorts for Shawn to put on after his bath then placed a matching cream towel and washcloth on the sink. "Hand me your clothes before you get in the tub so I can start washing them for you." She left the bathroom to give him privacy.

Within seconds, Shawn cracked the bathroom door and handed her his dirty clothes. "Here you go."

She was horrified when she saw all the bruises on his upper arm.

"Shawn, what happened to your arm?" She fought the urge to pull him from behind the door and examine his whole body.

"I don't want to talk about it." He firmly shut the bathroom door.

"I'm sorry, but we're going to talk about it. Wrap a towel around your waist and come out here."

Shawn slowly reopened the door and walked out of the bathroom. And Dominique stared in disbelief as she saw the numerous bruises. His chest, arms, shoulders, and back were all black and blue. Some of the bruises looked like they were trying to heal, but some were very recent. They shadowed his frail body. There was no way she was going to allow whoever was doing this to get away with it. She would have to intervene.

"Shawn, who did this to you? I want you to tell me the truth and right now."

Humiliated, he lowered his head. "My father."

"Why would he do this to you?" Dominique, unwilling to accept any vague answers from him, because of the sensitivity of this matter, tried to keep her voice even.

"He's mean and I hate him!" Shawn started to cry again. Dominique reached out to embrace his fragile body, full of sympathy and remorse. From the look of his body, Dominique felt he wasn't able to defend himself. She needed to talk to his mother and make her aware of all the support organizations that were available to her and her children. And to encourage her to take advantage of their support as soon as possible.

"Shawn, is your father hurting anybody else in your house?"

Shawn stared at Dominique sadly. "Yes. He does things to my sister, too."

"Is he beating her too?" Dominique asked.

Shawn's gaze dropped to the floor. "He touches her and makes her do things with him she doesn't want to do." Shawn continued to cry. Dominique could tell it was painful for him to confess, but she had to know everything in order to help him if his father was indeed hurting him and touching his sister.

Dominique repeated Shawn's words: "He's touching her and making her do things she doesn't want to do. What type of things does he make her do?"

Shawn sat silently, not answering her.

"Shawn, I know this might be uncomfortable for you to talk about, but I really need to know so I can help you and your sister get out of there. You can trust me. You really can. I want to help you, and the only way I can do that is if you share with me all the details."

"He makes her touch his private area and he sleeps with her. Please, I don't want to talk about this. That's why I come over here, so I can get away from all of that." Shawn dropped his head.

"Where is your sister now?" She cupped his chin in her hand and raised his head to meet hers.

"She's at home."

"What do you think your parents would say if I asked if both of you could spend the night with me?" Dominique wiped his tears from his face.

"My father isn't going to allow her to come over here."

"Why not, if they don't care where you stay?"

"She's only six. Besides, my father doesn't allow her to leave the house unless she's going to school."

Dominique was curious about what role Shawn's mother was playing. "Does your mother know what he's making your sister do?"

"Yes. It's because of her he does it."

Dominique was confused. "What do you mean, it's because of her that he touches her?"

"My mother is sick," he answered somewhat vaguely.

"She's sick. Sick how?" Dominique asked, eager to hear his response.

"She had a nervous breakdown one day and hasn't been the same since. She went crazy like Eric thinks you're about to do." Shawn paused as more tears rolled down his face. "She doesn't talk anymore. She doesn't even look at me anymore. She's in a comatose state, trying to escape her life living with my father and us. I hate my mother for allowing my sister and me to suffer because she wasn't brave enough to leave."

"Shawn, does your father touch you, too?"

Shawn looked down at the floor again and nodded his head yes.

Dominique embraced his fragile body. "Your father is sick and he needs help."

"I hate when he touches me or my sister."

"I know you do. Is that when he bruises you?" She released Shawn's body to see his face.

"Yes. If I don't allow him, he beats me until I give in."

Dominique's chest tightened, as she tried not to imagine what he was experiencing. "How long has this been going on?"

"For a long time. He just started touching my sister. It makes me so mad when he does that, but there's nothing I can do. I've thought about just killing him myself."

"Don't do that. I don't want you to get in trouble, but Shawn, you're going to have to allow me to tell somebody about this so I can get you and your sister out of there as soon as possible."

"No! You can't tell anybody! He threatened to kill me, my sister, and my mother if I ever told anybody!" Shawn pleaded with Dominique.

Now Dominique understood why he didn't want anyone to know about him. "Shawn, you can't allow your father to continue to hurt your sister, can you?" Dominique shifted the focus from him to his little sister. He didn't respond right away. "You're her big brother and she's counting on you to protect her now that your mother isn't able to do that."

"I know. I don't want anything to happen to her. I love my sister. I hate what he's doing to her, but I can't even protect myself from him."

She was familiar with how weak and helpless he was feeling. There were periods during her attack that night she felt the same way. Luckily for her, she managed to end the horrible night without being sexually assaulted.

"Shawn, I have a close friend at my office who can help us. You can trust him."

"Absolutely not," Shawn pleaded. "I don't want my father to kill my family because I told you and you told someone else."

"I know you're afraid, but you have to believe in me. I handle cases like yours all the time. Don't worry about anything. I'm going to do my best to get your sister and you out of this safely. This way I can also get your mother out of there so she can get some help."

Shawn paced the floor. "No way. He'll kill everybody. I know he will. He's mad."

"Just calm down and let me think about what I'm going to do next."

"I knew I shouldn't have said anything." Shawn paced the floor frantically.

"Don't be sorry. Shawn, you have no idea how hard it is for me to see you and know your sister is going through the same thing. The two of you don't deserve to be treated like this. I would be less than a person and friend if I ignored your situation. Besides, I care about you like family now. Family don't allow family to hurt," She sat back down on the edge of the tub beside him.

Dominique thought about what her next step would be as she stared at all the war bruises on Shawn's body. If she took him to a doctor to examine him, they would definitely notify the authorities to investigate. She did the next best thing and examined the severity of his bruises herself.

She watched Shawn flinch as she touched certain areas of his chest. Tears filled her eyes. "I want you to get in the tub and take a nice warm bath while I wash your clothes. I'll be right back to check on you. It's going to be okay." Dominique leaned over and kissed him on the forehead before rushing out of the room.

Dominique held Shawn's dirty clothes to her chest as tears rolled down her face. She had to find a way to get them out of there without anyone getting hurt in the process.

"Mommy, where did you go?" Devin appeared out of nowhere. "I was looking for you."

"Is everything okay?" Dominique tried to wipe her tears away before Devin noticed them.

"Mommy, why are you crying?" Devin ran toward her for a closer look.

Dominique looked down at Devin's little face. She could see the concern. What she was crying about, she prayed her daughter would never have to experience: living a life of constant fear, pain, and violation, a life Shawn and his sister were forced to live day in and day out.

"I just found out one of my friends has been badly hurt, and it made me sad."

"Did the same bad man who hurt you hurt him?" Devin asked, looking up at her mother fearfully.

"No, sweetheart. The same bad man didn't hurt him."

"Will your friend get better?" Devin's concerned voice touched her heart.

She prayed to herself Shawn would get better. "I hope so."

"Where is your friend now?" Devin asked.

"He's in my bathroom taking a bath. I'm sorry I left you by yourself this evening."

"Mommy, do you think if I drew your friend a picture it would make him feel better? Daddy always tells me my pictures make him feel better when he's had a bad day at work or isn't feeling well."

Dominique didn't want to tell Devin her picture wouldn't help Shawn's situation, but she knew Devin was only trying to help. She adored the fact that Devin was thinking about someone else's feelings. And who knows, maybe Devin's drawing would bring some sunshine to Shawn.

"Why don't you draw him a really happy picture? I think it might help him." Dominique patted her on the shoulder.

"Okay." Devin smiled back at her mother.

"Why were you looking for me?"

"I just wanted to know where you were."

"I need to go downstairs to put some clothes in the washing machine, but I will be right back."

Dominique rushed downstairs. Now she was glad she had allowed Shawn to spend the night. Otherwise, she wouldn't haven't discovered how serious his family situation was. She had to figure out how to convince him to let her help him and his family without his father killing or harming anyone.

Dominique returned upstairs and walked down to Devin's room. She was coloring diligently.

"Devin, how would you like to have someone else stay with us while Daddy is away?" Dominique asked from Devin's doorway.

"Is Ms. Anderson going to stay with us?"

"No. I'm talking about someone else."

"Does Daddy know they're going to be staying with us?"

"No, but I plan to tell him."

"Who is it?"

"His name is Shawn."

"Shawn from your office?" Devin started to get excited. She liked Shawn Silver. He always played with her when he came over to visit.

"No, not that one. I have another friend name Shawn."

"Did he get dirty when he hurt himself?"

"Kind of," Dominique answered, not being completely truthful.

"Did someone beat him up?"

"Yes." She marveled to herself how they both had become victims to unexpected violence neither deserved. Unfortunately for Shawn, his situation wasn't a one-time occurrence.

"Can we play tea party together after he finishes?" Devin asked, still drawing all the while.

"I don't know. It's kind of late."

"I'm not sleepy. Please, Mommy, just for a little while."

"I don't know."

"Please, Mommy. Please?"

"I'll have to ask him if he wants to play. Finish drawing his picture and I'll ask him."

"I'm going to set my tea party table up for us, while you ask."

"Let me make sure he wants to play."

"Okay." Devin answered, excited by the prospect of having someone new to play tea party with. Playing tea party was her favorite pastime. Dominique wished Devin had someone else to play with other than herself.

She returned to her bedroom to see if Shawn had finished his bath.

"Shawn, are you finished?" Dominique asked from the middle of her bedroom.

"Almost. Can I stay in here a little while longer? Your jets make the water feel funny."

"Sure. But when you get out, Devin wants all of us to play tea party with her." Dominique said, praying he would agree for her daughters' sake.

"Tea party?" Shawn shouted back.

"Yes. It would mean so much to her if you would play. I know it's late." Dominique crossed her fingers. There was long pause.

"I'll play this time, but I don't want to play tea party all the time. I'm a boy, not a girl. You better make sure you never tell anyone." His boyish voice made Dominique grin.

Dominique tried not to burst out in laughter. "I promise. Thanks, Shawn. Devin is going to be so excited to know you will be joining her for tea."

Delighted that Shawn had agreed to play with her daughter, Dominique rushed down the hallway to tell Devin the great news. They waited for Shawn to finish his bath, and she helped Devin set everything up. After a few minutes, Dominique heard her bedroom door open.

"Shawn, we're down the hall in Devin's room." Dominique stood to meet Shawn in Devin's doorway.

Shawn observed, "Your house is huge. It's three times the size of my house. You guys are rich." He had been admiring all the original artwork hanging on the walls along the way.

Dominique smiled back at Shawn, remembering how small some of the foster care homes were where she lived and how as a little girl riding the school bus, she would marvel at the larger homes along the way. She always wondered how it would feel to have a lot of space to move around in, and how it would feel to have her own room, never having had any privacy of her own.

"Thank you. Devin has been getting everything ready for you."

He was now moving at a snail's pace because he knew the worst was just around the corner. "I can't believe I'm going to play tea party," Shawn whispered.

Dominique laughed as she noticed how cute he looked in Eric's oversize T-shirt and shorts. She thought about taking him shopping while he was staying with her this week. It was obvious he could use some new clothes because the few times he had visited, his outfits looked worn and dingy.

"Devin, I would like for you to meet Shawn." Dominique moved to the side to allow Shawn to enter her room.

Devin didn't say anything at first. She just stared at Shawn and then back at Dominique with a hilarious expression on her face. Dominique assumed Devin was finding it amusing how he looked in Eric's oversize clothes.

Devin greeted him slowly— "Hello, Shawn"—as she pulled out chairs for him and her mother to sit in.

"Hello, Devin."

"I drew you a picture with all of us in it. I hope you like it." Devin placed the picture in front of him.

Dominique watched as Shawn glanced over the picture. He didn't say anything at first. Then he looked over at Dominique with a big smile on his face and handed the picture to her.

Dominique glanced over it. It showed four people standing outside and holding hands beside a big white house. The house had orange, yellow, and purple flowers surrounding it, and a big blue sky accented with a bright yellow sun in the center. There were two trees in the distance with a table and chair outside. Devin had drawn their home, with all of them, including Shawn, standing outside. Dominique looked at Shawn and smiled.

"Shawn loves your picture, Sweetie."

"Good. I'll draw you another one later," Devin said as she began to fill everybody's cups with make-believe tea.

"I'm out of sugar. I hope cream will do," Devin explained with her English tea party accent. Dominique was always amused by Devin's imagination. She could tell Shawn was, too, by the big smile on his face as he watched Devin fill everyone's cup.

"Cream will be fine for both Mr. Shawn and me," Dominique answered as Devin started to pour her imaginary cream into their cups. Before Dominique realized it, they had been playing tea party late into the night. She was surprised how well Shawn and Devin were getting along and disappointed she would have to end the wonderful evening together.

"Guys, we need to go to bed. It's really late," Dominique said as she stood up.

"Mommy, where is Shawn going to sleep tonight?"

"He's going to sleep in our guest room. I want you to get in your bed now and get some sleep." Dominique kissed Devin on the forehead and pulled back the sheets on her bed.

"Good night, Mommy. Thanks for playing tea party."

"Don't forget to thank Shawn, too.

Devin looked at Shawn sitting in her little chair and smiled at him. "Thank you, Shawn."

Shawn rose from his seat and stood in the hallway outside of Devin's room. He waved goodnight to Devin as he watched Dominique tuck her into her bed.

"Good night, sweetheart. I love you." Dominique gave her a final kiss on the forehead before leaving her room to show Shawn where he would be sleeping.

Once Dominique and Shawn were in the hallway, she thanked him again for playing tea party with Devin. She decided not to ask him any more questions. She wanted him to get a good night's sleep. Tomorrow morning, she would tell him the good news. She was going to allow him to spend every night while Eric was away. She felt that was the least she could do for him, still emotionally torn from knowing about Shawn's situation at home.

His situation was similar to Kimberly's. They were both innocent children who were victims of their fathers' cruelty. Tears rolled down Dominique's eyes later as she lay still in her bed. Her heart ached with sorrow. She started to question the ways of the world. Why did awful things happen to good people? Why were so many people suffering?

Her thoughts drifted to the atrocity she personally experienced. Why had her parents abandoned her? She wasn't a bad child. She was good. She made good grades in school. She helped around the house. She never talked back. *Why?* continued to fill her mind until her ringing telephone snapped her back to reality. She reached over to Eric's side of the bed to answer it, figuring it was him checking in for the evening.

"Hello?" Dominique wiped her tears from her face.

"Did I wake you?" Eric asked.

"No. I was still waiting up for your call. Are you finally settled in?"

"Yes. I miss you guys already."

"We miss you, too."

"You sound funny."

"I'm fine. I'm just lying down," she answered, wiping more tears away.

"Are you sure?" Eric asked with concern.

"Positive. I'm just tired, that's all," Dominique responded, trying to reassure him.

"I'm not going to hold you long. I just wanted to let you know where I'm staying. I'll call you tomorrow night." Eric rattled off his hotel information before saying good-night for the evening.

After they hung up, Dominique realized she'd forgotten to inform him of their guest.

CHAPTER 17

Dominique rose early and quietly entered the guest room to wake up Shawn for school. She experienced a sense of peace, knowing he had been safe last night under her roof, away from his father's abuse. She only wished she had been fortunate enough to have protected his sister from their father last night, too.

Dominique waited downstairs in the kitchen while Shawn dressed. She placed a big plate of pancakes on the table for him.

"Is that my plate?' Shawn asked as he sat down in front of the stack of pancakes.

"Yes."

"I love your pancakes," Shawn said as he cut up his pancakes with his fork and stuffed his face.

"Good. Eat up." Dominique set her own plate of pancakes down and joined him.

"How did you sleep last night?" Dominique watched Shawn as he devoured his breakfast.

"Good. Your mattress felt like I was sleeping on cotton. My bed doesn't feel like that. It's hard like the floor," he explained between bites. She laughed, remembering how hard some of her beds were growing up.

"I'm glad you had a good night's rest last night."

"Dominique, can I sleep over tonight, too?"

"Sure." She attempted to block out any thoughts of him having to go home.

"Will I have to play tea party again?" He asked, his mouth filled with pancakes.

"Maybe not." She smiled at him and looked down at her watch.

"Shawn, I think you better get going before you're late for school. Do you want me to drop you off this morning?"

"No. I'll walk." He took his last bite, grabbed his school bag and tote, and stood to his feet. "Thank you for not bringing up you-know-what up this morning."

Dominique knew exactly what he was referring to. Luckily, the opportunity didn't present itself, but she'd had every intention of bringing it up again over breakfast.

"Be careful and have a good day." She walked him to the front door and waved goodbye as he ran down the street. Then she returned to the kitchen to clean up so Ms. Anderson wouldn't arrive to a sink full of dirty dishes.

"Good morning, Mommy." Devin came running into the kitchen.

"Good morning, sweetheart."

"I smell pancakes." Devin's mouth salivated.

Dominique stared back at Devin, feeling bad that she had forgotten to prepare her breakfast this morning. She had been so consumed with making sure Shawn got breakfast that she forgot about Devin's pancakes. "Sweetie, I'm sorry, we ate all the pancakes this morning. I'll make you some more right now." Dominique raced around the kitchen to prepare her daughter's breakfast. Within minutes, Dominique managed to fix Devin two little pancakes. She poured her a glass of milk.

"Your pancakes are the best, Mommy." Devin spoke with a mouth full of pancakes.

"Thank you," Dominique answered as she heard the front door open. She assumed Ms. Anderson had arrived for the morning.

"Good morning, ladies." Ms. Anderson's cheery tones announced her arrival.

"Good morning. I'm going to head out now. Devin, I'll see you later."

"Bye, Mommy. I love you!" Devin called to her mother as she sat finishing her breakfast.

"I love you, too," Dominique responded. She kissed Devin on the forehead one last time and turned to face Ms. Anderson. "See you later this afternoon. You ladies have a wonderful day together."

"We will. We always do," Ms. Anderson said as she smiled over at Devin. "I'm going to get groceries this morning. Is there anything you would like for me to add to the grocery list?" Ms. Anderson handed her the list to review.

"No." Dominique glanced over the list quickly. Grocery shopping was another perk Ms. Anderson offered Dominique and her family. She made sure the house was fully stocked with food and other household supplies. Dominique had become spoiled by all the wonderful duties Ms. Anderson performed around her house. She couldn't imagine life without her now.

Dominique winked at Devin and left for work. By now things were back to normal for her. The attention was no longer centered around her attack, but on the new affair that was simmering between the new paralegal and one of the senior attorneys, Jack, the office playboy. Somehow, he managed to date every new female employee that entered the office. His predictable quest became an office lottery, and everyone enjoyed the thrill at the young ladies' expense.

By midday, the office lottery had reached its highest bid ever, and Dominique had to admit her curiosity was growing along with that of the caddish office staff. She tried desperately to stay focused on preparing for Kimberly's preliminary hearing. Now, with Mrs. Buchanan's willingness to testify, Dominique felt confident she would be able to convince the court of Buchanan's guilt without Maria's testimony. The only thing she worried about was eliminating any possibility of Buchanan's team discrediting Mrs. Buchanan. She would have to be at least two steps ahead of his defense always until the end of the trial.

Dominique swung around in her desk chair and admired the city's beauty from her high-rise office, wondering how her life had become so complicated so fast. One day she was breezing through life happy as a clam. The next, she was having unexplained attacks.

Startled by her ringing telephone, Dominique snapped out of her daze to answer it.

"Hello?"

"Dominique, your nanny, Ms. Anderson, is on the other line."

"Please put her through," Dominique demanded. She started to worry, knowing Ms. Anderson never called unless it was crucially important. Dominique appreciated Ms. Anderson for understanding how demanding their careers were and shielding them from unnecessary worries.

"Dominique, Devin and I were almost in a car accident," Ms. Anderson blurted out as soon as she switched over.

"Are you two okay?" Dominique asked, praying to God no one was hurt.

"Yes. Someone ran us off the road, and I think they tried to do it intentionally." Ms. Anderson sounded shaken.

"Where are you now?" Dominique rushed around her desk, gathering her belongings, to be by their sides.

"We're at home now, but Devin is still very upset. I did my best to calm her down, but she won't stop crying for you and Eric. Dominique, please come home if you can and be careful."

"I will. Tell Devin I'm on my way." Dominique rushed down the hall to Shawn Silver's office.

Shawn rushed to get off the telephone when he saw her expression. "Dominique, what's wrong?"

"Shawn, I think Buchanan just tried to hurt my daughter. My nanny, Ms. Anderson, just informed me someone tried to run them off the road just a few minutes ago. I'm going to kill that son of a bitch if he's responsible." Dominique paced around in a circle, furiously thinking about Buchanan's likely involvement.

Shawn embraced Dominique's frantic body. "Calm down. Where are Devin and your nanny right now?"

"They're home now, and my daughter is frightened. I'm on my way home, but I need you to arrange twenty-four-hour surveillance on Buchanan. If he so much as coughs, I want to know. He's absolutely insane, Shawn."

"I know."

Dominique could tell by the tone of his voice that Shawn was holding something back from her. "What's wrong?"

"Dominique," He hesitated before finishing. "Just before you walked in my office, I received a call from Kevin informing me they found Maria."

"And?" She couldn't wait to find out what he was about to tell her.

"Dominique, Maria is dead."

Dominique's legs nearly buckled. She had to know how and why. If only Maria hadn't run that day at her apartment, she might still be alive. She felt partially responsible for her death. If she hadn't tried to force her to talk, maybe Mr. Buchanan wouldn't have considered her a threat and had to eliminate her.

"Where did they find her?"

"Someone found her body lying in a stall in the bathroom at the bus station. The police said it looked like someone robbed her, too."

"Shawn, I'd bet my life that Mr. Buchanan had Maria killed." Dominique fought back the urge to track him down and eliminate him personally.

"So, would I. I'm going to go to the station to see if I can learn any details that might help us connect Mr. Buchanan to her murder."

"Call me as soon as you find anything out."

"I promise." Shawn grabbed his coat. "I'm going to arrange protection for both you and myself. I don't trust this man. It's obvious he's not going to play fair."

"I know. I'm glad I placed Mrs. Buchanan in protective custody. She might have been next." Dominique was pacing in circles.

"I agree, but we still have to be careful. Buchanan has a lot of connections, and I don't want to underestimate his reach." Shawn patted Dominique's shoulder.

"I have to get going. Devin is calling for me and Eric is out of town. I have to assure her everything is going to be all right until her father returns from his business trip." She was trying to convince both Shawn and herself that she could do it.

"Let's pray this was just a coincidence," Shawn said, trying to lessen her worry.

Normally, Shawn wasn't fazed by anything, but something was definitely bothering him. She wondered if something else had happened that he was protecting her from?

"Shawn, is there something else I need to know?"

"No. I'm just worried someone else will get hurt in the process of convicting this man."

She had to agree. Never before had she feared for her life or her family because of representing a client. She hadn't bargained for this part of the case, but it was too late to back out. She had to finish. Now it was personal.

"Call me as soon as you find out anything." Dominique was too worried about Devin to wait around.

"I will," Shawn called to her as she walked through his doorway.

The safety of Dominique's family was now in question. There was no way she could go against Buchanan in the fashion he chose to fight back. Buchanan was playing by another rulebook, and she didn't like it. Furthermore, Eric was going to go through the roof and demand she walk away from this case, but she just couldn't do that because then Buchanan would win, and Dominique wasn't going to give him that satisfaction.

Afraid he might have someone following her, she constantly checked her rearview mirror on the way home. She couldn't concentrate when all she wanted to do was get home to her daughter and comfort her. Devin was too young and innocent to be dealing with this confusion. Buchanan was not a rational thinker, and irrational thinkers can be very dangerous.

Dominique parked her car and ran inside to find that Devin had already cried herself to sleep. She made her way upstairs to Devin's bedroom and stood by her bedside. Tears filled Dominique's eyes as she thought of the possibility of losing the only person on the earth that she could prove was her blood relative. The thought made her sick to her stomach.

While feeling sorry for herself, she didn't notice that Ms. Anderson was standing beside her until she tapped her on the shoulder. Dominique wiped the tears from her eyes.

"Shawn Silver from your office is on the phone," Ms. Anderson whispered.

"Thanks." Dominique smiled at Ms. Anderson and quietly left to answer her call.

Dominique cleared her throat. "Shawn, what's up?"

"How are Devin and Ms. Anderson doing?"

"Devin is asleep and Ms. Anderson seems to be okay. Shawn, please be careful. I can't afford for something to happen to you."

"I agree." Shawn chuckled. "I've arranged for someone to follow both of us. You won't even know they're there. How is Eric taking all of this?"

"I haven't told him about this Devin and Ms. Anderson incident yet. He's going to flip. But I have to see this case to the end."

"Dominique, you *don't* have to see this case to the end. I can call Judge Bacon right now and explain what has been happening and have someone replace you immediately."

"I don't want anyone to replace me. Shawn, I want to convict Buchanan myself. He has attacked me and my family now. I can't just let him get away with that."

"I don't understand you, but I'll do my best to respect your position in this matter. I hope you know what you're doing because I don't."

"I do. That's all that matters. I'll talk to you later."

Dominique didn't know how she was going to tell Eric that she thought Buchanan had attempted to harm Devin. He was already furious because he suspected Buchanan was responsible for attacking Dominique. Now she wasn't sure whether she was more worried about Eric's response or about what else Buchanan had in store for her. She stood in the middle of the floor, worried and frustrated.

Later that night, as she put Devin down for bed, she tried to reassure her daughter that everything was going to be okay. Afterward, Dominique made herself a drink to help herself relax before bed. Today had been a whirlwind of events, and she prayed that tomorrow wouldn't prove to be similar. She took a big gulp of her wine and poured another glass before heading upstairs to her bed.

Deep in thought, Dominique took her clothes off and changed into her nightgown. She felt her back muscles tightening up again. Wishing Eric was home to massage her back, she sipped her wine and accepted that a good night's sleep would have to do tonight. When she went into her bathroom to remove her makeup before getting into bed, she heard a strange sound coming from her bedroom. She figured it was Devin climbing into her bed to sleep with her tonight since Eric was out of town. Normally, she would tell Devin she had to sleep in her own room, but tonight she would permit it after the terrible ordeal she'd experienced.

"You couldn't sleep, sweetheart?" Dominique called out to Devin as she entered her bedroom again. Her heart almost stopped when she saw Michael Buchanan standing in the middle of her bedroom, smiling devilishly at her.

She didn't know what to do. She didn't want to scream and wake Devin. What good would that do? If she was lucky, he wouldn't harm her innocent daughter.

"No, I can't sleep, sweetheart." Buchanan laughed as she stood in the middle of her floor and stared at him.

"What are you doing in my house?" Dominique asked as she struggled to think of what object she could grab quickly to protect herself.

"I thought I would pay you a personal visit," Buchanan said, with an evil smirk was on his face.

"Don't you come near me, or I'll yell and wake my nanny," Dominique threatened, knowing full well she was alone with Devin in the house. Oh, how she wished Eric or Shawn were here now. They would be able to help her.

"Dominique, I know you're alone with your precious little daughter. By the way, she looks a lot like you," Buchanan teased. When he started to walk toward her, Dominique's fear increased.

"I told you not to come near me!" She moved toward her telephone on her nightstand.

"Obviously, you don't know who you're dealing with. I own this whole damn city, and there's nothing you can do about it. I've tried to be patient with you, but you don't seem to get it, so I thought I would make it very clear for you this evening." Buchanan was only six feet from her.

Her heart raced uncontrollably. "Have you lost your mind? You better get out of my house before I call the police." She picked up her telephone receiver.

"Call?" Mr. Buchanan laughed. "There isn't a policeman in this city or surrounding cities that will cross my path." He chuckled. "It's amusing to me how little you know about this real world we live in. I found your little performance in the courtroom quite charming, but now it's getting old. I highly advise you to end this case and drop all charges against me before someone else gets hurt. And if you don't, I'll turn your whole damn world upside down." She shivered at the pure evil in his eyes. "And I will take great pleasure in watching you suffer."

"You are one sick bastard. Get out of my house now!" Dominique demanded as she tried not to show how scared she was.

"I will, but not before you've heard everything I came here to say to you. I've done a little research on you and learned you've done a great job of covering your own little ass. Normally, when people have something to hide, they make sure there is no evidence to be found … Dominique Shephard." A sneaky smirk appeared on his face.

"I have nothing to hide."

"Oh, yes you do. I'm sure you don't want me to expose your little secret. You'll wish you never crossed my path." Buchanan backed away from her. "Don't even think about calling the police or telling anyone about my visit this evening after I leave, or your darling husband, Eric, will have the misfortune of having an unexplainable accident this evening. You wouldn't want his death on your conscience, would you? Besides, I hear its hell raising a young girl as a single parent." Buchanan smirked at Dominique, who was shaking as she held her phone in her hand.

Dominique didn't find Buchanan's threats amusing, but she dared not take any chances. She didn't want anything to happen to Eric and didn't know what to do next. Buchanan's threats were serious, and every bit of energy she had to fight him seemed to abandon her. She felt vulnerable as she listened to Buchanan destroy her case against him.

The preliminary hearing was in a few days. Now she knew why he pleaded not guilty. He never intended to let her prosecute him fairly. And she understood why Mrs. Buchanan's and Kimberly's lives had become such feeble tragedies.

"Wasn't it a pity what happened to Miss Maria Gonzales?" Mr. Buchanan chuckled again.

"You didn't have to kill her."

"Miss Gonzales was a little example of what happens to those who betray me. And as for my wife, please let her know her days are numbered." Mr. Buchanan licked his index finger and made an imaginary nick in the air.

"You are truly one sick son of a bitch. Why can't you fight this case like a real man?" Dominique challenged him.

"Oh, I am fighting this case like a real man. Mrs. Wallace, you haven't begun to see what type of man I can be. If you insist on continuing to try to convict me, I will definitely have to show you how much of a man I am." Mr. Buchanan pointed his finger at her.

"Oh, I hope you enjoyed watching my video collection. Maybe one day you and I can make our very own movie. I know I would definitely enjoy it." Mr. Buchanan winked. "Heed my threats because I will do everything I promised. I will personally destroy you with my bare hands, and I'll have great pleasure doing so.

"But enough rough talk tonight. Good night, my dear, and get plenty of rest. You have a lot of work to do to fix this mess you've created, and I expect you to fix it at the preliminary hearing. I know you'll do the right thing if you want to continue to live the perfect life you've been living. It would be a pity to make your family suffer because of your ego."

Buchanan turned and exited the bedroom, leaving Dominique frozen in place. Her body shook like a leaf as she heard what sounded like a door closing. She prayed it was Michael Buchanan leaving her house.

Dominique felt violated. Buchanan had crossed every line there was with her, and now she felt unable to fight back. She slammed the telephone receiver down and rushed to check on Devin. Dominique was outraged to know that Buchanan had been alone with her daughter, in her house, and without her knowledge. Rage built up inside of her, and she fought back the urge to run after him and make him suffer for everything he'd done to her, her family, and now, for every threat he had made tonight.

As she continued to watch Devin sleep, the telephone rang in her bedroom. Quietly, she tiptoed out of Devin's room and ran to answer it.

"Look outside of your window now. See that car parked in front of your house?" It was Buchanan. Dominique walked slowly over to her window and looked out. There was indeed a car parked in front of her house that hadn't been there when she arrived earlier. "That's your sorry protection. Or do they work for me?" Buchanan burst out laughing and hung up. Dominique looked at her caller ID for a number, but there wasn't one. He had been smart enough to block the number.

Dominique didn't know what to think. Shawn Silver told her he was going to arrange protection for both of them, but she didn't know who was outside of her house. Buchanan had made it clear how well-connected he was. Dominique stood shaking in the middle of her floor, remembering her first conversation with Kimberly in the hospital. Now she knew why Kimberly couldn't believe her father didn't influence her, too. Until now, Dominique didn't realize he did, but after tonight she wasn't sure herself.

Dominique jumped when the telephone rang again. She hesitated to answer it for fear it was Buchanan calling to torture her again, but she answered it anyway.

"Stop calling here!" Dominique yelled into the phone.

"Dominique, it's me, Eric. Who's been calling you?"

She had to think fast. There was no way she could tell Eric what was going on over the telephone. She was afraid he would try to retaliate against Buchanan and make matters worse. She wasn't prepared to deal with the consequences, so she froze, having no way out.

"Dominique, what's going on?" Eric responded with panic in his voice.

"I thought it was some telemarketers calling," Dominique lied.

"Calling this time of night?" Eric said irritated.

"Yes. That's why I was so upset when I answered the telephone. Is everything okay?"

"Yes. I'm just calling to check on you and Devin. And to tell you I will be able to return tomorrow."

Desperately, she tried to hold back the urge to burst into tears and beg him to come home and protect her from Michael Buchanan.

"Great. What time will you get home?" Dominique prayed it was early.

"My flight lands around three thirty tomorrow afternoon. What's up?"

"Nothing, Devin and I are eager to see you, that's all." Dominique continued to fight back her tears and fear.

"I can't wait to see you guys, too. Give Devin a kiss for me. I'll give you one tomorrow." Normally, Dominique would have found Eric's statement romantic, but tonight she needed him to make her feel safe. She was scared.

"I'll be waiting," Dominique replied as silent tears started rolling down her face.

"I better let you go so you can get some sleep. I love you."

"I love you too." Dominique said before she hung up.

"You guys are so in love, it makes my stomach hurt," an unexpected voice from her bedroom doorway said.

Dominique's heart almost stopped when she heard the voice.

"I'm sorry I scared you," Shawn said as he noticed how frightened she looked when she turned around.

"Shawn what are you doing here?" Dominique reached for her heart as she stared at Shawn's young body frame in her doorway. He looked so little and helpless after her encounter with Buchanan.

"You said I could stay over while Eric is away," He reminded her with his boyish plea. "Or have you changed your mind?"

"No. I just forgot, that's all." She started to exhale to help calm herself. His presence provided a sense of comfort.

"Are you okay?" He asked.

Still looked shaken, she answered, "Yes." She wondered how he got in and whether he'd seen Buchanan leaving. "How did you get in?"

"Your sunroom door was unlocked. I thought you left it unlocked for me because you said I could spend the night."

Dominique jumped when the telephone rang again. Afraid it was Buchanan again, she answered hesitantly.

"Hello?"

"Mrs. Wallace, my name is Travis Wilkerson. I've been ordered to follow you during Mr. Buchanan's case. You probably have noticed our car in front of your house."

"Yes, I noticed it." She looked out her bedroom window again to see if it was the same car as earlier.

"We thought so. We saw you looking out tonight. Is everything okay?"

"Yes."

"We thought we saw someone running on your property, but when we checked it out, we didn't find anyone."

Dominique started to wonder whether they'd seen Buchanan or her young friend Shawn. Either way they both got in without a problem, which really worried her about how effective they were going to be protecting her.

"Maybe you guys need some backup to help you out."

"I think we'll be fine, but if you feel you need more, don't hesitate to request more." Mr. Wilkerson offered.

"I will." Dominique looked at Shawn, who was standing in her bedroom, listening to every word. "How do I know you are who you say you are?" Dominique was fearful they were working for Mr. Buchanan.

"You can call downtown to check us out. Shawn Silver requested protection for you and for him. If you'd like to make a call and verify before we come up to the house, please do so."

"I think I will."

"After you verify our information, just wave in your window to let us know it's okay for us to come up and introduce ourselves personally."

"Okay." Dominique immediately called to verify who was supposed to be assigned as per Shawn Silver's request and was relieved when their identity was verified. She returned to her window to let Mr. Wilkerson and his partner to come up.

"What are you doing?" Shawn listened to Dominique from her doorway, confused.

"I'm letting my protection know it's okay for them to come up to the house and introduce themselves to me." She brushed past him to open the front door before they rang the doorbell and woke Devin.

"What if they want to come in and look around and they see me?"

"Don't worry. They just want to talk to me to see who is here."

"I've got to get out of here!" Shawn said in a panic.

"Shawn, calm down. I won't let them in the house. I'll just talk to them outside if that will make you feel better." She peeked out the side window to see where the men were.

"I'm going into the sunroom to wait just in case they want to check the house out. If they do, I'm out of here and I'm never coming back again."

"I told you I'm not going to let them in," she insisted.

He rushed toward the sunroom in case he needed to make a quick getaway.

Dominique looked out her side window again and saw them standing in front of her door, waiting for her to open it. She looked back over her shoulder to see if Shawn was out of sight before she opened the door. Then she turned back around and opened the door to meet the men who were supposed to provide her protection. They had already let her down twice, and she couldn't even tell them they had. Both visitors she had tonight had threatened her to silence.

"Good evening, Mrs. Wallace." The gentleman on the right extended his hand. "My name is Travis Wilkerson, and my partner here is Frank Evans."

Dominique shook their hands without saying a word. She examined them thoroughly and asked to see their identification to be certain.

"Mrs. Wallace, would it be okay if we came in and looked around to make sure everything is okay this evening?"

"That won't be necessary. I've already checked the house myself." Dominique hoped Shawn wouldn't panic and run out the back door.

"If you need us this evening just wave to us from one of your windows."

"I sure will."

Mr. Wilkerson handed Dominique a business card. "Mrs. Wallace, here's our number for you to call if you need to reach us for anything."

"Thanks." She took the card in her hand and looked it over. She still didn't feel safe, even after verifying all the information. Now she wondered whether Michael Buchanan had any influence over them in any way. If he did, she wasn't safe at all. She would need protection from them, too.

Dominique thanked the gentlemen and said goodnight.

"I thought they would never leave." Shawn reentered the foyer area where Dominique was standing alone.

"Now don't you feel foolish, panicking like you did?" Dominique said, frustrated and still shaken by Mr. Buchanan's visit.

"No. If they saw me here, it would have caused a lot of problems for me."

"Well, they didn't, so relax." Dominique gave Shawn a pat on the back. "It's time for us to go to bed now."

"Do you want me to sleep in the same room I slept in last night?" Shawn asked as he followed Dominique upstairs.

"Yes. I'll come tuck you in after you put your pajamas on." Dominique turned the guest bedroom light on for him.

"I'm not a baby. You don't have to tuck me in," Shawn said smartly.

"I know you're not." Dominique said and kissed him on the forehead.

She left Shawn and headed for Devin's room to make sure she was still asleep. Thankfully, she hadn't woken when Buchanan was there earlier. Things might have gone much differently if Devin had walked in. She prayed to God that nothing would happen to her family just because she wanted to do the right thing by convicting Michael Buchanan for his crime. She returned to her own bedroom and tried to fall asleep.

CHAPTER 18

Dominique was anxious to get to her office that morning. When she reached her office floor, she rushed directly to Shawn Silver's office to inform him about her unexpected visit by Michael Buchanan.

"Good morning," Shawn said, looking up from his desk.

"I need to talk to you in private." Dominique closed his office door behind her.

"What's going on?" Shawn sat back in his chair.

"Buchanan showed up at my house last night." She said in a secretive voice.

"He did *what*?" Shawn yelled in shock. He sat up in his chair and picked up his telephone.

Dominique rushed across the room and jerked the telephone from his hand. She placed it back on the hook. "You have to promise me you won't tell a soul. Buchanan threatened that if I tell anyone about him coming to my home last night, my family will be harmed. I can't afford to take that chance."

"How did he get past the protection I had arranged for you?"

"I don't know." She shrugged her shoulders. "I'm not sure whether they are protecting me from him or just watching me for him."

"What do you mean?" Shawn asked with a puzzled look.

"He alluded to the fact he has a lot of connections on the force. To be honest, I believe him. He knew someone was sitting in front of my house before I realized they were there. Shawn, this man is insane. He doesn't plan on going down without taking somebody with him." Dominique took a deep breath.

"What do you want to do now?"

"I don't know. I want to convict his behind so bad, but I'm torn by the fear of my family suffering in the process."

"Dominique, please walk away from this case. I can get one of the other guys here to step in and help me." Shawn stood and ran a hand through his hair.

"No. If I walk away, he wins, and I don't want to give him that satisfaction."

"What does Eric think you should do?"

"I haven't told him, and I don't think I'm going to. Eric will explode and try to kill Buchanan himself."

"I don't blame him. But do you think it's smart to keep his visit a secret from Eric? He needs to know what he's up against if you're going to proceed with representing this case."

She knew he was right but just couldn't bring herself to tell Eric, even though he deserved to know.

"Can't we have someone follow Eric without him knowing?" She worried whether that option was really safe, especially given that both Buchanan and Shawn got into her house without getting caught.

"I guess we can. I really think you should at least tell Eric how dangerous this man is."

It wasn't fair for her not to be honest with Eric, especially if his life was in danger. But she was going to have to find a way to do it without compromising her family's safety in the process.

"Shawn, how are we going to convict this man if he's not going to play fair?"

"We have to play the same game but smarter." Shawn scratched his chin. "I have a few ideas about how we can beat him at his own game."

"What ideas?"

"First, I'm going to get your attacker, Jaret Bell to testify against Mr. Buchanan. I want him to confess that Michael Buchanan ordered him to attack you that night."

"And if you are unable to get that, what then?"

"I'm sure if I dig around, I'll get lucky. Someone like Buchanan always has some little secret they forget about. I'll find it out and use it against him. I'm sure there's something he doesn't want us to find, and it's not those videotapes."

"Are you sure you want to go digging around, trying to find out stuff about this man when you know he will kill you?"

"He won't even know until it's too late." Shawn said, laughing confidently. "I have my people, too."

Dominique didn't like the way Shawn was talking. She didn't want things to get any more complicated than they had already. All she wanted to do was convict Michael Buchanan and get on with her life.

"Dominique, don't worry about anything. You concentrate on the evidence we have now, and I'll do the rest. We will convict this man and no one else will get hurt," Shawn assured her.

"I hope you're right."

"Dominique, I haven't always worn a suit. I grew up in the streets, and I understand the streets well, so I know what I'm doing. Just relax and prepare for the preliminary hearing with what we have so far. I'll notify you with other evidence as I get it. Be ready to run with it when I do."

Shawn pressed his lips together. "Look ... I think you should start working from home. It might be safer."

Dominique didn't argue with Shawn's suggestion. Working from home did sound more appealing since Buchanan threatened her safety and that of her family.

"You might be right. I'm going to clean out my desk today and start working from home immediately. Call me with anything you find."

"Dominique, don't worry. I'll take care of everything. You just stay safe and keep your family out of harm's way. Please be careful."

CHAPTER 19

"Mommy, you're home!" Devin ran down the hallway toward her.

"Yes, I am. What have you been doing today?"

"I've been playing with Ms. Anderson," Devin answered excitedly. "I made you a picture for your office. You want to see it?"

"I sure do. Where is Ms. Anderson?"

"She's in the kitchen cooking dinner. She's making Daddy's favorite, spaghetti and meatballs, because he missed it last time."

"She is? Your daddy is going to be glad."

"I know. I love Ms. Anderson's spaghetti and meatballs, too."

"Do you like them better than mine?" Dominique joked, trying to see if she would be honest enough to tell her the truth. Dominique knew Ms. Anderson's spaghetti and meatballs were way better than hers.

"I like yours, too, Mommy," Devin answered politely and laughed back at her. Dominique followed Devin into the sunroom where she had her picture. As they walked through the kitchen, Ms. Anderson told her Dr. Martin had called again.

"I must have missed my appointment again." Dominique stopped in her tracks and opened her planner. Sure enough, she had forgotten her appointment this afternoon. She would call Dr. Martin's office first thing in the morning and reschedule again. She didn't like to miss her appointments with him. Besides, she promised him she wouldn't.

"Thank you for staying over to cook, Ms. Anderson. I want you to know we really appreciate it. This case has been taking up all my time."

"You know I don't mind. I understand your career is very demanding. Besides, I have nothing else to do when I leave. Being here allows me to spend more time with Devin."

"Ms. Anderson, you have no idea how much we appreciate you. I hope you never feel we take you for granted because we don't. Really, I don't know what we would do without you."

"Mommy, I want to show you your drawing," Devin said as she dragged her into the sunroom where her drawing table was located. She picked up the drawing for her mother and handed it to her.

Dominique examined the picture carefully. "Devin, this is so beautiful! I can't wait to put it up."

"Good."

A loud voice came from the other room. "I'm home!" It was Eric, back from his business trip.

"We're in the sunroom!" Dominique was relieved he was home, but still unsure how to tell him about Michael Buchanan.

"It smells great in here. Ms. Anderson, you have outdone yourself again." Eric gave Ms. Anderson a kiss on the cheek.

"I'm just glad you like it." Ms. Anderson smiled.

Eric whispered, "Don't tell Dominique, but I like your spaghetti and meatballs better than hers."

"I heard that. You'll see the next time I fix you spaghetti and meatballs," Dominique joked as she entered the kitchen.

Eric gave Dominique a kiss on the lips. "How long have you been home?"

"I just arrived a few minutes before you."

"How's your case coming along?" Eric pulled off his jacket and placed it on the back of one of the kitchen chairs.

"Bad news."

"What?"

"You remember me telling you I spoke with one of Buchanan's housekeepers by the name of Maria Gonzales?"

"I think so."

"Well, she was found dead at the bus station yesterday."

"What?" Eric shouted. "What happened to her?"

"They said it looked like someone beat her to death and left her in one of the restroom stalls."

"Do you think Michael Buchanan had something to do with it?"

"Yes. The police haven't been able to connect him to anything yet."

Dominique prayed Eric wouldn't start demanding she walk away from the case again.

Eric didn't say anything but started to pace the floor, looking back at her. He was obviously unhappy to hear the news about Maria's death. It would have been suicidal at this point to tell him Buchanan showed up at their house and threatened their family, too.

"Don't worry. Shawn is working on getting more evidence against Buchanan that will help us seal the case shut. I really want to convict this bum now."

"Mommy, I thought you said we shouldn't use that type of language?" Devin put her small hands on her hips.

"You're right, I'm sorry. Mommy shouldn't have used that language," Dominique said, forgetting once again that she was present in the room while she was telling Eric about her case. This time she was relieved, because now she would have an excuse to change the subject and buy more time before telling Eric everything.

CHAPTER 20

Dominique rose early the next morning and contacted Katherine Buchanan. Until now, their interaction had been limited. She prayed she was still holding it together.

Mrs. Buchanan sounded calm. "I'm very nervous, but as each day passes I'm starting to relax," she sighed. "Have you been able to arrange for me to see Kimberly yet?"

"Mrs. Buchanan, I know I told you I would try to arrange for you to see your daughter, but something has come up."

"What has come up? Is Kimberly okay?" Dominique heard her calmness change to worry.

"Kimberly is okay. But Maria Gonzales, your old housekeeper, was killed. We believe your husband was responsible for her death because he found out she was being asked to testify against him. Because of that, I don't want to compromise your safety by allowing you to go to the hospital. I think he will be waiting for you to show up there. I know you really want to see her, but it would not be a smart move. My recommendation is to have one of Kimberly's nurses place the telephone up to her ear so you can talk with her that way."

"I told you my husband didn't like disloyal people. You know he's going to try to kill me." Mrs. Buchanan sighed. "What he doesn't realize is I'm already dead." She laughed. Dominique sympathized with Mrs. Buchanan, but she had to make sure the woman would agree to communicate with her daughter by telephone.

"Mrs. Buchanan, will you agree to speak with your daughter only by telephone to ensure your safety?"

"Yes. What good will I do her if he kills me before the trial? I at least

174

want to testify against his sorry ass before he does anything to me. When can I speak to her?"

"Give me an hour to set something up."

"I'll be waiting."

"I want you to relax."

"I will. What else is there for me to do here? Can you arrange for me to have some books to read?"

"I'll have some reading material delivered to you as soon as possible. Meanwhile, I want you to relax and prepare yourself mentally for the trial."

The telephone rang seconds after their call. It was Shawn Silver. "Have you seen the paper this morning?"

"No. What's in it?"

"They have Maria Gonzales's attack all over the front page along with Mrs. Buchanan missing. They also talked about how she allowed her daughter to be sexually abused by her husband and chose not to do anything about it. They completely trashed her."

Mrs. Buchanan was going to lose it when she read about it. Instead of calling her, she decided to order no newspapers be delivered to her room, only novels. Dominique didn't know how long she would be able to protect Mrs. Buchanan from the media bashing.

"You better let her know. She'll probably hear about it over the television if she doesn't read about it in the paper."

"She's going to lose it, she's so concerned about what everybody else is going to think. I'd better call her now." Dominique dreaded making the call.

"Let me know if you need me. I'll be in my office. I'm going to go down to the hospital and see if I can make some headway with Mr. Bell."

"Good luck." Dominique felt nervous again about proceeding forward with Mrs. Buchanan's case.

Dominique sat at her desk, wondering what she was going to tell Mrs. Buchanan. Clueless, she located her newspaper and read both articles about Maria's death in their entirety. The newspaper was accusing Mrs. Buchanan of being a bad mother. Dominique reached for the phone to call her, but realized she hadn't arranged for her to speak with her daughter yet. She quickly made the arrangements and decided to use that for leverage when breaking the bad news.

"Mrs. Buchanan, this is Dominique. I need to talk to you about something."

"What bad news do you have to tell me that the news hasn't already tried to portray? They are convincing everyone of exactly what I didn't want them to. What a lousy mother I am! Please explain how you are going to overcome their accusations against me now. I am all ears if you have any suggestions." Mrs. Buchanan was slurring her words. She hadn't noticed her slurring earlier, but it appeared she was drunk.

"Mrs. Buchanan, have you been drinking?"

"Yes. How else do you expect me to deal with all this mess? I've found over the years, alcohol can become one's best friend."

"Well, on a good note, I've arranged for you to speak with your daughter today. But it is crucial that you follow my instructions carefully."

Dominique gave her the instructions to follow, hung up the telephone, and looked down at her planner, where she saw the note she made for herself to call Dr. Martin. She dialed his number and waited for someone to answer.

"Good morning, Dr. Martin's office. How can I help you?"

"Yes. This is Dominique Wallace."

"Good morning Mrs. Wallace. You missed your appointment yesterday."

"I know. I need to reschedule. When is your next opening?"

"We have an appointment two weeks from now if that's okay. Let me check with Dr. Martin to see if he wants to see you sooner."

Dominique waited for the receptionist to return with a response.

"Mrs. Wallace, Dr. Martin says he would like to see you before then. Can you come this afternoon at your usual time?"

Dominique glanced over her schedule. She was free for now. Maybe it would be good for her to see Dr. Martin. She had a lot to tell him since her last session with him. The thought sounded refreshing to her and she agreed.

"I'll come in this afternoon."

"Good, he will see you then, Mrs. Wallace."

Dominique hung up the telephone. As she wrote her new appointment time in her planner, she looked across her desk at her clock. It was almost lunchtime, and she felt the need to get out of the house for a while. She picked up her telephone and dialed Eric's office number to see if he would be able to slip away for lunch with her today.

"Hello, QTSU. How may I help you?" Eric's assistant, JoAnn answered.

"Hello, JoAnn. Is Eric available?"

"Let me check. He's not on his phone. Let me put you through. Hold, please." JoAnn placed her on hold and transferred her to Eric's extension.

"Hello. What's going on?"

"I was calling to see if you were free for lunch today."

"Actually, I think I can slip away for a few minutes. Where would you like to meet?"

"I'll come to you and we can have lunch in the deli one block from your office. I have a taste for chicken salad."

"Sounds good to me. Are you on your way?"

"Yes. I'll meet you downstairs in your lobby in thirty minutes. See ya." Dominique left her desk as is, grabbed her purse, and headed out. Almost to her car, Dominique was surrounded by several reporters with microphones and cameramen in her driveway. They surrounded her like starving game.

"Mrs. Wallace, is it true Michael Buchanan might be connected to Maria Gonzales's murder? Is Mr. Buchanan a possible suspect?"

"Excuse me, please!" Dominique pushed her way through the mob.

"Mrs. Wallace, is it true you also have Mrs. Buchanan in your possession? Are you taking better precautions with her safety than you did with Maria Gonzales?"

"Mrs. Wallace, is your husband as supportive of your psychiatric therapy as Mr. Buchanan is of his wife's?"

Dominique froze in her tracks, disarmed. How could he? She stood, furious, trying to ignore the microphones blocking the pathway to her car.

"I want all of you to get off my property right now before I file charges!" Dominique jumped into her car and raced down the street to meet her husband for lunch. She was boiling with anger as she thought about Buchanan's cowardly attempt to make her private life a public spectacle. She parked her car and rushed to meet Eric in front of his building.

"What's on your mind?" Eric asked as he wrapped his arms around her and placed a soft kiss on her forehead.

"Somehow Michael Buchanan found out about my sessions with Dr.

Martin, and he tipped off the media about it. They were camped outside of our front door when I left a few minutes ago," Still angry, she told Eric everything as they walked in the direction of the deli for lunch.

"What do your sessions with Dr. Martin have to do with anything? You go to Dr. Martin because you want to, not because you have to. Thousands of people see psychiatrists, for different reasons."

"I know, but the media is going to have a field day with this little gossip he has leaked out."

"Dominique, I think he's trying to discredit you before you go to court because you have more evidence then he does. You know what he's trying to do."

"I know," she agreed.

"He wants you to get upset and distract you. He definitely achieved that a few minutes ago because I saw you drive past my building."

"I know, and you're right. I have to stay focused and concentrate." Dominique kissed Eric on the cheek as they continued to head toward the deli. "I knew there was a reason I married you."

"Really!" Eric joked casually. "Ladies first." Eric opened the deli door for Dominique to enter. They were ushered to a private table and enjoyed a wonderful lunch together until an uninvited young lady intruded.

"Mrs. Wallace, is it really true you have been seeking psychiatric therapy? If so, does your psychiatrist think it's a good idea for you to handle this case in your present mental condition?"

Before Dominique could respond, Eric answered. "Mrs. Wallace is very capable of presenting her case. And as far as her present mental state, I assure you she's as sharp as any attorney around."

"Are you one of Mrs. Wallace's clients?"

Dominique responded before Eric could. "Miss, in case you haven't noticed, we're having lunch. I would appreciate if you would let me finish my lunch in peace."

"I'm sorry, I disturbed your lunch, Mrs. Wallace. I just don't want the defense to try to discredit you before you have an opportunity to present before the jury. I believe Michael Buchanan is guilty. I hope you convict him."

Dominique forced a smile on her face. "I appreciate your support. I plan to do my best."

"Good luck." The news reporter excused herself and left.

"We'd better go. They must have followed me down here. I'm anxious for this case to be over. I really don't care about all this publicity. I just want to do my job, that's all. I've never cared about the fame, like some attorneys."

"I know, but when you present a case like this one, what do you expect? Just stay focused and do your job. If you do that, Buchanan won't stand a chance. You're a great attorney, and you've demonstrated that over the years."

"I know!" Dominique responded.

"We better get out of here. Where did you park?"

"Two blocks from your office."

"You better take a cab back to your car," Eric said as he stood to his feet, walked around to her side, and pulled her chair from the table. "I would hate for them to surround us on the sidewalk and be unable to get away."

"You're probably right," She admitted as they walked up to the counter to pay for their lunch.

They cautiously exited the deli. Eric flagged down a cab. Dominique jumped in and slid over for Eric to get beside her.

"You're not going to ride with me?" Dominique asked when Eric didn't follow.

"No. I could use the walk back to the office. Call me when you reach your car." Eric closed her door behind her.

Dominique waved goodbye as her cab pulled off in the direction of her car. She sat back in the cab and stared out of the window at the crowd of people walking up and down the streets, wondering what dramas were invading their lives. Were they having a good day or a bad day?

Over the years, Dominique had become good at channeling negative energy into positive. It had become one of her strong suits in life. Growing up in the foster care system, she had two choices: be weak or be strong. Dominique learned to be strong. And during the last year of law school, she was nicknamed Tiger Lady by her classmates because she was savvy and aggressive as she dominated her classmates during court debates.

Dominique stepped out of the cab and rushed toward the garage entrance to locate her parked car. She scanned the garage for any reporters.

Home free, she jumped into her car and raced back home to finish working on Kimberly's case.

As she drove, she started thinking about her childhood. Why did her family give her away? Why didn't they love her enough to keep her? She wondered if she was the only child they gave up. Or were there more? She wondered whether her mother or father was still alive? And if they were, would they even want to know how she was doing now that she was an adult? Would they be proud of all that she had accomplished over the years as an attorney? Dominique had become one of the most respected attorneys in the state. She was proud of her accomplishments, considering her unpalatable childhood.

Four years ago, Dominique debated trying to locate her family. She was curious about her parents' medical history since she was starting a family. She knew nothing and prayed her child would be healthy.

Dominique smiled as she remembered how excited she was to hold Devin as a newborn, knowing a true blood relative for the first time in her life. She became emotional when the nurse came to take Devin away for her nap time. Dominique pleaded with the nurse to allow her to stay by her bedside. She didn't want Devin to leave her sight, fearing she, too, would disappear from her life.

During an appointment with Dr. Martin, she shared her concern about losing Devin, and how hard it was to return to work and not feel she was abandoning her child. She felt torn between her daughter, whom she loved so much, and a career she loved too.

Being an attorney was like therapy for Dominique. It filled that empty void she had growing up and crafted a sense of accomplishment and self-worth in her life.

Motherhood brought her mind to Mrs. Buchanan and Kimberly's situation. Kimberly had grown up in a household with her mother and father. They were very rich and could give her everything. They sent her to the best schools and camps and allowed her to participate in every program they could find.

But for Dominique, there were no private schools, camps, or programs. Those all required money and time that would inconvenience her foster care families. She had to do without.

Looking from the outside you might think Kimberly had it all, but that was far from the truth. Kimberly's life was far from perfect. She was living in a personal hell of her own, living with a painful secret, a secret that Kimberly could no longer deal with alone. Dominique could relate to Kimberly's taciturn suffering.

Dominique's chest tightened as she thought about how their lives were so parallel in dealing with so much pain. She tried to think optimistically about Kimberly's situation. She was still very young and had most of her life to look forward to after all this was over. She still had a chance to turn her life around. She prayed Kimberly would be able to block out all the bad memories about her past. Somehow, she had managed to suppress all the ghastly memories from her own mind and discover a place of peacefulness.

Dominique jumped at the sound of her cell phone ringing and reached to answer it. "Hello, Mrs. Wallace."

"Dominique, I don't know if I can do this!" Mrs. Buchanan shouted frantically.

"Mrs. Buchanan, please calm down. What's going on?" Dominique braced herself for the emotional flood.

"Have you been watching the news? I'm all over the newspapers and television. Everybody thinks I'm the worst person ever. They think I remain silent because of my husband's money. I knew this would happen. Dominique, I can't handle this type of ridicule." Mrs. Buchanan cried helplessly.

"Mrs. Buchanan, please don't cry. The media is only reporting what they think they know or what your husband has tried to convince them of. The media doesn't know that you've decided to testify against your husband now because you know what he's been doing is wrong. You have been abused over the years, like Kimberly. All they know is that your husband has been accused of a crime, and they're not sure of your involvement. During the trial, we'll have an opportunity to show the court and the media how you have been there for your daughter."

"I was abused by him," Mrs. Buchanan repeated, as if for the first time she was willing to admit the awful truth. "He has dragged my name and reputation through the mud. I can't even go to our clubhouse or be around our friends for the shame of what he has done. The media is right about me abusing my daughter, too. I didn't do anything about her situation because of my own shame and disbelief. I don't know if I can face the public again."

Dominique could tell Mrs. Buchanan was drunk, and she would have to address that with her, but right now she had to convince her to calm down again.

"Mrs. Buchanan, please don't fall apart. You are doing exactly what your husband wants you to do, and if you do, he wins again. Kimberly is counting on you. Don't allow your husband to continue to defeat you and Kimberly. I want him to see you up on the stand strong and confident. This is your opportunity to pay him back for all the years he has hurt you and Kimberly."

Dominique heard a door slam in the background. "I can't believe this place. I don't see anything else to drink."

"Mrs. Buchanan, I need you to stop drinking."

"No. It helps me calm my nerves. How in the hell do you expect anybody to deal with all this negative publicity? Dominique, I can't deal with all this pressure. Maybe I should just kill myself before Mike does it first."

"Please don't talk like that. You don't want to die. I know you are very upset about what the media is saying right now, but you'll have an opportunity to change that perception once they hear you testify in court. And I promise you, I will do my absolute best to convince the court you are not a bad mother and that you did not allow your daughter to be subjected to your husband's abuse because of his money. Actually, this is a good time for you and me to talk about what to expect during the trial."

"Like what?"

"I have several questions I'm planning to ask you about your knowledge about your husband and daughter's situation. I need you to answer these questions as honestly as possible." Dominique asked each question and waited for Mrs. Buchanan's responses.

After a few rounds of questioning, Dominique felt comfortable with the answers. And she felt comfortable she would be able to answer Buchanan's team's questions, too. It was vital to the success of Dominique's case.

After her call with Mrs. Buchanan, Dominique went to visit with Kimberly. She took the next exit to turn around and head for the hospital.

Dominique's telephone rang as she parked her car in the hospital garage.

"Mrs. Wallace, this is Nicole from Dr. Martin's office. I just wanted to remind you about your session with us this afternoon."

"Thank you for calling, I'll be there." She was thankful Nicole had reminded her because with all the confusion that morning, she'd forgotten her appointment already.

CHAPTER 21

Dominique couldn't wait to tell Dr. Martin everything she had been through since her last session. As she flipped through one of Dr. Martin's magazines, she saw him come around the corner with a young lady who was much younger than herself. Dominique wondered what her story was. She looked pleasant as she smiled back at Dominique, but then Dominique imagined as she laughed to herself the young lady probably thought the same thing about her. She would never have guessed either one of them would have been in a psychiatrist's office if she had seen herself or the other young lady walking down the street. No one at the firm knew she was seeing Dr. Martin until Michael Buchanan announced it to the world.

"Hello, Dominique. I'm sorry I kept you waiting." Dr. Martin motioned for her to follow him to his office.

"No problem." she returned a big smile.

"I've seen you all over the news. You're a celebrity now," he teased.

Dominique didn't see herself as a celebrity. She wanted her case to be over to get her privacy back.

"So how are you feeling today?"

"I feel fine. I'm just trying to stay focused until my case is over."

"Are you having a hard time with that?"

"Yes and no."

"Explain yourself."

"Dr. Martin, I have to ask you to keep what I'm about to share with you confidential because my family's safety is on the line."

"Of course, what's going on?" Dr. Martin sat up in his chair, waiting for her to fill him in.

"The other night, while Eric was away on a business trip, Michael Buchanan showed up at my house unexpectedly. He broke into my house and threatened me, saying that if I proceed with this case or tell anybody about him coming to my home that night, he would harm my family and me."

"So, what are you going to do now?"

"I'm not sure. I want to convict this man more than ever. He tried to run my daughter and nanny off the road the other day. He was trying to send me a message."

"Are Devin and your nanny okay?" he asked, with a worried look on his face.

"Yes. But they don't know Buchanan was behind it. They think it was a freak incident. And I haven't told Eric yet either about the Devin incident or about Buchanan breaking into our home."

"Why?"

"I'm afraid of what he might do. I know he'll demand I walk away from this case, but I'm not sure if that's what I want to do."

"When do you go to trial?"

"In a few days. I refuse to allow him to win by trying to scare me off. The other part of me is terrified of what he might do to my family. He has already threatened Eric's life."

"Why haven't you informed Eric that his life might be in danger?"

"I know I should tell him, but I'm afraid of his response. I promised Kimberly before she went into a coma that I would be there until the end. If I walk away, I'll be just like everybody else who turned their back on her. I want to keep my promise."

"Even at the expense of your own family?" he asked, leaning forward in Dominique's direction.

His question was hard for her to swallow. No, she didn't want to risk her family's safety, but she felt obliged to help Kimberly, too. She wanted to be able to tell her when she came out of the coma that she had kept her promise and convicted her father.

"Dominique, I can't tell you what to do, but I will remind you that your family is not dispensable. You won't be able to replace your daughter or your husband if anything happens to them because you want to continue with this case. Are you prepared to suffer the consequences behind your decision?"

Dominique knew she wouldn't be able to live with herself if anything happened to Devin or Eric because she was too stubborn to walk away. Tears rolled down her face as she wrestled with what decision to make.

"No. I'm not prepared to suffer the consequences." She wiped the tears away.

"Well, you need to make that decision and be able to accept everything that comes along with it." Dr. Martin shifted in his chair. "Has Buchanan done anything else besides trying to run your daughter and nanny off the road?"

She cleared her throat before answering. "Yes. We think he murdered our witness, Maria Gonzales."

"I just heard about her horrible murder on the news. They said she was found dead in the bus station bathroom."

"Yes. Michael Buchanan had something to do with it. I just haven't been able to prove it yet. Maria was the person who told me about Buchanan's videotapes. Thanks to her, I at least have those for evidence now that she's dead."

"Maria was going to testify against Mr. Buchanan in court?"

"Well, she said she would before she ran away. She was so afraid of what Buchanan might do to her. But if she had let me put her in protective custody, she might be here today."

"Do you have any more witnesses willing to testify against Michael Buchanan?"

"Yes. I have Buchanan's wife in protective custody now. She has agreed to testify that she knew he was sexually abusing their daughter for years. She's scared, too, and I can understand why. She knows firsthand what he is capable of. But I'm gravely worried about Katherine Buchanan's mental state. One minute she's fine. The next she's a raving lunatic. I just pray I can keep her sane long enough to testify."

"Has Mr. Buchanan been in contact with Mrs. Buchanan since she decided to testify against him?"

"No. But she's afraid he'll find her and kill her for being disloyal."

"Well, good luck with her. She has a lot at stake, and I'm sure that's all she's been thinking about."

"I keep trying to remind her she's doing the right thing for her daughter's sake."

"Have you been able to prove the man that attacked you is working for Buchanan?"

"I still haven't been able to prove it, but I know he's involved."

"How did you discover Buchanan's involvement with Maria?"

"Kimberly told me she thought something had been going on, so I investigated. Maria admitted to everything and told me about his videotapes with other women. He repulses me."

"Did Mrs. Buchanan know all this was going on?"

"Yes. She tried to ignore it and pretend it wasn't happening. She admitted firing Maria because she knew her husband was having sex with her."

"How do you feel, knowing Michael Buchanan is capable of such violent acts?"

"It makes me angry and scared at the same time. A man like Michael Buchanan will still have power in prison, but I can complicate his life a little. Life in prison for Buchanan will be difficult when the other prisoners find out why he is in there. They frown on people who sexually abuse children, and I will make sure everyone will know why he is in there."

"Do you feel like your anger toward Mr. Buchanan is really driving you to handle this case now?"

"Kind of. I still want to do it to help Kimberly. She is my client, and I haven't lost sight of that. She's my first concern."

"No. Your family is your first concern," Dr. Martin interjected.

"I know they should be," Dominique mumbled. "But as a professional attorney, I have vowed to present my clients' interests until there is a verdict."

"Does Kimberly want anything else to do with her father when all of this is over?"

"No, and I don't blame her. If he were my father, I would never want to see him again."

"Dominique, I want to change the subject for a moment. I thought a lot about our last session at your house. Have you had a chance to introduce Shawn and Eric yet?"

"No. The opportunity hasn't presented itself yet."

"Are you committed to doing it as soon as you can?"

"Believe me, Dr. Martin, I would love nothing more than to be able to introduce Shawn to Eric."

"Have you seen Shawn again since our last session?"

"Yes." Dominique paused, realizing she had nothing to gain by holding the truth from him. "Before you say anything, hear me out completely. I allowed Shawn to spend the night while Eric was away on a business trip. And I discovered his father has been sexually abusing him and his little sister."

Dr. Martin raised his eyebrow. "How do you know that for certain?"

"He told me after I discovered marks all over his body."

"How did you see marks all over his body?"

"I asked Shawn to take a bath before he went to bed. When he handed me his clothes through the bathroom door I noticed his arm was all bruised up. So, I asked him to wrap a towel around his body and step out of the bathroom. When he did, I saw that his whole body was bruised up. It was awful."

"So, what are you going to do?"

"I don't know. I've been trying to convince him to allow me to involve one of the attorneys I work with to help him, but he doesn't want anyone to know what's going on. He said his father threatened to kill his whole family if he ever told anyone."

"Sounds like another complicated situation you are faced with."

"I know. It's bizarre that I'm faced with two similar cases of this magnitude. They both rip at my heart. The only difference between the two is, one wants help and the other doesn't. Dr. Martin, I feel so torn about Shawn's situation. I can't stand by knowing what he is going through along with his little sister and do nothing. If I don't do something now, I'm no different from anyone else who turns their head and ignores it."

"What can you do if he doesn't want your help? You will only push him away. Do you know any more about his family? Where does he live? What's his last name?"

"No. I still don't know any more than what he has told me."

"You definitely don't want to scare him off before you get that information out. If you could learn his last name, you could find out what school he attends and get his information there."

"He must go to school near my house because he walked to school when he spent the night over."

"Are you sure he went to school?"

Dominique never considered the possibility he might not have gone to school. She had taken his word for it. "I don't know. I just assumed he went to school."

"Dominique, you and I both know there is more to your little friend than what he is sharing with you. I would be very interested in meeting him for myself. I would like to talk to him about his situation and emphasize how important it is for him to help both himself and his little sister."

"Dr. Martin, I'm one hundred percent sure he won't agree to that. He still runs when he thinks someone is going to see him. The other day, when he thought my police protection was going to see him at my house, he threatened to never come back to visit me."

"Can you give the police a description of him and see if they can help you find any information?"

"No. I definitely don't want to do that. He would never trust me again."

"So, what now?"

"I don't know. I guess I have to pray he will come around. Hopefully, it will be soon."

"I don't feel good about this," Dr. Martin said. "I still encourage you to convince him to allow you to introduce him to your husband. I know Shawn has made it very clear he doesn't want anyone to know about him, but let him know your husband is very important to you, too."

"He asked me to promise not to tell anyone about him, and before I knew it, he convinced me to let him spend the night."

"It seems he has some type of control over you. Are you aware of it?"

"No, he doesn't. I just feel sorry for him that's all. I can understand why he is so afraid. I have to find a way to win his trust."

"You don't want to risk Eric finding out you allowed Shawn to spend the night. I'm assuming Shawn must be spending the night when Eric is away on business?"

"Yes. Shawn feels he is protecting Devin and me when Eric is away."

"Does his parents know he is spending the night at your house?"

"He says he tells them. I haven't spoken with them myself." She could tell Dr. Martin disapproved of her concessions when it came to Shawn.

"How would you feel if Devin told you she wanted to spend the night at a complete stranger's house?"

"Of course, I would say no."

"Why are you changing the rules when it comes to Shawn?"

"I don't know. His situation is different."

"Why?"

"Dr. Martin, Shawn's father is sexually abusing him and his sister. When he spends the night with me, at least I know he's safe. Giving him that little bit of safety makes me feel better at night. I only wish I could help his sister."

"Why can't you? Can he bring her over when he spends the night?"

"No. She's much younger than he is. And he said his father is really strict with her. Dr. Martin, trust me, I want to help both of them. I just need a little more time."

"Have you ever tried to drop Shawn off at his house?"

"Yes, but he insists on walking home from my house every time."

"What do you think Eric would say if he knew Shawn was spending the night when he was away?"

"He would be upset because he hasn't met him yet. And I would completely understand his argument, but Shawn really needs me. Dr. Martin, I feel like I'm all he has that is safe in his life right now."

"You have developed some strong feelings for Shawn in a short period of time."

"I know. A part of me feels like I've known him all my life. It's the strangest thing. He's a sweet boy who is in a bad situation."

"I know you feel some sense of obligation to protect him, but please keep your wits about you."

"I plan to."

"Good. Dominique, I would like for you to think about our session today. Keep me posted on your progress with Shawn. And good luck with whatever decision you make about continuing with Kimberly's case. I want you to think about all the consequences that could result from your being the one to prosecute this case. For starters, the possibility of losing your daughter, your husband, and even yourself. Try to remove your personal feelings and emotions. Pretend you are trying to assist someone else with making this decision.

"I also want to point out today that I heard you express strong feelings of commitment for both Kimberly and Shawn. But your commitment for each of them has allowed you to sacrifice being honest and up front with your family. This is the first time I have ever witnessed this type of behavior from you. And I have to admit it troubles me greatly. However, I want you to think about everything we have talked about today and make the right decision for you. Remember: your family is not dispensable."

Dominique dropped her head and sat for a moment before leaving Dr. Martin's office. He had given her a lot to think about, and she didn't have a lot of time to make her decisions.

As Dominique pulled into her driveway, she breathed a sigh of relief. She was at home and could relax. All she wanted to do was take a nice warm bath and go to sleep. When she entered the house, she saw Eric's briefcase in the foyer.

"How was your day?" Eric asked as she entered the foyer.

"Okay. How was yours?" Dominique placed her briefcase on the floor beside his.

"Demanding as always," Eric answered. "Unfortunately, I have to go out of town again first thing next week. They need me in LA."

"Will you be gone all week?"

"No. I should be back on Wednesday, but if we finish everything without any problems, there is a possibility that I might be able to return on Tuesday. I know it's going to be hard for you and Devin to make it without me," Eric said jokingly as he pulled Dominique's body closer to his and kissed her gently. Dominique could feel Eric's nature growing against her body but tonight she didn't feel romantic and hoped he wouldn't be too disappointed.

"You want to slip upstairs before Devin discovers you're home?" Eric whispered in her ear.

"No. I'm not in the mood, Eric."

"Is there something wrong?" Eric released her body to look at her.

"No. I'm just tired, that's all. I'm sorry. Another time." Dominique gave him a quick kiss on the cheek and ran upstairs to take a bath.

When Dominique reached her bathroom, her body was shaking. She sat down on the edge of her tub and tried to calm herself while her tub filled. She felt herself being pulled in many directions, and she didn't know what to do. Exhausted from her present confusion, she slipped out of her clothes and slid down into her warm bathwater. She laid her head back and tried to escape her stressful week.

Her thoughts drifted to her young friend Shawn. She wondered where he was. Until now, she hadn't realized he hadn't been by to visit her since the night Michael Buchanan showed up in her bedroom.

Dominique's back and chest tightened as she continued to wonder whether Shawn and his sister were safe. Tears filled her eyes as she imagined how awful it would have been if her father had sexually abused her and not knowing if it was ever going to stop. Tears streamed down her face uncontrollably as she burst into a helpless cry. She couldn't understand how someone could do something so horrible to their child or to anyone else.

Dominique started to think about Kimberly and all the years she had to deal with what her father had been doing to her—little by little, losing herself and surrendering to the realization that no one was going to help her, day after day, month after month, year after year, and feeling suicide was the only option for any type of freedom.

Dominique continued to cry. She accepted the reality that she had placed her own family's life in danger by deciding to help Kimberly. Oh, how she prayed she had not made the wrong decision in proceeding with Kimberly's case! She couldn't understand why she was being punished for doing the right thing. All she wanted to do was help Kimberly out of her awful situation and give her a chance to start her life over.

Dominique dropped her head and said a long prayer to God. She prayed He would hear her prayer and would not refuse her plea for help as she tried to do the right thing. Then she prayed for Shawn and his family's well-being.

Silently, she entered her bedroom with her towel still wrapped around her body. Eric was in their bed watching television, so she quickly got dressed in her nightgown and slid into their bed without saying a word.

"Do you feel better?" Eric turned his attention away from the television to acknowledge Dominique.

"Yes. I just need a good night's sleep," she said as she closed her eyes.

CHAPTER 22

All weekend long, as Dominique prepared for her preliminary hearing, she waited for her young friend Shawn to drop by. She prayed no harm had come to him that would prevent him from visiting with her.

As she sat in their sunroom surrounded by paperwork, Eric asked, "Dominique, I hate to desert you, but my plane leaves in two hours. Are you still going to take me to the airport?"

Dominique acknowledged Eric's presence. "Sure. Let me get dressed." Dominique rushed upstairs to change her clothes and went downstairs to join Eric and Devin in the foyer.

The telephone rang as Eric gathered his luggage. "I got it."

"Dominique?" Mrs. Buchanan called out in a high-pitched voice.

"Yes, is everything okay?"

"I can't testify against Mike."

"What's wrong?"

"Dominique, I can't face the court after what Mike has done to our family," she confessed.

"Please calm down. Trust me, after the trial everyone will be focusing their attention on him, not you. You have nothing to be embarrassed or worried about," Dominique pleaded.

"I don't want to hear that anymore. I can't wait until the trial is over. My life is a complete disaster. My daughter is in a coma, and there's no guarantee she's ever going to come out of it. And it's all my fault for not stopping her father sooner. Let's not forget my daughter doesn't even want me in her life. And I can't blame her. I've been an awful mother to her. Hell, how can I be any good to her when I don't even have control over my life? For God's sake, my husband gave me and my daughter gonorrhea. How embarrassing is that?"

"Mrs. Buchanan, stop it right now! Yes, what your husband has done is awful, and he will pay for it dearly. I don't want you to spend another second crying or worrying about what anyone is going to say or think about you and your family. You have been to hell and back, and I want you to stop this emotional roller coaster you have allowed yourself to ride on all these years. It's time for you to get off, you hear me?"

"Don't you tell me not to worry! You're not in my shoes right now. I'm the one whose face and name is plastered all over the news. You're going to be able to walk away and never have to deal with my case again, but I have to live with this for the rest of my life. My life will never be the same again. I won't be able to show my face anywhere. No one will be knocking my door down to see how I'm doing. They won't give a shit about me, like they don't right now."

"You're right. It's not me. All I can do is ask you to remain strong for your daughter if you feel that you can't be strong for yourself."

"Are you deliberately trying to ignore what I'm telling you? My daughter doesn't want to have anything to do with me. I've lost my daughter! I lost her a few years ago when I lost myself!" Mrs. Buchanan was screaming.

"Have you been drinking again?"

"Yes. Who gives a damn whether I've been drinking or not? I've told you already, I'm not strong enough to deal with this sober. I just can't. I just can't," Mrs. Buchanan wailed, slurring her words.

"Yes, you can. I really need you to calm down." Dominique heard something crash in the background on the other end of the phone. "Mrs. Buchanan, what's going on?"

"Nothing. I need to lie down," she said calmly. Someone else's voice was in the background. Someone asked Mrs. Buchanan if she was okay, probably her security guard, checking in on her after hearing the noise. "Yes, I am. I just dropped my glass. I'm fine."

"Are you sure?" Dominique asked, worried about Mrs. Buchanan's mental state.

"Yes. I'm awfully tired right now all of a sudden. I'm going to lie down."

"I'm going to give you a call a little bit later. Please get some rest. Remember, you are in control right now, and you have to keep telling yourself that. I know you don't think so, but you are. You're stronger than you realize. I know it took a lot for you to call me that night, and I respect you very much for doing so. I know you can't believe it now, but others will feel the same once they hear your side."

"I hope so," Mrs. Buchanan answered, still slurring her words. "I need to sleep this wine off, that's all."

"I agree. I'll call you later," Dominique promised, feeling a sense of relief that Mrs. Buchanan was calm again. She would have to insist that no more alcohol be permitted in her room until the trial was over.

"Who was that?" Eric had been waiting for Dominique to hang up the telephone and open the door for him to carry his luggage out to the car.

"Mrs. Buchanan," Dominique answered, relieved to be off the telephone. She followed Eric and Devin to the car. "She was having another one of her panic attacks. I only pray she can maintain until after the trial."

"How do you think she will do in court?" Eric got into the car on the passenger side.

"Fine, if she can hold it all together. One minute she's fine, the next she's off in a rampage. A lot of it comes from the negative coverage that has portrayed her as a neglectful mother because of selfish greed."

"Are they right?"

"Yes and no. I really believe she didn't know what to do. I think it took her daughter almost killing herself this time to make her realize enough is enough. I'm not sure I told you—Mr. Buchanan gave his wife and daughter gonorrhea."

"That's awful."

"She's embarrassed about everybody finding out in court."

"Wouldn't you? Hell, I would be furious if you gave us gonorrhea and I had to tell the world about it. I can understand why she's upset."

"I can too, but I need her to realize that she has to stay strong until the trial is over."

"Has her daughter shown any improvement?"

"No."

"I've always been told that people in a coma need to be around family and friends. Hearing their voices sometimes helps them recover."

"She doesn't have any family and friends," Dominique said sadly.

"So are you ready for the trial tomorrow?"

"Yes, as ready as I will ever be." She was exhausted from all the preparation and she had been doing all weekend with her partner Shawn.

"I'm sure you'll do fine." Eric turned around in the front seat to look at Devin in her car seat. "Devin, Daddy wants you to promise to be a good girl while Daddy's away. I want you to take good care of your mother, too. Will you do that for me?"

"Yes. Daddy, will you be gone long?"

"I'm not sure. I'm hoping I'll be able to come home early if everything goes according to plan."

Dominique pulled into a space in front of his airline's outside check-in terminal.

"Daddy, I'm going to miss you, and I love you," Devin said as Eric got out of the car and grabbed his luggage from the back of the car.

"I'm going to miss you and Mommy. I love you both," Eric said and blew them a kiss.

"Be careful, and don't forget to call us after you land in LA," Dominique called after him as he headed for the entrance.

"I will. Love you. Drive carefully," Eric called back.

All the way home, Dominique prayed Eric would be safe during his business trip. She hated herself for not telling him his life could be in danger. But all weekend long, she couldn't find the words to tell him. She submerged herself in Kimberly's case work to distract her guilt. And she prayed desperately God would protect him, knowing he had no clue. She also prayed her decision was the right one—a decision she wrestled with all weekend long.

After Dominique and Devin settled back in at home, they lounged around and relaxed. She didn't want to think about Michael Buchanan at all while she was waiting for Eric to call her to let her know he was safe in LA. Dominique watched the clock until it was time for Devin to get into her nightclothes. She started to review her notes once more before calling it a night. She sat diligently with each piece of evidence. When her telephone rang, she reached across her bed and answered it.

"Just wanted to let you know I arrived safely and to give you the number to the hotel."

She was relieved to hear Eric had arrived safely. Now she prayed he would return safely. She promised herself she would tell him everything. After hanging up, she headed off for a warm, relaxing bath.

Completely covered with bubbles, she stretched out in her tub and allowed the warm water to massage her muscles. Slowly, she gave in to the wonderful feeling and closed her eyes to enjoy the moment.

Her telephone rang. Irritated, she climbed out of her tub, wrapped her towel around her wet body, and rushed into her bedroom to answer it, dripping water onto the carpet.

"I have great news!" Shawn Silver said excitedly.

Dominique glanced over at her alarm clock. It was after midnight, and she couldn't wait to hear what he had to tell her. "What is it?"

"Got us another witness to testify against Buchanan."

"Who is it?" she asked, sharing Shawn's enthusiasm.

"Jaret Bell has agreed to testify that he was paid to attack you that night in the garage. If we'll make a deal with him, he is also willing to testify that he has been paid on several other occasions to perform illegal jobs for Buchanan."

"What kind of deal?"

"He wants to pull his time in a maximum security facility where Buchanan can't get to him."

"We can't get that approved by tomorrow morning before court starts," Dominique replied with disappointment.

"I have already taken care of everything. I pulled a few favors to place Jaret Bell in an undisclosed location while he pulls his time for protection. Just be ready to present him as a possible witness."

Dominique couldn't believe what she was hearing. The same man who attacked her was now going to be a part of her case to help convict Buchanan. She didn't know what to say. Was this God's way of letting her know he was going to grant her blessing?

She hung up and quickly got dressed for bed. Her telephone rang again.

Dominique wondered whether Shawn forgot to tell her something.

"I see you're still up. I hope you have thought about our discussion long and hard. Tomorrow will be a big day for you. I'm sure you will do the right thing. Trust me—you don't want to cross me. By the way, tell Mr. Silver, 'Nice work today.'" Michael Buchanan hung up.

Dominique ran into her bathroom and threw up in the toilet. She allowed her chest and arms to hug her toilet as she cried out of control. Slowly, she dragged herself back into her bedroom to call Shawn. She had to let him know Mr. Buchanan knew Jaret Bell was offering to testify.

"Shawn, Mr. Buchanan just called me. He knows about Mr. Bell. What are we going to do? You know he will try to eliminate him before we can get to trial." Dominique was both nervous and nauseous.

"Don't worry," Shawn said, still confident in his accomplishment. "I've taken care of everything. Just calm down and get ready for tomorrow. I'll handle everything else."

Sitting on the edge of her bed, Dominique replied, "Shawn, I have a really bad feeling about everything. How did he find out so fast?"

"I'm not sure, but I have some people watching him, too. So, don't worry."

"You keep talking about 'some of your people.' Who are you talking about?"

"Don't worry about that. Forget I even said anything. You just need to concentrate on presenting evidence tomorrow before the judge."

"Shawn, I want to know."

"In time. But for now, it's best you don't know. Trust me," Shawn assured her and hung up, leaving Dominique even more unsettled than before.

CHAPTER 23

Preliminary Hearing

Dominique entered the courtroom with Shawn Silver two feet behind her. Without saying a word, she laid her briefcase on the table and allowed the new courthouse energy to intoxicate her. She felt a rush surge through her body as she scanned the crowd of people. There were reporters everywhere in the courtroom and in the hallways, even lined up outside along the sidewalks. The courthouse was now a headquarters for a curious mob of spectators coming to verify all the information that had been reported about the Buchanan's case in the news.

There were rumors that several important activists from high-profile abuse organizations were planning to attend the hearing today. Mr. Buchanan was allowing more attention to brew by delaying pleading guilty—attention she hoped would rally behind her, forcing Buchanan to reconsider his plea and derail any plans to persecute her for her decision to proceed forward. This morning, Dominique welcomed their interest as she absorbed the whispering, notepads rattling, lights switching, and recorders clicking throughout the courtroom while everyone waited for the session to start.

"Dominique, who are you looking for?" Shawn watched Dominique twist around in her seat.

"No one in particular, I'm just amazed how full the courtroom is this morning."

"Well, don't let their presence distract you. You need to concentrate and get ready."

Dominique didn't respond. She caught a glimpse of her young friend Shawn in the midst of the curious mob. Surprised to see him, she got to her feet and started to make her way from behind her table to question why he wasn't in school.

"Dominique, where are you going?"

Dominique glanced over her shoulder. "Shawn's in the back."

"Shawn who?"

"The boy from my attack, he's here in the courtroom. I'll be right back." Dominique stepped from behind their table.

"Dominique, what are you talking about?" Shawn Silver stood to look around. "Dominique, I don't see any young boy in here."

"He's over …" Dominique turned back around to find Shawn in the crowd again but stopped mid-sentence when she realized he was gone.

Shawn Silver stared at her. He looked concerned about her present mental stability. "Dominique."

"I'm not crazy. He was sitting on the back row."

Shawn leaned closer to Dominique and whispered in her ear. "Dominique, please sit down. We don't have time to question him. Judge Bacon is about to start any moment now. What are you thinking?" Shawn was clearly irritated by Dominique's careless behavior.

"How dare you question me?" Dominique snapped at Shawn as she took her seat again.

Trying not to create a scene in front of everyone, Shawn lowered his voice. "Maybe he decided to leave after you spotted him. He's supposed to be in school right now anyway."

Dominique ignored Shawn's attempt to appease her. She opened her briefcase and pulled out her preliminary folder. A little note was paper-clipped to her folder that she didn't remember putting there. Questioning its origin, she quickly read it.

Dear Dominique,

I'm so glad Eric will be out of town for a few days. I miss our time together. I don't like how we have to hide being together. I can't wait until we can be a family and never have to be apart. I worry about your safety when

I'm not around and pray someday we will never have to be apart.

Love, Shawn

Dominique stared at the note, not knowing what to say or think. She wondered when he had placed the handwritten note inside of her briefcase for her to read. She didn't know what to think because her new relationship with Shawn was very special to her, but he was making it very difficult for her to see how it would work if she couldn't introduce him to her husband, Eric. She knew she wouldn't be able to continue to hide their relationship much longer. Something would have to give and soon.

Dominique folded Shawn's note back up and placed it back in her briefcase for safekeeping. She took a deep breath and thanked God that he was at least safe for now.

"All rise," the courtroom deputy announced. Dominique stood as Judge Clarence Bacon entered the courtroom. He took his seat and motioned for everyone to sit.

"Good morning, Mrs. Wallace and Mr. Silver," the judge greeted from his chair.

"Good morning, Your Honor."

"Good morning, Mr. Jennings and Mr. Peters."

"Good morning, Your Honor."

"Before we proceed with this case, I feel it necessary to remind everyone present in this courtroom to remain silent at all times. Anyone who disrupts my courtroom will be escorted out, as well as anyone else not directly participating in this hearing this morning. There will be no lights shone in my courtroom, and no notepads or recorder where I can see them. I will allow microphones to be visible to me, only against the back walls of the courtroom.

"Now that I have set a few ground rules, if anyone feels they will be unable to comply, I ask that you remove yourself immediately." Judge Clarence Bacon hesitated. The courtroom was silent and still. No one wanted to leave before the trial had finished.

"Good. I will proceed with the hearing scheduled this morning. This preliminary hearing will be the ruling of contested point of evidence.

Attorneys, you will stay within those guidelines or disciplinary action will be brought against anyone who does not. Have I made myself clear, attorneys?"

"Yes, Your Honor," they said in unison.

Dominique smiled back at Judge Clarence Bacon. She was glad he was presiding. He was fair and always listened to all the facts before making his decision. Because of his prestigious upbringing, he didn't have to be concerned about politics like other judges. He didn't owe any favors, nor did he care if he was asked to step down. He was financially well off and ready for an early retirement from the legal system when that day presented itself.

"Good. Is the prosecution ready?"

"Yes." Dominique stood and inclined her head. "Your Honor, the state will present medical records to establish that both Miss Kimberly Buchanan—Mr. Michael Buchanan's daughter—and Mrs. Katherine Buchanan—Mr. Buchanan's wife—have gonorrhea. We can then show that it is extremely likely that they both were infected by the same person because both of their test results presented identical strains of gonorrhea. We will also present Michael Buchanan's medical records and show that he has also tested positive for gonorrhea and his strains are identical to those of Miss Kimberly Buchanan and Mrs. Katherine Buchanan." Dominique handed Judge Clarence Bacon the folder containing medical histories. While he reviewed the folder, Dominique waited in silence.

"Do you have any more medical records to present to the court, Mrs. Wallace?" Judge Clarence Bacon asked.

"No, Your Honor."

"Mr. Jennings?"

"I have nothing at this time, Your Honor." Mark pretended to take some notes.

"Mrs. Wallace, you have the floor."

"The state will present a videotape of Mr. Michael Buchanan and Miss Kimberly Buchanan having sexual intercourse." Dominique paused briefly, as if to gather her thoughts, but cleverly exploiting an opportunity to feed off the energy resonating behind. There was a bit of muttering, and Judge Clarence Bacon immediately reminded everyone of his earlier threat.

Dominique took heed of his warning and proceeded. "Due to the nature of the videotape, Your Honor, we requested that you review the videotape prior to this hearing. Have you done so?" Dominique asked, grateful the videotape wasn't going to be permitted to be played during this hearing.

"Yes, I have," Judge Clarence Bacon responded with a heavy voice, one that indicated to Dominique he did not approve of the contents of the videotape. And she couldn't imagine any jury approving of its contents either. "You may continue."

"Thank you. We can then show that Miss Kimberly Buchanan was coached into performing sexual favors for her father, Mr. Michael Buchanan. I would also like to add to the record that Miss Kimberly Buchanan is presently only thirteen years old. She was under the guardianship of Mr. Michael Buchanan during the making of the videotape presented as evidence." Dominique watched Judge Clarence Bacon rub his chin. She resisted the urge to stare in Mr. Buchanan's direction as she expressed her disgust before the court.

"Is that all, Mrs. Wallace?" Judge Clarence Brown asked.

"Yes."

"Defendant?"

Mark half-rose. "I have nothing at this time, Your Honor."

Dominique wasn't surprised Mark was remaining quiet during the preliminary hearing. Most good defense lawyers did, and took plenty of notes to use against the prosecution during the grand jury. Her evidence this morning was solid, and there was no way he would be able to effectively debate it with a grand jury. She wondered how he was going to advise Mr. Buchanan behind closed doors.

"Mrs. Wallace, is there anything else?" Judge Clarence Bacon leaned back in his chair and studied Mark.

"Your Honor, I have two witnesses who I move to keep their identities withheld from the public for their safety. Our third witness, Maria Gonzales, was murdered prior to this hearing. So, our defense will be requesting that the identities of our two witnesses be withheld for their safety, Your Honor." Dominique was aware that it was Mr. Buchanan's constitutional right to know who was going to be testifying against him. But as a strategic gamble, Dominique and Shawn decided to withhold Katherine Buchanan's and Jaret Bell's testimony from the preliminary hearing. They were confident that Judge Clarence Brown would find sufficient proof with the medical records and videotapes to send the case on to the grand jury. And there they would reveal and subject both of their witnesses to the maliciousness of the witness stand and cross-examination.

Judge Clarence Brown stared at both Dominique and Shawn silently then glanced over at Michael Buchanan and his team before speaking. "Normally, I would require the identities of witnesses to be disclosed. However, I agree with Mrs. Wallace that I, too, am very concerned for the safety of the two remaining witnesses of this case. I will grant their identities to be withdrawn at this time."

Dominique glanced over at the defendant's table. Mark was smiling faintly back at her. There was something unusual about Mark's calmness. He was too calm, and she questioned what ammo he had up his sleeve that could possibly cripple her case.

"Now that I have heard all the evidence that will be presented before the court today, the court definitely finds sufficient evidence that a crime has been committed. I would like to set a date," Judge Clarence Brown announced. He leaned over to his assistant and whispered and proceeded to speak again after she answered. "I am setting a date for two weeks from today. I want to conclude this case as soon as possible. This type of case is very hard on parties. Therefore, a speedy case will be best preferred in order to review the evidence and come to a speedy and acceptable verdict."

"Great preliminary evidence," Mark complimented Dominique. "Thank goodness I have two weeks to prepare." Mark switched to his old arrogant demeanor. "You know I'm famous for finding one piece of evidence that wins the whole case. By the way, I hope you've taken the necessary steps to prevent another witness from not being able to testify for you. Haven't you? Especially since you didn't reveal their identity today," Mark taunted and laughed strangely.

Dominique stared back at Mark as if she was looking at the Devil himself.

"Well, you have two weeks to protect your witnesses or kiss your tired case goodbye." Mark walked off in the direction of the exit, his team and Mr. Buchanan following closely behind.

"What were you two talking about?" Shawn whispered in Dominique's ear.

Unsettled by Mark's cryptic remarks, she slowly turned around. "He joked about the safety of our witnesses. I have a bad feeling, Shawn. God, I pray nothing will happen to Katherine Buchanan."

"Don't worry, it won't." Shawn assured Dominique as they grabbed their briefcases and headed for the exit.

News reporters surrounded Dominique and Shawn as they stepped out into the noisy and crowded hall. After her unsettling briefing with Mark, she felt a need to make a quick statement for the press.

Reporter, microphones, and lights surrounded her. "Mrs. Wallace, how do you feel about your case, since the defense didn't interject once during the hearing?"

Immediately, it became difficult for her to breathe. Afraid of having a panic attack in front of the cameras, she quickly gave her statement.

"I feel very confident the prosecution will provide the court with all the necessary evidence needed to make the right decision. As you know, this is a very serious charge against Mr. Buchanan. The prosecution will also make a great effort to keep our witnesses safe from harm's way. If the court finds that our witnesses have been threatened or harmed in anyway, criminal charges will be brought against them. That is all that I have to say for now. Thank you."

Dominique pushed her way through the crowd and gasped for breath. She prayed she wouldn't have another panic attack, discrediting herself single-handedly.

"Mrs. Wallace, is it true Michael Buchanan's wife is now one of your witness?" reporter one asked.

"We noticed she wasn't present today for the preliminary hearing this morning," reporter two observed.

"Was she absent because she's afraid someone's going to try to attack her like they did you?" a third reporter asked.

"Is it also true Mr. Buchanan had something to do with your attack?"

"Has your psychiatrist recommended you step down from representing this case due to your inability to handle stress?"

Reporter after reporter fired questions at her as she continued to force her way through the crowd, trying desperately to hold it together.

"I have no more comments." Dominique repeated until she made it safely into her office.

"Good going, Dominique!" Shawn Silver cheered as he watched Dominique walk around her desk to sit down. "I think you were smart to announce something about our witness protection. If anything happens to them, the media will automatically think Michael Buchanan has something to do with it."

Dominique sat down at her desk gasping for air, completely ignoring Shawn while her legal partner stood in the middle of the office floor, grinning like a Cheshire cat.

"Dominique, are you okay?" He asked noticing how she looked a little flushed as she struggled to catch her breath.

"Yes, but I'm really concerned about Mrs. Buchanan's and Mr. Bell's safety. I don't want to take a chance that Mr. Buchanan can do anything to harm them. I think Mark was trying to send me a message, and I have no intention of ignoring it." She was calmer now.

"Don't worry, I'll take care of everything. I can guarantee their safety long enough to stand trial." Shawn's eyes shone with confidence.

"I hope so. I'm going to the hospital to visit with Kimberly."

"Listen to all the people in the hallway. Don't you get a rush?" Shawn said, growing excited from all the noise.

"I can't say I do. I have too much on my plate to be excited about the media right now. Maybe after all this is over, I'll reflect and enjoy, but for now I have to stay focused and win this case." She felt very much in control of the situation.

"Well, I need to go and secure our witnesses. I'll call you later." Shawn disappeared into the noisy hall.

Dominique waited until the noise and crowd of people emptied the hallways, allowing her to slip out to her car without being harassed with more questions. She drove straight to the hospital, sat by Kimberly's bedside, and watched her sleeping peacefully. She wondered if Kimberly was able to hear anything while she lay in her comatose state.

Dominique took her hands and gently rubbed her forehead. Her skin felt smooth under Dominique's hand, like that of her own daughter. How fragile and precious they were—naïve and vulnerable to the ways of the world as they extended their unconditional love.

"Kimberly, it's me, Dominique. I'm not sure if you can hear me, but if you can, I really want you to listen. I have something very important to tell you. I received a call from someone who is willing to testify against your father and confirm everything you have said to be true." Dominique continued to rub her forehead gently. "Kimberly, I hope you can hear me, because that person willing to testify on your behalf is your mother. Your mother called me and told me she can't allow another day to pass knowing that you have been suffering because of her silence. She feels extremely sorry, Kimberly. She really does. And all she wants now is for the two of you to be together and start over because she really loves you," Dominique noticed a tear roll from Kimberly's eye.

"Kimberly, can you hear me?" Dominique wiped the tear from Kimberly's face. Excited, she ran out into the hallway to share the good news.

"What happened?" The nurse asked Dominique as she rushed into Kimberly's room and checked her vitals.

"I believe she heard me talking to her. I saw a tear. Isn't that a good sign?"

"Yes. Let me notify Kimberly's doctor. Let's pray you have said something causing her to fight back." The nurse paged Kimberly's doctor.

"I hope so too." Dominique turned her attention back to Kimberly. "I know you can hear me now. Please fight for me."

"Good afternoon. How is she doing?" The doctor asked as he entered the room.

The nurse replied, "She's still in a coma, but Mrs. Wallace noticed Kimberly showed some sign of emotion when she was talking to her."

"Good. What were you telling her?"

"Some great news pertaining to her case."

"I do see a change in her monitor readings. I would highly recommend those permitted to visit her to come and try to talk to her. Obviously, she can hear us. I always recommend that family and friends talk with coma patients. Many are able to reach them."

"I only want those individuals whose names are on the list to be permitted to visit her. Mrs. Buchanan has been added to the list, but she's only able to communicate with Kimberly by telephone."

"Just inform the nurse station that Mrs. Buchanan will be allowed to speak with Kimberly by telephone only." The doctor closed the chart. "I need to finish making my rounds, but I'll come back to check on her later."

CHAPTER 24

Dominique drove home excited, knowing Kimberly may have responded to her during her visit. And if she was lucky, she would be out of her coma before the grand jury. Trying to be optimistic, she ignored her gut, which was telling her to prepare for the worst. So Dominique turned up her jazz music and absorbed the soothing melodies as she blocked out any thoughts related to the Buchanan's.

By the time she drove into her driveway, she'd decided to spend the remainder of the evening with Devin, who was playing with her dolls on the floor.

"Devin, what would you like to do this evening?" she asked as Devin leaped into her arms to greet her for the afternoon.

"Can we go to the movies?" Devin screamed with excitement.

A movie sound great, but Dominique wasn't sure if was a good idea under the present circumstances, with Michael Buchanan lurking around and making deadly threats.

"Sweetheart is there anything else you would like to do?"

"No. I want to see that new movie, Mommy. You promised me you would take me." Devin started to whine.

Before Dominique could respond, it started to pour down rain.

"Mommy, I don't want to get wet," Devin said as her face frowned up.

"Good, because I don't either. Let's order a movie on pay-per-view and a pizza," Dominique recommended, relieved of the thought of having to chance going out with Devin.

"I'm going to get my dolls so they can watch the movie with us," Devin suggested and ran off to her room to get her friends.

Dominique walked into the kitchen to put away the wonderful casserole dinner Ms. Anderson prepared for them. Her stomach started to growl as the aroma filled her nose; She wished she hadn't agreed to pizza, but she knew Devin's little heart was set on having pizza for dinner now. She had just placed the last of their dinner away when she heard someone knock at her sunroom door.

She peeked cautiously around the corner into her sunroom to see who was knocking at her door in this weather. A big smile appeared on her face when she recognized her young friend Shawn, standing with his face pressed against the glass window and water running down his face and body, waiting for her to let him in. Excited to see him, she rushed across the room and opened the door for him to enter.

"How are you doing?" Dominique asked, excited to see him.

Shawn didn't respond. Instead he wrapped his arms around her and burst into tears.

"Shawn what's wrong?" Dominique asked as she held Shawn tightly in her arms.

"I hate him, Dominique! I don't know how much longer I can take living in my house!" Shawn screamed as he sobbed helplessly in her arms.

"Calm down. Did your father hurt you and your sister again?" Dominique asked as she rubbed his back to comfort him.

"He's always hurting one of us. I hate him! I hate him!" Shawn continued to scream out loud.

Dominique pulled Shawn's body away from hers so she could see his face. "Calm down. Stay here tonight. Eric's gone out of town."

"Dominique, I don't ever want to go back, but if I don't, there won't be anybody there to protect my sister. I'm all she has, and I can't even protect myself from him," he said, wiping his tears away.

"Try not to think about your father right now. I have a good idea."

"Are you going to help me kill my father?" he asked with a serious look on his face.

Killing his father wasn't what she had in mind—more like a simple PG-13 movie.

"Shawn, I can't help you kill your father. I don't want you to think or talk about killing him, either. You would go to jail, and who would be there for your sister and mother?"

"I know, but you have no idea what I'm going through," he said, exhausted.

"Believe me, I can relate."

"Your father didn't force you to have sex with him?"

"Shawn, I never knew my father, so as far as I know, he might have. I know how it feels to be in a family without cuddling and love. But I'm certain it will get better," she tried to assure him.

"I don't think so. Killing him is all I've thought about the last few days. I almost killed him the other night, but my sister walked in."

"Shawn, don't talk like that!" Dominique demanded, afraid things had gotten out of control. She could tell from the sound of his voice that he wasn't joking. Mentally, he was in a dangerous place, and if he didn't calm down, he just might kill his father.

"Mommy where are you?" Devin yelled from the foyer area, interrupting the crisis.

"I'm coming. Wait for me in the family room," she yelled back, not knowing what to do now. She needed to talk to Shawn before he did something he would regret for the rest of his life.

"What are you guys doing?" Shawn asked with a sad look on his face.

"I promised Devin I would order a movie and pizza tonight," Dominique answered.

"What movie are you going to order?"

"I'm not sure. I'm going to let Devin pick something out. I want you to relax and watch the movie with Devin and me." She led him into the family room.

"Devin, do you remember Shawn? He played tea party with us the other night," she reminded her.

"Yes." Devin answered, looking unhappy.

"I've invited him to spend the evening with us."

"I thought it was going to be just you and me," Devin said, pouting and making it obvious she wasn't pleased with the idea of Shawn joining them this evening.

"I know, but I think Shawn could use our company this evening."

"I don't have to stay if she doesn't want me to," Shawn whispered to Dominique. He shrugged his shoulders, feeling out of place.

"No, I don't want you to go. Devin, I want you to stop being selfish. I'm still going to order your movie and pizza."

"I want to pick out the movie," Devin demanded, trying to remind everyone the evening was still going to be about her.

"Fine. We can see whatever you want," Dominique said, relieved Devin hadn't put up a big fuss and deterred Shawn from joining them.

But Devin made it clear she wasn't going to entertain Shawn because she remained silent the whole evening. And Dominique tried her best not to allow Devin's selfish attitude spoil her time with Shawn. She wondered what she was thinking. She was surprised Devin wasn't okay with him watching the movie and eating pizza with them, especially after he played tea party and they had such a great time together the other night.

"Devin, thank you for being a big girl and allowing Shawn to share your mother with you this evening," Dominique whispered to Devin when Shawn got up to go upstairs for bed.

"Is he going to live with us now?" Devin asked, with an uneasy look on her face.

"No, but occasionally I might allow him to spend the night."

"Does Daddy know Shawn spending the night with us?" Devin asked.

"I haven't talked to him about it yet, but when he gets home, I will see what he thinks. For now, I need for you to make him feel like a part of our family. Can I count on you to help me with that?" Dominique was kneeling so they would be on eye level with one another.

"I'll try," Devin answered. She grabbed her baby dolls and ran to her room to prepare for bed.

Dominique cleaned up the pizza dinner and headed upstairs to tuck everyone in for bed. She rushed to her bedroom when she heard her phone ringing.

"Hello," Dominique answered.

It was Eric calling to check in. "Hello, I didn't wake you?" Eric asked.

"No. How did your meeting go today?" Dominique asked while she changed out of her clothes into a nightgown.

"The meeting was long as usual. Ron and I went to get a drink afterward. That's why I'm calling you so late."

"That's okay."

"Is Devin sleep?" Eric asked.

"Yes. We ordered a movie and had pizza for dinner." She left out the part about Shawn joining them.

"Cool!" Eric responded.

Dominique jumped when she heard her phone beep. She wondered who was calling her this time of night. The clock read ten thirty p.m. She prayed Mr. Buchanan wasn't trying to call her with any more threats.

"Eric, hold on for a moment. The phone is beeping." She clicked over to answer the call.

"Hello." Dominique answered apprehensively.

"Hello. May I speak with Mrs. Dominique Wallace?" A female voice asked on the other end of the phone.

"Yes, this is Mrs. Wallace. Who is this?"

"This is Yvonne Saunders. I'm a nurse at the hospital. I was instructed to call you if there were any changes with Ms. Kimberly Buchanan."

"Yes. Is there a problem?" Dominique sat up in her bed.

"Actually, Ms. Buchanan is doing much better. She's come out of her coma. If you can reach her mother, please inform her of her daughter's condition."

"Thank you, God!" Dominique said out loud. "Thanks for calling. I will get in contact with Mrs. Buchanan right away." She clicked over to tell Eric the great news.

She called Mrs. Buchanan's number as soon as she hung up with Eric. She prayed the good news would give her a new sense of strength as she waited to testify against her husband in court. Dominique allowed the phone to ring several times before she called her security to have them check on her.

Dominique waited on the other end of the line while Roger, one of Mrs. Buchanan's security guards, checked her condition.

"Mrs. Wallace, Mrs. Buchanan is not responding." Roger said. "I think she tried to OD. There are pills all over her nightstand. I need to get her some help,"

"Is she still breathing?" Dominique shouted, sitting on the edge of her bed and paralyzed by the information.

"I can't tell. If she is, it's really faint."

She couldn't believe what she was hearing. Mrs. Buchanan tried to OD, and now she was on her way to the hospital. Dominique started to shake as an unnerving cold chill surged through her. Her heart raced, and her breathing became difficult.

Her telephone fell to the floor, and her bedroom started to spin around. She grabbed onto the side of her bed and held on to it as if her life depended on it. Slowly, she slid to the floor. How did she allow this to happen? She should have seen this coming. She knew Mrs. Buchanan was upset. What was she going to do if she ODed?

Dominique pulled herself together when the dial tone from the phone jolted her from her daze. Dominique looked up. Shawn was standing above her with a scared look on his face. Before she could speak, he ran out of her bedroom. She dropped her head and took a deep breath. Slowly, she stood to her feet. She called Shawn Silver's phone but it went to voice mail. She prayed he would call her back while pacing back and forth in her bedroom, not knowing what to do.

Almost an hour had passed before Roger called her with an update about Mrs. Buchanan. He informed her that Mrs. Buchanan was admitted to the ICU. Her condition was critical. Dominique's stomach started cramping. She felt herself becoming nauseous at the thought that Mr. Buchanan was able to reach Mrs. Buchanan with all the security around her. She knew now his influence and power were truly real.

She walked over to her window and looked out at the car sitting in front of her house and wondered who they were really working for. She had no way of knowing, and she felt vulnerable. She badly wanted to call Eric, but she was afraid to. All she wanted was for him to come home safe and sound. Dominique sat down on the edge of bed, regretting her decision to remain on the case.

"Dominique," Shawn whispered from the doorway of her bedroom.

"Yes," she answered, preoccupied with what to do next.

"Can I come in?"

"Sure. What's on your mind?" she asked, making a space on the edge of her bed for him to sit. Shawn's eyes were teary as he sat down beside her.

"Shawn what's wrong?" Dominique asked, wrapping her arms around his shoulder.

"I'm afraid I'm going to lose you," he said softly.

"You're not going to lose me," she assured him.

"You're all I have right now. If I lose you, I won't have anyone," he said, allowing his tears to stream down his face freely.

"Shawn, where is this coming from?" Dominique asked.

"I'm afraid Eric is going to put you away. And if he does, we will never see each other again. I don't want to lose you like I've lost my mother."

"Shawn, Eric is not going to put me away. There's no reason why he should. I'm fine, so don't you worry about a thing. I'm sorry you found me the way you did. But I assure you, I'm not going crazy." She said as she gave him a kiss on the forehead.

"You promise?" he asked, needing reassurance.

"I promise," she said, smiling back at Shawn. "It's late. You better go to bed so you can get up tomorrow."

"I know. I think you need some rest, too."

"I agree. I will in a few minutes. I'm waiting for an important call." She leaned over to kiss him goodnight. Without another word, Shawn left the room and went to his room to go to sleep. Dominique went down to her office to get her briefcase. She opened it, pulled out the letter Shawn had written her, read it several times, and laid it down on her desk.

What was she going to do? Now he was worried she was going to abandon him like his mother had. The last thing she wanted to do was scare him off when he needed her the most. Dominique held his letter close to her heart and burst helplessly into tears.

CHAPTER 25

"Mommy," Devin whispered in her mother's ears as she shook her limp body resting on her desk.

"Good morning," Dominique answered, forcing her eyes open to acknowledge her daughter hanging off the side of her desk chair.

"Mommy, why didn't you sleep in your bed?"

"I accidentally fell asleep," she answered. She glanced over at her clock to see what time it was. It was eight thirty in the morning. "How long have you been up?"

"I just got up. I'm hungry, Mommy." Devin jumped into her mother's arms.

"What do you want to eat this morning?"

"I want some pancakes."

"Let me wash my face first. I'll meet you in the kitchen." Dominique lowered her back to the ground and stood to her feet.

"Can I help you make the pancakes, Mommy?"

"Sure. I'll let you help me stir up the mix."

"Hurry up, Mommy. I'm really hungry." Devin ran into the kitchen to wait for her.

Dominique ran upstairs to wash her face and brush her teeth. She stared at her reflection in the mirror, and was frightened by the dark bags under her eyes. She felt exhausted and looked it. She rushed over to her phone to call Shawn Silver. Still he didn't answer. She called Rogers, who informed her that Mrs. Buchanan's condition had not changed: still critical.

She felt anxious, but she couldn't do anything about it now. Devin was up. She was going to have to figure out what her next step was going to be. She was running on fumes and would have to make do with the little rest she did manage to get. She pulled her hair back and headed back downstairs to make her famous pancakes for Devin.

"Good morning," Shawn greeted her as she entered the kitchen.

"Good morning," Dominique replied, having forgotten that Shawn had spent the night with them last night.

"Mommy, I'm hungry." Devin interrupted.

"I know. Let me get everything out so we can start. Shawn, Devin has requested pancakes this morning. Would you like some, too?" Dominique asked as she moved around the kitchen, pulling out all the ingredients and tools.

"Yes. Make my pancakes larger," Shawn requested.

Dominique placed the bowl of batter in front of Devin to mix. Then she poured the batter into the pan and made five very large pancakes for them to eat. She gave Devin one and hoped she would finish it all. Then she placed two pancakes on Shawn's plate for him to eat, and the remainder on her plate and ate up.

"Shawn, you need to get going before your principal calls your home. I don't want you to get in trouble because I allowed you to oversleep this morning."

"Don't worry. School ended last week. I'm on summer vacation right now. What are you going to do today?" Shawn asked.

"I have to run some errands this morning. Why?" Dominique asked.

"I just wanted to know. I'll wait for you here—if you don't mind?" Shawn asked Dominique.

"Okay. Before I leave, both of you need to take a bath," Dominique joked and ordered both of them upstairs after they finished their breakfast. Dominique ran Devin's water in her bathroom while Shawn took a bath in the guest bathroom. After everyone finished bathing for the morning, she decided to take Devin with her to the hospital. Ms. Anderson wasn't going to be able to come over until after lunch because of her doctor's appointment scheduled months ago. Dominique thought it would be best if Shawn waited at home for them.

Dominique noticed Devin staring at all the filled beds lined up against the hallways, with moaning sick patients that occupied them.

"Mommy, I don't like it here." Devin whispered to her mother as she gripped her hand tighter.

"I don't either."

"Who are we going to see?"

"My client. She's been very sick, and I need to see how she's doing now."

"If you get sick again, will you have to come here?"

"Let's hope not."

Dominique knocked on Kimberly's door.

"Who is it?" Kimberly called from her bed.

"Good morning, Kimberly." Dominique greeted Kimberly with Devin by her side as she entered her room.

"Good morning, Mrs. Wallace." Kimberly replied in a weak tone but with a big smile.

"How are you feeling this morning?" Dominique asked.

"Okay, I guess." Kimberly answered.

Dominique walked around the bed and gave Kimberly a big hug. "I want to introduce you to my daughter, Devin," she said as she rubbed Kimberly's shoulder.

"Hello, Devin," Kimberly responded. She tried to sit up and get a good look at Devin's little face peeking around her mother's side.

"Hello." Devin answered shyly.

Kimberly turned her attention back to Dominique. "Is it true my mother is going to testify against my father?"

Dominique's stomach started to cramp again. She hadn't planned on telling Kimberly about her mother's condition yet. Her visit this morning was supposed to be causal, not about business.

"Yes," she answered, forcing a smile.

"You're kidding. I bet she's only doing it to piss him off because she caught him cheating on her again. So, this is her way of getting back at him. I'm sure she doesn't care anything about me." She laid back against her pillows for support.

"No. Your mother decided to testify against your father because she thought it was about time for her to be there for you. She feels guilty about not saying anything until now. She wants the two of you to start over, Kimberly. She really loves you." Dominique hoped these words would change her feelings about her mother.

"I don't believe that." Kimberly said and glanced out of the window.

"But I believe she really does love you. Your mother has been deeply worried about you, anxious for you to get better."

"If she's so worried, why hasn't she come down here to visit me?" Kimberly asked, staring back at Dominique.

Dominique bit her bottom lip. There was no way she could cover her mother's hiding from her. "Kimberly, I have some bad news," she said slowly. She dreaded telling Kimberly the awful news and prayed it wouldn't send her back into a coma. "Your mother is in the hospital right now. She had an accident last night."

"What kind of accident?" Kimberly struggled to sit up in her bed.

Dominique regretted bringing Devin with her now. She was afraid she was going to witness Kimberly become emotional, and she was definitely too young to be exposed to the Buchanan's dysfunction.

"Kimberly, I don't want to upset you with the details," She tried desperately to avoid a scene in front of Devin.

"Mrs. Wallace, I want to know what kind of accident my mother had!" Kimberly demanded. "Has she tried to kill herself again?"

She didn't know whether to tell her she tried or her father had tried. Right now, Dominique didn't know which scenario was the truth. All she knew was Mrs. Buchanan had tried to OD, and she was still waiting to hear something about her condition.

"Your mother tried to OD," Dominique said remorsefully.

"Do you think she's going to make it?" she asked.

"I don't know."

Kimberly looked away again and started to cry. Dominique caressed her shoulder for comfort.

"My father is responsible, and you know it," Kimberly asserted, staring Dominique straight in the eyes.

"Kimberly, I would prefer not to discuss this in front of my daughter." Dominique finally admitted.

"This is my mother we're talking about," Kimberly snapped.

"I know, but I don't have any proof yet."

"And you won't ever," she responded, resenting her father's power. "I've watched my father destroy both of our lives. He destroyed my mother a long time ago. He cheated on her and stripped away all her self-esteem. At first I thought she deserved whatever he did to her. I felt that was her

218

punishment for not being there for me." Kimberly started to cry. "Together they robbed me of everything."

"Your mother wants to reach out to you and make amends. And I want you to at least give her a chance."

"I don't know if I can."

"If you can't do it for yourself, at least do it for me. Do it because I didn't get that chance." Dominique pleaded.

"It's not that easy."

"Yes, it can be. You have your mother, who truly wants you in her life now. Kimberly, you owe it to yourself and your mother."

"What's going to happen to me if she doesn't make it this time?" she asked, terrified of losing her mother.

"Well, let's pray she will."

"I will."

Dominique leaned over and gave Kimberly a kiss on her forehead. "That's more like it. I don't want to hear you talking negatively anymore. I want you to think and act positively. I'm going to expect good things out of you, Kimberly."

Dominique looked down at her watch and realized it was getting late and she needed to drop Devin off at home so Ms. Anderson could watch her while she attended her session with Dr. Martin this afternoon.

By the time Dominique reached her house, she realized she forgot to tell Shawn that Ms. Anderson was going to be coming to the house. But if Shawn was consistent with himself, he would have managed to leave without her seeing him. She chuckled to herself as she parked the car and helped Devin out and into the house.

Dominique called from the front door. "Ms. Anderson, I'm dropping Devin off. I have an appointment with Dr. Martin."

"Okay. I'm upstairs changing everybody's sheets. Devin, come up here with me."

Devin ran upstairs to join Ms. Anderson.

"When you arrived, was anybody here?" Dominique asked Ms. Anderson.

"No. Were you expecting someone?" she asked from the top of the staircase.

"No one in particular." As she figured, Shawn ran away again when he realized Ms. Anderson wasn't her.

"I'll be back in about two hours," she said and left for Dr. Martin's office.

All the way over, she peeked in her rearview mirror, wondering who was following her today and whether they were really trying to protect her or were they waiting for the perfect opportunity to knock her off, too. By the time, she reached Dr. Martin's office, she was completely paranoid. She grabbed her pocketbook and rushed inside his office.

She signed in at the front desk and waited for Dr. Martin to usher her back to his office. While waiting for her turn, she tuned into a vacation commercial, advertising a beautiful and relaxing stay on a romantic island. A vacation away from all of this sounded great to Dominique. Falling further in love with the idea of getting away, she wrote down the number on the screen and committed to calling it later, when Kimberly's case was over.

"Are you thinking about taking a trip?" Dr. Martin asked, seeing her write down the number to the vacation getaway.

"Yes. I could really use the vacation now, but I have so much work to do." Dominique stood and followed Dr. Martin to his office.

"Are you referring to the Buchanan case?" he asked as he shut the door behind them and sat down across from her.

"Yes. I can't wait until this whole case is over." Dominique said as she rotated her head in a circle to help relax her neck muscles.

"So, you decided to stay on the case?" Dr. Martin asked.

"Yes." She felt like a little child after being told not to do something.

"How did you come to that decision since the last time we spoke?" Dr. Martin asked as he wrote something down on his notepad.

"It was a hard decision to make, I assure you. Last night I started to question my decision again when I found out Mrs. Buchanan tried to OD. But after visiting with Kimberly again this morning, I started to feel again that I'd made the right decision."

Dominique allowed her body to fall back into the comfortable cushions of Dr. Martin's couch.

"Even at the risk of endangering your own family?"

"Dr. Martin, I've prayed about my decision. I've already asked God to support me during this case because I truly believe I'm doing the right thing by trying to convict Mr. Buchanan."

"So you will be able to forgive yourself if anything happens to your family because you decided to handle this case, knowing the possible danger?"

"No, I will never be able to forgive myself if something happens to my family, but I have to have faith that God will protect them because I'm trying to protect one of his children, too."

Dominique was preaching back at Dr. Martin. She believed God was the only being that could help her now, and if Mr. Buchanan was able to defeat God, then there was no hope for her regardless of her decision. She felt the fear of uncertainty creeping in.

Dr. Martin changed the subject. "So, have you been able to introduce your husband to your young friend Shawn yet?" Dr. Martin asked.

"No, I haven't had an opportunity yet."

"Have you seen him again since our last visit?" Dr. Martin asked.

"Yes I have. Yesterday he showed up very upset with his father. He didn't say for what, but I had a pretty good idea why, knowing what his father has been doing to him and his sister."

"Why did he come to your house?"

"He says he feels safe with me," she said softly. A comforting smile appeared on her face.

"How do you know?" Dr. Martin asked.

"He told me so," she said, allowing her thought to drift to the letter he wrote her. "He wrote me a beautiful letter the other day, telling me how much he cared about me."

"Do you think he might allow you to help him and his sister now that he's starting to trust you?"

"I hope so. I didn't say anything about it last night. I just wanted him to feel safe and enjoy the evening with Devin and me while Eric was away."

"So you allowed him to spend the night again because Eric was out of town?"

"I did. I shouldn't have because I didn't get permission from his family, but if you could have seen how upset he was, you would have allowed him, too."

She didn't regret her decision to allow Shawn to spend the night, and she would allow him whenever she could until he was safe and sound. At least when he was with her, she knew he was safe from his father's abuse.

"Why do you continue to allow this young boy to manipulate you so?" Dr. Martin asked causally.

Dominique didn't feel like Shawn was manipulating her at all. She felt very much in control of their relationship. "Shawn's not manipulating me, Dr. Martin. I made the decision to let him spend the night. He hasn't twisted my arm."

"Why haven't you allowed him to spend the night when Eric is home?"

"Normally, Shawn doesn't come around when Eric is around. So, the opportunity hasn't presented itself." She said this, knowing full well that Eric probably wouldn't have allowed any overnights without permission from his parents. And she knew he would have to speak with them personally before believing anything Shawn might have told him.

"How does he know when Eric is home or not?" Dr. Martin asked.

"I don't know. Maybe he checks my driveway for Eric's car."

"So you think he might be watching your house?"

"I don't know."

"Have you been able to find any information about his last name or address?"

"No."

"Have you asked him if he would be willing to come speak with me?"

"No, but I will."

Dr. Martin wrote down a few more notes in his notepad. "I would like to change the subject back to your case again. Is there anything that has happen recently regarding the case that you would like to talk about?"

"Yes. Last night, Mrs. Katherine Buchanan was rushed to the hospital. I'm not sure whether Mr. Buchanan had something to do with it, but she tried to OD on some pills."

"I thought you said she was placed in protective custody."

"She was. I'm sure she brought them with her. I still don't know how she is doing."

"Do you think her husband has something to do with it?"

"Yes, I do, but I can't prove it. Mr. Buchanan has a lot of connections. Now I'm not sure how secure Mrs. Buchanan's security was, nor the security that's been following me."

"Why do you think that?"

"After Mr. Buchanan came into my house and threatened me, I'm not sure about anything—especially now that Mrs. Buchanan has tried to OD. I pray I can keep her alive long enough to convict her husband."

"Dominique, do you think it's safe for you to be driving around alone?"

"I know I need to be careful. I do have someone following me. I pray I will be safe."

"I think you need to go straight home from here and think carefully about your safety while you are working on this case."

"I promise, but while I'm here I want to finish my session with you," she said, looking helpless.

"Very well. I've been thinking about our last few sessions. Your unexplainable attacks gravely concern me. I know you are under a lot of stress because of this case, but I'm not certain whether your attacks are stemming from this case only. I'm starting to wonder if there is something else causing them. I've been seeing you for several years now, and I know very little about your past, besides the fact you grew up in the foster care system. I'm curious to know more about your experiences at each foster care family."

"I don't want you to start running through this now. I want you to go home and start writing down some of your experiences in a journal so we can begin discussing them during our future sessions together."

She didn't know what her past would have to do with anything, but she was willing to try anything if it would stop her from having attacks. "Okay," she said in agreement.

"Good. Do you have anything else you would like to discuss before we conclude today?"

"No," she replied and slid to the edge of the couch.

"Start on your journals right away. Be as detailed as you can be." Dr. Martin walked Dominique back out to the waiting room.

Dominique drove straight home, thinking about the assignment. Having to recall all her unpleasant foster care experiences didn't appeal to her, but Dr. Martin had good reasons for her to do this exercise, and she was going to comply.

When she arrived home, she told Ms. Anderson she could go home early. She thought it would be a great opportunity for her to spend some time alone with Devin. They played in her sandbox, on her swing set, and they even played tea party for a while before it was time for Devin to turn in for the night.

Dominique bathed Devin, gave her a big kiss, and tucked her in for the night. Afterward, she decided to drink a glass of wine and take a nice warm bath to help her unwind for the evening. After her bath, she went back downstairs to make herself another drink—and heard a knock come from her sunroom.

Cautiously, she made her way to the kitchen and peeked around the corner into her sunroom, praying desperately that no harm was about to come to her or Devin. It was her young friend Shawn standing outside.

"Shawn, where did you go today?" Dominique asked.

"I needed some time to think alone," Shawn said, giving her a half smile.

"Is there something wrong?" she asked, worried.

"I know I'm not supposed to be discussing Kimberly's case with you, but I have a really bad feeling about you handling it. I think her case is going to destroy your life."

"I don't think so. Yes, it's causing me a lot of stress, but as soon as it's over, I'm going to take some time off." She was trying to hide the fact she agreed with him.

"So, what are your plans after the case?" he asked, looking anxious.

"I'm going to spend a lot of time with my family and will take it easy for a while."

"Is that all?"

"Yes. What do *you* think I should do?" Dominique asked, chuckling softly. She couldn't imagine anything she wanted to do more than be with her family and relax.

"What about me? You didn't mention anything about spending time with me."

"You know I love to spend time with you. I'm looking forward to taking you and Devin to the museums, parks, and movies. We are going to have so much fun together. I can't wait. You just wait and see."

Shawn searched Dominique's face, trying to measure the truth of their future together. "It didn't sound that way at first. You just said you were planning on spending a lot of time with your family and taking it easy. You said nothing about me. Nothing!" Shawn shouted back at Dominique.

She wondered where his ambiguity was coming from. "Shawn what is wrong with you?" she asked.

"I can see it happening already. You're not going to have any time for me. You're going to be spending time with everybody else and forget about me. Everybody I ever love is always taken from me. I don't know why I thought that it would be different with you," Shawn said, raising his voice again.

"Shawn, no. I plan on spending time with you, too," she reassured.

"Sure, I don't want you spending time with me because you think I'm a charity case."

"I don't think of you as a charity case. What your father is doing to you and your sister is no reason for you to be ashamed. It's not your fault. You didn't ask your father to abuse you."

"I know, but I don't want you to see me as different. I noticed after I told you everything, you started treating me differently. Dominique, I don't want you feeling sorry for me."

"I don't. Whether you believe it or not, you mean a lot to me."

"Have you heard anything about Mrs. Buchanan, yet?" Shawn asked, changing the subject.

"No."

"I hope she will be okay."

"I hope so too."

Shawn plopped down on the couch and smiled back at Dominique. "Dominique, can I stay with you tonight? Eric's not here."

Dominique's thoughts drifted immediately to her session with Dr. Martin, when he questioned how Shawn knew when Eric was around. "How do you know that?" Dominique asked.

"He's never here."

"Shawn, are you spying on me?" Dominique asked as she placed her hands on her hips.

"I'm not spying on you. I'm just afraid Mr. Buchanan is going to try to hurt you again. I don't think it's safe for you and Devin to be here alone without a man in the house, especially with that crazy Buchanan guy on the loose out there. You need protection." Tears rolled down Shawn's face.

"Shawn, where is all this coming from?" Dominique asked as she embraced him in her arms.

"I don't know what I will do if I can't be with you." Shawn said wearily. "I wasn't going to say anything, but why was Dr. Martin asking you questions about having an attack in your bathroom?"

"What are you talking about?" Dominique asked as she released Shawn.

"I don't want you to think I was trying to eavesdrop on your conversation. I just happen to be in the bushes that day Dr. Martin stopped by to see you. I remember him asking you something about another attack you had in your bathroom?"

"Why do you ask?"

"Have you always had attacks?"

"No."

"When did they start?"

"They just started recently. They're not a big deal."

"They *are* a big deal," Shawn insisted.

"No, they're not."

"Yes, they are."

Dominique shrugged her shoulders. She wasn't intentionally trying to ignore her body. She just had a lot going on with this case. Afterward, she would rest. "I don't know. Sometimes we don't listen as well as we should to our bodies."

"Dominique, my mother didn't listen to her body and went crazy. If you don't be careful, you will go crazy, too." Tears started rolling down Shawn's face, which he quickly wiped away.

"Shawn, I'm fine." Dominique gave him a big hug and held him for a while before letting him go. "I want you to go upstairs and go to sleep."

Silently, they headed upstairs to the guest bedroom. Dominique waited outside while Shawn got in bed. She entered and tucked him in. "Shawn, I will always be here for you. Please don't forget that." She leaned over to kiss him on the forehead.

"You promise?" he asked, snuggled comfortably under the sheets.

"Yes." Dominique answered and said good night to Shawn.

CHAPTER 26

Half asleep, Dominique answered the telephone so Eric could inform her that he would be returning later that evening. When he arrived, she prepared a wonderful meal for them. Afterward, they retired to the family room to relax and enjoy each other's company.

"Dominique, I've made plans for us for tomorrow night." Eric shared.

"What type of plans?" she asked excitedly.

"I'm going to keep it a surprise. But I will tell you this: It's going to require you to wear something formal. I've already planned everything out," he said eagerly.

"Have you? I can't wait to see what it is. What would you like for me to wear?" Dominique asked, smiling.

"For starters, I would like for you to get out of what you have on now and wear your birthday suit." Eric leaned over and kissed Dominique on the lips. He pulled her body closer to his and let his hand explore her body. Dominique felt a cold, chilling feeling go over her body. Eric's touches were normally pleasing to her, but tonight she couldn't enjoy them. She felt like she was being violated. Her body started to shake, and she pulled away.

"What's wrong?" Eric asked, perplexed.

"I don't know. I'm just not in the mood right now. I'm sorry." Dominique raced upstairs to their bedroom to be alone.

Eric was confused now, and wondered if her behavior was due to the attack. If so, he was sorry and would be patient. He didn't mean to upset her. Eric got up and went upstairs to find out what was wrong. Their bedroom door was closed, so he quietly opened it, entered, and closed it behind him. He saw Dominique on the bed with her back to the door. He wanted to apologize and comfort her. How could he have been so thoughtless and insensitive?

"Dominique, I'm sorry." Eric walked around the bed to her side. Dominique was crying, and this made him feel especially bad. "Please don't cry."

"I don't know why I reacted the way I did," she said, still emotional about what just happened.

"I'm sorry for not being more sensitive about your feelings. Don't worry about it. Get some rest." Eric said. He wanted to touch her, but he was afraid that he might upset her even more. So he watched Dominique fall asleep without saying another word.

The next morning, Dominique looked over at Eric still sleeping. She didn't disturb him, but he woke up as she started to get out of the bed.

"Good morning," he said, still half asleep.

"Good morning to you."

"Where are you going?" Eric was wiping his eyes.

"I'm going to make you and Devin some breakfast this morning."

"Would you like some help?"

"No. I can manage." She got dressed to go downstairs and started breakfast.

After breakfast, Eric said he needed to run some errands this morning, and he would be back later that afternoon. She kissed him off and went outside. While Devin played, Dominique would work on the new assignment Dr. Martin had given her.

"Good morning," called a soft voice from her bushes.

She immediately turned to greet the familiar voice. "Good morning."

"What are you doing?" Shawn asked.

"Making a journal." She closed her notebook.

"Can I see what you are writing?"

"No. It's private." She picked her notebook up from the table and held it close to her chest.

"Were you writing about me?" Shawn wore a childish smile.

"No!"

"So can I just hang out with you today?" Shawn sat down across from her.

"I don't mind. What do you want to do?"

"Nothing, really." Shawn rocked side to side playfully.

Dominique thought for a second or two about what they could do together. They already worked in the garden, and now it looked beautiful. Maybe they could play a board game. "You want to play Scrabble?" Dominique asked.

"Sure," he said, smiling. Dominique went into the house to get her Scrabble game, returned, and set everything up. As they played, Dominique became amused by Shawn's vocabulary. He used words that she didn't know herself at his age. She was also surprised by how competitive he was while they played.

As they continued to play, she heard Eric calling her name from the house. This would be the perfect chance for Eric to meet Shawn for the first time. If Eric saw him, he would have to allow her to introduce him.

"Shawn, I want to introduce you to my husband, Eric." she said.

"No. I don't want to meet him. I told you that. Besides, I don't trust him." Shawn's voice was defensive.

Dominique didn't understand why he still wouldn't allow her to at least introduce him to her husband. Eric was harmless. "Eric's my husband. He won't do anything to harm you. I know you can trust him because I trust him with my life." Dominique *did* trust Eric with her life and was sure he would do whatever he could to protect her or Devin.

"He doesn't know me and has no reason to want to protect me," Shawn responded defensively.

"Shawn, please. I know how you feel. It took me a long time before I started to trust anyone after everything I went through growing up. Eric changed all of that for me. He showed me it's okay to trust some people. It's true you can't trust *everybody*. Don't you trust me now? Otherwise you wouldn't continue to come visit me."

"I know, but there's something about him I don't trust."

"What is that?"

"I don't know." He shrugged his shoulders again. "You're like a sister to me. I just knew I could trust you."

Dominique heard Eric calling her name from inside the house and wondered how long it was going to take him to realize she was outside in the backyard. If she could stall Shawn long enough, Eric would see him, and then she would have to introduce them.

"If you think of me like a sister, you can definitely think of Eric like a big brother."

"I'm not sure. Maybe in time I will, but for now I don't want to be introduced to him." Just then, Eric came out onto the sunroom, but the telephone started to ring at the same time.

"I'll get it," Eric hollered as he turned around to answer the telephone.

"Well, I guess I'll have to introduce you now that he's seen you sitting out here with me." Dominique said, smiling victoriously.

Shawn stood up from the table and yelled, "I don't care. I'm leaving. I told you I don't want to meet him or anybody else!"

"I haven't told him anything you have shared with me. I've kept my promise to you. I just want you to meet him, that's all." Dominique pleaded.

"I don't want to meet him. Besides, I don't need for him or anybody else to feel sorry for me. Now I wish I hadn't told you!" Shawn wailed and ran toward the bushes.

"Shawn, please don't leave!" Dominique cried out as she stood to her feet to go after him.

"Don't follow me. I told you I don't want to meet anybody," he repeated.

"Shawn!" Dominique followed him until he disappeared into the bushes. Stopping in her tracks, she wondered if he was going to come back again to visit. She hoped she hadn't run him away by insisting that he meet Eric. She did that only because she knew Eric wouldn't harm him.

"What are you looking at?" Eric asked as he approached her standing by the bushes. She hesitated for a moment before answering, not knowing what to say. She didn't want to tell him he just missed Shawn again.

"Dominique?"

She was going to have to answer him, or he was going to think something was wrong. "Yes?"

"What are you looking at?" he asked. "You didn't hear me calling your name just a few seconds ago?"

Eric's face showed worry. She needed to tell him the truth because he probably already saw Shawn outside with her when he first came outside before answering the telephone. "I was saying goodbye to my friend." Dominique answered reluctantly.

"What friend are you talking about?" Eric asked, confused.

"The one you saw out here with me before you answered the telephone," she blurted out.

"I didn't see anybody out here with you. Where was he?" Eric's confusion and concern were increasing.

"He was sitting right here across from me playing Scrabble. How could you have missed him?" Dominique asked, raising her voice. She couldn't believe he hadn't seen Shawn. He had been sitting at the table big as day when Eric walked out of the house.

"I don't know. Maybe you were blocking him. Why did he leave?" Eric asked.

"He's still too afraid to meet you," she explained, still stunned that Eric hadn't seen him sitting across from her.

"Why is he afraid of meeting me? I won't hurt him," Eric said, still not convinced of his reasons.

"I know, that's what I told him, but he was still afraid."

"Well, try to convince him next time. I really want to meet him." Eric reached out to hold Dominique in his arms.

"I would like for you to meet him, too. He's really a nice boy." Dominique allowed herself to be held by Eric. She really did believe Shawn was a nice boy, but he was just living in a bad situation right now.

"What is his name?" Eric asked.

"His name is Shawn."

"Shawn. Isn't that one of the names you said you would like to name our son if we ever had one?" Eric asked as he released her body to look at her directly.

"Yes." she said, smiling.

"Maybe we could just adopt him instead because it's taking us a long time to have another child," Eric joked. Then he realized his comment might have been in poor taste. He didn't want to upset Dominique again by being insensitive.

"Ha … ha … ha," she said, knowing Eric wanted more children.

"Dominique—you do realize I was only joking? Besides, he won't even allow you to introduce us. What is he going to do, come around only when I'm gone? Tell him I need to at least meet him if he's going to continue to spend time with my wife. A man might think he is trying to do something tricky behind my back with my woman," Eric joked in a primitive caveman voice.

"Eric, he's just a boy." Dominique laughed.

"So, what? He might be trying to get a jump-start. He might be looking for a woman to take care of him, you never know nowadays." Eric joked.

"Sure." Dominique laughed as Eric leaned over and kissed her.

"You two are always kissing," Devin yelled out.

"We kiss so much because we love each other. One day you will have someone you love and want to kiss and hug all the time, too. But for now, I will be the only man you will be kissing and hugging." Eric reached and grabbed Devin.

"Oh, Daddy!" Devin laughed as Eric kissed and hugged her.

"I love you too, just like I love your mother."

"I love you too, Mommy. I love you both." Devin said, giggling.

"Mommy and Daddy will always love you, no matter what. So don't you ever forget that." Dominique insisted. She bent over to kiss Devin on the forehead.

"Daddy, I have something I want to give you. I made you something today."

"What is it?"

"It's a surprise."

"Can you give me a hint?"

"It has a lot of colors."

"A lot of colors. Give me another hint."

"No, you have to wait to see. I want you to be surprised." She was excited about giving her father his surprise.

"Okay."

Devin opened the sunroom door and directed Eric and Dominique to come in so they could see her surprise. Devin ran across the room to her workstation. She picked up a piece of paper on which she had drawn a picture of her, Eric, and Dominique on a beach and handed it to Eric. He looked the picture over and was impressed by Devin's efforts.

"Devin, this is good. Is this your mommy and me?"

"Yes. We are on the water."

"I see. Can I take this to work and hang it up?"

"Yes. That's why I made it."

"I can't wait to hang it up and show it off. It's beautiful." Eric passed the drawing over to Dominique to look at.

"Thank you. Mommy, do you like it?" Devin asked, desiring her mother's approval.

"Yes, it's beautiful. Your drawings are always beautiful."

"I'll make you something tomorrow."

"I can't wait to see it." Dominique leaned over to give Devin a kiss.

Eric said, "I like the way the water scene looks in this picture. Maybe we need to go on a trip to the islands to get away for a while. I could sure use the relaxation myself. What do you think? Can you get away for a while?"

"I've been thinking about suggesting a trip myself," Dominique responded, recalling the phone number she wrote down in Dr. Martin's office.

"You decide, and I'll call our travel agent and book it."

"Let me think about it."

"Devin, I'm taking Mommy out tonight. Ms. Anderson is going to come over and babysit you while we are gone."

"Where are you taking Mommy tonight?" Devin asked.

Eric knew Dominique was hoping he would answer, but he wasn't going to tell her yet. He had it all planned. He had arranged for a limo to pick them up and take them out for a romantic dinner and night on the town. It had been a long time since he had done something like this for Dominique. They had gone to dinner, but this time he had taken the time to get a driver and everything. He really wanted to show Dominique a nice time tonight. He was looking forward to a vacation to get away, too. He was very tired from the long hours he had been putting in the office lately, and he felt bad leaving Dominique home since her attack.

"It's a surprise," Eric said. "What do you want Ms. Anderson to fix you for dinner?"

"I want some spaghetti and meatballs. I love Ms. Anderson's spaghetti and meatballs."

"I don't know, Dominique. Maybe we should eat here instead. I love Ms. Anderson's spaghetti and meatballs, too," Eric joked.

"Why don't we just tell her to make you some and put it away for you?" she said. "I'm looking forward to our outing this evening. It's been a while since I've had a reason to get dressed up."

"I'm looking forward to it, too." Eric leaned over and kissed Dominique.

"What time are we leaving this evening?" Dominique asked. Eric looked down at his watch.

"We leave in about two and a half hours. So, start getting ready. I want you to be absolutely breathtaking tonight."

"Oh, don't you worry, I will. You need to be as well."

Eric nodded his head for the challenge and responded, "Oh, don't you worry, I will be."

"I'm going to take a bath now and start getting ready," Dominique said. She kissed Devin on the forehead before heading inside to get dressed.

"I'm going to hang out with you for a bit while Mommy is getting ready." Eric said.

"Daddy. You want to help me draw?"

"If that's what you want me to do."

Devin motioned for Eric to sit down at her workstation.

"Devin, I need to talk with you about something," he said. He turned her chair around so they would be face-to-face. She looked up at Eric.

"I want you to be a big girl and help me take care of Mommy."

"What do you want me to do?" Devin asked.

"I need for you to watch Mommy during the day for me. If something should happen to Mommy, I want you to call me to let me know right away."

"Okay."

"You know Mommy and I told you never to keep secrets from us, but I don't want you to tell Mommy I asked you to help me watch her. She might get upset."

"Why would she get upset?" Devin asked. She tilted her head to the side, not quite understanding.

"You know how your mommy likes to take care of everybody. Now she needs for us to take care of her for a while. I need for Mommy to get some rest to relax."

"Okay."

Eric picked one of Devin's pencils up and started to write a few numbers down for her to memorize. "Here is my number at work and my cell number. Do you know how to dial them on the telephone?"

"No."

"I know what. I will program both numbers in our telephone so all you will have to do is press a button to dial my number." Eric quickly programmed their telephone and showed Devin what buttons to press to reach him at the office or by his cell number. Eric was amused by how fast Devin caught on to what he was telling her. He also programed some more important numbers for Devin to press if there was an emergency. He explained each one to her. Then he colored with her for a while before going upstairs to join Dominique in getting dressed.

Dominique slid down into the warm bubble bath. Her body started to tingle from the massaging water. Her muscles began to relax as soon as she sat down in the water. She laid her head back and closed her eyes for a moment as she took in the serenity of her bath. She tried to clear her mind of everything, but her conversation with Dr. Martin plagued her thoughts. She decided not to fight the temptation to think about her past. Instead, maybe now, while she was able to concentrate in peace, she would be able to think clearly.

Dominique rubbed the bubbles all over her body as she tried to remember each foster care family she spent time with and anything significant she could think of to write down in her journal and share with Dr. Martin. But nothing seemed noteworthy enough to associate with her present attacks. So she kept her eyes closed as she continued to rub the bubbles all over her body, wondering what surprise Eric had planned for her this evening. She still hadn't decided what dress she was going to wear. She had plenty to choose from. Then she remembered the evening dress Eric had bought her on their last trip to New York. She decided she would wear that one to please him. He would like it because he picked it out. She also fell in love with it herself after she tried it on. It hugged her body perfectly, revealing just enough.

The doorbell rang, and Eric got up from playing with Devin to answer it. It was Ms. Anderson.

"Hello, I thought I better get here a little early so you two could get dressed," she said.

"I appreciate that. I taught Devin how to use the telephone in case of an emergency. I was surprised how fast she caught on."

"I'm not. Devin is a very bright little girl. She surprises me every day with something new. I've learned a lot from her."

Eric shook his head in agreement with Ms. Anderson. "She's growing up so fast. I hope I don't miss it."

"I'll take good care of her if you do miss it. She's so excited about Dominique spending more time with her at home," Ms. Anderson said.

"Dominique is going to take some time off after her current case is over to spend with Devin. I'm sorry it's taken what happened to get her to slow down, but things happen for a reason. I'm just glad she's okay."

"Me too. Where are you taking Dominique this evening?" Ms. Anderson asked.

"I'm not telling. It's going to be a big surprise. I can't wait to see her reaction."

"I know she will love it. That's one of things I love about Dominique. She appreciates anything anyone does for her."

"I love her so." Eric said with a big smile on his face.

"Daddy, I want you to see my drawing." Devin yelled from the sunroom.

"I need to get dressed before I'm late taking Mommy out for her surprise. I want you to show me later when we get back." Eric replied.

"Okay."

"Go get dressed before you are late." Ms. Anderson waved her hand for Eric to go upstairs to get dressed.

"Thanks for coming early," he said and rushed upstairs as directed.

Dominique got out of the tub and dried off. She rubbed her lotion on and pinned her hair up for the evening while she was still in the bathroom. She rewrapped her towel around her body and headed for her closet to pull out her lingerie and dress for the evening. She unwrapped her towel and hung it on her towel rack to dry. Then she slipped into her lingerie and dress. Unable to zip it all by herself, she decided to wait for Eric to finish zipping it up when he came up to get dressed. It wouldn't take him long to be ready. So she sat down in front of her vanity mirror to put on her makeup. She looked through her selection of eye shadows and lipsticks to see which ones would work better for the evening.

As she was putting the finishing touches on her makeup, she heard her bedroom door open and someone enter. A strange, chilling feeling came over her body. She sat staring into the mirror at herself, unable to move. Her heart raced faster and faster as she heard the unknown visitor move closer and closer. It became harder to breathe as her chest tightened. Completely paralyzed by the heavy voice calling her—"Dominique"—she closed her eyes and sat there praying he would go away. But deep down inside she knew he would stay and she would feel herself suffocating.

She felt the cold hands of the unwanted visitor as they caressed her shoulders. They were strong hands with a lot of power—power she knew she couldn't compete with. She felt naked as the unwanted lips explored her neck and back. The cold hand slipped slowly down her back and into the opening of her unzipped dress. Her body started to tremble, and tears formed in her eyes as the warm heat from the stranger's breath filled her ears along with the piercing words: "I love you."

Dominique just sat as the cold hands continued to explore the naked areas of her body. With her eyes closed, she tried to disappear deep inside to escape the repulsion. She couldn't understand why this was happening to her, but she prayed it would be over soon.

When Dominique woke up, Eric was standing over her. She jumped up to a sitting position. She felt strange.

"Dominique, are you okay?" Eric asked with a worried look on his face.

"What's wrong? Why are you looking at me like that?" Dominique asked, still disoriented.

"You had another one of your attacks."

In disbelief, she started touching her body all over before responding. "I don't remember having an attack."

"I want you to see a doctor," Eric demanded.

"I'm fine," Dominique replied sharply.

"I think you do. You really scared me." Eric debated.

Dominique moved away from Eric. "I'm sorry, but I don't think I need to see a doctor. Really, I'm fine." As she continued to move away from Eric, she caught a quick glance of herself in the mirror. She was dressed up and suddenly remembered Eric was taking her out for a special evening. She immediately turned around to face Eric apologetically before saying a word. "Is it too late for us to go now?"

"I'm afraid so. I called and canceled our reservations. We can do it another night. Don't worry about it. I want you to get some rest, and don't argue with me. I'm going to help you take your dress off, and I want you to get back in bed," Eric demanded.

"Eric, I really feel fine." She really *did* feel fine. She couldn't understand what was going on.

"So explain to me what happened tonight."

Dominique knew he was worried about her, but she couldn't really explain it herself. "I can't. All I remember is sitting at my vanity and putting on my makeup. This strange feeling come over me, and I blanked out."

"What type of strange feeling?"

"I can't really explain it. Like I said, I was putting on my makeup and heard the bedroom door. I never turned around to see who it was. I just sat frozen. I guess I closed my eyes because I didn't get to see who it was, but I felt someone touching and kissing me. After that, I can't remember."

"Dominique, that was me," Eric said with a worried look. "I was trying to zip up your dress. Then you became unhinged."

"It was you?" Dominique couldn't understand why she would react to Eric that way. Something was strange, but she didn't know what it was or how to explain it. Maybe she did need to see a doctor. She would call Dr. Martin in the morning and see if she could move her appointment up.

"Yes. You started crying and shaking. I tried to calm you down, but you rolled up in a knot again and wouldn't let me touch you. Dominique, I think you need to go see someone. Maybe you could go see Dr. Martin if you don't want to see our family doctor. But you need to see someone."

"I think I'll call Dr. Martin."

"Good, I want you to call him first thing tomorrow morning. If you would like, I will go with you."

"No, I don't think that will be necessary." She didn't want him to feel he had to hold her hand. She could take care of this situation all by herself.

"Are you sure? I don't mind." Eric rubbed her shoulders.

"I'm sure."

"I want you to tell him about everything. The actual attack, the attack you had in the bathroom that night, and tonight. I don't feel comfortable leaving you here by yourself. Devin wouldn't know what to do if you were to have another attack and I wasn't here. You would scare her, and I don't want that to happen."

"I don't want that to happen either. But Eric—truly I think everything is going to be fine."

"How can you say that? You couldn't explain why you had either of those other attacks."

Dominique sat thinking for a few seconds before responding. She tried to remember the first attack and what brought it on. But Dominique wasn't sure what was causing her attacks. Nothing was similar about any of the attacks except she had an overwhelming sense of fear come over her. They never happened at the same time or place. She didn't have any answers, nor had Dr. Martin been able to give her any explanations. All he told her to do was relax. Well, she had been relaxing. She felt perfectly fine. She was excited about spending a wonderful evening with her husband alone. So what brought this attack on? She wasn't stressed about anything.

Dominique didn't know what to tell Eric but understood that he had become deeply worried about her condition. She tried to think of anything that was similar between the attacks Eric had experienced with her. All she could remember was standing in front of her mirror and feeling the same type of feelings she did this evening sitting in front of her vanity. The only thing similar was her standing in front of a mirror on both occasions.

"I'm not sure. The only thing similar is me being in front of a mirror before both attacks, but I can't explain why."

"What do you see in the mirror?"

"I don't see anything specific. The first attack, I thought I saw someone entering the bathroom. But I wasn't able to identify who it was. This time, I didn't see anyone, but I felt someone touching me. Then I became completely fearful and everything went blank."

"Can you explain how you felt?"

Dominique tried to remember the feelings so she could explain them to Eric. She felt the same type of fear every time. She felt weak and vulnerable The fear was overwhelming. She felt she was in danger with nowhere to turn. "It's hard to describe my feelings, but they are awful. I just have this sense of fear like I'm in danger, but I don't know why. It's real strange. Maybe I have some pent-up emotions about the attack. Maybe Dr. Martin can help me sort through them and all of this will be over soon." She wanted to offer Eric some comfort or hope.

"I hope so because I don't like to see you like this. It worries me because I can't help you. I never know when you are going to have one of these attacks, and all I can do when it happens, is try to help you through it."

"I know. I promise you I will go see Dr. Martin as soon as possible."

Eric leaned over to give Dominique a kiss, but she jumped back. He tried not to make a big deal about it because she was just recovering from another attack.

"Are you hungry?" Eric asked.

"Yes. I'm starving." Dominique answered while folding her arms together.

"What would you like to eat?"

"First, I want to know what I missed this evening," she said with a half smile. She felt awful she had ruined their evening.

"I'm not going to tell because when you get better, you will see. So you have to get better."

"Please give me a hint. I can't wait," she pleaded.

"No, but I will give you one of your surprises. Wait right here while I get it." He returned quickly with a dozen big red roses.

"They're beautiful!" She loved roses, her favorites. She reached to take possession of her flowers and admired them in her arms. She noticed a card and removed it to read it. It read:

> To my dearest Dominique, the woman of my life. I thank God every day for bringing you into my life. You are my lover, friend, and spiritual mate. I hope I have been the man of your dreams as you have been the woman of mine. There isn't anything in this world I wouldn't do for you because I can't imagine my life without you. I love you. Eric

Tears filled her eyes as she read the note. She knew Eric loved her, and she loved him, too. Eric had been a wonderful husband and friend to her. He meant the world to her, and there wasn't anything she wouldn't do for him. She thanked God for bringing him into her life. She leaned over and kissed Eric on the lips to thank him for the beautiful flowers, card, and life. Dominique couldn't imagine what other surprises Eric had planned for her, but he could be extremely romantic when he wanted to be. And after reading his note, she knew he had planned a breathtaking evening for her.

"I'm so sorry for messing everything up," Dominique said as she wiped tears from her eyes.

"Don't worry. Just get better and you will see what I had planned for you. But for now, I want you to relax and tell me what you want to eat." Eric took the flowers away and placed them on the table.

"What about a light salad?"

"One light salad coming up," Eric shouted like a short order cook in a restaurant. "I'll be right back," he said and headed for the kitchen.

Dominique just lay in the bed, trying to understand what was going on with her. She couldn't remember ever having panic attacks like these before. She felt fine and in control of her emotions besides the stress Michael Buchanan had created in her life. Yes, she had been a victim of his attack, but she had been victorious. She couldn't wait to tell Dr. Martin about her attack tonight. And she prayed he would be able to help her.

CHAPTER 27

Dominique woke up with an awful headache. She slowly got out of bed and went into the bathroom to see if she could find some pain medicine to help ease the headache, but there wasn't any in her medicine cabinet. She went downstairs to see if she had any in the kitchen. She hadn't noticed Eric was already up until she walked into the kitchen and saw him sitting in the sunroom, reading the paper, and drinking coffee. She greeted him.

"Good morning," Eric responded. "How do you feel?"

"I have an awful headache, and I can't find any pain medicine anywhere," she answered, standing in the doorway of the sunroom and rubbing her head.

Eric folded his newspaper and stood to his feet. "Why don't you come and sit down while I go and get you something from the store?"

"I would appreciate it very much."

"Is there anything else you want me to get you while I'm out?" Eric asked.

"No. I'm going to go outside and relax. I could use the fresh air. Maybe that will help my headache," she said as she took a deep breath.

Eric helped Dominique outside to the yard chairs. "Would you like some juice?" he asked.

"Actually, I would. Would you bring me a glass, please?" She got comfortable on her chaise chair.

"Sure. I'll be right back."

The outdoor breeze was cool and soothing to Dominique. With this headache, she was glad she didn't have anywhere to go this day. She seldom had headaches, but when she did, they were painful. When she was in school, she thought she had migraines, but her doctor told her she didn't and recommended that she relax more. Lately, that was all she was hearing from everybody: relax and relax.

As Eric stepped outside, Dominique called to him to bring out the telephone so she could call Dr. Martin. He turned around and got the telephone for her.

"Who are you about to call?" he asked, placing her glass of juice on the table beside her.

"I'm going to call Dr. Martin."

"I'm glad to hear that. I hope he can fit you in soon."

"Me too," she said, knowing she already had an appointment scheduled with Dr. Martin because of everything going on. She took a sip of her juice before dialing Dr. Martin's number, then another while she waited for someone to answer the phone.

"Hello, Dr. Martin's office, how can I help you?" a female answered.

"Yes, this is Dominique Wallace. I need to make an appointment with Dr. Martin."

"Mrs. Wallace. Is this an emergency?"

"No. But I would like to come in as soon as I can to see him."

"Let me look at his schedule ... Mrs. Wallace, have you forgotten you already have an appointment scheduled?"

"No. I need to see Dr. Martin sooner than that."

"Let me see what we have ... How about tomorrow? We have a nine o'clock appointment available tomorrow. Will that work okay for you?"

"Yes, that's perfect. I will see you then."

"Good, I will pencil you in, Mrs. Wallace."

When Dominique hung up the phone, it rang again, and she immediately answered it. Eric's office was calling him for something.

Eric walked away to take his call. When he returned, he told Dominique he had to go out of town that evening on a last-minute trip. She could tell he wasn't very happy about it.

"When is your appointment with Dr. Martin?" he asked, still concerned about her health.

"I have an appointment tomorrow at nine o'clock," she said.

"Good. I feel better knowing that. I want you to tell him everything. Don't try to withhold any information because you think it might not be important. I mean tell him everything. Tell him about all the attacks and your visits with this Shawn person," he demanded.

"Listen to you. I'm not a child. I will tell him everything."

"You promise?"

"Yes. I want to take care of whatever is going on just as much as you."

"How is your headache?" he asked.

"It still aches." she said, raising her hand to her head to comfort the aching throbbing.

"I'm going to the store. Is there anything else you want me to bring back? I have to pack to leave for the airport." He leaned over to kiss her on the lips before leaving.

"No."

"I'll be right back." He left for the store.

Dominique stretched out on the chaise and finished her orange juice while waiting for Eric. She closed her eyes and enjoyed the fresh, cool breeze that was blowing.

"Dominique," a voice called softly from the bushes.

She raised her body from her comfortable chaise couch and acknowledged the voice. "Shawn, is that you?" she asked, seeing bushes move.

When he stepped out, Dominique saw that Shawn's clothes were torn up, and several bruises were visible on his body.

"Shawn, what happened to you?" She jumped from her chaise and ran over to him to examine his bruises. "Who did this to you?"

"My dad did this," Shawn answered slowly.

"Why?" she asked, with panic in her voice.

"I don't want to talk about it. Where did Eric go?" he said harshly.

Dominique wasn't ready to change the subject. She wanted to know what had happened to him. She wondered what his mother said when she saw him. Shawn had a black eye, and there was no way she couldn't have noticed it. She wondered if she should take Shawn to the hospital.

"Don't change the subject, Shawn. Why did your father give you a black eye and all these bruises?" She continued to question Shawn even though he didn't respond.

"I don't want to talk about it." Shawn started to cry. Dominique reached out and pulled Shawn's body into hers and held him tightly.

"Please don't cry, Shawn. I'm here now. Shawn, do you want to see a doctor?" She asked as she pulled him away from her body to look him directly in the face.

"No. Promise me, Dominique, that you won't go away. I'm afraid Eric is going to send you away." Shawn continued to cry as he looked at Dominique.

"Eric's not going to send me away. Why would he?" she asked, puzzled by his comment.

"You had another attack, didn't you?" Shawn asked.

"Yes," she answered, wishing her answer had been no.

"I knew this would happen!" he responded with frustration in his voice. He started pacing in a circle, wearing a worried expression.

"You *knew* what would happen? Shawn, what do you mean?"

"I'm going to lose you, too," he blurted out.

"No, you are not!" Dominique said. She reached to grab his face gently. "What did your mother say when she saw you?"

"She didn't say anything," he said angrily. "She never says anything. I told you she's gone crazy. I'm not sure if she even knows she's alive half the time. I hate her, too," He removed his face from Dominique's hold.

"Shawn, don't say you hate your mother. I know you are angry with her. But I can't believe your mother doesn't care about your safety."

"Well, she doesn't."

"Did she even acknowledge your black eye?"

"No. Dominique, my mother doesn't even look at me. She hasn't spoken in a long time, and I don't think she has any plans to do so."

"Shawn?"

"She never says or does anything. All she does all day is look out of the window and rock back and forth in her rocking chair. She won't do anything for herself. My sister has to bathe and clothe her. If my mother messes up anything, we have to clean it up. My father doesn't help us do anything. He keeps threatening to send her away. At times, I think that's what she wants him to do. I know I want him to send *me* away. We have to do everything for her. My sister is the one who normally tends to our mother. My father doesn't want me to help with some things. I feel sorry for my sister. She's like a slave."

"Shawn, you haven't been able to get your mother to speak when your father isn't home?" Dominique asked, shocked by everything Shawn had told her.

"No. She doesn't say a word. All she does is look out of the window while rocking back and forth in her rocking chair."

"How long has she been doing that?"

"For a few years now. My father destroyed her. He always told her she was no good. He called her names, and I guess she had enough and just went crazy one day."

"Did she just stop talking one day?"

"Kind of. I remember coming home from school one day and the house was a mess. I knew something was wrong because she always had the house clean by the time I returned home. The first thing I thought was my mother finally left, but she left without telling my sister and me. I ran through the house looking for her. I didn't see her at first because she was sitting down in a corner on the floor with her head tucked in between her legs. Her whole body was shaking like she was afraid of something or someone. When I reached to help her up, she started shouting and crying for me to leave her alone.

"I think my mother had a nervous breakdown that day. My father didn't even take her to the hospital. He told us to help her to their bedroom. She's been in there ever since. My mother never said much anyway. She just cleaned up around the house and made sure food was always ready before my father got home. She was always nervous when he came home. I used to hate to see her rushing around, trying to do everything he wanted and being afraid he would get upset if it took her too long or if she didn't do it the way he wanted it done. She was a bundle of nerves. I never understood why she didn't just pack us up and leave one day while he was at work. I mentioned it to her one day, and she slapped my face. I never said anything about it again."

Dominique shook her head in disbelief. "Why didn't your father take your mother to the hospital?" she asked, more curious than ever.

Shawn shrugged his shoulders as he spoke. "I guess he was afraid she would tell someone what was going on at our house."

"Are you sure your mother won't talk to you or your sister when your father is gone?"

Shawn shook his head as she answered. "No, she won't say a word. My mother hasn't spoken since that day. Sometimes I wonder if she can even hear us anymore. She doesn't respond at all to us. She just sits there looking into space. She's like a prisoner in our home."

"Do you think your mother would respond to your sister if it were just the two of them?"

Shawn shook his head again as he answered. "No. She doesn't respond to anyone. My sister did tell me one day while she was combing my mother's hair that my mother started to cry, but she didn't say why she was crying. She's never shown any type of emotion or anything when I'm around. My sister normally is the one who helps my mother. My father doesn't help at all. He just tells my sister and me what to do."

"I'm really sorry to hear that. Your mother needs professional help, Shawn. If she can get out of there, she might have a chance to get better. Right now, she can't. Your mother is like a lot of women who have been abused by their husbands, whether physically or mentally. She has found a way to escape without actually leaving."

"I wish she had packed us up instead of leaving the way she did. I don't understand how she is able to sit there and watch what my father is doing to us. I don't understand why she doesn't love us enough to do something about it."

"Shawn, your mother probably doesn't know what to do. From what you have told me, your father has gradually been destroying your mother mentally for years. People deal with stressful matters in different ways. And you are right, this was her way of checking out and not having to deal with it. Unfortunately, for you and your sister, she could have gone about it differently. Your mother probably feels helpless about not being able to help you and your sister. She's probably torn apart inside. Shawn, that's why it's so important for you to trust me now. The sooner I'm able to tell the appropriate people, the sooner I can help your mother, you, and your sister get away from your father."

"Believe me, Dominique, I want to get my family away from my father. I'm just afraid he might find us and kill us."

"Shawn, your father won't be able to find you. You and your family will be placed in protective custody. No one will know where you are. We will find you somewhere else to live where your father won't be able to find you. We will also try to get help for your mother so she can get better."

"Are you sure you can promise me my father will not find us? He knows people everywhere. He always tells me he has friends at the police station, and if I ever try to tell, they will tell him before I leave the station."

"Your father is just trying to scare you. Shawn, what does your father do?"

"I'm not sure. He never talks about his job."

"Does he have to wear a uniform to work?"

"He wears a blue uniform. I think he works in the maintenance department somewhere. I don't know where he works, though."

"So, your father isn't a policeman himself?"

"No, he's not a policeman. He just says he knows a lot of people on the force who would tell if I tried to tell someone."

"Well, I'm glad you told me that. I will try to make sure I'm very careful, just in case he does know someone on the force. I will keep everything very secretive."

"Why can't you leave Eric and start a new life with me and Devin?" Shawn asked with a serious look on his face.

"I can't just leave my husband for you! I love my family and I love you, too. Besides, I would have to get custody from the state. I can't just let you live with us without your family giving us guardianship. Shawn, what about your mother and sister? Don't you want to be with them?"

"Yes, I do," Shawn said, nodding.

"Then stop thinking only about yourself. Try to think about your sister and mother too. They are depending on you to help them. They need you now more than ever."

"Dominique, I don't want to talk about this anymore. If you won't leave Eric, then there is nothing for us to talk about. Anyway, I need to get going."

Shawn looked away from Dominique with a sad look on his face. Then he left through the bushes, leaving Dominique speechless. She couldn't believe he wanted her to leave her husband in order for him to be with her. She cared a great deal for Shawn, but she wasn't going to leave her husband for him or anybody else for that matter. Yes, she felt like she was losing her mind, but she hadn't gone completely insane yet.

****

Dominique laid back on her chaise chair and took several deep breaths. Her headache intensified as she thought about her conversation with Shawn.

"I'm back," Eric called to Dominique as she stepped out of the sunroom heading in her direction with a bag in his hand.

"Here is your pain medicine and some water." Eric handed her everything. "Do you feel any better?"

"Not really, but I'm sure this pain medicine will help." She took the medicine, then smiled back at Eric.

"I'm going to pack now. I'll drive myself to the airport. I want you to get some rest. I've called Ms. Anderson and asked her to stay with you guys until I return. I don't want you to argue with me because I won't change my mind. I don't want to take any chances that Devin may find you alone. She's too little to deal with it, and it would probably scare her to death. End of discussion."

Eric rushed into the house to pack for his trip. Dominique just sat in her chaise, staring in space. She felt helpless, knowing that Eric didn't trust her to be alone with Devin. She fully understood his position, but she didn't like it one bit. But she couldn't debate under the current circumstances because she didn't know when and where she would get sick again, and she didn't want Devin to be alone to deal with it. She closed her eyes and tried to escape.

CHAPTER 28

Ms. Anderson quietly got dressed for the morning, then decided to find out what Dominique and Devin wanted her to prepare for breakfast. When she walked down the hall to inquire about Dominique's breakfast request, her bedroom door was closed. Afraid of waking her, she continued down the hall to Devin's room.

"Good morning, sweet pea," Ms. Anderson greeted Devin, who was already up for the morning.

Devin jumped and turned around to face Ms. Anderson nervously, holding her wet bedsheets in her hands. "Good morning," Devin answered slowly as she lowered her head.

"Devin why are you pulling your bed sheets off?" Ms. Anderson asked.

As Devin stood staring at Ms. Anderson, her eyes filled with tears. She had been discovered and would have to confess she wet her bed. There was no way around it. She was holding the wet evidence in her hands. Devin dropped the wet bedsheets to the floor. Afraid of being punished, Devin ran across the room and wrapped her arms around Ms. Anderson's body helplessly and started to cry.

"Devin, what's wrong? Why are you crying?" Ms. Anderson asked as she held Devin's weeping little frame.

"My bed is wet." Devin answered honestly, still crying.

"Did you use the bathroom in your bed by accident?" Ms. Anderson asked, knowing if that was the case, all they would have to do is pull her protective padding, clean it, and replace it along with some fresh bedsheets.

"No," Devin answered. "Shawn did."

"Shawn."

"Yes. Mommy's new friend did it." Devin mumbled.

Ms. Anderson wondered what he was doing in Devin's bed and where he was now. She looked around the room to see if he was hiding in Devin's room, but it was only the two of them.

"Where is Shawn now?" Ms. Anderson asked, looking back at Devin.

"He's gone," Devin answered as she wiped some of her tears away.

Ms. Anderson was curious to know why Shawn was in Devin's bed. "What was he doing in your bed?"

"He said he was scared to sleep by himself," Devin answered. She lowered her face again.

"Well, the next time he gets scared, I think you better wake your mother or father and let them know … so he won't wet in your bed again." Ms. Anderson explained. She was confused now, because Dominique never mentioned to her Shawn would be spending the night with them last night.

"Ms. Anderson, please don't tell my mommy and daddy about him wetting my bed," Devin pleaded with Ms. Anderson.

"Devin, I don't know if I should keep this a secret from them."

"Please. I don't want to get him in trouble. She's going to get mad with me," Devin continued to plead.

"Why would your mother get mad with you if he wet your bed?"

"Because she likes him so much," Devin answered, then paused for a few seconds before speaking again. "He's the reason my mommy is so sick. I know Daddy told me he wasn't, but he is."

"Why would he be the reason your mommy is so sick?"

"He's bad, Ms. Anderson. Shawn is bad. You see he wet my bed and now I'm going to get in trouble for it."

"Well, don't worry. You are not going to get in trouble."

"Please don't tell." Devin pleaded with Ms. Anderson.

"I won't tell this time, but if it happens again, I'm going to have to tell your parents he's wetting your bed."

She wasn't sure whether Devin was telling her the truth. She hadn't officially met Shawn. She had heard about him, but never saw him. This was the second time he had managed to escape her without her meeting him. Now she was really curious to meet him for herself, especially after how frantic Devin had been about her mother finding out he wet her bed. What kind of bond had Dominique and Shawn developed?

"Thank you, Ms. Anderson." Devin said as she reached out to give Ms. Anderson a hug of gratitude.

"Let me help you out of those wet clothes," Ms. Anderson said. She helped her out of her clothes and pulled the protective sheet off the bed. Silently, they walked into Devin's bathroom. As Devin sat on her toilet releasing any remaining urine, Ms. Anderson ran some bathwater for Devin to bathe. After helping her into the tub, she rushed downstairs and put Devin's wet sheets and clothes in the washer. Before going back into the bathroom to check on Devin, she went to make the other guest room bed up too, but it hadn't been slept in. The sheets hadn't even been pulled back. She thought that was strange. Ms. Anderson checked the sheets to see if maybe he wet the sheets and tried to cover it up by making up the bed again. She pulled the comforter and sheets back but it was dry. Nothing was wet about the bed. She made the bed up and went into Devin's room and made her bed up with fresh sheets. Then Ms. Anderson joined Devin in the bathroom.

She didn't know whether to question Devin about where Shawn had slept there that night. She decided to let it go. Devin had been through enough this morning and felt bad about her bed being wet. This was the first-time Devin's bed had been wet. So, she would let it slide this time.

Dominique opened her eyes and rolled over to check the time. It was seven twenty-five. She rolled back over to wake herself up. She needed to get up. In five minutes, her alarm clock was going to buzz for her to get up. She had another appointment to see Dr. Martin. She couldn't wait to see him today. She had so much to tell him. Dominique rolled back over and pressed the alarm button before it buzzed. She threw the covers back and rolled her body to the edge of the bed. She allowed her feet to fall to the floor, then she forced herself to a sitting position. She looked around her bedroom. It was a mess. She had clothes everywhere. She quickly gathered all her dirty clothes and put them in the dirty clothesbasket in the bathroom. Then she pulled the sheets off her bed for Ms. Anderson to replace with fresh ones. She opened her blinds to let the light in. When Dominique looked back at her clock, it read eight o'clock. Her appointment with Dr. Martin was at nine o'clock. She selected an outfit to wear before jumping into the shower.

Dragging herself into the bathroom still sleepy, she turned the water on and took a quick shower, grabbed her towel, and stepped out of the shower to dry off. Someone was calling her name.

"Dominique."

She quickly wrapped her towel around her body and looked around her bathroom for somewhere to hide as the fear grew inside of her. She didn't want whoever was calling her to find her. She had to hide, but she didn't have anywhere to go. Dominique continued to look around the bathroom. She wouldn't fit into the linen closet or in the cabinet under the sink. The only place she would be able to fit would be in her shower. She quickly stepped back into the shower and pushed her body as far as she could into the back corner and slid to the floor. She held onto her towel tightly as if it was a shield to protect her. She tried not to breathe too hard for fear she would give herself away.

"Dominique, are you in there?" the voice called out, but Dominique just sat in silence, unwilling to answer and prayed the unwanted voice would go away if whoever it was thought she wasn't there. But the voice got louder, and she knew it was getting closer and closer to her. Tears started to fill her eyes as she heard the bathroom door open and the sound of footsteps coming closer and closer.

"Dominique, can you hear me? Are you in the bathroom?"

Dominique couldn't move, and her heart was racing so fast that her chest was starting to hurt.

"Dominique?" The words pierced her ears as she hid in fright for her safety. She closed her eyes when she saw a tall-built figure appear in front of the shower glass window. She knew she would have to pay the consequences of hiding.

"Dominique, are you in here?"

Dominique never opened her eyes. She couldn't bear to see what punishment she was about to receive. She felt someone leaning over her body. She became completely numb when she felt her towel being pulled at. She tried to hold onto it to cover her body, but she wasn't strong enough. She was losing the tug-of-war for her towel. She allowed her tears to fall from her eyes as she surrendered.

"Dominique. Can you hear me? It's me, Ms. Anderson. Can you hear me?" Ms. Anderson called out to Dominique as she started to come through.

Dominique was still out of it when she heard Ms. Anderson's voice. She felt chilly and wet. She wasn't sure where she was.

"Dominique. It's me, Ms. Anderson. Can you hear me?" Ms. Anderson continued to ask Dominique.

"Yes. What wrong?" Dominique asked in a faint, disoriented voice.

"You had another attack. Are you okay?"

"I think so." Dominique wondered what had happened to cause this attack. She prayed Devin hadn't seen her having this one. "Where is Devin?"

"Devin's in her room."

"Please help me up." As Dominique stood up, she realized she was naked. She quickly reached for her towel lying on the bathroom floor. She was so embarrassed that Ms. Anderson had found her like this. Dominique wondered what was going through Ms. Anderson's mind now. If she wasn't worried before, Dominique was sure she was now. This was all she needed now—someone else thinking she was losing control.

"Dominique, what happened?" Ms. Anderson asked as she helped Dominique to the bed.

Dominique shook her head as she answered. "I don't know."

"I want you to lay down for a while," Ms. Anderson instructed.

Dominique slid under the sheets and looked over at her clock. It was eight thirty . She had only thirty minutes left to get to Dr. Martin's office. She didn't want to miss her appointment with him.

"Ms. Anderson, I need to get dressed. I have a doctor's appointment this morning. I don't want to miss it." Dominique said.

"Dominique, I'll take you. I need to get Devin dressed. I don't want you driving yourself in this condition."

Dominique didn't feel like arguing with Ms. Anderson. All she wanted to do was get to Dr. Martin's and she didn't care how she got there. "Okay. My appointment is at nine o'clock this morning."

"Are you going to be okay while I get Devin dressed?"

"Yes. I'm fine now," Dominique answered Ms. Anderson, but then she burst into tears crying. She was so embarrassed and angry at the same time. Embarrassed that Ms. Anderson had found her naked in her bathroom. Angry that she hadn't been able to control the attack. She didn't have any control at all. Her attacks were in control of her now. She was just the vessel from which they happened. What was she going to do? She couldn't continue to live like this. Why was this happening to her?

"Sweetheart, don't cry. Calm down. It's going to be okay." Ms. Anderson said as she sat down beside Dominique and wrapped her arms around her for support.

"I'm not sure if it is. I can't control my attacks and I never know when they are going to happen. Eric thinks I'm losing my mind, and I'm not so sure he's wrong." Dominique cried as she laid her head down on Ms. Anderson's shoulder.

"Eric doesn't think you are losing your mind. He is just worried about you. He doesn't know what's wrong, and you know how men are. They want to fix it for you. But he doesn't know how. Eric loves you, Dominique, and he doesn't want to see you hurting."

"Mommy, you're up." Devin yelled as she came running around to her side of the bed. Dominique tried to wipe her tears away as fast as she could before Devin saw them.

"Why are you crying, Mommy? Did Shawn make you cry again?" Devin asked with a worried look on her face.

"No. Shawn didn't make me cry," she answered, still trying to hide her tears from her.

"So why are you crying?" Devin asked, wondering what else could be making her mother cry.

"Mommy was sad before you came in, but now I feel much better." Dominique reached out to give Devin a hug, but Devin moved away.

"Did you have another attack?" Devin asked. Dominique stared back at Devin speechless. She wondered how long she had known about her attacks.

"I heard you and Daddy talking about you having attacks," Devin explained.

Dominique looked over at Ms. Anderson first before answering Devin. She didn't want to tell her a story. She had to tell her the truth.

"Yes, I had another attack." Dominique answered. She hated having to tell Devin she had another attack because she knew Devin was worried about her.

Devin just stood there for a second or two and then she ran out of the room.

"Don't worry. I'll go check on her. I want you to get dressed. She's just a child, confused about what is going on. She's scared, too." Ms. Anderson tried to assure her.

"I know she is. I feel so bad that I'm hurting her like this."

"I know you do. First, you have to get better, so get dressed so you won't be late for your appointment. I'll take care of Devin. That's why I'm here."

Dominique removed the comforter and got out of bed. She reached for the clothes she had pulled out earlier to put on. After she finished dressing, she stood in front of her vanity mirror and looked herself over. Dominique was amazed how her outside appearance looked the same as always, but her inside was clearly different. She didn't know who she was anymore and neither did her family. Dominique felt as if a big hole inside her was growing larger and larger. She was losing herself and her family slowly. Eric was trying to deal with everything the best way he knew how, but she could tell it was taking a toll on him. His patience was running thin, and he was constantly questioning her decisions and her capability to care for herself and Devin, something he never did before.

"Dominique, we're ready to go," Ms. Anderson called out from the hallway.

"I'll meet you guys downstairs, I'm almost ready." Dominique answered, as she continued to stare at herself in the mirror. She pointed her finger at her reflection and began to speak to the reflection that looked like her in the mirror.

"I don't know who you are, but I will not allow you to destroy my life and my family any longer. I will defeat you because I'm a survivor. *I'm a survivor, you hear me?* I'm a survivor."

CHAPTER 29

Dominique rode in silence as Ms. Anderson drove them to Dr. Martin's office. After Ms. Anderson pulled into a parking space, she stayed behind to help Devin out of her car seat while Dominique went inside for her appointment. Dr. Martin was standing behind the receptionist desk when she entered his office. He immediately waved for her to go directly to his office. Without making eye contact with his receptionist, Dominique followed him into his office.

"Good morning, Dominique." Dr. Martin greeted her.

"Good morning to you," she responded, with trouble in her voice. "Here is my journal you asked me to start." She handed it to Dr. Martin.

"You don't sound very happy today. What's going on?" Dr. Martin asked as he sat down and started flipping through her journal.

"I've had two attacks since my last appointment with you. They are getting worse. I don't know when they are going to occur and I have no control."

"What do you mean you don't have any control?" Dr. Martin started to write in his notepad.

"They just happen, and I still don't know what is triggering them."

"How do you feel right now?"

"I feel fine right now, but that's not to say I won't have another attack before I leave here today. Eric's very worried, and so am I. I'm losing a little bit of myself every time I have one."

"What do you mean by 'losing a little bit' of yourself?"

"I'm not my strong, independent self anymore. Eric doesn't see me that way either. He hasn't come out and directly said that, but I'm sure that's how he feels."

"How do you know for certain?"

"Eric is out of town right now, but before he left, he asked our nanny to stay with Devin and me until he returns. He has never asked our nanny to stay overnight while he was away unless he knew I was going to be working late on a case. I'm actually working from home on the case I'm handling now."

"Why did Eric feel it necessary for your nanny to stay overnight while he was out town?"

"He said it was because of the attacks. He didn't want to take a chance that I would have one with only Devin at home. She wouldn't know what to do. I understand his concern, but it makes me feel bad. He doesn't see me the same anymore. He's acting like he has to take care of me like our daughter. Now he's having our nanny watch me, too."

"Dominique, you just said you understand his concern."

"I know. I didn't say I *like* it. I *don't* like it."

"Tell me everything you can remember about each attack." Dr. Martin reached for his notepad and began to write something in it.

Dominique started to rattle off all the details of her last two attacks as Dr. Martin took notes.

"You mentioned hearing a heavy voice both times. Did they sound like the same heavy voice?"

"Yes."

"Do you recognize the heavy voice?"

"No."

"You mentioned someone touching you."

"Yes." Dominique nodded.

"What did the hands look like?"

"I didn't see the hands, I just felt them, but I remember how strong they felt. I can't remember anything else about them because I fainted again."

"Did they feel like Eric's hands?"

"No. These hands felt rougher then Eric's."

"Where were they touching you?"

"They touched my neck, shoulders, and back, which were exposed because my dress was still unzipped."

"Where was Eric when all of this was happening?"

"I'm not sure. I think he was downstairs with Devin."

"Do you think it might have been Eric who you heard entering the bedroom and touching you?"

"It could have been Eric because when I came to, we talked about everything. He told me he did kiss and touch my shoulders while I was sitting there in front of my mirror."

"You might still be bothered more than you realize by the attack or some of the cases you have worked on in the past. Let me make sure I'm clear on a few things we have discussed."

"I don't understand. I've never experienced anything like this before because of working on a case. This just started." Dominique couldn't figure out what was so different about this case. Yes, she had become quite fond of Kimberly, but she had also become fond of a lot of her clients over the years.

Dr. Martin flipped silently through his notepad to locate the information he needed to question Dominique. "I have it here. You decided to take the case immediately after you spoke with Miss Kimberly Buchanan at the hospital."

"Yes." Dominique nodded.

"That same day you had another funny feeling on the elevator leaving her room?"

"Yes."

"Then you felt like you were suffocating when news reporters surrounded you after leaving the court after Mr. Buchanan's bond hearing?"

"Yes."

"Then you were attacked in the hospital garage?"

"Yes." Dominique was impressed by Dr. Martin's notes. He had been keeping close track of things.

"Then you had another attack that very same night in your bathroom where Eric found you?"

"Yes."

"You had another attack the night you learned Mrs. Buchanan tried to OD? This time Shawn found you?"

"Yes."

"Your next attack occurred in your bedroom where Eric found you in front of your vanity mirror?"

"Yes."

"And your last attack your nanny found you in your shower?"

"Yes." Dominique answered, not realizing how many attacks she had already had.

"Dominique, I'm certain your body is trying to tell you something. You did say you had your first panic attack when you took on the Buchanan case, didn't you?"

"Yes."

"And you have handled other sexual abuse cases before without having panic attacks?"

"Yes."

"Would you also agree this case has been a little more stressful because of the defendant's threats and related complications?"

"Yes." Dominique fully agreed with Dr. Martin. Michael Buchanan had created quite a bit of stress in her life since she agreed to handle this case.

"Both of your last two attacks seem to have had a male present during them." Dominique just watched as Dr. Martin flipped through his notes quickly. She didn't say a word while she waited for him to finish, curious to see where he was going.

"Dominique, would you say that the initial feeling you experience with each attack has been the same?"

"Yes. I always experience a feeling of fear."

"And you feel like it is getting worse with each attack?"

"Yes. They are more real now."

"You are able to see and hear more than before?"

"Yes. Why do you think that is the case?"

Dr. Martin made some notes in his notepad before speaking.

"I want to backtrack to when you decided to handle Miss Buchanan's case. So far I have observed you approach this case much differently from any other case I have witnessed before. What I mean is that you have made decisions that I believe you normally wouldn't have before."

"I don't understand what you mean," Dominique said, interrupting.

"Do you think you might have gotten too involved with your last client's problems?"

"I don't know. I must admit, I have been more intense with preparing for this case than some of my others. I want to help Kimberly, yes. But why would this case cause me to have panic attacks?"

"Maybe you didn't realize how involved you are with Kimberly."

"But I've gotten involved with other clients in similar situations before and walked away just fine after everything was over."

"Yes, but this case isn't over. Nor have you ever before had anyone threatening your family and attacking you. Unless you haven't shared that information with me. And if that's the case, why not?"

"No, I've been very honest with you over the years." Dominique sensed she was on trial herself.

"You did say earlier you had a fondness for the girl you were representing. Why is that?"

"I can't explain it. When I heard what her father was doing to her, the idea that he thinks he can get away with it because he is so influential made me sick to my stomach. This man is incredible. He's pleading not guilty, knowing full well he *is* guilty.

"Her mother had been unsupportive until recently. She finally came to her senses and admitted he had been sexually abusing their daughter. Then she tried to OD—we think. So every time I think about Kimberly, my heart goes out to her. I thought I could relate to her feeling of being alone and abandoned by her family."

"How were you able to relate?"

"I felt no one really cared about me until one of my elementary or middle school teachers took an interest in me, which was before I met the Franklins. The Franklins were the last foster family I lived with before I went to law school. I felt I could be that person to reach Kimberly if she would allow me. I think she has responded well, and I plan to try to help her through this. I have to admit her case took me by surprise. It has been a very difficult case."

"Why was this case more difficult than some of the other sexual abuse cases you have worked on in the past?"

"I don't know. It just feels different besides the fact her father is trying to kill me and my family," Dominique joked. "Winning her case will allow Kimberly to see her father receive punishment for what he has done to her. She didn't deserve to be sexually abused by this man or anybody else. No one deserves to be forced to have sex or participate in any part of the act if they don't want to. Besides, Kimberly—like everybody—never asked to come into this world. Her existence was determined before she ever took her first breath. Yet Kimberly has been paying a horrible price for her existence because of her own father's personal sickness." Dominique had tears in her eyes as she spoke. Her rage toward Michael Buchanan surfaced again as she told Dr. Martin everything.

"Dominique, you are giving vent to strong emotions right now, something I rarely see from you. Where is it coming from?"

"Her father," Dominique admitted. "It's my job to make sure he receives proper punishment for his actions."

"You have a lot of anger toward Mr. Buchanan which I'm not sure isn't associated with some of your attacks." Dr. Martin shook his head, still clueless why she was having these attacks. "I don't know, Dominique. I started thinking about what might be the cause after your last session. I've looked over my notes repeatedly to see if I might have missed something."

"So, what do you think you missed? Because I don't know." Dominique wondered what his plan of action would be.

"Dominique, I've been working with you for a few years now, and I still don't know a whole lot about your past. I'm not trying to imply your attacks stem directly from your past. I just feel I need to know a little more about your past in order for me to rule that out as a cause. I looked over your journal, but you were vague about your experiences in the foster care homes."

"What do you need to know? I don't remember much about it, except having to move from family to family."

"What can you tell me about your foster care experiences?"

"They were all the same for the most part. I always felt like an outsider. None of the foster care families showed a genuine interest in me until my last home with the Franklin family. They were nice. Mrs. Franklin was unable to have children. She was good to me. She made sure I got my hair done on a regular basis. She polished my fingernails for the first time. She taught me how a woman should care for herself, something none of the other foster mothers did. She taught me how to cook and wash clothes. She also explained to me the birds and bees. Mrs. Franklin was a good woman. I always wished I had been placed in her home first because she wanted to adopt me. But by then I was almost old enough to be on my own."

"Do you still stay in contact with the Franklins?"

"Yes. We still communicate. I haven't told them about my panic attacks. I don't want them to worry about me."

"Tell me about Mr. Franklin. What was he like?"

"He was very nice, too. He used to let me help him fix things around the house. He believes a woman should be independent. He helped me with my homework sometimes. He would talk to me about life. He took me to my first college orientation in high school. I always felt bad they weren't able to have children of their own. If there were two people who truly deserved children, it was Mr. and Mrs. Franklin."

"Tell me about the family before the Franklins."

Dominique tried to think about the foster family she stayed with before the Franklins, but she couldn't quite remember. They all seemed to blend in together. She had tried to forget about her other foster families because her memories were not all pleasant. It was easier and less painful to remember living only with the Franklins. It made her feel like she had some family past to hold on to that was positive.

"Dr. Martin, I can't remember." Dominique answered and sighed.

"Why can't you remember?"

Dominique shook her head as she spoke. "I don't know. I moved around so much, I can't remember."

"It's important. Try to remember something about any of your foster families. You don't have to try to remember the order, just something."

Dominique raised her hands and placed them over her shoulder to massage her collar bone while she tried to think. Nothing came to her. It was as if she had completely erased her past before the Franklins. She just sat there staring into space, waiting for memories to come rushing back. Tears started to fill her eyes, and she desperately fought not to cry in front of Dr. Martin.

"Dominique, tell me what you are thinking about," Dr. Martin leaned forward and requested.

"I'm not thinking about anything. I can't remember anything before the Franklins except feeling alone and abandoned." Dominique responded with a crackling voice. "I can't remember any faces or names."

"Why did you feel alone and abandoned?" Dr. Martin asked writing more notes in his notepad.

"I guess because I never had a family of my own who loved and wanted to care for me until the Franklins." Dominique was continuing to fight back her tears.

"Do you remember anything about your real parents?"

"No. I remember asking one of my foster mothers about helping me find out about my past. She told me some things are better forgotten and left in your past. Since that day, I never asked anyone else to try to help me find anything out about my real parents."

"Why do you think she told you that?"

"I don't know. I just assumed she knew my parents didn't want me."

"What about now? Are you curious to know about your parents?"

Dominique wasn't sure whether she wanted to know now. It had been easy, telling herself the Franklins were her family. They had been the only true family she ever knew. She wasn't sure if she wanted to know anything about her parents that might cause her any more pain. She had already been through enough as a result of being abandoned by them.

"Dr. Martin, I don't know. I used to think I wanted to know, but now I'm not sure. I've managed just fine without knowing."

"Are you curious to know about their medical history?"

"I used to be. I make sure I have a physical examination on a regular basis. I've been doing fine until now."

"So now there is more of a reason for you to try to find out about your past, don't you think?" Dr. Martin raised his eyebrow.

Dominique didn't know how to respond. She just sat there staring back at Dr. Martin. She felt torn inside, trying to decide how she felt about finding out about her real parents. A part of her still wanted to know while the other part didn't want to know.

"I don't know," she said with hesitation. "I really don't know if I want to."

"I want you to think about it. Our time is up for today, but I want you to try to remember anything you can about your past. I also want you to think seriously about finding out about your real parents. I want to reemphasize that I'm not trying to imply that your past is the reason for your attacks. I just want to know more about your past so we can rule it out as a possible cause."

Dominique nodded.

The telephone rang again. Dominique wondered what the emergency was this time. This was the second time he had been called during one of their sessions.

As they stood and walked toward the doorway, Dominique wondered how Ms. Anderson and Devin made out. Devin was asleep in Ms. Anderson's lap, and Ms. Anderson was reading a magazine.

"Sorry you had to wait so long for me."

"Don't worry. It gave Devin a chance to catch up on some sleep." Ms. Anderson answered.

"Devin, it's time to wake up. Mommy's finished," Dominique said, shaking her awake.

Devin pulled away from her, reaching and grabbing hold of Ms. Anderson.

"Don't worry about it. She's still sleepy." Ms. Anderson whispered as she embraced Devin.

Devin cried out, "I want to go home."

"We're leaving now. There's nothing to cry about." Then Ms. Anderson stood to her feet with Devin in her arms.

Dominique walked ahead of them toward the car and toward the driver side, but Ms. Anderson wanted to drive so she could relax. Dominique didn't challenge her request but changed directions toward the passenger side and got in. Dominique waited in the front seat as Ms. Anderson put Devin in the back.

"Everybody in," Ms. Anderson said, sounding like a mother on a grocery outing. "Dominique, is there anywhere else you need to stop before we go home?" she asked before pulling out.

"No." Dominique answered as she laid her head back on the headrest.

"Home it is." Ms. Anderson responded and backed the car up and headed home.

Dominique rode in silence. All she could think about was how her life was changing so fast. She tried to replay each attack in her head. Was there something she had missed? She tried to keep her thoughts straight, but everything was running together, and she was having a hard time concentrating. Tears started to fill her eyes. She tried to fight them back as she looked out the window, trying to focus her attention away from her sadness. She didn't want Ms. Anderson and Devin to see her cry or to worry about her any more than they had.

At home, Ms. Anderson parked the car and got out, then opened the door to help Devin out.

"Ms. Anderson, will you play with me outside?" Devin asked.

"Sure. What do you want to play?"

"I want to make you a sand castle."

"First, let me prepare some lunch."

"Can I help?" Devin asked.

"Yes, you can. Dominique, is there anything particular you would like for lunch today?"

"No, whatever you fix is fine with me," Dominique said. She unlocked the front door of the house and went straight upstairs. She wanted to be alone while she tried to get herself back together again.

When she reached her bedroom, she stretched out across the bed, closed her eyes, and embraced the empty darkness. She took several deep breaths to help her relax, and continued to free her mind of thoughts. Slowly she felt herself calming down and relaxing.

She heard a knock at her bedroom door, opened her eyes, and turned over to face the door. "Yes?"

"Dominique, can I come in?" Ms. Anderson asked from outside. "Yes."

"I just wanted to let you know, I've finished preparing lunch. Would you like for me to bring you your lunch up here?"

"Yes. Thank you." Dominique answered.

"Dominique, I want you to know if you ever need to talk, I'm available. I know you are very private about your personal business, but I promise you, whatever you share with me will stay between the two of us."

Dominique gave Ms. Anderson a big smile at this offer of loving assistance. Ms. Anderson had been like a mother to her over the years. She always made sure her house and family were well taken care of in her absence. She always made herself available to them, like a mother would. Dominique really did appreciate Ms. Anderson's offer.

"Ms. Anderson, I really do appreciate the offer. I might just take you up on it later." Dominique said as she gave Ms. Anderson a half smile.

"Why don't you come outside with Devin and me and just relax on your chaise? I think it would be good for Devin to see you up and about. She's confused right now. Give her some time to come around. I remember when my mother would get sick I would feel like my whole world was upside down. It seemed like the house went to pieces. Everyone tried to take on her responsibilities while she got better. I would always develop a little resentment toward my mother during that time because she got sick and wasn't her usual strong self. I felt my mother was too strong to get sick; for her to get sick meant she wasn't strong anymore. I never liked to think of my mother as being weak.

"Eventually, I realized she was human, just like the rest of us. I think that's what Devin is experiencing right now. Dominique, all her life Devin has seen you juggle a million things and be able to handle each one with ease. Now she feels that you are unable to juggle your attacks, and she doesn't like it. She doesn't understand why. Give her some time."

Dominique felt a little comfort from Ms. Anderson's story. She only hoped Devin would come around like she did. She didn't like seeing Devin act toward her as she'd been doing.

"I hope you are right. It bothers me she doesn't want me to touch her."

"I know. I was like that, too. I eventually got over it as I got older."

"I pray Devin won't have to deal with my attacks much longer. I can't continue like this. I won't be able to practice law, having attacks like these. I never know when they are going to happen. I can't afford to be in court when one starts. I will lose all my creditability."

"You're right. Well, let's think positively. Hopefully, with Dr. Martin's help you will be able to figure out what is causing them."

"I hope so, and I hope it happens soon. I don't know how much more Eric is going to be able to handle."

"Eric is a strong young man. He will be able to handle it. He is worried about you, but he's going to be by your side until the end. What he needs from you is for you to relax and try to get better. That's what Devin needs, too."

"I wish it was just that easy."

"You can start by coming outside and having lunch with Devin and me. You could use the fresh air."

Dominique sat up, slid off the side of the bed, and followed Ms. Anderson outside.

After everybody finished eating, Ms. Anderson took the dishes in to clean and Devin went back to her sandbox to play. Dominique tried not to get upset when Devin didn't say much to her while they ate. She was going to take Ms. Anderson's advice about giving Devin some time.

She reclined in her chaise outside and closed her eyes to clear her mind and relax. As she slipped into a peaceful state, she heard the bushes rustling behind her. When she opened her eyes, she focused her attention on the moving bushes. A body appeared. It was Shawn, coming to visit her. She was excited to see him, but as he approached, she detected something was bothering Shawn. She wondered if something had happened at home again.

"Shawn, what's wrong?" she asked, sitting upright on her chaise.

"I've been thinking about all the fun I have with you and Devin. I wish my sister could come and hang out, too. I wish I didn't ever have to leave." Shawn sat down beside Dominique on her chaise.

Dominique felt the same way. She was never ready for him to leave. She enjoyed him sleeping over and fixing him meals. She knew he was safe when he was with her. "I've enjoyed your company, too. I wish you could stay, too. But we both know that's not possible right now."

"It really is. You just don't want to make the sacrifice necessary to be with me. Anyway, I just wanted to see you one last time," Shawn said.

"What do you mean 'one last time?'" Dominique asked.

"You don't have time for me, Dominique. Besides, you're sick, and it's just a matter of time before Eric tries to commit you. I can't stand to watch you deteriorate like my mother before my eyes, so I have to leave you now while I still have good memories of you."

"Shawn, don't talk like that. I'm not going crazy. I'm just a little stressed, that's all. My situation is very different from your mother's."

"No, it isn't," he interrupted. "Neither my mother nor you have control of your mental state. You can't stop yourself from having another attack. And she can't stop herself from drifting further away from my sister and me. I want to remember you just the way I first met you: strong and determined. I don't want to see you weak and broken down. I can't stand to see that happen to someone else I love." Shawn leaned over and gave her a quick kiss on the cheek, then disappeared through the bushes.

Dominique sat on her chaise, stunned by Shawn's words. He really thought he was losing her because of her attacks like he lost his mother to her breakdown. In her mind, she wasn't going to have a breakdown, she just needed to relax and with time everything would work itself out. Dominique turned around to see what Devin and Ms. Anderson were doing. They were no longer outside, so she decided to go inside, too, and join them.

CHAPTER 30

Dominique walked back into the house and sat down on her sunroom love seat. She looked back outside at the place she and Shawn once stood discussing her mental condition. Her reminiscing was interrupted by her ringing telephone. Not sure whether Ms. Anderson was free to answer the telephone, Dominique reached over and answered her cordless telephone sitting on her coffee table. Devin blew her a kiss as she opened the sunroom door and went back outside to play.

"Hello," Dominique answered.

"Dominique," Shawn Silver said wearily.

"Where have you been? I've been leaving you messages." Dominique said, afraid of knowing.

"I'm sorry, Dominique. I've been trying to keep Kimberly's case together."

"What do you mean, 'keep the case together?'"

"Jaret Bell has been killed," Shawn replied and allowed silence to fill the air.

Dominique felt her chest tighten as she started to gasp for air, not believing what she was hearing. Another witness had been eliminated from testifying against Mr. Buchanan. She couldn't imagine what could have happened. Bell was supposed to be in maximum security. She now feared Buchanan's unlimited boundaries and influence more than ever.

"Dominique, are you still there?"

Finally, able to speak, she choked out, "Yes. What happened to him?"

"Someone slashed his throat in his cell, and no one saw a thing."

Dominique sat in disbelief. "I thought he was in maximum security."

"He was. The security guard watching his cell said he didn't see a thing. You and I both know that Michael Buchanan ordered that hit."

Dominique knew it, but she didn't want to believe it. There were no limits to Mr. Buchanan's reach. If he was able to eliminate Mr. Bell in maximum-security, then he was probably responsible for Mrs. Buchanan's trying to OD the other night, too. But what puzzled Dominique was why he didn't kill her. Now he still risked her testifying against him.

"Shawn, what are we going to do about Mrs. Buchanan? If Mr. Buchanan got to Jaret Bell, Mrs. Buchanan is a sitting target right now in that hospital."

"Don't worry, I've arranged for some of my people to watch Mrs. Buchanan. Believe me, she will make it to trial."

"Shawn, what people of yours are you referring to?" Dominique asked hesitantly.

"Don't worry about it. Forget I said anything. The less you know the better off you are."

Dominique sat on her couch, numb as she listened to Shawn's discomforting words. Obviously, she didn't know Shawn as well as she thought. As Michael Buchanan had put it: she was definitely out of her league now. She knew nothing of this world, nor did she want to. She wanted to stay in her own little world and pretend none of this was really happening.

"Dominique, I think you better come clean with Eric about everything. He needs to know what he's up against right now," he warned, sparing no punches.

She sat petrified as she listened. When she glanced outside, she saw that Devin was standing by the bushes and talking to someone. She dropped the phone and ran outside to rescue her child from the stranger.

"Devin!" Dominique yelled and ran as fast as she could toward her.

Devin, not realizing the danger she was in, turned around as the stranger disappeared into the bushes. Dominique snatched Devin into her arms and ran back toward the house, operating off sheer adrenaline.

"Mommy, what's wrong?" Devin asked as her mother rushed inside the house and locked the sunroom door behind her.

"Who was that talking to you outside?" Dominique asked frantically as she lowered her to the ground again.

"I don't know. He said he was a friend of yours," Devin answered, unaware that she may have been in danger. Calmly, she handed Dominique a dollar bill. "He gave me this to have."

Dominique snatched the money from Devin's hand and tore it into little pieces. "Don't ever talk to strangers again without your father or me being present! Do you hear me?" Dominique was yelling at Devin and shaking her.

Devin burst into tears as her fragile body jostled back and forth. "I won't, Mommy!"

"Dominique!" Ms. Anderson called from the kitchen doorway.

Dominique released her hold on Devin and turned around, delirious from her scare.

"What's going on?" Ms. Anderson asked, reaching out to receive Devin's frightened body.

"Someone tried to abduct Devin from the backyard. They almost had her until I glanced out by the bushes. Why weren't you outside with her?" she screamed. Tears raced down her face.

Obviously, blaming Ms. Anderson wasn't right. It would have been Dominique's fault because she insisted on prosecuting Michael Buchanan. How would she be able to tell Eric and expect he would not blame her, too? And how would she be able to live with herself? She was in too deep, and it was too late to turn back. Shawn was right, she was going to have to tell Eric everything whether she wanted to or not.

"I'm sorry," Ms. Anderson apologized. "We have to call Eric and the police." She held Devin tightly in her arms, grateful that Dominique had been there in her absence.

Dominique started to pace the floor. "No, we can't call the police," she said, trying to think of her next move.

"Why can't we call the police?" Ms. Anderson asked.

Dominique's telephone rang and interrupted her thoughts. Disoriented, she answered it.

"Lucky you. You almost lost your precious little girl." It was Michael Buchanan. "I thought you had protection watching you and your family. Oh, I forgot … They work for me," he said, bursting into loud laughter.

"Leave my family alone, you bastard," Dominique yelled back at Mr. Buchanan.

"No need to call names. You knew the risk when you decided to continue with this case. Now you deal with the consequence. And just in case you forgot what I told you about calling the police, I'm watching your husband at the airport as we speak. What a fine specimen he is! I see why you chose him. Goodbye for now." Buchanan hung up the telephone.

Enraged by Buchanan's call, Dominique threw the telephone across the room. Devin screamed in horror as she watched the telephone crash into the wall and broke into pieces.

"Dominique, who was that?" Ms. Anderson asked, now frightened too by Dominique's violent behavior.

"That bastard Mr. Buchanan," she yelled, terrified because she knew Eric was in danger and had no clue. She had to contact him and tell him everything before it was too late.

Dominique ran into her kitchen to call Eric on his cell phone, but his phone was off. Paranoid about her own safety, she ran to her front window to see who was outside guarding her house. She stood there vulnerable as she searched her street for any signs of her designated protection. The street was empty except for her neighbors' cars that lined the streets. No one was outside protecting her and her family right now. Dominique ran back to the kitchen and dialed Shawn Silver's cell phone again.

"Dominique, what just happened?" he asked, without saying hello. He recognized her number on his caller ID.

"Mr. Buchanan tried to abduct Devin from my backyard a few minutes ago," she explained, shaking nervously.

"Have you told Eric yet?" Shawn asked.

"No. His cell phone is off."

"Where is Eric now?"

"He's out of town on business, and Buchanan knows it, too. He told me just a few minutes ago he was watching him in the airport." She was praying to God nothing would happen to Eric. Right now, she didn't even know which airport he was at.

"Dominique, as soon as you can, you need to tell Eric everything. Don't you or your family leave your house until this case is over," Shawn said without confidence.

"What are you going to do now?" Dominique asked. She was afraid for his safety too.

"I have a few things I need to wrap up around here before I make myself a ghost."

"Shawn, please be careful. Maybe you should go into hiding for a while."

"I have a lead I need to follow up on first," he replied vaguely. "I prefer not to say what, just in case our telephones are bugged. I'll tell you the details as soon as I've confirmed and secured everything," With that, they hung up.

Dominique wondered what lead Shawn had and how it would help them win the case. With Katherine Buchanan fighting for her life and Maria Gonzales and Jaret Bell dead, all Dominique had was Buchanan's videotapes and his daughter's testimony.

Then Dominique wondered about how secure Buchanan's videotapes were down at the police station. She had to get them before he did. Dominique rushed to get her pocketbook and keys. She had to go down to the police station and get those videotapes. Otherwise they wouldn't make it to court as a part of her evidence.

CHAPTER 31

Dominique drove as fast as she could to the police station, breaking every safety regulation. After she parked her car, she ran straight into the police station and demanded to see whoever handled the evidence labeled top security. As she waited to be ushered back, she prayed nothing had happened to the videotapes of Mr. Buchanan, because if they were gone, she didn't know how convincing she could be with just Kimberly's testimony.

"Mrs. Wallace, please follow me," a police officer said as he led the way down a long hallway.

Dominique didn't say a word. She just followed the officer until they reached a room where thick security bars surrounded them. She looked around the room until another officer appeared in the window to assist her. "Mrs. Wallace, how can I help you?" he asked.

"I have several videotapes stored here for protection. I need you to pull them for me," Dominique answered. She watched as the officer disappeared into the back for a little while and returned empty-handed.

"Mrs. Wallace, your videotapes have been checked out," the officer said as he stood behind the barred window holding a clipboard full of papers.

"Checked out!" Dominique screamed. "Who checked out the videotapes?"

He looked down at his clipboard to retrieve that piece of information for Dominique. "I don't know. My records show that someone with top clearance has checked the videotapes out. Unfortunately, I'm not privy to that information."

Dominique's stomach started to become upset as she became faint, knowing Mr. Buchanan had beaten her to the punch. She couldn't believe she and Shawn had been so stupid to leave their evidence here.

"Mrs. Wallace, are you okay?" The officer asked. "Someone get her a chair before she falls!" he yelled from behind the gated window.

The officer who escorted her to the evidence room grabbed her arm and helped her into a chair. "Would you like something to drink?" he asked, seeing how flush Dominique looked.

Feeling ill and defeated at the same time, Dominique yelled back. "*No!* I didn't give anyone permission to release my evidence."

"Mrs. Wallace, whoever checked out the videotapes had the authority to do so without your permission," the officer behind the window answered.

"What kind of operation are you people running here?" Dominique yelled. "Your people haven't been able to protect any of my people. Now you haven't been able to protect simple videotapes. What good are you? I don't know who I can trust now!" She ran out of the police station and headed home. She tried to call Shawn Silver's cell phone but there was no answer, so she left him an urgent message.

Dominique's mind raced as she drove back home. She didn't know what to do next. Everything was falling apart, and she couldn't stop it. Michael Buchanan was winning the boxing match, and she wasn't sure how many more rounds she would be able to go. And she was sure he wasn't going to allow her to walk away with just a loss. That didn't seem like his style at all.

Panicking about her unfortunate fate, Dominique tried to dial Shawn Silver's cell number again, but still there was no answer.

When Dominique finally reached her house, she parked her car, raced back inside, and locked all the doors and windows. She was going to have to protect herself now. No longer would she rely on the assigned protection, especially not knowing who their true allegiance was to.

"Dominique, what's going on?" Ms. Anderson asked as she watched her race around the house in a panic.

"I need you to make sure all the doors and windows are locked. I'm afraid Michael Buchanan might try to hurt us. I have to secure us here until Eric gets home," Dominique said, never slowing her pace.

"Where is Eric now? Are you sure Eric is safe out there?" Ms. Anderson asked.

Dominique stopped in her tracks and slammed her fist against the wall as she burst into tears. "No. I'm not sure."

Ms. Anderson rushed over to Dominique's side and pulled her body into hers for support. "He's going to be okay," Ms. Anderson tried to assure her, not realizing the danger she had been placed in herself.

"I honestly didn't think things would get to this point. I really thought everything was going to be okay. What have I done?" Dominique continued to cry.

"Why don't you go lie down for moment?" Ms. Anderson suggested. "I'll stay up and keep a watch on everything. You won't be any good if you fall apart right now. You need to stay strong until Eric gets back to help us figure out what to do next."

"I can't sleep right now," Dominique replied.

"I think it would be best. Dominique, I don't want you to work yourself up and have another attack. So do as I say and at least go lie down for a moment or two," Ms. Anderson insisted.

Dominique decided not to argue with Ms. Anderson. She agreed she didn't want to have another attack, so she slowly walked upstairs to her bedroom and lay down. Afraid of the danger she had placed Eric in, she prayed he would make it home safely. She was so disappointed in herself for not being honest with him from the beginning. Now her lies and deceit were catching up with her.

CHAPTER 32

Devin heard funny sounds coming from her parent's bedroom as she played in her bedroom down the hall. Hesitantly, she walked down the hallway and opened her parents' door. When she entered the room, her mother was crying and moaning as she lay across her bed. Confused and scared by her mother's strange behavior, Devin stood by the door and watched Dominique rolling around the bed frantically.

She wanted her mother to stop, so she ran over to her mother's side, and yelled. "Mommy! Stop crying!" But Dominique ignored her and continued.

Frightened by her mother's behavior, Devin started shaking her mother's body.

"Please don't touch me," Dominique cried out, trying to wave Devin away.

Devin fell backward off the bed. Her head slammed against the floor, causing her to bite her tongue. A sharp pain shot through Devin's mouth as blood started filling her mouth. In pain and dizzy, she tried to raise her head from the floor with her head and mouth throbbing. She rubbed her mouth gently. Realizing she was bleeding, she started to scream as blood continued to pour from her mouth. The sight of the blood terrified Devin and distracted her attention from her mother's condition.

Frantic because of her bleeding mouth, Devin started running in circles, afraid that she might have bitten her tongue off. Screaming at the top of her lungs, she started to choke on the blood going down her throat. She fell on the floor and bent over, trying to catch her breath as she threw up the blood and everything else she had eaten for lunch that afternoon.

"Devin, what's going on?" Ms. Anderson shrieked when she entered the room and saw Devin kneeling and throwing up everywhere.

Unable to answer, Devin continued to throw up.

"Devin, what happened?" Ms. Anderson asked, rushing to Devin's side.

Lightheaded and terrified, Devin managed to answer, "I'm bleeding!"

"Calm down!" Ms. Anderson demanded. She helped Devin get to a sitting position, then pulled up the bottom of Devin's shirt and stuffed it in her mouth to stop the bleeding. Now that Devin was a little calmer, Ms. Anderson saw Dominique on top of her bed, crying and rolling around.

Devin sat on the floor and held her shirt in her mouth while Ms. Anderson tended to Dominique. Devin was devastated that her mother had pushed her off the bed and caused her such pain. She wondered if this meant that her mother didn't love her anymore and started to cry again.

"Please don't hurt Shawn! Please!" Dominique yelled. Devin was confused. There wasn't anyone in the room but the three of them. Why was she yelling Shawn's name?

"I'm not hurting Shawn," Ms. Anderson pleaded.

"Please don't hurt Shawn! Please!" Dominique continued to yell.

"I'm not hurting Shawn, Dominique. Please stop saying that. I'm not hurting him. Please wake up!" Ms. Anderson yelled as she wrestled with Dominique on top of the bed.

Devin wanted her daddy now, but he was gone. Then she remembered that he showed her how to reach him in an emergency. Devin ran downstairs to the sunroom, dripping blood along the way, and leaving Ms. Anderson behind to deal with her mother. She pushed the phone button her father told her would dial his cell number and waited for him to answer. "Daddy!" Devin screamed when Eric finally answered his cell phone.

"Devin, is this you?" Eric asked, surprised to hear her voice.

"Yes. Something is wrong with Mommy. She's crying and fighting with Ms. Anderson in your bed and she won't wake up. I tried to wake her, but she pushed me off the bed and I bit my tongue really bad." Trying to catch her breath, she added, "Now she keeps telling Ms. Anderson to stop hurting Shawn. She's not hurting Shawn. Shawn isn't here, Daddy. It's just Mommy, Ms. Anderson, and me. I'm scared. Daddy, please come home," Devin screamed and started crying again.

"I'm on my way home now. Where are you?"

"I'm downstairs in the sunroom," Devin answered, still holding the bottom of her shirt in her mouth.

"Stay put. I'm on my way," Eric said as she rushed to his car from the airport terminal. "Sweetheart, stop crying. It's going to be okay. Devin, I'm going to stay on the telephone with you until I get there."

"Hurry up. I'm really scared and, my mouth is bleeding, too."

"Your mouth is bleeding?"

"Yes, Mommy pushed me off the bed, and I bit my tongue," Devin answered.

"Devin, is your mouth bleeding a lot?"

"Yes. I have my shirt in my mouth now. Daddy, I threw up on the floor in your bedroom. I couldn't help it."

"Don't worry about that. I'll get it up. Has your tongue stopped bleeding?" Eric asked.

She removed the shirt from her mouth and saw that her blood wasn't dripping anymore. "I think so."

"Good. Devin, you did the right thing to call me about Mommy's condition. She's not feeling well right now. She's very sick, and we have to be patient with her."

"She didn't start getting sick until Shawn started coming around. Now she thinks we're hurting him," Devin said resentfully.

"Devin, calm down. I'll talk to Mommy about Shawn when I get home. I don't want you to worry about him right now. Mommy doesn't realize what she is saying right now."

"I don't want him to come around anymore. I don't like her hurting me because of him."

"Shawn isn't the reason Mommy is hurting you," Eric responded, realizing Devin didn't understand what was really going on.

"She was fine until he started coming around. That's when she started getting sick," Devin repeated, convinced of her belief.

Eric thought it was strange how Devin thought Shawn was the cause of Dominique's attacks. Then he wondered why Dominique was talking about him during the attack. He wondered if she was having a flashback about that night of the attack. Maybe she *had* seen him that night and was dreaming it all over again. He knew now they would have to explain to Devin what happened to Dominique that night. He didn't want her to blame someone else for her mother's attacks.

"Devin, calm down. When I get home, I need to talk to you about something. But right now, you have to stay strong for me. Can you do that for me?"

"Yes, I can be strong. Daddy, are you almost home?"

"Almost. I'm going as fast as I can," Eric responded as he accelerated down the interstate, trying to get home. He was glad his meeting had been postponed at the last minute. Now he would be able to help Ms. Anderson with Dominique.

"My head and my mouth still hurt, Daddy," Devin said, feeling better from knowing he was almost home to comfort her.

"Do you think you could go back upstairs to check on Mommy?"

"I think I can. Please don't make me try to wake her up. I'm afraid she's going to hurt me again," Devin pleaded.

"I just want you to tell me what Mommy and Ms. Anderson are doing now, that's all."

Devin agreed and headed upstairs to her parents' bedroom with the cordless telephone still to her ear. Slowly, she entered the room. Her mother's eyes were still closed, but now she was calmer and lying in a knot while Ms. Anderson sat on the edge of the bed watching her. Devin watched as her mother continued to cry, and she told her father every detail while standing in the doorway and watching.

"Good job, Devin. I'm in the driveway now. I'm on my way into the house. You can hang up the telephone now," Eric said, racing from his car. He saw Devin standing at the top of the stairs crying and immediately ran to comfort her. She was scared, and he wished she had not seen Dominique having an attack. Before going to comfort Dominique, he ordered Devin to go to her bedroom until he joined her. He didn't want to scare her any more than she already had been.

Ms. Anderson jumped to her feet when Eric entered the bedroom. "Eric, I'm so glad you are home. She's having another attack, and I can't wake her this time."

"I'll take care of Dominique while you stay with Devin in her room," Eric said, making his way over to Dominique's bedside.

"Dominique? It's me, Eric—your husband. Can you hear me?" Eric said repeatedly, but she didn't respond.

Finally, she answered yes in a faint voice.

"It's me … Eric. Do you recognize me?" He gently rubbed her back to help calm her.

"Please don't touch me! Please leave me alone!" Dominique yelled and started to swing at him.

"Dominique, it's me … Eric, your husband."

"I hate you," Dominique yelled back. Then she covered her face and turned it side to side as if someone were slapping her. "Please stop! Stop, you're hurting me," Dominique yelled.

"Dominique, please calm down and let me help you," Eric cried out.

"Stop! Please don't touch me. Please," Dominique continued to yell.

Eric let her go and watched her cry out, not knowing how to help her. He could only watch her lying there suffering. Tears filled his eyes because he couldn't help her. He didn't like her suffering like this, and now Devin had seen Dominique have an attack.

Feeling helpless, Eric stood to his feet and paced around the floor until he noticed Devin standing in the doorway and crying with Ms. Anderson holding her hand. When Eric made eye contact with Devin, she ran to her room and slammed the door. He didn't know whether to go after her or stay at Dominique's side. He turned back around to face Dominique when the yelling stopped. She had stopped yelling and now was crying. He watched as she continued to curl up in a tight knot. She was shaking and appeared to be coming out of it. She always seemed to calm down once she went into this position, so he waited patiently by her side, waiting for the right moment to call to her.

"Dominique. It's me, Eric … your husband." He sat on the edge of the bed waiting for Dominique to answer and praying that his wife would recognize his voice and end this horrible scene. He was afraid Devin would be traumatized forever by this experience.

"Eric," Dominique responded as tears continued to roll down her face.

"I'm right here. What happened?" Eric asked as he took Dominique into his arms to comfort her shaking body.

"I don't know what happened."

"It's going to be okay," Eric assured her. "Just calm down." He rubbed her back gently and continued to repeat: "Just relax."

"I feel a little strange," Dominique responded.

"You just had another panic attack."

"I don't know what caused it."

"I know. Just relax. I want you to go see Dr. Martin as soon as possible."

"I have another appointment first thing next week."

"I want you to see him before then. I'm going to call him for you."

"I just need to relax, Eric. I will be fine."

"You have been relaxing."

"I think I know what happened this time."

"What?"

Dominique dreaded telling Eric everything, but no longer could she keep the truth from her husband. He needed to know the true danger they were in because of her.

A loud crash came from down the hallway. Eric jumped up and told Ms. Anderson to watch Dominique as he ran out of the room. He looked down the hallway to see what might have caused the noise. But everything was in its place, so he rushed down the hallway toward Devin's room to make sure she was okay. When he opened her bedroom door, he saw her bookshelf had been turned over, and her toys were all over her room. Devin was sitting in a corner, crying, with her head down between her legs.

"Devin. What happened?" Eric asked, rushing over to her, but Devin didn't answer.

"Devin, don't you hear me talking to you?" Eric called out to her.

"Yes." Devin finally answered, with the bottom of her shirt still in her mouth.

"Why didn't you answer me the first time?"

"I don't know," Devin answered, crying.

"What happened to your room?"

"Shawn did it!" Devin yelled out.

"Devin, why are you blaming this on Shawn? You know he didn't do it."

"Yes. He did," Devin insisted.

"No, he didn't. He's not even here."

"He was. He just left. I hate him, Daddy," Devin yelled.

"Don't say that. You don't hate anybody," Eric told Devin as he took Devin into his arms.

"Yes, I do. I hate Shawn like Mommy hates you and me." Devin continued to cry.

"Mommy doesn't hate you and me."

"Yes, she does. She just told you she hates you, and she pushed me onto the floor. She doesn't love us anymore. All she cares about is Shawn."

Eric just stared at Devin, thinking about how to explain everything to her so she would understand. He didn't want to scare her, nor did he want her to be afraid of Dominique. But he definitely didn't want her to think her mother didn't love him or her anymore. He had to explain to her that her mother was sick now. And hopefully, with time, she would get better. Eric wished he could tell his daughter when it was going to be over, but this was the first time he had ever experienced anything like this. He wanted Dominique back just as much as Devin did, and was willing to do whatever was necessary to help her get better.

"Eric, let me explain it to her," Dominique interrupted as she stood in the doorway of Devin's bedroom.

"I don't want to talk to you," Devin yelled at Dominique.

"Devin!" Eric yelled at Devin.

"Eric, it's okay. She's just upset. Try to explain to her what is going on. I'm going to give you two some privacy to talk," Dominique said then closed Devin's bedroom door behind her, disheartened.

"Devin, I didn't like the way you spoke to your mother," Eric said with disappointment in his voice.

"I'm sorry, Daddy," Devin said as she reached out to hug her daddy. She held Eric tight and continued to cry.

"Devin, I want you to calm down and listen to me." He stood up with Devin in his arms, walked over to her bed, and laid her in it.

She looked up at her daddy with tears in her eyes.

"Mommy isn't feeling well now. She is going through something very difficult. I don't know when she is going to feel better, but I'm praying she will get better real soon."

"I'm trying to be a good girl so she can get better," Devin said.

"I know you are, and we appreciate you doing that. But we didn't tell you everything. You remember that morning when you found out someone hurt Mommy?"

"Yes."

"Since then, Mommy has been having bad dreams about that night," Eric explained.

"How long is she going to be having bad dreams?"

Eric shrugged his shoulders and shook his head as he answered Devin. "I don't know. Mommy's seeing a doctor to see if he can help stop the bad dreams."

"Can she go back because she didn't stop having them?"

"She's going to see him again. Hopefully, he will be able to help her," Eric said, praying that Dr. Martin would be able to help her end her attacks.

"I don't understand why Mommy was telling you she hated you."

"Mommy wasn't telling me she hated me. She didn't realize she was saying those things to me. You remember when you found her? She was saying things then, too, right? She wasn't saying them to you. She didn't even know you were in the room with her. Her eyes were closed."

"I remember," Devin nodded.

"She was having one of those bad dreams again. That's why she was crying when you found her. She was dreaming. Do you understand what I'm telling you?"

"Kind of. I don't like Mommy having bad dreams."

"I know. I don't either. All we can do is make sure Mommy relaxes so she can get better. So that means you are going to have to clean up all this mess in here for her," Eric said as he pointed to all her books and toys scattered about her bedroom.

"Do you think Mommy hates me now because I was mean to her?"

"No. Mommy is more upset that she upset you."

"Will I cause Mommy to have another bad dream?"

"I don't think so. I think if you go apologize to her and clean up your room she will feel better."

"Okay. Will you go with me, Daddy?"

"Yes. But let me look at your tongue first." Eric pulled Devin's shirt bottom out of her mouth. He could see her little teeth marks in her tongue but the bleeding had stopped.

Eric reached out and gave Devin a big hug. He knew she was feeling awkward about everything. Even he was feeling awkward. He was as concerned and confused as Devin was. He wanted his wife back. He didn't like seeing her losing control like she was. He felt tears coming into his eyes as he thought about how his family had been affected by that troubled night in the hospital parking lot. Since then, things hadn't been the same. He felt helpless, and that bothered him.

He hated himself for not being there for his wife and daughter when they needed him most. What kind of husband and father was he? His job as a husband and father was to protect his family, and he hadn't done a good job of that. Not only had he not been there for Dominique that night, he wasn't able to keep her from having those attacks, nor protect Devin from experiencing what she had today. They meant the world to him and he would give his life for them.

Eric started feeling angry because his manhood was at stake now. He was angry with the attacker who caused all these emotions to become bottled up inside of him. He wished he could have been the one who was in the parking lot that night, not Dominique. He felt defenseless because he was unable to protect them. Eric wanted revenge, but of course that wouldn't solve anything. It would only give him instant gratification. He would have to try to put his anger aside for now and be there for his wife and daughter. He had to be strong for them.

Eric kissed Devin on her forehead and whispered to her, "I love you so much, Devin. Don't you ever forget that."

"I love you too, Daddy."

"I feel bad that I wasn't here today with you and Mommy. I will try to never let that happen again. I owe you an apology. Will you forgive me?"

"I forgive you, Daddy." Devin responded.

"Thank you," Eric responded as he helped her out of the bed to go apologize to Dominique. He took her by the hand and walked with her into the sunroom, where Dominique was reclining on her chaise.

"Mommy, I have something I want to tell you," Devin said in a soft, whispery voice. Dominique rose from her reclining position on her chaise to address Devin and Eric as they walked toward her.

"What is it?" Dominique asked, just now noticing that Devin had

286

blood all over her clothes. "Devin, where did all that blood on your clothes come from?"

"I bit my tongue when you pushed me out of the bed," Devin answered.

Dominique looked up at Eric before responding. "I pushed you out of the bed?"

"Yes. I was trying to wake you up, and you pushed me out of the bed. I fell off the bed and hit my head on the floor and bit my tongue. I'm sorry I threw up in your room. I couldn't help it."

"Don't worry about that. I'll get it up," Dominique said as she slid to the edge of the chaise to examine Devin's tongue.

"No. I'll get it up," Eric interrupted. "I want you to relax. I'll take care of it."

"You don't have to. It was my fault she got hurt. Devin, let me look at your tongue." Dominique reached out to get a closer look at Devin's mouth when she opened for her. She could see Devin's teeth marks in her tongue. She pulled Devin closer to her and gave her a hug to apologize for causing her to bite her tongue. "Devin, I'm so sorry. Will you accept my apology for hurting and scaring you?"

"Yes." Devin started to cry. "Please get better. I don't want you to get sick again."

Dominique looked up at Eric again before answering. She was so sorry for making her family suffer like this. She prayed after this was over, they would be able to forgive her. "Did Daddy explain to you what's going on?"

"He said you are having bad dreams because you weren't relaxing like you were told. Will you start relaxing so you won't get sick again?" Devin asked.

"I promise I will," she replied.

"Devin, let's go upstairs and clean up your room so Mommy can rest," Ms. Anderson spoke up, alerting everyone to her presence.

"Okay," Devin said and followed Ms. Anderson upstairs to clean her room.

Dominique looked out of the window as tears started to fill her eyes again. She had to tell Eric about her other attacks as well as the danger she had placed them in because of being the lead attorney in the case against Michael Buchanan. "Eric, I have something I need to tell you," Dominique said sadly.

"What is it?" He picked up on the sad tone in her voice.

"I haven't been completely honest with you about everything," she said, not looking directly at Eric.

"How so?"

It was time to tell Eric about her attacks first, and then the situation with Michael Buchanan. "I've had several panic attacks."

"Several. How many?"

"I started having attacks before the physical one in the parking garage. I didn't think anything of it at first. Then they got worse."

"How have they gotten worse?"

"They're now starting to feel real. I hear, feel, and see now, whereas before I didn't."

"So how do you explain the panic attacks before the physical attack?"

"Dr. Martin was right about my body trying to tell me I needed a break. I was afraid to tell you because I knew you would demand I stop working."

"You're right. I want you to call Shawn now and tell him you can't finish prosecuting this case," Eric demanded.

Tears rolled down Dominique's face because she knew she had to confess to Eric everything. "There's something else I haven't told you."

Eric just stared at Dominique without responding.

"I've put our family in danger by continuing to prosecute this case," Dominique confessed.

"What are you talking about?" Eric asked.

"Sit down," Dominique insisted as she felt herself becoming extremely nervous thinking about his reaction to what she was about to tell him.

Dominique took a deep breath before elaborating. "A week ago, Michael Buchanan showed up here uninvited in our bedroom while you were away on business."

Eric jumped to his feet and shouted, "What? Did he touch you?"

"Calm down. No, he didn't. I don't want Devin and Ms. Anderson to hear you," Dominique pleaded.

"What did he want?" Eric asked.

"He told me if I insist on trying to convict him, he will harm my family," Dominique finally admitted.

"Did you call the police and report his threat?" Eric asked.

"No. I couldn't. He threatened me that he would harm you guys if I did. I was afraid to tell you, Eric. I didn't know what to do," Dominique said remorsefully.

"Dominique, I can't believe you didn't tell me this," he shouted back as he started to pace the sunroom floor. "Do you realize how serious this is? He has already killed one of your witnesses. What makes you think he won't kill you or us too?"

Dominique nodded. "He also killed Mr. Jaret Bell while he was in maximum security."

"Who is Mr. Jaret Bell?" Eric asked curiously. Dominique couldn't remember if she ever told Eric his name.

"Bell was the man who attacked me in the hospital garage. Shawn and I believe Mr. Buchanan had him killed when he found out he was going to testify against him in court."

"You mean he was going to help you try to convict Buchanan?" Eric asked, shocked and confused at the same time.

"Yes. He was willing to make a deal to reduce his sentence, but now he's dead. Now I'm worried he is going to try to kill Mrs. Buchanan, too. She's in the hospital now. She tried to OD. They said she tried to commit suicide, but now that Bell has been murdered, too, I believe Michael Buchanan managed to get to her. And I'm praying she's going to make it,"

Dominique paused. "He also tried to abduct Devin in our backyard."

"What?" Eric shouted. "What happened?"

"I was talking on the phone to Shawn Silver when I looked outside and saw Devin talking to someone in the bushes."

Eric paced the floor, trying to take in everything he had been told. "What exactly did Buchanan say to you the night he showed up here? First of all, how did he get in here?"

"I don't know how he got in here because I had people watching the house that night, but he managed to get past them. I thought it was Devin coming into our bedroom because she didn't want to sleep by herself."

Eric interrupted. "He was in our bedroom?" He was outraged. Buchanan had crossed the line.

"Yes. Nothing happened. He just told me he would turn my perfect world upside down by hurting you and Devin. He let me know he had a lot of connections all over. I didn't realize to what degree he was talking, but now I know. I was afraid to tell you because I didn't know how you would react. I was afraid to take that chance. So I told Shawn, and he had twenty-four hour protection placed on you and me."

"Why didn't you tell me you had someone following me?" Eric asked.

"I was afraid," she said. "You would have wanted to know why, and I wasn't prepared to tell you."

"Were you afraid I might tell you not to prosecute him, or afraid for my safety? Because what it looks like to me is you were afraid I might tell you to walk away from this case." Eric stared disappointedly at Dominique.

She didn't know what to say. She was concerned about Eric's safety, but she also wanted to convict Mr. Buchanan. She hadn't expected things to get out of control the way they had.

"Dominique, I don't know what to say or think right now. Who are you?" Eric asked as he continued to stare.

"I'm your wife."

"I'm not so sure. My wife would have put her family first. She wouldn't have put her family in jeopardy to prosecute some case. She wouldn't have thought twice about walking away. Dominique, since you decided to handle this case, you haven't been yourself. You are allowing it to destroy this family, like you are allowing that boy Shawn to come in here and destroy everything, too. It seems to me everything else has taken precedent over your family." Eric was outraged.

"That isn't true. I'm not trying to destroy my family."

"How can you say that with a straight face?" he replied angrily. "You have some deranged man out there waiting to kill us when we walk out that front door, yet you still want to help his daughter. Now you're having attacks where you're calling out Shawn's name while you abuse your daughter."

"I didn't intentionally try to hurt Devin," Dominique shouted back.

"You might as well have. I've asked you constantly since the attack to introduce me to him, but you haven't. Why haven't you?" Eric demanded.

"Because he's afraid," she responded defensively.

"Afraid!" Eric chuckled. "There's that word 'afraid' again. Well guess what? I'm fuckin afraid, too, that my damn life is in danger. But do you care? No. You have been so selfish about everything. Everything has been about you and what you want."

"It hasn't," Dominique shouted back.

"Yes, it has. Dominique, you didn't even tell me you had someone following me because you knew I would insist on you getting off this case. So, you decided to be deceitful and go behind my back and order protection, hoping I wouldn't find out. Let me ask you this: Do you think the car incident with Ms. Anderson and Devin was a fluke?"

"Eric, I don't know for certain whether Mr. Buchanan was involved with that car incident."

"Sure, you don't, and right now, even if you were telling me the truth, I don't believe you. So let me ask you this. What is your plan now?"

"I don't know."

"You don't know." Eric repeated. "Dominique, I don't even feel safe walking out of that front door with Devin not knowing who is around the corner waiting to follow me. I hope this case is worth your family's life."

Dominique felt like Eric had dumped the world's burdens on her shoulders as she stared back at him, speechless.

"Daddy, why are you and Mommy fighting?" Devin asked.

"Devin, I need for you to go back to your room," Eric demanded forcefully.

"Stop yelling at me," Devin yelled back at her father and fell to the floor. She started rolling all over the floor, kicking and screaming.

"Devin, stop it. Get up!" Eric yelled at her.

Devin continued to throw a fit. Then her body started to shake frantically, like Dominique's had been doing during her attacks. Was Devin having an actual attack or pretending? Eric's body froze as she shook in the middle of the floor.

"Devin, what's wrong with you?" Dominique cried. She rushed over to Devin and bent down to grab her. "Eric, call an ambulance. Something is wrong with her," Dominique shouted frantically.

"Don't touch me," Devin said as she tried to push her away.

"Devin, please calm down. Eric what's wrong with her?"

"I don't know." He rushed over to help calm Devin down.

"Devin—this is Daddy. Devin—this is Daddy," he continued to repeat.

"Daddy," Devin whispered as her body stopped shaking.

Eric held her body tightly to his as tears streamed down Devin's face.

"I'm going to take you upstairs and put you in bed. I want you to relax," Eric said. He carefully carried her into her bedroom and laid her across her bed.

"Please don't leave me, Daddy," Devin pleaded.

"I won't leave you. I'm going to be right here by your side. Close your eyes and get some rest."

"Okay." Devin closed her eyes and went to sleep. Meanwhile, Eric, Dominique, and Ms. Anderson remained sitting by her side in complete shock.

"Eric, do you think we should take her to the emergency room?" Dominique asked.

"No. She's going to be fine. She just needs to rest," he said calmly.

"I'm not sure. Didn't you just see how she was acting?"

"Dominique, what you saw is how you look when you have an attack," he said. Eric walked over to the door then motioned for everybody to follow him.

"What do you mean, how I look?" Dominique covered her mouth in disbelief.

"I'm not sure if she was doing it for attention or what. Remember: She did see you have one of these attacks. This episode may have been her way of getting back at us for fussing and at me for yelling at her." Eric was feeling exhausted from everything that had just transpired.

"Eric, what are we going to do? I don't want her to think she can just fall out when she can't get her way."

"I know and fully agree. I'm going to talk to her when she wakes up. I'm going to let her know she can't play around like that."

"I'm so sorry," Dominique apologized as tears rolled down her face. She felt so bad about what just happened. She felt responsible for destroying her whole family. Everything was falling apart, and she needed to clear her head. Dominique ran downstairs to look for her keys so she could get out of the house to be alone.

"Dominique, where are you going?" Eric followed behind her as she raced down the stairs.

"I need to get out of here for a while. I need some space to think," Dominique said as she grabbed her purse and tried to race for the front door, but Eric stopped her.

"Dominique, you can't leave here. You know it's not safe."

"Let me go, Eric. I really need to get out of here for a while," she insisted as she tried to pull away.

"Dominique, I can't let you. I don't want anything to happen to you. Please be reasonable right now. I know you are upset, but please don't do anything you will regret later."

Dominique just looked at Eric before responding. Then she handed over her pocketbook and started to cry uncontrollably. "I don't know what to do. I'm so sorry for tearing our family apart," she said. She cried as her body fell to the floor.

"Dominique, Devin's breakdown is not all your fault. It's my fault, too. She saw us arguing." Eric knelt down beside Dominique and wrapped his arms around her to comfort her.

"Eric, it's all my fault. None of this would be happening if I never agreed to take on the Buchanan case." Dominique felt weak and defeated inside. She couldn't pretend to be strong anymore. Her daughter was upstairs, all messed up because of her. Her family was trapped inside of their home, not knowing whether someone was waiting outside to kill them.

Dominique continued to cry because she was convinced that either the Buchanan case was the cause of her attacks, or it was the catalyst that triggered an underlying condition. Now she was worried it might be a hereditary condition that might have been passed on to her daughter. She didn't know anything about her real parents' medical history to rule the possibility out.

She felt awful, like her whole world was crashing down around her as she sat on the floor crying. "Eric, I don't know who I am."

"What do you mean?"

"I don't know anything about my past. I don't know whether my attacks are heredity. I don't know whether our daughter upstairs had an attack or pretended to have an attack. And I haven't been able to remember anything about my past," Dominique confessed, continuing to cry.

"That's what Dr. Martin is there for. Isn't he trying to help you remember?"

"Yes. But I still can't remember a thing. I don't know why. I have been trying to remember, but nothing is coming back to me."

"Does he have an explanation for why you can't remember?"

"He's not sure yet."

"Haven't you tried to find your records yourself?"

"Yes, a long time ago, but I couldn't find anything, so I stopped trying."

"That's strange," Eric said. But now he wondered whether she was telling him the whole truth. "Dominique, is there something you aren't telling me? You know you can tell me anything no matter what."

"I know. I remember asking one of my foster mothers to help me find out some information about my past, and she told me to leave my past in the past. Since then, I've never tried to find anything out. I guess subconsciously I've been afraid to know."

"Does Dr. Martin think your past has something to do with your attacks?"

"I'm not sure, but I think he does."

"Do you want to call him to see if he has found anything yet?"

She didn't respond right away, unsure whether she wanted to do this. A part of her wanted to know but another part didn't. Until now, she was fine without knowing. Her life had been perfect since she met Eric, but erasing her past had been necessary for happiness.

"Let me help you up. Why don't you come in here and rest on the couch while I call Dr. Martin? I'm curious to see if he has found anything." Eric helped her to her feet and onto the couch in the family room.

"Eric …" Dominique called his name but stopped mid-sentence. She wasn't sure if she wanted him to know either. She didn't know if she could handle any more bad news right now.

"It's going to be okay. I will support you no matter what we find out. Don't worry about it. Dominique … I think we need to know."

She didn't answer. Of course, she needed to know, but it had been easy all these years just to tell herself she didn't need to, that she was better off *not* knowing. She closed her eyes and tried to escape.

"Dominique, I just called Dr. Martin's office. They said he is out of town. I didn't leave a message." Eric sat down across from her.

"Did they say when he will be back?"

"No."

The telephone rang, and Eric rushed to pick it up before it woke Devin from her sleep.

"Hello," Eric answered.

Dominique watched from the couch as Eric's facial expression revealed the news he was receiving wasn't good. And the cold stare he gave her was another indication it involved her. Dominique waited nervously as Eric hung up the telephone and stared at her without saying a word.

"Eric what's wrong?" Dominique asked, apprehensive of his response.

"Your damn case!" Eric shouted at Dominique.

"What about my case?" Dominique asked, confused.

"It seems your Mr. Buchanan is on the board of several of my biggest accounts. He's made some phone calls, and now they are pulling out," Eric said furiously.

"I'm so sorry," she responded. A sharp pain raced through her chest. She had truly underestimated how powerful Mr. Buchanan was, and now she was paying the price dearly.

"Now my ass is on the line thanks to you and your precious case. Everything I have worked so hard for all these years, gone up in smoke with just a few phone calls." Eric shook his head still in disbelief.

"What are you going to do?" Dominique asked ruefully.

"Nothing, because my partners think I should take some time off until they can decide the proper action to take. I find this absolutely amazing. I've given that company so many years of hard work and loyalty, and in a matter of seconds I'm nothing. To be honest with you, you might have done me a favor because until now, I was willing to give that company everything I had." Eric walked out of the room shaking his head.

Dominique followed Eric out into the sunroom and watched him from the doorway, picking up everything he threw around earlier. "Eric, I'm really sorry."

"Not as sorry as I am," he responded.

Dominique didn't know what else to say. She needed to be alone to think everything through. Michael Buchanan's threats were haunting her, and she wasn't sure if she was strong enough to ignore them any longer. She couldn't afford to cause anyone else to suffer because of her decisions. Without saying another word, Dominique left Eric to his picking things up and headed back to the family room to be alone.

Eric continued to pick things up until he noticed a note hanging from the side of Dominique's briefcase. Normally, he would have ignored it and tucked it back into her briefcase, but after everything she had dumped on him today, he was curious to know as much as he could about this case that was so dear to her. Eric pulled the piece of paper from her briefcase and read its contents.

Eric stood in the middle of the floor in disbelief. He couldn't believe how Dominique had been able to keep so many things from him. Now he was reading a letter from Shawn that confessed how deeply he felt for her. Eric read the letter again as the words pierced his heart.

Eric paced in a circle as he accepted the fact that his wife was having an affair. Now he wondered how long her affair had been going on. How stupid he felt, welcoming co-worker Shawn into their home, thinking he and Dominique were working on cases late into the night when they were really having an affair right in front of his face. He felt naive and angry with himself for placing Dominique on such a high pedestal—believing she was different and wasn't capable of such. Now he knew she wasn't. He didn't know who she was and didn't care to find out, either.

Dear Dominique,

I'm so glad Eric will be out of town for a few days. I miss our time together. I don't like how we must hide being together. I can't wait until we can be a family and never must be apart. I worry about your safety when I'm not around and pray someday we will never have to be apart.

Love, Shawn

Eric folded the letter up, stuck it in his pocket, and headed out of the sunroom to find Dominique. He at least wanted her to know he knew now and she didn't have to sneak any longer. If she wanted to be with Shawn now, she could.

Eric spotted Dominique in the family room, looking out of the window.

"Dominique, I found something that belongs to you," Eric said as he entered the family room. Dominique turned around to face Eric as he pulled the letter out of his pocket and threw it at her.

Dominique was confused by Eric's behavior as she leaned over to pick up the piece of paper. Clueless, she opened the folded piece of paper and recognized it was the letter her young friend Shawn wrote her. Before she could say a word, Eric spoke.

"You don't have to lie about your affair. I know now. Now you can be with Shawn Silver without having to sneak."

"Eric, it's not what you think," Dominique tried to explain.

"Dominique, please. How can you say that? It's there plain as day in black and white. Shawn is in love with you, and you have been spending time with him when I've been out of town."

Before Dominique could say a word, she spotted her young friend Shawn standing behind Eric in the hallway with a knife pressed against his wrist. He mouthed to her not to tell it was him who wrote the letter. Dominique didn't know what to do. She was torn as she stared back at Shawn threatening to cut his wrist if she told the truth, but she couldn't afford not to tell her husband the truth.

"Shawn!" Dominique yelled.

Shawn mouthed silently "Don't do it" as he pressed the knife deeper into his wrist.

Dominique felt panic starting to set in as she stared at Shawn then back at Eric, trying to maintain her composure.

"Yes, Shawn Silver. I have to admit, Dominique, you had me fooled. I really thought you were different. Wow, it's my lucky day. All your bones seem to be falling out of the closet."

"Eric, it isn't what you think it is. I'm not having an affair with Shawn."

"Sure. Now you are going to tell me all those late nights at the office you were really working on cases together. I'm no fool. I just hope he's worth you destroying our lives."

"I'm *not* having an affair, Eric. Shawn and I are just colleagues and that's it. I'm not in love with him, and he's not in love with me," Dominique said, pleading with Eric.

"So explain to me why he would say he was waiting anxiously for my departure so you two could be together again and how he felt empty when he wasn't with you? Those are words a lover would tell someone they love. I wonder if Shawn's wife knows about his wonderful affair. Maybe I should inform her now, since you have the green light to walk right out that door and be with him. I would hate to keep him waiting." Eric walked toward the telephone to call Shawn's wife.

"Eric, don't do that. Please trust me. It's not what you think," Dominique pleaded.

"Dominique, please tell me then why not. I really want to hear your explanation," Eric said sarcastically.

Dominique stood speechless as she glanced back over at Shawn, who continued to hold his knife against his wrist while Eric waited for Dominique to explain.

"Just as I thought," Eric said before Dominique could say another word. "Well, do you want to tell her, or do you want me to call her? It's up to you."

Dominique stood still, feeling her words escape her.

"I'll do it. That's the least I can do for his wife," Eric said, reaching for their phone—when it started to ring. Dominique froze in place as she stared at Shawn standing in the distance and then back at Eric.

"Hello," Eric answered, still pumped up from all the stress. "Yes, this is Mr. Wallace. Who is this?"

Dominique stood across the room and watched Eric's face turn pale as he listened to whoever was on the other end of the telephone. Slowly, he hung up the telephone and dropped into the seat next to him without saying a word.

"Eric who was that?" Dominique asked.

"It was the police station calling to tell you they found Shawn's body in his office. Gunshot to the head."

Dominique fell to the floor.

CHAPTER 33

Dominique opened her eyes. Her head was throbbing as she lay still in her bed. She glanced over her shoulder and noticed Eric was sound asleep next to her. She didn't want to wake him, so she quietly slid out of bed, struggling to keep her balance. Her legs felt weak under her as she made her way downstairs to her kitchen to get herself something to drink.

She opened her refrigerator and decided she needed something stronger than a glass of orange juice right now. Her life was a mess, and she feared for her life. Slowly, she made her way to her bar, poured herself a shot glass of straight vodka, and took it down in one try. She poured herself another and decided to peek out of her front window to see if her protection was still outside protecting her. She saw the same car as always sitting across the street from her house. She didn't know what to feel about their presence. After hearing about co-worker Shawn's death, she didn't believe it mattered if someone was outside or not. If Michael Buchanan wanted her next, he would get her no matter what. But was she ready to go yet?

Dominique struggled with the thought of death as she made her way back to her sunroom and reclined on her chaise. Terrified by the thought of dying, she sipped her glass of wine while trying to make peace with herself.

Dominique's heart almost stopped when she saw someone standing outside of her sunroom door. After a few seconds, she recognized her young friend Shawn standing and staring back at her with his faced pressed against the glass door. Dominique quickly made her way over to him and opened the door.

"Shawn, we really need to talk," Dominique said with her voice elevated.

"I know," he responded.

"You put me in a really bad position today with my husband."

"I know. I didn't know what to do. I came here earlier to tell you I need your help."

"What do you mean?" Dominique sat down.

"Dominique, you know my situation at home. I can't stay there much longer, and I have to find a way to get my mother and sister out soon. And I know you have offered to help me, but until now I didn't know whether I could trust you. Now I know." Shawn sat down across from Dominique.

"Shawn, we really need to talk about what you did. I can't believe you would come in here and threaten me like that. I stood there risking my marriage to keep your secret. I want you to know I plan to tell Eric everything first thing in the morning. I'm not going to allow him to go another second believing I was having an affair with my co-worker Shawn when I wasn't."

"I'm sorry, Dominique. I was afraid of what he would say if he knew I wrote the letter. You and I both know he would have asked you to stop seeing me, too."

"Maybe not. Shawn, you don't know Eric. He's a good man. I know he will want to help you."

"I don't think he's going to go out of his way to make my life better. Dominique, I came earlier to tell you I was ready to meet Eric. But, after seeing him blow up over that letter, I don't want to ever meet him face-to-face," Shawn confessed.

"Shawn, I hate to say this, but if we are to have a friendship or any kind of relationship, I'm going to have to introduce you to Eric. I'm sorry; I have obeyed your wish far too long, and it has caused me a lot of heartache and trouble. I care a lot about you, and I don't want any harm to come to you or your family, but I have a family here that cares about me, too. And I owe them the truth no matter what."

"I knew you would turn on me, too. It was just a matter of time," Shawn said as she stood to his feet.

"I'm not turning on you. Shawn, I have a life of my own, too, and I want to keep what's left of it. Why can't you understand that and stop being so selfish?"

"Me being selfish—are you kidding me? I've sacrificed myself to protect my sister over and over. I can't count the number of times I protected her. So how can you sit there and question me? If it wasn't for me that night in the hospital garage, there's no telling what might have happened to you. Or have you forgotten already?"

"No, I haven't. I'm still very grateful to you. I will always be, but I have a husband upstairs who I care a lot about and a daughter who is counting on me to protect her. I've offered to help you get out of your situation, but you are so stubborn that you won't allow me. So, don't try to make me feel bad."

"You have no idea all the times I have been there protecting you. I've been there for you when you didn't even realize you were in danger. You are so naïve." Shawn stated walking to the door.

"Shawn, don't you leave before you explain yourself to me!"

"No, you left me when you chose everyone over me. Dominique, I can't continue to be there for you if you can't return the same type of loyalty I have to you. You won't find anyone else on this planet that has been as loyal to you as I have. Eric doesn't come close, and I know you think he does, but he doesn't. You think he's your family, but what you don't realize is I'm your real family." Shawn ran out the door.

Dominique stood in the doorway, watching his body disappear into the dark. She was stunned by Shawn's words. Tears filled her eyes because she didn't know who her real family was. Overwhelming emotions of sorrow swept over Dominique as she fell to the ground, weak and crying helplessly.

"Dominique," Ms. Anderson rushed to her side.

Dominique tried to sit up and wipe her tears away. She was embarrassed that Ms. Anderson found her this way. And she didn't want to consider what Ms. Anderson might be thinking about her now.

"Let me help you up," Ms. Anderson offered as she helped Dominique from the floor to the chaise. "I'm going to make you some coffee."

"I have something to drink," Dominique said as she located her glass of wine sitting on her coffee table.

"Coffee would be better than that glass of spirit. Whatever is troubling you will pass. Dominique, you know you can talk to me. I'm not here to pass judgment on you. You're like family to me," Ms. Anderson said as she sat down beside Dominique.

Dominique burst into tears as she allowed the word family to echo in her head. Why did others want to be a part of her family and her own parents didn't? Why didn't they want her? Why didn't they leave her a note or something that would have given her some type of closure?

"Dominique, honey, what's troubling you?" Ms. Anderson asked as she pulled Dominique's body closer to her to comfort her.

"I don't know who I am nor my real family," Dominique answered as she continued to cry on Ms. Anderson's shoulder.

"You do know who you are. You are Mrs. Dominique Wallace. You're a wife and mother. You're a successful attorney, and you're the daughter I never had. I love you, Dominique and I have watched you over the last few weeks struggling with something I can't understand. Dominique, you have a dark cloud following you around."

"I know, and its name is Mr. Michael Buchanan," Dominique joked.

"Dominique, I don't trust this Mr. Michael Buchanan. I think he will stop at nothing to protect himself. I realize you want to help this young girl Kimberly, but is it worth risking the family you have now over her? I didn't want to say anything before, but I think I will now. Your friend Shawn Silver lost his life over this case. Dominique, I can't lose you over this case, because it wouldn't make sense to me. And I don't want to have to explain to Devin why you aren't there for her sweet sixteen party, her graduation or wedding day. I love that little girl upstairs like she was my grandchild, and I don't want her to grow up like you had to without a mother there to wipe her tears away when she's hurt or to give her a kiss and hug when she has done something great. She didn't ask for all this high-profile case stuff nor did Eric. And you know Eric would die if something ever happened to you. I've watched you over the years create this incredible life with Eric and Devin. I don't know where your parents are or why they gave you up, but I do know people who would die for the family you have living under this roof. Please don't lose everything because of this case." Ms. Anderson pleaded with Dominique as she wiped the tears from Dominique's face. "I overheard you and Eric arguing over some letter Shawn wrote you. Dominique, I know and I believe with all my heart, you didn't have an affair. I know you love Eric, just as much as he loves you."

"I do, Ms. Anderson, and I wasn't having an affair with my co-worker Shawn Silver. Trust me, I wasn't. The young boy Shawn—the one who helped me in the garage the night of the attack—*he* wrote that letter," Dominique explained.

"Honey, I believe you. I also believe things happen for a reason. It was real eerie that you received that call about Shawn's death when you did. I fell to my knees and prayed because the Devil is working overtime around here," Ms. Anderson said as she started to hum an old church hymn.

Dominique sat silently as she listened to Ms. Anderson hum softly in her ear. She felt at peace and safe for the first time in a long time. She knew Ms. Anderson was right: Her family meant too much to her to risk them over convicting Mr. Buchanan. The first thing in the morning she would call the judge presiding over the case and tell him she needed him to replace her on the case. Ms. Anderson's advice had enabled her to see clearly now, and she felt at peace with her new decision.

"What's going on?" Eric asked from the doorway, where he was watching Ms. Anderson holding and humming to his wife like a little girl.

"Nothing you couldn't take over for me," Ms. Anderson said as she released Dominique's body for Eric to replace her. "I'll be upstairs if you need me," she said as she left the room so Eric and Dominique could be alone.

"Ms. Anderson," Dominique called out.

"Yes?" Ms. Anderson answered.

"Thank you for loving me so much," Dominique said and blew Ms. Anderson a kiss.

"Thank you for loving me," Ms. Anderson responded and blew Dominique a kiss back.

"Who loves me?" Eric joked.

"I do," both Dominique and Ms. Anderson said simultaneously.

"Just checking," Eric laughed.

Eric waited until Ms. Anderson disappeared into the darkness before he spoke. He wanted his conversation with his wife to be in private. There were so many things he wanted to say as his heart filled with joy, knowing his wife had been telling him the truth about her possible affair with Shawn. He overheard Dominique confessing to Ms. Anderson that she wasn't having an affair, and he knew deep down she was telling the truth. He still was confused by the wording of the letter, but for now he was going to let it go. He wasn't sure Dominique could handle any more drama after everything that had transpired earlier that day. He wasn't sure even he would be able to handle anything new.

"Dominique, I owe you an apology for my behavior earlier. I should never have doubted you," Eric said.

"You don't owe me any apology. I'm the one who owes you one. I've done the unforgivable, and I don't know if you will be able to forgive me. I just want you to know that I plan to call Judge Clarence Bacon first thing tomorrow morning and let him know I can't stay on the case. I know he won't make me stay on the case after everything that has happened. I'm just sorry it took all of this to happen before I could think straight."

"Well, just be glad you are still here to make that decision," Eric said, holding her body close to his.

"I love you, Eric, so much," Dominique said as tears rolled down her face.

"I love you, too, and I never want to lose you," Eric responded and leaned in to kiss Dominique on her forehead.

"Can we make a vow to never keep any secrets from each ever again?" Dominique asked.

"I vow," Eric responded.

"Good."

"What were you drinking," Eric asked as he leaned away from Dominique.

"Wine."

"I think you better go to bed so you can sleep it off," Eric said, helping her up from the chaise.

"I'm exhausted," Dominique said. Her body felt tired when she stood up. Silently, they made their way to their bedroom and fell asleep.

CHAPTER 34

Dr. Martin pulled out all his notepads containing Dominique's session notes over the years and reviewed them all. He sat for hours looking them over, hoping he could possibly make a connection, but there was none as far as he could tell. He wanted answers, and now he knew they definitely weren't in his notes in his office. And the more he thought about everything, the more curious he became about her childhood past, a past he didn't have any records of. Rarely did they discuss her past. She would mention a few things, but not much. She mostly talked about what was going on in her life at the present time. He knew Dominique had been raised in the foster care system for most of her younger years. He asked her to make a journal of her foster care experiences for him recently, but she had also been vague about that information in her journal.

Dr. Martin started calling around, trying to gather any information he could about Dominique's past. But each call turned out to be a dead end. There was no information on her past out there. It was as if she didn't exist, and this sparked his curiosity even more.

Dr. Martin continued his pursuit until he finally located someone who was able to pull some information on Dominique, but all they were able to pull was her birth certificate. Unfortunately, Dominique's birth certificate was so damaged they couldn't read her parents' name on it. Once, again, he found himself at a dead end.

Frustrated, he decided he needed to visit the hospital and foster care offices in person. Maybe he would be able to find someone who would be able to remember Dominique and give him some history about her past. Right now, anything was better than what he had.

Dr. Martin packed his bags and headed for the little town called Chase City, which was recorded on Dominique's birth certificate. Chase

City was less than two hours from Richmond. He prayed someone would still remember her and be able to provide him with any information that would be helpful.

As he entered the town limits, Dr. Martin admired how peaceful and modest the little town looked. Everything was well manicured, and the people looked very friendly as they walked about, smiling back at one another. As he continued to drive through the little town, he noticed a large white building straight ahead at the end of the street. It was the largest building he had seen since entering the town limits. And as he approached it, he realized it was the building he was looking for. He parked his car and got out, noticing the building had been recently renovated. The yard was neatly cut, and there were trees and benches on the property for leisure sitting and two large flags hung out front. He stood beside his car and glanced over the surrounding township. He couldn't believe how tranquil everything around him looked and felt as he breathed in the fresh, cool air that was blowing about. He observed how everybody was waving and talking to each other. No cars were racing up and down the street or blowing their horns for people to get out of their way. No noise or gas fumes filled the air. He could hear the birds chirping. It felt great, and for a second or two Dr. Martin almost forgot why he was there.

Quickly gathering himself, he headed for the entrance of the large white building and walked straight over to the front desk to ask for assistance. He prayed she would be able to help him obtain information on a foster child who was in their system about twenty-five years ago. Dr. Martin waited as the lady made a call and returned with instructions for him to speak to a lady by the name of Pat Jones.

Dr. Martin quickly made his way to Pat Jones's office, eager to speak with her. This was his first positive break. He hoped it wouldn't end in disappointment as his other attempts had. When he reached her office, she was on the telephone and motioned for him to take a seat. He sat down across from her, glancing around her office as he waited for his turn. She had several crates of files stacked up all around her office. He couldn't understand how she was able to find anything. Then he figured it explained why his process had been so difficult, assuming that all the other offices were operating under the same unorganized system. Dr. Martin sat quietly for what seemed like over twenty minutes, waiting for her to hang up. He felt himself becoming restless and irritated with every second that passed. Finally, she hung up.

"Sorry to make you wait so long. How can I help you today?" Ms. Jones asked Dr. Martin.

"My name is Dr. Martin. I'm a psychiatrist from Richmond, Virginia. I'm trying to locate any information on Mrs. Dominique Wallace, one of my patients. Dominique's maiden name was Shepard. Does that name ring a bell?" Dr. Martin asked.

"Not really. How long ago was it since Mrs. Shepard was here in our system?"

"I'm estimating about twenty-five years ago."

Ms. Jones laughed before responding. "I don't mean to laugh, but this place has been through many changes since that time, and I don't know if I'm going to be able to help. Ten years ago, we had a bad fire, and we lost a lot of our records in the fire. Unfortunately, we didn't have anything backed up on computers. So if no one was able to pull Mrs. Shepard's records for you then, we don't have anything on her now. I'm really sorry you had to drive all this way to hear me tell you that."

"You mean you don't have any information anywhere else?" He asked wondering if she was mistaken and Dominique's information was among the stacks of files in her office, but chose not to look.

"Dr. Martin, I'm not sure if you realize how many children come and go around here. After they leave the system, we never hear from them, and many don't want you to get in contact with them afterward either. They want to erase this part of their lives, and rightfully so in my personal opinion. Unfortunately, I don't have any more information to give you about Mrs. Shepard. I wish I could have been of more assistance in this matter, but unfortunately I can't," Ms. Jones said as she sat back in her office chair and started to rock.

Dr. Martin could tell she was enjoying her control over the situation. He disliked her type. She was arrogant and desired titles to identify herself. She would compromise a situation just to be in control, and Dr. Martin felt she was abusing her power to accomplish that goal right now.

"Is it possible for me to speak with any of the case workers who were staffed during that time? Maybe they will be able to help me."

"Turnover has also been a problem here. I doubt very seriously anyone during that time is still working here." Ms. Jones played with her pen while continuing to rock back and forth.

"Can you at least look that information up for me?" Dr. Martin asked, still trying to be polite.

"Dr. Martin, in case you didn't notice when you entered my office, I was very busy," Ms. Jones responded arrogantly.

"I'm sorry. I wasn't sure if it was a sign of how unorganized you are, especially from the looks of your office," Dr. Martin responded. Immediately he regretted his response. After saying it, Ms. Jones rose up in her chair with an expression of disapproval on her face.

"Dr. Martin, if you haven't forgotten, it was you who came to me for help. Not the other way around," she reminded Dr. Martin. "If you would excuse me, I need to get back to work."

"Ms. Jones, I apologize for my comment. It was unnecessary, but I really need any help you can provide. Mrs. Shepard is really sick now, and I think her past history can help me treat her better."

Ms. Jones sat back in her chair and stared back at Dr. Martin for a second or two before responding. Then she picked up her telephone and made a call requesting names of all the caseworkers who were employed twenty-five years ago.

"Ms. Jones, I appreciate your help," Dr. Martin said. He was glad she had decided to help. Maybe he had misjudged her. But he couldn't celebrate yet. He had to wait to see if any were still employed and prayed they would remember.

"Well, don't thank me yet. I don't know if we have anyone left," Ms. Jones said as her telephone rang. "Please excuse me while I answer this call."

Dr. Martin waited eagerly for his answer.

"Good and bad news. We do have one caseworker who was employed here during that time, but she is out on medical leave."

"When do you expect her back?" Dr. Martin answered excitedly.

"I'm not sure. Ms. Brown is close to retirement now, so I doubt that she will return."

"Do you have a number where I can reach her?"

"We do, but I think it might be best if you give me your number and

I get in contact with Ms. Brown. If she wants to reach you, she can return your call."

Dr. Martin had been correct about Ms. Jones. She was desperate to be in control over the situation. He wanted to set her straight, but he needed her to get in contact with Ms. Brown right now. And maybe later he would take the time to tell her about her character flaw. Dr. Martin handed Ms. Jones his card and insisted that Ms. Brown call his cell number as soon as she could.

"Well, Ms. Jones I appreciate your help and I'm sorry I took up so much of your time. I pray Ms. Brown will be able to help me. Any information she could remember will be greatly appreciated." Dr. Martin stood up and reached out his hand to shake Ms. Jones's hand as she maintained her sitting position, barely leaning forward to return his handshake.

Dr. Martin left Ms. Jones's office wondering whether or not she was going to call Ms. Brown. As he turned back around, he noticed her tossing his business card in her trash, not caring whether she was affecting someone's life. He decided to get a room. Then he would locate a telephone book and call every Brown listed.

Dr. Martin left Ms. Jones's office disappointed but hopeful. He was determined he was going to speak with Ms. Brown before he returned to the city. So he checked into the only lodging place available in town, which was a bed and breakfast inn at the end of town, a cute colonial home. He could tell the owners had done a lot of renovations to make the house cozy and inviting to their guest. And even Dr. Martin appreciated their efforts. He was glad he hadn't had to stay in an old, dirty motel tucked in the middle of nowhere and wondering whether he was going to be safe all night until the sun rose the next morning. He paid the owner for at least one night and headed straight for his room. He unpacked his clothes and located the local telephone book on the little nightstand. Immediately, he flipped to the B's and strolled down to Brown, where he saw over thirty Browns. He had a feeling it wasn't going to be easy locating Ms. Brown because her name was so common, but he prayed she didn't have an unlisted number. He started to dial all the numbers with the last name Brown. Almost halfway through, a pleasant voice answered the phone. Dr. Martin introduced himself and told her the nature of his call. She told him she didn't remember Dominique's name right then, but she did have personal journals of everybody she helped. She said she started keeping her own personal journals after their first fire. Since then, the agency has had two more. Dr. Martin started wondering if someone was starting them on purpose, but he didn't come there to find that out. He was there to get information about Dominique.

Eager to help, Ms. Brown agreed to go through her journals to see if she had made one for Dominique. And if she did, he was welcome to stop by the next day around lunchtime to review it.

After Ms. Brown gave Dr. Martin directions to her house, he hung the telephone up and began to dance around the room. He was getting closer to finding out about Dominique's past, and if he was lucky, tomorrow he would learn all he needed to know to help Dominique.

CHAPTER 35

Dr. Martin kept his eye on his watch all morning long. He couldn't wait to meet with Ms. Brown for lunch. All night long he wondered if she had been lucky in locating a journal on Dominique's past, praying he wouldn't have to return to the city empty-handed.

With time to kill before lunch, Dr. Martin decided to take a little tour of the town. He parked his car and casually walked up and down the streets, window shopping as he enjoyed the beautiful flowers and trees that filled the plant boxes along the streets. Then he came across a little antique shop where he admired several old picture frames from the window. Enticed by their unique variety, he entered the little store. Immediately upon entering the store, he saw an old, rustic silver frame he thought his wife would love. Taking pictures was a hobby of hers, and she had many different types of frames throughout their home. At first, he thought she was going overboard, but as time passed, he enjoyed the warm feeling the pictures brought to their home.

He remembered coming home one day, exhausted from work, and glancing over at a picture she had sitting on the coffee table next to their couch. It was a picture of him when he was in middle school, dressed up in his basketball uniform. He remembered how excited he was when he made first string on the basketball team, and how proud his father was, too. That same day his father took him out and bought him a new basketball rim so he could practice. And together they spent countless hours playing together, nurturing a wonderful relationship between the two of them. And for a few moments his wife had allowed him to escape the stresses of his life as an adult by reminiscing. And since that day, he embraced her hobby. He hoped she would like the old, rustic silver frame he was buying her today and would fill it with another wonderful memory.

Dr. Martin looked at his watch as he purchased the frame for his wife. It was almost lunchtime, and he needed to get going. Dr. Martin went back to the bed and breakfast to gather his belongings and checked out. He placed his wife's frame and luggage in his trunk, got in the car, and headed to Ms. Brown's house. The drive to Ms. Brown's was beautiful. The countryside was bright and full of blossom flowers. Ms. Brown's house was right outside of town, just off the main road. Dr. Martin turned into her driveway and slowly drove up the graveled driveway. He parked his car beside an old green Impala, then he got out. Before he could reach Ms. Brown's front door, she opened it, welcoming him to come in.

"Dr. Martin, I made us some lunch to eat," Ms. Brown said with a pleasant smile on her face.

"Thank you," Dr. Martin responded.

"It's nothing special, just some sandwiches and lemonade."

"Well, I appreciate it. Ms. Brown, were you able to locate any information about Dominique Shepard?"

"Yes, I was. I didn't recognize her name at first, but after you left I did. Here is the journal I kept on Dominique," Ms. Brown said as she handed the journal over to him.

"Thank you so much for taking the time to look through your things to locate this for me."

"No problem. Luckily for you, I kept personal journals at home. Otherwise you would have been out of luck."

"I know. I spoke with Ms. Jones at your office, and she wasn't too helpful."

"I know. She's really mean. Since she's been in charge, just about everybody has quit or been fired. I have less than six months left, and I'm trying to stretch my medical leave till then. But please don't tell anybody I told you that," Ms. Brown said as she leaned over as if to whisper her plan.

"I won't. I can completely understand you not wanting to go back and work for her anymore. I hope I never have to see her again myself," Dr. Martin joked.

Ms. Brown laughed at Dr. Martin's remarks and told him to follow her to her back porch and have a seat. Ms. Brown went back inside and returned with their lunch on a tray. She set the tray down on a little table that sat in between her chair and Dr. Martin's and started to serve Dr. Martin some lemonade to drink.

"Yes, I remember Dominique Shepard. Did she ever get married and have a family of her own?"

"Yes. She got married. She has a husband and daughter now."

"What does she do for a living?"

"She's an attorney."

"You don't say? I would always tell Dominique I thought she would be a good attorney."

"She told me one of her teachers encouraged her."

"I also tutored Dominique in the evenings. Dominique was real special to me. I guess I was like a teacher to her. I would take her to the library and let her check out books to read. She loved to read. It took me a while to reach Dominique and develop a friendship with her. She was really messed up when I first met her. She had been in and out of a lot of foster care homes and felt abandoned and lost. Dominique just grew on me for some reason. She would have these real bad panic attacks all the time. I prayed that with time she would grow out of them, but from what you are telling me she is still having them?"

"Actually, she just started having them again."

"She used to have them really bad. They would just come on and we never knew when she was going to have them."

"That's how they are now."

"What do you think caused her to start having them again?" Ms. Brown asked as she took a sip of her drink.

"I'm not sure. Dominique has been through a lot recently. Dominique was attacked a few weeks ago."

"Was she raped?" Ms. Brown asked, gasping.

"No, but she was really lucky. He shook her up pretty badly."

"Do you the think the attack caused her to start having the attacks again?" Mrs. Brown asked with a worried look on her face.

"I don't know because she had other panic attacks before that attack. But they all started when she was working on her last case."

"What type of case was it?"

"A sexual abuse case," Dr. Martin answered. Ms. Brown slid back into her chair.

"Poor girl!" Ms. Brown shook her head as she started to rock back and forth. "I think you better read this. I hope this journal will be able to help you."

Dr. Martin opened the journal with Dominique Shepard's name written across it. Then he flipped through the pages, reading all the notes Ms. Brown had kept on Dominique. She had been very thorough with her notes, and Dr. Martin was appreciative of it. Page after page, the words weighed Dr. Martin down. He was aghast at everything Dominique had been through during her childhood. He didn't know how she had managed to keep everything under control this long. Now he understood what was going on.

By the time he finished reading the whole journal, the missing pieces to his puzzle had been found. He just sat there taking everything in.

When Dr. Martin left Ms. Brown's house, he was worried about how Dominique was going to handle the information. Ms. Brown allowed him to take Dominique's journal with him. She asked him to promise to take good care of it and tell Dominique she was praying for her.

Dr. Martin was in deep thought all the way back to the city, trying to figure out the best way to present the journal to Dominique. He had to be careful because Dominique was in a vulnerable state right now. He didn't want to push her over the edge and not be able to reach her. He would have to proceed with caution.

Dr. Martin's pager went off. He looked down at the number and recognized his answering service number and returned the call.

CHAPTER 36

"Hello, Dr. Martin's answering service. How may I help you?"

"This is Dr. Martin. You paged me?"

"Yes. A Mr. Eric Wallace called. His wife, Dominique Wallace is your patient. He said they had an emergency and they need to speak with you right away."

Dr. Martin wondered what was going on. He figured Dominique must have had another panic attack and wanted to tell him about it. He also had something he wanted to tell her, and he hoped she was going to be strong enough to deal with it. Dr. Martin dialed Dominique's number and waited for someone to answer.

Eric answered. "Hello."

"This is Dr. Martin returning your call." Dr. Martin assumed it was Dominique's husband, Eric answering the phone. "Is everything okay?"

"I'm not sure. Dominique just had another panic attack. This time she saw a face and she wants to talk to you about it."

"Where is Dominique now?"

"She's right here beside me."

"I want to speak with her."

"Hold on." Eric pressed the speaker button on their phone so he could listen to their conversation.

"Hello," Dominique answered.

"Hello, Dominique. Eric said you saw a face during your last attack?"

"Yes. I saw Shawn. I was able to see his face clearly and talk to him."

"Which Shawn are you referring to?" Dr. Martin asked for clarification.

"Shawn from my physical attack," Dominique answered.

"What was he doing?"

"He was trying to help me hide from that heavy voice I always hear."

"Did you see the face of who the heavy voice belonged to?"

"No."

"Tell me what happened."

"The man found us and pulled Shawn out of our hiding space and beat him."

"Did the man do anything to you?"

"I woke up before he touched me. All I can remember is him beating Shawn as he dragged him from our hiding spot."

"Do you know where Shawn is now?"

"No."

"Dominique, I have some information I need to share with you and Eric."

"What type of information?"

"Information I need to tell you in person."

"Where did you get it?"

"Do you remember a caseworker by the name of Ms. Brown, Ms. Cynthia Brown?"

She'd worked with a lot of caseworkers over the years in her line of work, but the name Ms. Brown didn't ring a bell. "No, that name doesn't sound familiar to me."

"I'm on my way over to your house now. I have some information that I think will explain why you are having panic attacks and why Shawn was present in the last one."

Dominique felt relief rush through her body. She would finally be cured of her unexplained attacks. "Sure. Do you think it's because he saved me from my attacker and I want him to protect me from whoever is scaring me during my panic attacks?"

"There's a connection there, but it's much deeper than that. I'll explain everything to you when I get there. Right now you need to get some rest."

She hung the phone up and stared at Eric. They sat in silence both anxious to find out what information Dr. Martin had that would explain her panic attacks and Shawn's deep connection. Eric held Dominique in his arms and prayed their misfortunate would soon be over.

Eric broke the silence, "Dr. Martin asked you about someone named Ms. Cynthia Brown. Are you sure you don't remember her?"

"Her name doesn't sound familiar, so I don't know how she is connected with my attacks."

"Hopefully Dr. Martin will be able to explain it to both of us."

"I just want to know what's going on with me. I want my life back again."

"I know."

Dominique lay back onto her bed and waited silently for Dr. Martin's arrival. She didn't know what to expect, but she had a feeling her life was about to change forever. She couldn't imagine anything topping the life-altering experience of handling the Buchanan case. Michael Buchanan had singlehandedly disrupted her life, her family's life, and the lives of anyone else involved in the case. He had managed to introduce her to a way of life she never wanted to experience again.

Tears filled Dominique's eyes as she thought about Shawn Silver's death and how he lost his life trying to convict Buchanan. Dominique wished things had turned out differently. She wondered whether Shawn would still be alive if she had walked away from the case that first day. Would Maria Gonzales still be alive? Had her own selfish wants assisted in their deaths?

The doorbell rang, and Dominique froze. There was no turning back. She would find out what was haunting her.

"Dominique, Dr. Martin is here," Eric said over the intercom system from downstairs.

She wiped her tears away. "I'll be down shortly."

Dominique slowly stood to her feet and walked over to her vanity mirror to look herself over before joining Eric and Dr. Martin downstairs. She stood there staring at her reflection. The reflection staring back at her looked like Dominique Wallace. But was it really? Or was it someone else? Then she heard Eric call her name again.

"Yes. I'm on my way down. Give me a second," she said. She finished wiping her face and headed downstairs. Finally, she was going to be able to find the missing pieces to the puzzle in her life.

"Thank you for coming, Dr. Martin," Dominique said and motioned for everyone to sit down in the family room.

"Dominique, how are you feeling right now?" Dr. Martin asked when he took a seat.

"I feel fine. Hopefully, I'll feel even better after you tell me your news," she tried to joke.

"Are you sure you feel up to it? What I have to share with you might be a lot for you to handle." Dr. Martin was sitting on the edge of the couch, not quite settled in for a long session.

Dominique felt butterflies flying in her stomach as she looked over at Eric for support.

"Dominique are you sure you're up to it?" Eric asked. He moved beside Dominique and took her hand to comfort her.

"If I don't hear it now, I'm going to drive myself insane wondering what Dr. Martin has to tell me. So, give it to me. I'm a big girl," Dominique responded, trying to convince herself and everyone else she was strong enough to handle whatever Dr. Martin had to tell her.

"Dominique, I don't quite know where to begin."

"The beginning would be a good start," she blurted out.

"We have been trying to figure out what has been *causing* your panic attacks …I've been seeing you for a few years now, but it's only recently that you have experienced them. I've seen you deal with a lot of stress over the years, but nothing like this. So I thought and thought about everything we ever talked about during our sessions together. I had to rule out that physical attack in the hospital garage as the main reason for your panic attacks because you had several panic attacks before that episode. The more I thought about everything, the more I realized I didn't know anything about your background. You and I rarely discussed your past during our sessions together. We have always dealt with your current issues. When I reviewed my notes, I couldn't find anything about your childhood because you were vague about it, and when I asked you to elaborate, you were unable to, which caused me to wonder even more about your past."

Dominique was becoming impatient. "Dr. Martin, where are you going with this?"

"I made a few calls to locate your foster care records, and I had a hard time locating any information on you. Your foster records were destroyed in a fire a few years ago, and I thought that was the end. Then I found someone who had some personal records about your past."

"So, what do you have to share with me?" she asked, eager to hear what there was.

"Just give me a second to finish. Do you remember me asking you earlier about knowing a Ms. Cynthia Brown?"

"Yes. I don't remember any caseworkers by the name Cynthia Brown."

"Well, Ms. Brown knows you, and she was your caseworker when you were in the foster care system."

"I still don't remember a Ms. Brown," Dominique answered, shaking her head.

"See if this will help you remember. Who was the person who first encouraged you to become an attorney when you were little?"

Dominique tried to remember, but no one came to mind. "I can't remember. Was Ms. Brown the one who first encouraged me?"

"I think so. At least she believes she was. Dominique, I had an opportunity to visit with Ms. Brown. She had records about your birth parents."

Dominique jumped to her feet and started to pace the floor as she allowed Dr. Martin's words to sink in. After all these years, she was finally going to find out who her parents were. Tears started to fill her eyes as she looked back at Dr. Martin.

"Can you remember anything about your parents or any siblings?" he asked.

A sense of sadness came over her as she stood there, unable to remember anything about them. "No, I can't. I've never been able to remember them. I even tried once to locate them but became discouraged, so I let it go."

"Dominique, I have information about your birth family here in this journal. I want you to take your time and read it. There are things in this journal that will be hard for you to handle at first, but remember I am here to help you work through it."

The room was silent. Dr. Martin watched as Dominique stared helplessly in Eric's eyes then laid her head down on his shoulder like a little girl. "Are you sure you are ready to deal with this?" he asked again.

Dominique looked at the black and white journal on her coffee table. It looked so thin lying there, waiting for her to open it and discover her past. Her mind drifted to the first time she held Kimberly's folder in her hand. It had felt thin and light in her hands, but she later discovered its contents were complex and deadly. Her heart raced, and her stomach continued to harbor butterflies. Her body went completely numb as she continued to stare at the journal, wondering what was inside that might change her life forever. Her desire to read the contents grew stronger with every second, but she just sat there staring at the black and white journal with her maiden name written across the cover in black ink: Dominique Shepard.

Her thoughts drifted to her childhood. She remembered well looking in the telephone book, wondering whether any of the last names *Shepard* were her parents, but being too afraid to call them and ask why they gave her up.

Dr. Martin observed Dominique's reaction as he handed her the journal with Dominique Shepard written across the cover. He watched as she slowly took possession of it.

She gently rubbed the cover with her fingers. It felt smooth and cool. Carefully, she circled the letters that spelled her last name, Shepard, with her index finger—a name that looked foreign to her now. With every second, she became increasingly overwhelmed with emotions as she realized she was finally going to find out who Mr. and Mrs. Shepard were.

Tears filled her eyes as the mixed emotions weighed heavily on her heart. She was afraid of the contents of the journal. What would the pages tell her? Would she like her parents after reading about them? Would she be able to forgive them for giving her up? Had they given up only her, or did she have sisters and brothers somewhere who were searching for their true identities, too. Full of so many questions, Dominique raised the journal to her chest and took a deep breath.

Sensing her growing emotion, Dr. Martin asked in a calm voice, "Dominique, would you like for us to leave the room for a while so you can review the journal?"

She didn't know what to say. She had to read it because knowing what it said might free her of her attacks. Surely everything she needed to know was in that journal. She looked helplessly at Eric as she laid it down on her lap. Tears streamed down her face onto her journal. She immediately wiped them away as if she was afraid they would destroy the journal.

Eric reached over and took the journal from Dominique's shaking hands and placed it on the coffee table in front of them. "Are you sure you are ready to do this?" He rubbed her back to comfort her.

"I don't know. I've always wanted to know about my birth parents, but now that I have the chance, I'm not sure I want to." She shook her head as she wiped the tears away from her face. She stood to her feet, overwhelmed with mixed emotions, and paced the floor, pulling her hair away from her face.

Eric rose to comfort her. "Dominique, I don't know if this is a good idea."

"Eric, stop it. I appreciate it, but you can't protect me from my past. That journal has who I am in it … And I'm not sure either you or I are ready to deal with it." Tears rolled down her face.

"Dominique, I love you, and there's nothing in that journal that could change that. I love the person you are now. That's what matters to me. I'm not concerned about who you were when you were a little girl. Whatever is in that journal, you couldn't help, nor can you change it now."

She stared back at Eric, praying his words were sincere.

Dr. Martin stood up to join Eric in calming Dominique down. "Eric is right. What's in that journal you didn't have any control over. You were just a child. Don't forget that. Take all the time you need. I want you to open the journal when you think you are ready. There's no rush. We don't have to do this right now. If you want, we can wait a day or two. Maybe by then you will be better prepared to handle everything."

"Mommy, what's wrong?" Devin asked as she walked into the family room and saw her mother crying.

"Devin, Daddy would like for you to go back upstairs right now." Eric said as he walked over to Devin in the doorway of the family room.

"Why is Mommy crying?" Devin asked again.

Dominique reached her hands out to Devin. "Devin, come here. I want you to know Mommy loves you and wants to apologize for putting you through so much these last few weeks. I'm sorry. Dr. Martin has brought me something that might help Mommy's bad dreams go away. In a few minutes, maybe Mommy's bad dreams will all be gone forever. But I need you to go upstairs like your daddy has asked and say a prayer for Mommy. Can you do that for me?" she asked, trying to force a calm smile on her face.

"Yes, Mommy, and do you want me to say one for Daddy too?" Devin asked.

"Yes. Please say one for all of us. Pray that everything will be okay and things will get back to normal." She gave Devin a kiss, not realizing it was the first time in a long time that Devin had allowed her to touch her.

"I love you, Mommy. I will pray for you to get better and for us all to be happy again. I don't want you and Daddy to fight anymore." Devin turned and ran upstairs to her room.

Dominique knew there was no turning back now. She had to do this for her family even if she wasn't brave enough to do it for herself. She looked at the journal on the table and decided she wanted to read it alone. She didn't know how she would feel about what she was about to find out. And she wasn't sure she wanted anyone to see her if she became emotional.

Dominique picked the journal up and walked across the room. This time it felt heavier in her hands, and she knew deep down inside the words would weigh heavily on her heart. "I think I want to read this alone. I'm going to go outside so I can be alone," she said.

She walked over to Dr. Martin and gave him a hug. "I thank you so much for finding my past for me, whatever it might be. I've been wondering all my life, and now you have brought it to me in this journal."

To Eric she said, "I thank you for being the great, loving husband you have been over the years. Thank you for giving me so much peace and love in my life, something I knew nothing of growing up. I will always love you and be grateful to you for that. I want to apologize for everything that I have put you and Devin through these last few weeks. I want to apologize for breaking our vows and the awful things that I have said. I only pray after I have finished reading this, you will have whoever was your wife before back again." She leaned over and gave Eric a kiss on the lips.

Then she glanced over her shoulder at Dr. Martin and gave him a wink as she headed outside to discover her past.

Dominique sat down at the end of the chaise, took a deep breath, and opened the cover of the journal. She started to read each page carefully, trying not to miss anything.

"Dominique, what are you reading?" Shawn interrupted. His unannounced presence startled Dominique, causing her to accidentally drop her journal onto the ground.

Shawn picked it up before Dominique could retrieve it. When he read the words Dominique Shepard written across the cover, he immediately started tearing the pages out of the journal.

"Shawn what are you doing?" Dominique yelled, trying to stop him.

"It's all lies." Shaw shouted. "Can't you see what they are trying to do to you?"

Dominique grabbed what was left of her journal away from Shawn. "Have you lost your mind?"

"It's all lies! Can't you see what they are trying to do to you?" He continued to scream at Dominique.

"Dr. Martin gave me this journal. No one is trying to do anything to me. What's wrong with you?" Dominique said furiously as she tried to pick up the torn pages scattered all over her yard.

"Why would he give you those lies to read? What kind of cruel joke is he trying to play?" Shawn asked. He watched Dominique scurry around to pick up the torn pages off the ground.

"He's not trying to play any cruel jokes. He found some information about my past for me."

"I thought you told me you couldn't remember anything about your past. How do you know whether that information in that journal is true? How do you know he didn't make it up?"

"Shawn, I know Dr. Martin very well. He wouldn't do anything to hurt me."

"That's what he wants you to think because he can't figure out why you are having your panic attacks. Can't you see what he's trying to do? It's a trick, and you are too stupid to see it."

"Shawn! How dare you talk to me this way?"

"I'm sorry, but it's all lies in that journal."

"How would you know? You don't even know what's in it." She continued to pick up the torn pages from the ground.

"Trust me. Don't believe it," Shawn said. He tried to grab the journal and torn pages from Dominique's hand again.

"Shawn, let go. What's wrong with you?" Dominique yelled as she fought to regain possession of her journal from Shawn before he ran through the bushes.

"Dominique, what are you doing?" Eric yelled from the sunroom doorway.

"Help me, Eric! Shawn tried to take my journal so I couldn't read it."

"Dominique!" Eric yelled as he ran toward her.

"Why would Shawn want your journal?" Eric asked as he picked up some of the torn pieces in the bushes.

"I don't know. He said he didn't believe it was true, then he started tearing up the pages." She started to help Eric pick up the remaining torn pages. But it was too late. Her journal was destroyed. Dominique burst into tears and fell to her knees, holding the torn pages to her chest.

"How much of the journal did you get a chance to read?" Dr. Martin asked as he leaned over to rub her shoulders.

"Just a few pages in the beginning, and I actually thought I was starting to remember until he took it and tore it all apart. What am I going to do? Now I can't read it."

"Dominique, sit down over here. Let's talk about what you *did* read in that journal," Dr. Martin said. He helped Dominique to her feet and over to her chaise to sit down.

"Dominique, I didn't share this with you before, but now I think I'd better. Ms. Brown also gave me your old address where you used to live with your birth parents when you were a little girl. It might be good for you to go there to see if you will be able to remember more that way, since Shawn has destroyed your journal. I don't want to tell you what was in the journal. I believe it's important for you to remember on your own. I don't want to influence your memories in any way."

"Is it near here?" Dominique looked over at Eric smiling with new hope.

"It isn't too far from here," Dr. Martin responded and handed her the address on a little white piece of paper.

"You're kidding!" Dominique said as she studied the address. She wondered whether she passed it on her way to work every day. What did it look like? How did her room look? Her mind was racing in circles. Could it be true? Her birth place had been right around the corner all these years?

"I want to go there. Is anyone living there now?"

"No one is living in the house right now."

Dominique was disappointed to hear that. She was hoping her parents were still living there and she would have a chance to meet them face-to-face.

"Dr. Martin, I have one last question to ask you. Are my parents still alive?"

He hesitated for a second before answering, unsure whether he should reveal that information right now. What he was curious about was the part she got to read and what she remembered now. If she remembered anything, then what?

"Dominique, are you sure you didn't read that in the journal?" Dr. Martin asked.

"No. I didn't make it that far. Why can't you just tell me now what it says? What harm would that do?"

"I want you to remember on your own," Dr. Martin insisted again.

"Well, let's go," Dominique demanded, standing to her feet.

"What about Devin?" Eric asked.

"Ask Ms. Anderson to watch her while we go." Dominique said, eager to find closure.

"Okay," Eric responded and went inside to tell Ms. Anderson.

"Dominique, sit down. I want to take advantage of this time while we are alone," Dr. Martin said.

"Is there something wrong? Are my parent's dead?" She sat down slowly and stared at Dr. Martin.

"Dominique, I'm not going to say right now. I want you to tell me why Shawn tore up your journal."

"He insisted the journal was full of lies and you were trying to trick me."

"Do you believe him?"

"No. And I told him that, too."

"How did he know what was in the journal?"

"I don't know. Shawn is so afraid you and Eric are going to commit me and take me away from him."

"Why would we want to commit you?"

"Because of my panic attacks. He's afraid I'm going crazy like his mother."

Dr. Martin stared for a second before responding. "Did they commit his mother?"

"No. He said his father won't take her to get help."

"What else has he told you about his mother?"

"Not much. He said one day he came home from school and she had a nervous breakdown. She stopped talking or caring for herself. Then his father made him and his sister start taking care of her."

"What is Shawn's sister's name?"

"I don't know. He never would tell me."

"Have you ever seen his sister?"

"No. I asked him to bring her over, but he said his father is very protective over her."

"Why does he allow Shawn to visit with you?"

"To be honest, I don't think Shawn has told them he's coming over here," Dominique admitted.

"I agree. What has he told you about his father?"

"He says he's mean. I think his father is a controller and he has beat Shawn's mother down emotionally. I've tried to convince Shawn he would be able to help his mother if he would only allow me to help him."

"But he resists?"

"Yes."

"Dominique, has Shawn ever told you his last name?"

"No. It was hard enough getting his first name out of him."

"You said Shawn was present in your last attack. Do you remember whether Shawn's presence during your last attack seemed real to you?"

"Yes. His presence seemed so real. I saw him clearly."

"What did he say to you?"

"He told me he was trying to protect me, but he ended up being punished."

"Why do you think he was being punished?"

"Because Father didn't want him in my room."

"Your father?"

"Don't answer him Dominique! Can't you see what he's trying to do? He's trying to trick you," Shawn yelled.

Dominique immediately turned around to face the bushes were Shawn's voice was coming from. "Shawn!"

"Who's father?" Dr. Martin asked as he stared at Dominique.

"Don't answer him, Dominique. He's trying to make you think you are going crazy," Shawn yelled.

"No, he's not. Why don't you calm down and come over here so I can explain to you what is going on?" Dominique said, patting her chaise cushion beside her for Shawn to sit next to her.

"I've heard enough. I can't believe you are sitting there believing all his lies. Don't you think it's awfully strange he has found your whole past in a single journal? How do you know he didn't make it up?"

"Because I trust him. He has no reason to lie to me." Dominique assured then looked over at Dr. Martin.

Dr. Martin had a blank stare on his face. He was surprised that Shawn had finally allowed himself to be present when someone else was around.

"Shawn, calm down. I want Dr. Martin to explain to you what is going on." Dominique told Shawn trying to gain control.

"I don't want to talk to Dr. Martin." Shawn said. He pulled out a knife and placed it to his wrist.

"Shawn, what are you doing?" Dominique asked, jumping to her feet. "Put that knife away."

"Dominique, I'm going to kill myself if you don't come with me!" Shawn threatened. "If you stay here, I want you to know you have my family's blood on your hands," Shawn said desperately.

"Shawn, what are you talking about?" Dominique asked.

"My father knows I've told someone about what he has been doing to me and my sister, so he's threatening to kill my mother and sister."

"Shawn, we need to call the police before it's too late," Dominique said frantically.

"No police," he answered.

"Are you crazy? Your father is threatening to kill your mother and sister. I can't just stand here and allow that to happen."

"Then go home with me and help me get my mother and sister out of there before it's too late."

"I have to get my keys. Meet me in my car," Dominique insisted as she rushed into the house and passed by Eric to get her keys and pocketbook.

"Dominique?" Eric reacted, looking worried.

"I don't have time to argue with you. Shawn's family is in danger and I need to help them."

"Dominique, calm down," Dr. Martin said as he rushed behind her and grabbed her by the arm.

"Let me go. Didn't you hear him say his father is going to kill his mother and sister if I don't help them?" She pulled away from Dr. Martin angrily.

"You won't be able to help anyone if you don't calm down first," Dr. Martin said, maintaining his position.

"I *am* calm," Dominique yelled back at Dr. Martin. "We're wasting time standing here debating while his mother and sister are in danger."

"What's going on?" Eric demanded, lost by all the sudden change of mood.

"Shawn needs my help with getting his mother and sister out of their house before his father kills them. I have to go get them now," Dominique shouted to Eric as she made her way to the front door.

"What?" Eric grabbed hold of Dominique's arm.

"Let me go," Dominique yelled as she fought to break free of Eric's hold.

"No, not until you calm down," Eric said.

"Eric let me go!" she demanded.

"No," Eric responded. He continued to restrain her. Ms. Anderson ran from the house to Dominique and Eric wrestling in the front yard.

"What's going on?" Ms. Anderson asked as she tried to break up the wrestling match. Dominique took advantage of Ms. Anderson's assistance, she managed to break free, and got into her car. Before starting her engine, Dominique locked her doors so no one would be able to pull her or Shawn out.

"I told you they were trying to prevent you from being with me," Shawn said as Dominique raced out of her driveway and down the block.

"Well, they didn't succeed. Now you need to tell me where you live," she said, half out of breath.

CHAPTER 37

"Ms. Anderson, I need to follow Dominique," Eric yelled to Ms. Anderson as he and Dr. Martin raced over to Dr. Martin's car.

"Please be careful," Ms. Anderson begged.

"I'll try," Eric responded. He slammed his car door shut and headed down the street after his wife.

Dominique adrenaline raced as she drove frantically to reach Shawn's mother and sister before it was too late. She only prayed she wouldn't be too late to save them.

"Dominique, you know Eric is never going to allow you to see me again after today. What are we going to do?" Shawn asked.

"Eric can't stop me from seeing you, Shawn. So don't you worry about that."

"You can't go back there again. Eric is going to put you away. He thinks you're crazy for sure. You have to stay with me now. All we have to do is get Devin when Eric isn't around and we can all be one happy family."

"Shawn, it's not that easy," she said.

"Yes, it can be. I know what's best for you. You don't know. I've been there for you all this time. Now it's time for you to be there for me," Shawn insisted forcefully.

"Shawn, I'm here for you now. I'm risking my life to save your mother and sister right now."

"What are you going to do if it's too late?" Shawn asked helplessly.

"Don't talk like that. We're going to make it." Dominique prayed she was right.

"And if we don't? What are you going to do about me?"

"I don't want to think about that right now."

"Turn here. It's the second house on the right."

She slammed on the brakes to make the turn. She glanced over the little neighborhood as she pulled up in front of Shawn's house and parked her car. Quietly, she examined his little white colonial style home with black shutters that was crying for a fresh paint job. A pair of old curtains hung in the front window. The front yard was in desperate need of a cutting. There were overgrown bushes in the front and side yards.

Shawn's driveway was empty. She breathed a sigh of relief. His father wasn't home, and if she was quick, she would be able to get his mother and sister out of there before he returned.

"It looks like your father isn't home," Dominique said, seeking confirmation.

"No, he's not, but I'm not sure when he's coming back," Shawn said. He opened his car door and got out. Dominique followed in pursuit as she walked around her car and headed for Shawn's front door.

"We need to hurry and get your mother and sister in my car before he returns," Dominique said as she followed him to the front door. Dominique was surprised that the front door was already unlock.

"Don't say anything. I want to make sure he's not here," Shawn whispered as he opened the door and entered the house with Dominique cautiously following behind him.

CHAPTER 38

Eric sat silently as his heart raced, wondering where his wife was headed, praying Dr. Martin was correct about his guess. He felt helpless sitting in the passenger seat and staring out of the window, waiting to be by his wife's side again. She needed him now more than ever, and he was desperate to be there for her.

"They're here!" Dr. Martin shouted with relief when he saw Dominique's car parked in front of the little white house.

"Thank God," Eric responded.

"I'm going to see if they are inside. Wait here for me," Dr. Martin said. He parked his car and got out.

"No. I'm going with you," Eric insisted as he jumped out of the car.

Eric saw a curtain move and someone peeking out. "I just saw the curtain move. They're in there."

The front door opened and Dominique appeared in the doorway. Eric's heart was racing faster than ever.

"You have to leave," Dominique said. They looked at each other for a moment without saying a word. "I don't want Shawn's father to catch all of us here."

Dr. Martin placed his arm in front of Eric to prevent him from chasing her away. "Dominique, where is Shawn?" he asked.

"He's inside getting his mother and sister. Please leave. I have everything under control," she pleaded and slammed the door.

"Dominique, what's going on?" Eric yelled, racing toward the closed door. Dr. Martin grabbed him to prevent him from bursting into the house.

"Calm down. Just follow me." Dr. Martin said calmly.

Dr. Martin cautiously walked up to the door with Eric following closely behind him. "Dominique, this is Dr. Martin. Please listen if you can hear me. Your husband and I are here to take you back home."

There was silence.

"Dominique, can you hear us?" Eric yelled.

"You need to leave," Shawn demanded from inside the house.

Eric pushed pass Dr. Martin and tried to open the door. "It's jammed." he said.

"Move back. Let me try," Dr. Martin grabbed the doorknob and shook it, then he pushed firmly against the door with his body. "It's open."

Slowly, they entered the house. A stale smell hit them in the nose when they entered because the house had been empty for some time, and the windows hadn't been opened to allow fresh air to circulate through it, leaving it stuffy. The only thing that occupied the little house was the old, torn curtains hanging from the window.

"Dominique, it's me, Dr. Martin." he announced, allowing his words to echo through the empty little house. "I want to help you," he continued.

"Dominique, this is Eric. Please let us help you," he pleaded.

"We don't need your help," a voice mumbled from down the hall.

"Dominique, please let me see you." Dr. Martin responded, searching the empty house as he cautiously stepped further inside. He walked slowly through the small family room into the kitchen area. On the other side of the kitchen he saw three more doors to the other rooms. He guessed they used to be bedrooms.

Like a ghost, Dominique stepped halfway into the hallway.

Dr. Martin observing her frightened stare and asked, "What's wrong?"

"I need you and Eric to leave," Dominique pleaded, as if she was afraid someone was going to catch them.

Eric was confused and afraid for his wife. "Dominique, what is going on?"

Dr. Martin grabbed Eric's arm. "We just want to help you." he said.

"You need to leave before he gets home," she insisted.

"Who are you talking about?" Dr. Martin asked.

"My father. He doesn't like for people to come over," she answered, then stepped back into the room and closed the door.

"Dominique!" Eric yelled as he rushed toward the door.

The mumbling voice from behind the door said, "Please leave us before you cause all of us to get hurt."

"Who is 'us?'" Dr. Martin asked.

"My brother and me," she answered.

Dr. Martin glanced over at Eric before responding. "What is your brother's name?"

"Shawn," she answered.

"Is Shawn the same Shawn who's been visiting with you?" Dr. Martin asked.

"Yes."

Dr. Martin now realized that Dominique knew who Shawn was, but he didn't know what else she knew about him and her past.

"Dominique, I want you to open the door." Dr. Martin said calmly.

"You need to leave our house!" a muffled voice said.

Dr. Martin wondered if it was Shawn speaking now.

"Shawn, is that you?" Dr. Martin asked.

"Yes. You can leave now," he said.

"Shawn, why don't you come out so we can talk."

"Leave now!" he demanded.

Dr. Martin calmly responded. "Let me come in there."

"Get out of here! She doesn't need you and Eric. I can protect her by myself," he yelled.

"Where is my wife?" Eric pleaded, grabbing the locked doorknob and shaking it.

"Dominique doesn't need your help," Shawn shouted back. "I'm going to protect Dominique from now on," Shawn said forcefully.

"Dominique, it's me—Eric, your husband. Please say something," The house was silent. Eric pleaded again for Dominique to respond. "Dominique, please answer me."

"Eric!" A faint voice called out.

"Dominique, is that you?" Eric asked.

"Yes."

"Are you alone in the room with Shawn?" Dr. Martin asked.

"Yes." she answered.

Dr. Martin placed his finger over his mouth to instruct Eric not to speak. "Whose room are you in right now?"

She didn't answer.

"Are you in your old room?" Dr. Martin asked, trying to see if she remembered living there.

"Your time is up," Shawn responded this time. They heard a loud noise coming from the other side of the door.

"Dominique," Eric shouted helplessly.

The house went silent again. Dr. Martin turned the doorknob. It was still locked. He reached into his pocket, pulled out his wallet, extracted a credit card, and slid it into the cracked area where the door lock was. He pushed it slowly downward until it unlocked the door. He placed his credit card back in his pocket and slowly opened the door. Dr. Martin and Eric slowly entered the small, empty bedroom. No one was visible, but then they noticed another door in the rear of the bedroom. Dr. Martin assumed it was a closet door. They heard movement on the other side of the door. Quietly, they approached the closed door.

Dr. Martin heard someone telling someone to be quiet. He listened as the voices in the closet whispered to each other.

"Dominique, are you in there?" Eric whispered calmly.

"Father is going to get us," Dominique answered frantically.

"Dominique, is Shawn in there with you?" Dr. Martin asked.

"Yes."

"Is this where you and Shawn hide from your father?"

"Yes. Father is going to get Shawn when he finds out he's been in my room again. He said he's too big to be playing in my room now. He's going to beat him."

"Where is your mother?"

"She's in her room. She won't help us. She doesn't love us anymore." Dominique responded remorsefully.

Dr. Martin glanced around the room. He wondered which room was her mother's outside her door. "Dominique, I'm going to open the closet door," Dr. Martin said as he reached for the closet doorknob.

"Please don't open the door. Father is going to find us." Dominique responded with panic in her voice.

"No. He won't. I'm going to help you and Shawn get out of here." Dr. Martin took hold of the closet doorknob.

"Get out of here before he finds us." Shawn's voice demanded from behind the closet door.

Dr. Martin jumped when he heard Shawn's voice. He had to think quickly to keep the situation calm.

"Shawn, I want to help you and your sister. You don't have to protect her by yourself now." Dr. Martin responded.

"I don't need your help." Shawn yelled.

Dr. Martin wondered if Shawn would tell him what happened that last night they all were together. "Tell me why you and Dominique had to be separated."

There was silence.

Dr. Martin continued to question. "You made your father really mad that night? Didn't you? You managed to stop your father from hurting her but something went wrong."

"Yes, I tried to protect her." Shawn answered as he started to get emotional. "I really did. I wanted him to stop hurting her. She was too small to help herself."

"Tell me what happened that night." Dr. Martin pressured Shawn to continue.

Shawn started to recall the events of that evening as it unfolded. As he recounted that evening, Dr. Martin noticed that Shawn no longer was telling the details. It was Dominique's voice.

Dr. Martin slowly turned the doorknob to the closet and opened it. His eyes made direct contact with Dominique's as the light filled the empty closet with only Dominique in it. Dominique had crawled into a ball and was holding herself as she relived the events of that horrible night.

Dominique felt the fear intensifying inside. Afraid of being discovered, she closed her eyes and held her body tightly. When she reopened her eyes, she was a little girl again. A towel was wrapped around her body, and she was preparing for bed. As she pulled her pajamas over her head, she caught a glimpse of someone standing in her closet. Startled, she jumped and turned around to get a better look at the intruder in her closet. Her brother, Shawn, was standing in her closet with his finger over his mouth, meaning she was to be quiet and join him in the closet to avoid being discovered. She obeyed and entered the closet.

"What are you doing in here, Shawn? You know he's going to punish us if he finds out you were in here while I was getting dressed," Dominique said, reminding Shawn of the punishment they would receive.

"Be quiet or he'll hear you. He's looking for you now. Come on. You better hide in here with me before he finds you," Shawn whispered to Dominique as he grabbed her by the arm and pulled her behind him to protect her.

"Be quiet," Shawn whispered to her.

Dominique heard her door open. Someone entered, calling her name with a heavy voice. It was her father. His voice echoed through her small room as he searched for Dominique.

Her body shivered as she listened to her father hunt her down like an animal. "Stay still," Shawn whispered.

Dominique prayed her father would not find them, and that tonight she would be free of his painful sexual demands. And now Shawn was the only thing that stood in between her father and her. He was her protector. And he unselfishly sacrificed himself on many occasions until their father's sexual appetite grew and Shawn no longer was able to satisfy him alone.

"I know you are in here. You better not be hiding from me, because when I find you I'm going to give you a beating," her father threatened. Dominique's heart raced. She prayed it would explode, freeing her from her father's painful pursuit.

"I hope you aren't hiding with her, Shawn. If you are, I'm going to beat you, too. So you better make it easy on yourself and come out," her father demanded. His voice grew louder and louder as he approached the closet where they were hiding. Dominique felt her heart beating in her throat. She closed her eyes, unable to watch what was about to happen.

Dominique held her breath when she felt the cold air fall upon her, replacing the warm heat that Shawn's body generated. They had been discovered, and they were going to be punished. She opened her eyes and watched Shawn's body being dragged away. "Please don't hurt Shawn, Father. I made him hide in here," Dominique pleaded with her father as she cried out loud.

"Shut up, girl. You should be worried about yourself, not your brother. When I finish with him, I will be back for you, don't you worry," her father promised and continued to drag Shawn, who was kicking and screaming.

Dominique wanted to run away while she had the chance, but she had nowhere to go. She was stuck, and she hated her mother for not helping them. In Dominique's eyes, her mother had been selfish. Because of her mother's inability to fight back, she had allowed her husband to defeat her and destroy their whole family.

Dominique remembered the first time her father came to her room. It was raining that night, and the house was quiet as Dominique played silently with her dollhouse in the corner of her room. Her father entered the room, closed the door behind him, and quietly approached her while she played on the floor. He explained that her role would be changing since her mother was sick. Dominique would assume the responsibilities of the woman of the house. She didn't know what that meant at first, but he quickly educated her. She watched him take off all his clothes in front of her and demanded she do the same. Unaware of his intent, she stood to her feet and undressed as told.

That night, Dominique's father made her perform duties her mother should have performed. He covered her mouth as she screamed in pain. When her father was done, he swore her to secrecy. She cried all night. She felt violated and dirty. She longed for her mother to comfort her, but she was not available. Dominique blamed her for the reason she was being molested. She hated both her father and mother that night.

Night after night he returned to her room, demanding a replay of that horrible night until one night when Shawn promised it all would be over soon. He hid with her in her closet and told her to stay quiet no matter what. Dominique waited in fear as she watched her father drag her brother away, beating him. She knew he would be back for her, but she was too afraid to run and had nowhere to go. So she stayed and waited her turn.

When her father returned for her, he was breathing hard from beating Shawn. He told her to come out of the closet and take off her clothes. Dominique pulled her pajamas off and kneeled to the floor. She cried with shame, until she heard her bedroom door open. She prayed it wasn't Shawn, if so, her father was going to kill him and her. Without looking to see who entered, her father yelled for whoever to close the door. Disgraced and fearful, Dominique kept her eyes closed. She wanted to disappear and never come back.

Dominique felt her father's body pull away from her. She fell back away from her father's body as he fell to the floor. When she looked up, she saw Shawn standing over her father with an iron rod in his hand. She looked back at her father's body lying between them. He was still then he started to move again.

Her father grabbed Shawn's ankle and tried to pull him to the ground. Shawn swung the iron rod with all his might trying to break free. Dominique watched in horror as her father and brother wrestled around on the floor.

Suddenly a loud bang echoed through the small room. Shawn's body fell to the floor as her father tried to stand up. Then there was another loud bang. Her father fell back to the floor, lifeless, as blood poured from his body. Dominique looked up to see who was responsible for her father's demise.

Dominique was horrified when she realized it was her mother who stood in her doorway, holding a gun in her hand. Dominique stared helplessly at her mother, terrified by the possibility that her mother might kill her, too.

Tears rolled down her mother's face. She shook her head, and her body rocked back and forth slowly.

Speaking softly and remorsefully, her mother said, "Dominique, I'm so sorry, my dear princess. You will never know how much I loved you and your brother. I never meant for you and your brother to be hurt this way, but I didn't know how to fix it until now. I pray you will be able to forgive me someday for not protecting you all these years. God, please forgive me." Then she placed the gun in her mouth and pulled the trigger again. Dominique sat there paralyzed as her mother's body fell lifelessly to the floor, as her brother and father had.

Dominique looked around her room. She was alone. Everyone was dead. She started to cry as she rocked back and forth, staring at her brother's dead body, which was lying on the floor across from her and bleeding. He was gone now, all because he tried to protect her. What would she do without him? Who would protect her in his absence?

Dominique rocked back and forth as she cried silently, staring at her family's dead bodies lying on the floor. She sat helplessly in the corner of her bedroom as the police and ambulance arrived and took her family away. Still shaking and in a daze, Dominique made her way to the police car with the assistance of a police officer. Reporters' cameras were flashing everywhere. The lights blinded her as she tried to walk to the police car for refuge while the growing crowd of people suffocated her. Dominique's head fell back into the cold leather seats, and she sat silently as she was driven away from the only place she knew as home.

CHAPTER 39

A month had passed, and Dominique's life seemed normal again. Dominique couldn't believe she was still standing after everything she had been through over a month ago: her panic attacks, Shawn Silver's death, and the unexpected news of Michael Buchanan's death before his case was tried before the grand jury.

Dominique had received a call informing her that Buchanan's body was found in his home with two gunshots, one to the head and one between his legs. The police were convinced that it was a revenge hit because they were not able to find any evidence anywhere. Everything had been wiped down. Katherine Buchanan and Kimberly Buchanan were not considered suspects because they were both in the hospital with around-the-clock protection. Dominique didn't care if they didn't find out who did it. All she knew was her own life and family life were safer now that he was gone.

Dominique was also free from her unexplainable panic attacks and secret visits. She had been set free of a haunting past, a past she had managed to suppress for many years in order to protect herself from the horrific pain. Dominique allowed her head to fall back onto the soft cushions of her chaise as she closed her eyes and took in a deep breath. "God, thank you for giving me my peaceful life back," Dominique whispered in prayer. "But mostly I want to thank you for the wonderful husband and daughter you have brought into my life now. You have given me the family I have always prayed for, and I owe you the biggest apology for doubting whether you were listening to my prayers all these years."

"Who are you talking to?" Eric interrupted as he approached Dominique carrying a tray of sandwiches, drinks, and the telephone.

Dominique opened her eyes and looked at Eric with a big smile on her face. "I was talking to God. I was thanking him for everything," she told him.

"Thank him for me, too?" Eric said jokingly.

"I already have," she replied as she sat up on her chaise. "Where is Devin?"

"I think she's playing in her bedroom. I'll go get her," he said as he placed the tray of sandwiches and drinks on the yard table.

"Devin, where are you?" Eric asked, pressing the button to their house intercom system and allowing his voice to echo throughout the whole house.

"I'm in my room," Devin called from her tea table, dressed for the occasion.

"Are you ready for lunch?"

"Yes! I'm coming," Devin answered.

In her room, she pulled off her tea party gloves and placed them on her table. "Everybody, I have to go now," she said in her tea party accent to all her make-believe guests. "My mommy and daddy would like me to join them for lunch." She turned to face her special guest. "Shawn, would you mind carrying on in my place?"

Shawn nodded yes, with a big smile on his face, and Devin skipped out of her room to have lunch with her parents.

Printed in the United States
By Bookmasters